Cruelty

Ellen Crosháin

kristell-ink.com

ISBN 978-1-909845-65-7 (Paperback)
ISBN 978-1-909845-67-1 (EPUB)
ISBN 978-1-909845-66-4 (Kindle)

Cover art by Evelinn Enoksen
Cover design by Ken Dawson
Typesetting by Book Polishers

Kristell Ink

An Imprint of Grimbold Books

4 Woodhall Drive
Banbury
Oxon
OX16 9TY
United Kingdom

www.kristell-ink.com

For Adam and for Mum and Dad. Thank you.

Chapter 1

THE TRAIN CHUGGED to a stop. The young woman in a navy coat and a grey beanie gazed out of the grimy window at the deserted platform. Her wan reflection, jaundiced in the harsh fluorescent light, revealed a haunted face. She drummed her slender fingers nervously on the stained melamine table. No one got on; only a few exhausted travellers stumbled off. As the train left the station, the woman allowed herself to exhale the breath she hadn't realised she'd been holding in.

She'd planned her escape for years. It would have looked suspicious to her family if her bank accounts had suddenly emptied. To feed the carefully constructed illusion, she had left a small fortune in her current and savings accounts. Subtly, she had taken money out, putting it into an account she hadn't registered with her father. She wasn't considered worthy of watching closely, so no one noticed her money was slowly going down and down, or that her wage packet no longer went into the account they had on file.

Her disappearance had been beautifully carried out; a car accident in Scotland, far away from home, a crash into a storm-swollen river. Dragging herself from the wreckage, she floated down the turbulent stream. For weeks afterwards newspapers mourned the tragic loss of the beautiful daughter of one of Ireland's most influential families. As they grieved, she dyed her hair, hiding its ice-blondeness with an ordinary brown, put in coloured contacts and applied a deep fake tan. She travelled across Scotland, leaving a thousand false trials without a hitch and soon, *soon*, London and her new life would welcome her.

Throughout the endeavour she'd tried to blend in, tried not to draw attention to herself. So far she'd succeeded, but now on the last leg of her escape, this final night of running, she was close to giving herself away. Every time the train stopped she sat bolt upright and scanned the platform for signs that they were on her trail.

The train slowed, jolting her out of her considerations. Panic stabbed at her as it shuddered to a halt. The next stop was supposed to be in an hour's time. The tannoy crackled into life and a nasal voice floated, muffled, above her.

'Apologies, ladies and gentleman, for this delay. We're currently experiencing signalling problems. The train manager has been in contact with control. We hope to be on our way in the next half an hour.'

The passengers around her tutted or groaned in frustration. She wanted to scream. For them a delay was an inconvenience, an irritant to be tolerated. For her, the consequences would be catastrophic. Trying to breathe normally and remain inconspicuous, she fought the terror rising inside her.

The lights flickered. And then she heard it. The heavy tread and rasping, panting breath of the one sent to collect her. *The Hound.*

Instinctively, she yanked her brown travel blanket over her head. Though she knew feigning sleep would not save her, she could think of nothing else to do. The footsteps stopped beside her. She squeezed her eyes tightly shut; tears of fear escaped her closed lids and ran down her face. Silently, she prayed he would move on.

He sniffed the air above her and she suppressed the shriek trying to force its way out of her gullet. He leant over her. Even with her eyes shut she could feel the shadow his huge form cast. He sniffed at her blanket and her heart thudded so quickly she thought it would burst. She felt the vibration of the growl before she heard it and her stomach dropped. She had been found.

But the blanket was not lifted and she was not revealed. The Hound retreated and carried on down the train. She felt no relief; the Hound's nose was never wrong. No amount of fake tan, perfume or soap could have concealed her scent, especially when she was afraid. She'd been discovered, so why had he moved away?

She waited, considering her options. If she ran, the Hound would chase her and he would catch her. Even if she could have outrun him, the doors of the train were locked, controlled by the conductors. Despite the fact she only carried a backpack, the windows did not open wide enough to let her through. She would never get out.

Another more horrible thought unravelled in her mind. If the Hound had been sent to collect her, he would have dragged her off the train and taken her directly home, where her mother would weep and her father deliver a lecture on how she had let down the Family. That's what would have happened if she'd taken off on a whim one afternoon, like her eldest brother had years ago.

This was different. She'd been missing for six months.

She'd plotted and schemed for seven years, hiding her earnings, not giving a proper share of her wealth to the Family. She'd betrayed them. Faked her death. There had been a *funeral*, for pity's sake.

And yet somehow they'd discovered she was still alive. The humiliation would be more than her parents could bear. The retribution would be slow and terrible, which meant the

Hound had not been sent to collect her and bring her home. He was to give her to someone far worse. *The Cruel.*

The Cruel was the Family's head of security, a hunter, spy and assassin, a role handed down from father to son since time immemorial. He was sent for when the worst crimes were committed against the Family. When she was a child, still fiercely loyal to her kin, she believed the Cruel a fantasy, a bedtime story to scare the naughty children of the house.

That was until her cousin Joshua ran away with a *Gnáth* girl from the village, taking a lot of money with him. He was sixteen, and the money was taken from the safe in her father's study. Her mother cursed the wiles of the girl, while her aunt Alexandria howled in shame at what her child had done, until the moment Jacob decided to send the Cruel after the errant child. Alexandria's howling ceased and her entreaties for mercy began; she would replace the money, she would take a flogging, she would do whatever they asked to spare Joshua the inhumanity of the Cruel's punishments. She was firmly told that Joshua must pay for his own sins.

The boy was dragged back to the Big House, beaten and broken, screaming, weeping and naked. The Cruel brought him to the library where her father waited. She had been playing hide and seek with her brothers, concealed behind the mahogany shelves of history books, missed when the boys were rounded up and sent to play elsewhere. From her vantage point behind a tome on the Napoleonic Wars, she witnessed the return of the wayward child. Every detail of that afternoon was etched on her memory, every colour, every smell, and every sound as vivid as the day it happened.

Joshua lay prostrate on the Persian rug before her father. The Cruel stood behind him, clad head to toe in raven black. At a nod from her father, the Cruel extended a bone white hand and dragged the child to his feet by his hair. She swallowed her screams at the sight of her cousin's body. The skin on his back was ripped from his bones, his torso covered in burns, scorched and blackened from the flames, and his left shoulder hung at an impossible angle.

Before all the poets, novelists and other great minds, in the sunlight that streamed through the stained glass window in the ceiling, the retribution that fell on Joshua terrified the little girl. Her father prowled around him, inspecting the wounds. As soon as he was satisfied, the boy was dropped to the floor.

Congratulated on his swift capture of the boy, the Cruel was led out of the library and to the study for his payment. The Physician, the Family doctor, another of her kin and a stooped, bespectacled man, entered the defiled library. He tutted over the prone body of the boy, using his ocular gifts to check there was no life-threatening internal bleeding. The Hound, a giant to her childish eyes, joined the small doctor. He gathered up Joshua with an angry grunt and took him to the medical room.

She watched it all from the hidden recesses of the library. Tears trickled silently down her face as she waited for them to leave. The Physician adjusted his glasses on his hawkish nose. His pinched face wrinkled in disgust at the congealing blood on the floor. He rubbed his bony hands together as if he were cold. Even then, nearly seventeen years ago, he acted like an old man, though he was barely thirty. Eventually he left, switching off the light as he went and plunging her into semi-darkness as a cloud passed across the sun.

Finally alone, she scurried out of her hiding place. She wept for Joshua, but she believed the punishment was just. But this was before it was made obvious her Family had no use for her. Before they began to ignore her, before they pushed her into the background and shunned her for being different.

Now on the train, she mulled over her options. Joshua had run away a long time ago, under the rule of a different Cruel, one who had always been fair to the penitent. When Alexandria drunkenly accused Jacob of cruel and unusual punishment, her father told her Joshua had fought, spat and cursed against his heritage; if he hadn't, he wouldn't have needed to be corrected by the Cruel. The man who had punished Joshua would have listened to her if she'd thrown herself on the floor and begged for forgiveness, explaining the reasons she left. He would have taken her home in one piece, her punishment lessened.

His son was not of the same ilk.

If the new Cruel was here to collect her she had very few options; she could give in immediately and agree to face her punishment. She would be beaten and she'd never enjoy a moment's freedom again. She could claim she had amnesia but they wouldn't believe her and she'd be tortured until she confessed. Or she could fight. And lose and be punished.

It was suffocating under the blanket. She dragged it off, gasping for air. The train seat which had been comfortable earlier seemed to tighten around her, restraining her. The sticky plastic table-top glued her to the spot. The long aisle of the carriage stretched for miles in front of her, removing all hope of escape. In her frenzied state, she noticed all the other passengers in her carriage were gone. *Fuck.* They had isolated her while she tried to hide in plain sight.

She feigned a yawn and stretched, twisting to get a better view. In the shadows, she made out the tall figure of the Cruel. Her terrified mind galvanised her into action, creating a plan she had no time to review. She reached into her bag as if reaching for her ticket, and brought out her purse. An icy hand fell on her shoulder.

'You can stop the charade, Eliza. You should have known we could still track you, despite your weak aura.'

The voice sounded disinterested and old, weary of life and its trials. It was a lie. The Cruel felt no such thing. He would have enjoyed chasing after her. She was the only the third child to run away since he took over, and the first he had been sent after. Though he had hunted and tortured the enemies of the Family, the thought of punishing Eliza must be delicious.

The Cruel took the seat opposite her. Eliza put her purse down and feigned confusion. 'I'm sorry?' Her carefully practised English accent sounded false and shaky. With those two words she had lost the first hand.

'You will be once I'm done with you.' He reached across the table to grab her wrist. Eliza snatched her hand away.

'Listen, I don't know who you are,' she said, fear strengthening her act, 'but you've got the wrong girl. If you don't back off, I'll report you to the conductor.'

The Cruel's face remained impassive but his navy eyes sparkled with annoyance. He tapped his long fingers on the melamine table top. Even the curls of his white-blonde hair flickered with irritation. Eliza stared defiantly at him, trying to make him back down.

'Eliza . . .' he began, his impatience obvious in his voice.

Eliza jumped to her feet and snatched up her belongings. 'Why don't you fuck off?' she snarled. 'Fucking weirdo.'

She attempted to walk away. The Cruel whistled and the Hound emerged from between the seats, blocking her way. Like his compatriot, he wore an expensive black suit. The material strained over the Hound's bulk, emphasising his muscles. His ham hock hands hung limply at his sides. His misshapen, shaved head was covered in scars, his face as ugly and as sad as a bulldog's.

When she had seen him years ago in the library, his face was twisted and snarling in rage. Today, his beady black eyes were full of misery.

'I'm sorry, Eliza, but orders are orders. You've got to be brought back.'

She took a step back and bumped into the Cruel. He gripped her shoulder with a cold hand. The chill sent a ripple of dread through her body.

'And punished,' his soft voice hissed.

The Hound whined pitifully. Despite her situation, Eliza felt for her dear Pup. She'd always been kind to him because she understood what it was to be different in a family of perfect people and he loved her for it.

'What if she was willing to come quietly, Cornelius? If she came now, we could wash off the tan and fix her hair. We could pretend she'd been in the hospital. Your dad was always kind to the willing . . .'

The Cruel held up a hand and the other man felt silent.

'That would be a lie. We punish liars as severely as we punish runaways. I'll forget that you said that, Julian. I appreciate your loyalty and, in time, so will Eliza.'

Eliza let out a terrified cry as the Cruel pulled her closer to him. She heard the wet parting of his lips as he bent to whisper in her ear.

'When I'm done with you, you will be the epitome of loyalty.'

His voice held a faint tremor of desire, and she felt the slight rise of his erection against her backside. He licked his lips and Eliza felt something in her snap. Before she realised she had moved, she elbowed the Cruel in the gut. He crumpled behind her. She spun around and kicked him in the face, feeling his nose crunch beneath her foot. She smacked him with her rucksack before scrambling over his back towards the next carriage.

'Julian! Stop her!' the Cruel howled from the floor.

The Hound dropped to all fours and ran after her. Eliza had almost reached the other carriage. She could see the other passengers. She could see safety. She jabbed the button to release the door. It wouldn't open. She banged on the glass in panic.

'Help!' she cried in desperation as Julian reached her. The conductor turned, too late, as he dragged her away from the door.

'Eliza, please. You'll only make it worse.'

'How could it be any fucking worse? Pup, please, let me go. I'm not like the rest of you. I'm of no use. Please!' She was weeping now. 'Please let me go!'

'It won't be so bad, Eliza . . .' Julian began.

'They'll kill me! Please Pup, please! They'll kill me.'

Cruelty

She flailed in his arms, one last futile attempt at escape. The Hound hitched her up on his shoulder, smashing her head on the luggage rack. She struggled on a moment longer before her world went black.

Chapter 2

IT HURT TO think. It hurt to breathe. She wanted to open her eyes. Why couldn't she open her eyes?

She felt like she was at the bottom of the ocean, the huge weight of all the world's water pressing down on her.

She wanted to scream for help but the words caught in her gullet.

A cool hand reached down through the miles of water and touched her face.

'Eliza,' someone called, far away, muffled.

Who is Eliza?

'Eliza.' The voice sounded again, clearer now. Other noises began to come through: the low hum of conversation, footsteps echoing on a floor. She struggled as consciousness flooded back.

'Eliza!' The voice was sharp this time and the chill hand shook her.

Eliza sat up, gasping for air. She stared around wildly, not registering what she saw for a moment. Then Cornelius was there, leaning over her. She punched him hard, jarring his broken nose. He fell back, swearing as she tried to scramble away. But she couldn't move. She was surrounded by blankets and there were bars on the sides of the bed. A clear bag on a long pole stood beside her. The damn thing was an IV, feeding saline into her arm, keeping her trapped for precious seconds as she pulled out the needle.

She tore at it with her teeth and tried once more to escape. But she was still tethered, lower down. Inside her. A catheter! She clawed viciously at the invader, barely registering the pain as she yanked it free. Cornelius scrambled up, eyes streaming as she pulled herself over the bars. He lunged, wrapping his arms around her. She screamed and kicked out, trying to break his hold as he clamped a hand over her mouth, stifling her cries. She swung her legs back, viciously aiming for his groin. He tried to sink to the ground but Eliza's fear had given her a rush of strength and he couldn't bring her down. He twisted, and her heel cracked off the wall.

Eliza screamed in pain and outrage. She slammed her head back but he dodged and his nose avoided another battering. In the struggle, she managed to wiggle her head free a little. She sank her teeth into the flesh between his thumb and index finger. He groaned, and his hold tightened, encouraging the bite. They stumbled backwards as Cornelius tried to bring her down once more.

Her feet found purchase against the wall and she pushed. They flew forward, knocking over the bedside locker and sending the vase on top of it skittering across the floor.

'Eliza, stop it!' Cornelius hissed. 'We're in a *Gnáth* hospital. Do you realise how much trouble we'll be in if your father finds out I brought you here? We'll have to go to Him.'

She stilled. Cornelius was bad, but the alternative was far, far worse. With a groan of protest, she released her grip on his hand and he let her go. Exhaustion washed over her as the adrenalin faded away. She sat down on the bed and glared at Cornelius. He brought his left hand to his mouth and sucked the bite, closing his eyes for a long moment. When he opened them, his pupils were dilated. She could see the faint outline of his erection.

'Why are we here?' she asked, deliberately ignoring his arousal.

Cornelius picked up the locker and restored the vase to its proper place. Eliza glanced around the room. They were clearly in a private hospital, tastefully decorated to look like a hotel. There was real art on the walls, rather than prints. A large window overlooked the hospital grounds and she could see nothing but parkland. A television was mounted on the wall. Of course he'd have brought her to a private hospital; he could pay the bill directly with cash and there would be no record of her in the NHS. Not that he'd have given her real name even if they had gone to an NHS hospital, but he was taking no risks.

The Cruel settled comfortably into the visitor's chair.

'You fought us on the train. You banged your head badly and passed out. We managed to get you into the car but then you started vomiting.' He wrinkled his nose in disgust and winced, raising a hand to his sore nose. 'I was half-way through fixing my nose and Julian took his eyes off the road for a moment. We were side-swiped by a drunk driver and he crashed the car. A *Gnáth* called an ambulance. With your head injury, they insisted we went to a hospital. I convinced them to bring us here rather than the local accident and emergency.' He frowned. 'I'm glad you aren't dead. I don't like dead things.'

Eliza pressed her lips together, fighting a fresh surge of vomit.

'How long have we been here?'

'Two days. They want to keep you in for observation for a while. And then . . .' a slow smile spread across his face, 'you're all mine.'

It took every ounce of Eliza's self-control not to show fear. 'Sounds promising.'

Cornelius blinked hard. He got to his feet and stood over her, pushing his bruised face into hers and forcing her to look him in the eye.

'Don't toy with me Eliza. You will be punished. You will cry. You will bleed. You will scream.'

'As I said, sounds promising,' she repeated, but the humour was gone from her voice. Instead, she mimicked his tone. Cold, hard, fearless.

The Cruel grabbed a fistful of hair and forced her head back.

'I have a thousand ways to inflict untold pain on you,' he said. 'I can paralyse you, spread fire through your muscles, turn your bones to dust, make you believe spiders are eating your eyes. Don't make the mistake of thinking that just because I don't have my tools or because we are amongst the *Gnáth* that I cannot touch you.'

He threw her down on the bed and stalked away. She watched him leave the room and heard the door lock before she allowed the fear to flow over her. One tear, then another trickled down her cheek. She pulled the covers over her head as the first sobs choked their way out of her throat.

A gentle hand smoothed the hair out of Eliza's face and her eyes opened. A middle aged nurse sat beside her, with kind eyes and a frown of concern.

'How are you, love?' she asked.

'I'm fine,' Eliza lied, sitting up. Her eyes were sore and puffy from crying and her throat was raw. Her head felt stuffed with damp cotton wool.

She gratefully took the water and the apple the woman offered, and glanced around the room.

'He's gone to get something to eat.' The nurse answered her unspoken question. 'He almost refused to leave . . .' She paused. 'You know, you could tell a nurse anything and we'd be able to help you.'

Eliza nearly spat her water out as she realised where the conversation was going.

'You whacked your head pretty badly for such a small crash and the bump's in a strange place.' The nurse paused again. 'I can help you get away. We have close links to a woman's shelter and lawyers who specialise in this sort of thing.'

It was tempting. The police could keep Cornelius away long enough for her to get away, at least long enough for her to escape England. She'd get to Europe or Asia this time.

She opened her mouth to speak but, over the woman's shoulder, she saw Cornelius coming up the corridor. He had permission to torture *Gnáth* humans if necessary, in his line of duty. He would work out who had helped her escape. His retribution would be painful and slow against this kind-hearted soul.

Cornelius reached the door, one questioning eyebrow raised. Eliza made her choice.

'I'm sorry?' She blinked hard to feign confusion. 'Do you think he's been beating me?'

'Well . . .' the nurse said.

Eliza covered her mouth, her eyes widening in horror. 'Oh God, no. *No,*' she stressed. 'He's my boyfriend; he'd never hurt me. We were hit by a drunk driver. We were both hurt. Look at his face. He smashed his face on the dashboard.'

Cornelius coughed. The older woman looked back and saw him.

'I'd never hurt her,' he said in a small voice, looking convincingly hurt and sad.

'Sweetheart, the lady is only doing her job. Don't be upset.'

The nurse got to her feet, putting herself between Cornelius and her patient. 'Why did you lock her in?' she asked, her voice full of suspicion.

'I asked him to,' Eliza said. 'I get anxious and I panic. I pulled my IV and catheter out earlier. He was giving me space to calm down.'

The nurse took a step towards the Cruel. She was tiny and slight in comparison to him but Eliza had no doubt she could handle any *Gnáth* man she perceived as a threat. She frowned as she inspected the bruises on his face. Cornelius gave her a charming smile and Eliza saw the blush rise up her throat before she scurried away, leaving them alone once more.

Cornelius sat on the edge of the bed and stared at Eliza as if perplexed.

'She was offering you an escape?'

'Yes.'

'Why did you refuse?'

'Because she's innocent,' Eliza said. 'She offered me refuge and protection, completely unaware of the repercussions. Her kindness didn't deserve to be repaid with whatever special kind of hell you bring.'

He tilted his head to one side as he digested her words.

'I didn't expect that from you. I thought you'd seize any opportunity to escape, no matter who got in the way. Maybe you're not as selfish as I first thought?'

He frowned and stood up. He threw a few trashy magazines on the bed. 'The doctor wants you to read something,' he said, turning on the television.

Eliza opened one glossy that screeched about Z-list celebrities and tales of amazing pets on the front cover. As she flicked through the pages, she knew he was staring at her, confusion playing across his face.

'Where's Julian?' she asked, uncomfortable with the intensity of his gaze.

'At the hotel. I couldn't leave my tools for your punishment unattended.' He continued to stare.

She suppressed a shudder but Cornelius must have seen the apprehension flicker across her face. He smiled.

'Pain isn't so bad, you know. After a while, you might enjoy it.'

Eliza said nothing, choosing to return to her magazine. Cornelius refused to be dissuaded.

'Being Barren, you'll never have anyone touch you. This will be the closest you get to sex. If I was you, I'd see it as a blessing.'

He didn't even see it coming. She flicked her wrist and the apple the nurse had given her sailed out of her hand and hit him on the nose.

'Oh for fuck's sake!' he growled. 'Would you ever leave off my nose? It's going to be hard enough to fix after leaving it so long.'

'Pain's not so bad,' she mimicked. 'Why haven't you fixed it?'

'Lends credence to the car crash story.' He winced. 'Just so you know, I'd have left the nurse alone. You're the guilty one. And if you managed to get me arrested?' He let out a long, low whistle. 'You might have actually been able to escape me altogether.'

She rolled her shoulders, refusing to rise to the bait. She knew his game. He wanted to torture her emotionally and mentally first, make her feel wretched and alone. She smiled wryly to herself. She'd felt that way for years; he would have to try much harder than that to shake her. She stared at him, refusing to break his gaze, until he shrugged and turned his attention back to the television.

The doctor had been friendly and firm. He reminded Eliza of her own father. She felt a pang of guilt, knowing how she must have broken his heart when they realised she wasn't dead, only hiding.

'I'm happy with your recovery. We'll keep you in for the rest of today to be sure. I'll prescribe some painkillers for that bump, but there appear to be no other ill effects after your accident.'

He too had raised the question of domestic abuse. If only she could tell them what they were tangling with, then they would leave her alone and stop putting themselves in danger.

'Are you absolutely sure there's nothing else?' he asked now.

'Nothing, Doctor. Thank you.'

Unlike with the nurse, there was no charming Cornelius to weave an enchantment and dispel the doctor's fears. The Cruel had been whisked away on the pretence of filling in some forms so the doctor could ask his delicate questions in private. Eliza had to rely on her own merits to convince him everything was fine.

'He's never touched me,' she said.

'The bump on your head and his possessiveness of you suggest otherwise.'

'What about his face? He was hurt in that accident too.' She fought to keep the tension out of her voice.

'His injuries could also be consistent with wounds inflicted in self-defence,' the doctor remarked quietly. 'If he's hurting you and you want to report him, let me know.'

He put his pen back in his pocket and frowned at her, as if unhappy with what he saw. *Shit*, Eliza thought. *He's going to figure it out. He'll realise we're not normal.*

But the realisation never came. The doctor nodded at her and walked away. Eliza fell back on the sheets and rubbed the heels of her hands into her eyes to quell the panic.

'Everything all right?'

She looked up. Her gaoler was back, holding two paper cups. She blinked in surprise.

'You got a drink for me? Thank you.'

'They're very suspicious of me. I don't seem to be much of a caring boyfriend. They're close to calling the police,' he said, dismissing her gratitude.

Eliza took a sip of tea as Cornelius pulled the visitor's chair up to the edge of the bed.

'Aren't they supposed to in car crashes?'

He nodded. 'I've managed to keep them from doing that so far but the more people we have contact with, the more difficult that will be.' He sighed. 'We need to get out of here soon. We can't bring any more scrutiny on us. Why the fuck did you run away? You've put us all in danger.'

She stared into her tea, ashamed. She hadn't meant to pull anyone else into her mess. She just wanted a life. She was a nobody back home, an outcast, a dreadful shame for the Greater Branch to bear. They had no need of her for the Ritual or in the house. She would never need the Ritual, because there was nothing to renew. What was the point of staying to be ignored?

Cornelius leaned forward, glaring at her. 'It wasn't a rhetorical question.'

She sighed but did not answer.

'Do you know who we are, Eliza? Do you know what we do?'

'We are the last of the People. We protect the ancient sites and Magicks,' she replied, the words learned by rote. 'We protect the last guardian of the Veil and He protects us.'

Cornelius scowled.

'You could be more reverent. It's far more than that. We protect the earth; we help maintain the balance between worlds.'

'How exactly? By blindly completing the Ritual year after year, acting like zealots? Do you honestly think it necessary? How can you justify what He requires of us?'

'That's blasphemy.' The Cruel paled. His hand closed around her wrist and he squeezed, digging his nails into the tender flesh underneath. She grit her teeth against the pain; she would not give him the satisfaction of seeing her show weakness.

'If we are to properly attend to our duty, we need what He gives us in return for our sacrifice. Eire is where the seams between worlds are thinnest. Our Master is bound to the seam beneath the House and so, as the last of the People, we protect the other ones.

'We stop the *Gnáth* from undoing the seals and the spells protecting them. We are the environmental lawyers and the *Teachtaí Dála* that decide where houses are built and which areas of Ireland get protected status. We maintain the holy places. There are people out there who know these places of magic and power exist and they want to abuse them, to open the Veil in vain attempts to get power. We stop ordinary mortals from waking forces they cannot control. '

Eliza knew she was sneering, and she didn't try to hide it. She'd suffered a lifetime having this speech spouted at her, usually when someone wanted to make her feel like a failure because she'd been born a dud. She didn't need to hear it again.

'And we make a fucking fuckload of money in the process. Don't try and sell me the idea that everything we do is pure, Cornelius. If it was, we'd have stayed in Ireland, doing our duty. As it is, we are supporting emerging economies, we have links with Big Oil and Big Tobacco. We're staying disgustingly rich, while the rest of Ireland tumbles back into poverty. How is that protecting her? And when was the last time we actually faced a threat to the holy places? Aren't you usually sent to deal with people who are muscling in on our investments, rather than those trying to access the Veil?

'The last of the People do not give a flying fuck about protecting the Veil. They care about the power.' He was gaping at her, rendered speechless by her lack of faith. 'Do you want to know why I left? I left because I can't stand the smell of bullshit.'

Cornelius twisted her wrist, forcing it back on itself. The bones cracked and protested under the strain. She bit back an instinctive whimper and held his gaze. It was only the door opening that ended their stand-off, forcing Cornelius to let her go. It was the well-meaning nurse. Eliza rubbed her wrist absently as her eyes sailed over the woman's name tag. *Angelica*. How apt.

'The doctor thinks you're almost ready to go,' she said. 'But he would like to see you up on your feet first. It's a lovely day. You two love birds can take a stroll in the Community garden. It will do you both the world of good.'

Eliza almost giggled at the absurdity of the situation. Angelica fussed around her, slipping her feet into soft booties. All the while Cornelius glared, his hot gaze threatening all kinds of Hell. Eliza extended her hand and Cornelius pulled her up. She lost her balance and fell against him. He smelt like fresh air and clean linen. She jerked back, reaching for the dressing gown the nurse offered.

'I have to say,' he muttered as they walked down the corridor, 'your boyfriend idea was a good one. Gave me license to stay with you.'

'I play chess,' she answered nonchalantly. 'We're playing a dangerous game here. You were never going to leave me on my own and they'd have grown suspicious. It was the best strategy at the time. I know we're related, somewhere in our twisted bloodline, but we don't look enough alike to pretend we're siblings.'

'That's actually a brilliant plan.'

'Careful, I hear a trace of admiration in your voice.'

He attempted a snort of derision, but it was oddly lacking in conviction.

'I was just wondering when you became such an accomplished liar.'

'The day I was born.'

Her quick reply made him smile and a laugh escaped his lips. Eliza raised her eyebrows in disbelief. 'Is that a sense of humour, Mr MacCatháin?'

'Oh no. Mine's far more twisted.'

A door on her right opened to the outside world. Cornelius slid his arm around her shoulders and drew her in tight.

'I wasn't going to try anything,' she whispered.

'I know. Just making sure.'

She wriggled. The way Cornelius held her was painful on her left shoulder. It felt like he was trying to push it out of its socket with his torso. She twisted and squirmed until she could slip her arm around his waist, relieving the discomfort. She reached out with her fingers to brush his left hand, feeling the welts where she'd sunk her teeth in. She pinched the flesh, not hard enough to make him loosen his hold but enough to make him jump.

The Cruel gazed down at her. He licked his lips.

'You're going to fight me, aren't you?' he said.

'Every step of the way,' she answered, calmly.

He swallowed. Eliza repressed a shudder.

Sick fuck!

'No one's ever fought me before. They always fold in on themselves, accept their fate. No one has ever been a challenge.'

'Well, we wouldn't want you to get bored.' Eliza wished she could untangle herself from him. 'You'll have to earn my screams.'

He chuckled at her bravado. 'I look forward to my reward.' He lowered his mouth to whisper in her ear. 'I will make you scream, Eliza, do not doubt that. I hope you enjoy the garden. It will be the last breath of freedom you ever have.'

The fresh air was a relief after so long in that small room. The Community garden was a pleasant space, an oasis in a place of pain and worry. There was a bench beneath the shade of two intertwining oak trees and a fountain in the middle of a pond full of lazy goldfish. It even had a picnic area in the middle of the large patch of grass. A family sat at the table, a wisp of a girl in a wheelchair, gazing into the abyss while her mother chattered away in a high, brittle voice and her father silently cut something up into tiny pieces.

'We'll get you another donor, Amanda. It will be fine. Just fine.'

Eliza's throat constricted at the scene. 'We should go back inside,' she whispered to her captor.

'It's a public garden,' he said, his eyes closed, clearly enjoying the sun on his face.

'But those people,' she insisted, 'their grief is so raw. We should leave them alone.'

Cornelius opened his eyes and looked at her in confusion. 'You don't take an offered escape because you don't want the nurse to get hurt. You don't want to stay out here because of this sad family. I don't understand. You care about everyone but your own people. What the fuck is wrong with you?'

He pressed his forehead to hers. To the outside world, they looked like a young couple cuddling up. But it was intimidation, an attempt to force her into silence. She would not be bullied. She refused to be cowed by his behaviour.

'That little girl is dying,' she said. 'She's in agony. Her pain, her looming death, her very existence is a constant source of misery and distress to those who love her. I know empathy isn't in your repertoire, but we should afford that child a little dignity.'

Her tone was calm and even. There was no anger in her words, only compassion. Cornelius glanced over at the little girl and then nodded his assent. They got to their feet and left the family in peace. Cornelius took her hand again, but held it loosely, distracted as they moved from the cool air of the garden into the fetid atmosphere of the hospital.

Chapter 3

ORNELIUS CHEWED HIS bottom lip as they made their way back to Eliza's room. His prisoner was a puzzle to him. He'd never had contact with the dud from the Greater Branch before, neither had he noticed her at many Family functions. She lingered in the background, sad and silent. She went to her job in the village library early in the morning and returned late. She stayed out of the way, almost invisible. No one expected her to be so devious as to fake her death and evade detection for six months. He thought he would confront a selfish, ungrateful brat who would do whatever it took, hurt whoever it took, to get away.

Despite her initial struggles against him, she'd instead proved herself kind, compassionate and able to listen to reason. She was clearly frightened of him and everything he threatened her with but when she realised they were amongst *Gnáth* people, she immediately stopped fighting him, adopting the default position of 'Protect the Family. Say nothing. Do not bring their attention to us.'

And she was strong. She did not look away, did not whimper in fear when he threatened her. She would fight. It was almost admirable . . .

He rubbed his forehead and pinched his eyes closed in frustration. Usually there was no thinking involved in his job. He was far from stupid, but normally he was sent after someone having been told they were evil and he dealt with them, quickly and aggressively. Eliza was an enigma.

'Is it all right if I have a shower?'

Eliza's question dragged him back to the moment. 'Are you asking my permission?'

She shrugged. 'You're my gaoler, aren't you?'

'There's a shower in your room. You can wash if you want.'

'Thank you,' she said. 'I appreciate it.'

She smiled then, a genuine, if sad smile of gratitude. His heart stopped. For the first time he saw her delicate beauty, rather than just the betrayal. He forced the feeling down. She was a traitor, a traitor who would be punished, no matter how pretty she was.

They swung past the hospital gift shop to pick up some shower gel and shampoo, as well as a new pair of pyjamas.

'Fancy hospital,' Eliza mused as Cornelius paid. 'Are the Family paying for it?'

'No,' he told her, as they walked away. 'I am. I'd become far more intimately acquainted with my own tools if your father found out we were here.'

'I thought the entire point of coming after me was to punish me.'

'It is. That does not extend to putting a Fae-child in a *Gnáth* hospital. I'm not into self-abuse.'

He caught her smiling to herself, amused despite it all.

'Careful. There's that sense of humour again.'

He said nothing and she looked away.

Back in the room, Cornelius settled into the chair while Eliza vanished into the en-suite. He turned on the television, flicking through until he reached a history channel. He tried to engross himself in a documentary on the Black Death but the puzzle of Eliza distracted him. Try as he might he could think of nothing but her and her plump pout.

'Ah feck,' he groaned aloud. 'Why did she have to be pretty?' He fished in his pocket for his phone and dialled a number. 'Hi, Kylie? It's Cornelius. How are ya? Yeah, yeah. I'm grand. Listen, I'm not too far from you. Fancy a drink sometime this week?'

The girl simpered and giggled down the phone. The last time he and Kylie went for a drink, it had taken a mere twenty minutes to get from their meeting in the hotel bar to his room. His date made, Cornelius turned back to the television and tried to ignore the fact Eliza was naked in the adjoining room.

Eliza locked the bathroom door and sank onto the toilet, covering her face with her hands. She had no tears left, only resignation. At least he'd let her shower. She stank, days of sweat and inactivity clinging to her skin and clothing. She sniffed and got to her feet, letting the ordinary action of washing keep the horror at bay. She turned the shower on and let it run until the room filled with steam, stripped and stepped into the cubicle.

Standing with her eyes closed, she let the hot water engulf her. She tried to let her mind float away, to enjoy the heat, but she was too distracted. The way Cornelius looked at her made her uncomfortable, his stare, as if he was trying to pierce her soul even as he made her cower before him. But there was the other side to him, a human side. She'd made him laugh, he liked the way she fought him and he respected her for not putting *Gnáth* people in danger. He even had a heart. He'd listened to her when she said they should leave the family in the garden alone with their grief. It also didn't hurt that he was handsome. Even with his broken nose, he was fine to look at . . .

'Whoa Missy!' Eliza opened her eyes. 'The man wants to beat the living daylights out of you. Behave yourself.'

She reached for the shower gel and found the knobs for a radio.

'Feck me. This *is* a fancy hospital.' She fiddled with the buttons until she found a song she liked, smiling as the opening bars of 'Ain't no sunshine' floated out of the speakers. Her father used to sing it about her mother when Ruby went away to reseal barriers or fight environmental cases. Those had been good days, when there was still hope for her.

Eliza sang throatily along with the music as she scrubbed away the last of the fake tan. The radio station must be an oldies one because the next tune was 'Lean on me.' She couldn't help herself. She sang along with this one too, louder this time as she washed her hair.

Eliza turned off the water and the radio but kept humming to herself. She opened the door, dressed in her new white pyjamas, her long hair pulled into a braid. She smiled wryly as she caught sight of her reflection; with her pale skin and dark hair she looked like a pixie. It was a cruel irony. She had no power. Her stomach rumbled, reminding her she'd eaten nothing since breakfast and even then she'd only picked at her food.

She took a step towards Cornelius, to ask him if they could get something to eat. Her captor had dozed off in the chair in front of the TV. Asleep, all the aggression in his face vanished. Long dark lashes fanned his cheek and a lock of white-blonde hair fell across his forehead. She swallowed, ignoring the intense flash that erupted across her belly. She tucked his hair back into place with trembling fingers, and he smiled in his sleep at her touch.

She glanced towards the door. Could she run? Would she make it?

She took a deep breath and decided against it. She wouldn't have got one step before the Cruel woke and inflicted a terrible mental punishment on her. Cornelius frowned while he slumbered. Eliza took one of the blankets from the bed and covered him with it, wondering when the lunch trolley would arrive.

Cornelius woke with a start, looking around in panic and cursing himself for drifting off. It took a moment to realise Eliza hadn't left. She sat on the bed, chewing an apple and filling in a crossword.

'I got you some lunch,' she said. 'The doctor will be back soon and then we can leave.'

The Cruel levered himself out of the seat. His back ached and he had a crick in his neck.

'You didn't run.' It was almost an accusation.

'I think I'm in enough trouble, don't you?'

He crossed the room in two strides and towered over her. 'What are you trying to pull?'

'Nothing,' she said.

'Really? Do you think being sweet and compliant will save you from being dealt with? You're a traitor, Eliza. You abandoned your post.'

'I didn't have a post to guard!' she snapped, leaping to her feet. 'I had nothing. I *am* nothing. I only became something when I left.'

'A problem,' Cornelius supplied.

'I was always a problem!' Eliza laughed bitterly. 'Do you honestly think being the only dud ever born to the Patriarch line isn't a fucking problem?'

Cornelius looked behind him. The door was shut but there was a little window through which their argument could be seen. He grabbed her arm and pulled her out of view, moving her easily even though she struggled.

'Lower your voice,' he said. 'Don't bring attention to us with your selfishness.' He craned his neck to see if anyone was coming.

'I'm not selfish.'

'Then why did you leave?'

'Because I love them, you moron.'

'Them who?'

'My mum and dad,' she said quietly. 'I left because I love them.'

He grimaced. Figuring out riddles wasn't his remit. 'What?'

'That little girl from earlier,' Eliza said. 'I know how she's feeling. She doesn't want to be here anymore, not because she wants to die but because her existence causes her loved ones so much pain and anxiety.' Pain danced across her face. 'Just like the pain I cause Mum and Dad. Duds aren't born in the Greater Branch. Certainly not to the Patriarch, not to direct descendants of the First Born.

'My very existence is a constant source of shame to my parents. I have no doubt they love me, but they *are* ashamed of me. How do you explain that you're the ones who produced the dud, when you're supposed to be the best? I left because my presence in the house causes them so much pain. If I'm not there, there are no accusations to answer, no pity to be inflicted. I faked my death because they could cope with a dead child. They cannot cope with a dud.'

Her voice cracked and tears streamed down her face.

'It's not my fault I was born without magic, but I still get punished for it.' She hiccupped between her sobs. 'I didn't do anything wrong and everyone hates me. I'm ignored all the time. I have no friends. I'll never be allowed a husband in case I taint the children. Nobody wants anything to do with me.'

She turned her bright, fierce eyes, wet with tears, to her captor. 'Can you even fathom how that makes me feel? And in turn how that hurts my parents? I figured if I was going to be a nothing, I could be a nothing elsewhere and stop hurting people.'

All the spirit left her. She dropped her head and gazed into emptiness, wiping away silent tears that wouldn't stop. Cornelius shifted uncomfortably. He had not expected that. He rubbed the bridge of his nose reflexively before the sharp sting of broken bone made him snatch his hand away.

'Whatever your reasons,' he said, 'you still broke the rules. You might have acted out of love but you can't just up and leave. That's not how it works.' He frowned. 'And you can't get out of your punishment either.'

A small, bitter laugh burst from her lips. 'I accept my fate, which is far worse than anything you have planned for me. It doesn't mean I'm not afraid. I'm terrified of the pain you will bring me, but you bring something far worse. You're sentencing me to a slow and painful death, suffocating under pity, shame and isolation.'

She looked up at him again, her eyes sad and resigned. 'Do you know something? This is the most I've spoken to anyone in four years. I'm glad my final real conversation was half-way meaningful, even if you don't understand.'

She got to her feet and dried her tears as the doctor came in to the room.

'Miss Smith, I've got your discharge papers. You can leave whenever you're ready.'

'I'm ready,' she said, her voice betraying a tremor as she looked at Cornelius.

Oh Eliza. No one is ever ready for what I bring.

Chapter 4

*J*ULIAN BROUGHT THE silver BMW round to the front of the hospital. It had a long, fresh gash down its side where the drunk had hit it.

'Rental company will have fun with that,' Cornelius said. 'Always tick the insurance box when you fill in the form.'

Eliza didn't reply. She felt sick and her jaw ached from clenching it so hard. As Cornelius tore his appraising gaze from her and opened the boot, Eliza felt like someone was standing on her chest, making her stomach lurch. Her ribcage tightened round her heart as she caught sight of a blackened choke pear. She felt the air catch in her lungs. Cornelius flicked the blanket over it, swearing at Julian for being so foolish. His words washed over Eliza like white noise.

Holy shit. He'll ruin me. He's going to rape me with that thing and then peel my flesh off in little pieces.

The Cruel threw Eliza's backpack into the boot. He had to guide her into the car; she was frozen to the spot. He followed her in while Julian guarded the passenger door.

'Put the child locks on, Julian,' Cornelius said, evenly. 'She's liable to try something stupid otherwise.'

'Why not just tie me up?' She tried to sound defiant, but her voice betrayed her.

'There will be time for all that fun later. Besides, if I want to bind you, I'll do it magically. Less suspicious to passing peelers.'

Eliza nodded as if he'd said something banal like 'Nice weather.' She was aware of every inch of her body. Every hair on her skin stood on end and her heart thumped so hard her chest hurt. She had so little left and he was going to take it all from her. She bit her cheek to keep from screaming. She closed her eyes and focused on taking slow, measured breaths to lower her heart rate.

Cornelius looked at her again. The dark hair suited her. She really was pretty. No, she was more than that. She was beautiful. And clever.

And devious. And a traitor. His Familial conscious niggled at him. *She's slippery and dangerous. Do not drop your guard.*

'I won't touch your face,' he said.

Eliza opened her eyes but made no other movement.

'It's more delicate,' he elaborated. 'I won't touch your face because I might break bones that never heal.'

She did not answer him, just kept staring forward at nothing as Julian put the car into gear and drove out of the grounds of the hospital.

As soon as they were on the motorway, Cornelius began repairing his nose, muttering to himself as the last of the swelling went down and the bruises vanished. It took fifteen minutes for all signs of Eliza's attack to vanish. He wrinkled his nose to test it for aches and pains.

'That's impressive.' Eliza's voice held reluctant admiration.

'Thank you. It's not my natural skill . . .' He stopped, realising he had fallen into ordinary conversation with her. Again. Feck. He had to stop that. She was a prisoner and he wasn't being a good gaoler. It was her. She was distracting. The way she looked at him made him feel . . . sorry for her. But he couldn't afford her any sympathy; sympathy led to doubt and doubt led to a job badly done.

'Julian. Pull over at the next service station. I want to drive for a bit.'

Eliza's ears pricked up. There was a chance, a tiny chance she could get away without putting anyone else in danger. She had a bank card sewn into the inside pocket of her jeans. If the opportunity presented itself, she was running.

At a service station? Where would you run to? Into traffic, fuck some poor driver up for life? She bit her lip, ignoring her doubts. She had to take the risk.

Luck was on her side. Julian pulled over beside a busy picnic area, close to fields and a walker's path. She was giddy when she saw him unlock the child locks. She released her belt, muffling the sound with her hand as Cornelius turned away. The moment his back was turned she threw open the car door and flung herself out. She was on her feet in an instant, tearing off towards the fields.

Behind her she heard Cornelius' shout to Julian. She lengthened her stride and risked a glance back. Cornelius pelted after her. Picnicking families gazed around in shock as first Eliza and then Cornelius ran towards the benches. The Cruel lost his footing and fell, swearing loudly. Eliza allowed herself a grin. She was almost at the path. She could do this. She could get away . . .

She heard him gaining on her, felt the anger boiling in his blood. Anger at her, anger at Julian, anger at himself for giving her the opportunity to escape.

Eliza felt him brush the sleeve of her jacket and tried to force her legs to move faster but it was no use. The Cruel grabbed her arm and pulled her to him.

Feck.

She slammed against his body. He wrapped his arms around her and pulled her close to him, looking down at her. His teeth were clenched but his eyes shone with the enjoyment of the chase.

'Is everything all right, love?' a middle-aged man shouted from the car park. He held his phone out, ready to call the police.

'What are you going to do?' Eliza whispered. 'There are dozens of witnesses who can put you in a cell. You can't touch me here.'

Cornelius smiled at her. He wound his hands into her hair.

'Is that what you think?'

Before she could object, he pressed his mouth to hers. She froze for a moment before she responded. She put her arms around his waist, snaking her hands up his back. She groaned as his tongue pushed into her mouth.

Cornelius let go of her hair and slid his hands down her body. He dragged her hips against his, pressing his erection into her. She gasped and instinctively pulled him closer. His teeth grazed her bottom lip and she felt her knees buckle.

'Oi! There are kids here, you two!' the by-stander shouted, miffed at the public display of affection but pleased the girl wasn't being attacked.

Eliza moaned in protest as Cornelius pulled away.

'You heard the man,' he said.

'That's not fair,' she breathed.

Cornelius grinned down at her. 'I don't play fair. Neither do you.' He put his arm around her shoulders and guided her back to the car. He pressed his lips against her temple as they passed the concerned citizen, who tutted, pointing to the kids at the tables. A thousand tiny shock waves passed over Eliza's skin and her lips tingled.

'At least I've been kissed,' she murmured as they reached the car. 'Ow!' There was a sharp scratch in her back as she bent to get in. She whipped round. Cornelius was crushing a syringe ruthlessly beneath his boot. She felt her limbs grow heavy and her eyes fluttered, trying to stay open.

'No,' she mumbled, as she crashed into darkness. 'No.'

When Eliza woke, she was in a soft bed in an expensively decorated room. Her head hurt and her eyes struggled to focus. When they finally did, she saw the Family's crest carved into the frame of the mirror on the far wall.

Of course, they'd have brought her to a Family-owned hotel. Being on Family ground would strengthen Cornelius' resolve to punish her.

She tried to roll over but she couldn't; her hands and feet were bound to the bed. She struggled to sit up, pulling hard against the ropes but she was bound in a series of complicated knots, looping and twisting, doubling back on themselves.

'Feck,' she growled, giving up the fight.

She'd already given him the slip once. There was no way Cornelius would be lax with her restraints. Survival was her only option. Joshua had survived the Family's retribution but his mind was forever broken. He was thirty-one and he still slept in the old nursery, too simple to work or to breed. The old Cruel had stripped even his sexuality from him, leaving him a hollow shell, a being that existed, rather than a person.

Eliza vowed not to become like her ill-fated cousin. No matter what Cornelius did, she would remain Eliza. She strained her head up to gaze at her reflection in the mirror. Her pale green eyes were colourless in the muted light. They stared back from her reflection, not afraid, but determined. No matter what he did, she would survive.

The door handle turned and she put her head back down. A rough paw shook her, and she twisted her head to see the Hound.

'I brought you some food, Eliza. Only a few bits of fruit, but I knew you'd be hungry.'

Faithful Julian; her dear Pup had been trained only to fetch, not to punish.

'Thank you, Pup.' She smiled as he broke up the banana.

He fed it to her carefully. He wouldn't untie her and Eliza wouldn't ask him to. She had already caused him enough grief.

'Would you like a cuppa?' he asked, as if she was a visitor, rather than a prisoner.

'Thank you but I'd need my hands.' She tried to laugh and he sighed sadly, his slumped shoulders telling her he was deeply unhappy with the situation. She knew he adored her because she had never been cruel to him, unlike her brothers and the rest of the Family, who were as cruel in their way to Eliza as they were to Julian. She knew what it was like to be an outsider, like he was, and she had only ever shown him kindness.

'If it was up to me,' he said, 'I'd have set you free years ago.'

'But it isn't up to you.'

'I wish I could stop it. You don't deserve this. No one deserves this. I'd hoped you get away when I took the locks off . . .' The door handle rattled once more and Eliza stiffened. Cornelius entered, a black suitcase in his hand. It looked like a bag carried by a Victorian doctor. He scowled at Julian, who slunk away, slamming the door shut in a small act of rebellion. Cornelius put down the bag and crossed to Eliza. He moved her so she was sitting up, legs crossed, hands in her lap as if she was meditating. She caught a hint of his scent again and her stomach contracted as the memory of their kiss roared back to life.

Eliza watched Cornelius in silence as he unpacked his torture kit. Nausea threatened once more as each tool was revealed. First came a cat-o'-nine-tails, its wicked fronds knotted at regular intervals. It was followed by the choke pear. Her legs twitched reflexively as she remembered its dreadful purpose. A set of thumb screws came next, followed by a cat's paw and a knee splitter. Finally, he withdrew a set of knives as thin as paper, designed to fillet her skin from her flesh as if she was a piece of salmon. She bit down on her tongue to stop the scream that was building. She would not give him the satisfaction. She glared at him the entire time, even as he withdrew a ball gag. The only moment her resolve faltered was when he brought out a jumbo pack of baby wipes. The pink packet was so bright and commonplace amongst the dark medieval weapons she nearly dissolved into hysterical laughter. Eventually, he turned to face her, his face puckered in a frown. He kept opening and closing his mouth as if trying to articulate a difficult thought.

'I have a problem,' he said finally. He sighed and sat down on the stool in front of the dressing table, his head in his hands. 'When I kissed you,' he continued, speaking to the floor, 'I felt all your sadness, all your shame and grief. I saw your life as you live it. I can't get it out of my head.' He looked up now and she saw the pain, her pain, in his navy eyes. 'It keeps repeating over and over. I couldn't sleep last night. I spoke with Julian and he told me all about you, how you treat him like a human being rather than the beast the rest of us see, how you spend your free time keeping Joshua company. He said before you left, whenever you had a day off you'd take Josh to the park or the zoo, just to get him out of the house, give him some quality of life.'

He paused and licked his bottom lip.

'My old man really did a number on him.'

'I was in the library when he was brought home. I saw . . . I saw everything.'

Cornelius covered his mouth in horror. 'How old were you?'

'Eight.'

'Fuck,' he breathed. 'I was thirteen and not even I saw the full extent of it. Why didn't they take you out?'

'They didn't see me.'

'Bloody Hell. Of all the punishments to see.'

He fell into silence again. They sat there for a long time, contemplating the revelation.

'As I said,' the Cruel said eventually, 'I have a problem. In my head, I know you broke the rules. I know you should be punished. But in my soul . . .' he touched his chest with his open right hand, '. . . I don't think it's the right thing to do. I don't want to punish you.'

Eliza's heart leapt in hope.

'But,' he continued, 'I can't bring you back without retribution. My own position with the Family is tentative. I don't have the authority to *question* the order, never mind bring you home whole. If I even attempted it, they'd send us both downstairs.'

He got to his feet and crossed over to her. Crouching in front of her, he rested his left hand on her knee and cupped her chin in his right.

'I won't touch your face,' he repeated, reaching behind him as he rose.

'Wait! Wait!' She grabbed his hand. 'Why is your position tentative?'

He looked down at her.

'When I was twenty-one,' he kept hold of her hand, 'there was a girl. A *Gnáth* girl. It's not unusual for the men to play with outsiders and have a little fun before we're paired up.' He pressed his lips together. 'I really fell for her. I would have given up everything for her. But she was a spy, sent by a New York Irish gang looking for a way to muscle in on our American investments. I brought her to the house only once and I caught her trying to break into Jacob's office.

'I tore her to pieces with my bare hands before going across the Atlantic to do the same to the men who sent her. I did the right thing. I dealt with the threat. But I had introduced the threat in the first place. I was punished, a lash for every time I'd fucked her, and I was warned. There can never be another slip up.'

He sighed deeply, frowning down at her. 'So although I'm sympathetic to your plight, I cannot be lenient. I need to survive.'

'That's all I want too!' Eliza felt the tears threatening. 'Maybe . . . maybe we can help each other?'

Cornelius smiled sadly at her. 'How? I'm a Lesser and you're a dud.'

Cornelius must have seen the glint of deviousness in her eyes as an idea began to form. He smiled in return.

'What if we turned you from the Family torturer into the conquering hero?'

He sat down beside her, mistrust fighting with interest on his face. 'Go on.'

Eliza leant forward conspiratorially. 'In all the world,' she whispered, 'there are three people who know for definite that I ran away. Me, you and Julian.'

'Your mother knows . . .' he said.

She shook her head. 'My mother suspects. Totally different thing. Who's to say I actually ran away? What if I was taken against my will? You said we have enemies, waiting to discover our secrets. What if one of them . . . ?'

'Was watching the house, looking for weakness,' he interrupted, a tremor of excitement in his voice. 'And they realised your working pattern was the easiest to interrupt and struck at the opportune moment?'

Eliza sighed and tears filled her eyes. A low, shuddering breath, ragged and harsh, escaped her lips.

'I didn't want to go . . . They made me . . .' Her voice cracked. She looked down, her free hand plucking at the blanket. 'They wanted me to . . . to . . .' Her voice vanished as sobs shook her body. She looked up finally, smiling through her tears.

'You really are cunning.' Cornelius was unable to hide his respect. He wiped her face.

'You're still holding my hand,' she said.

He flushed as he untangled his fingers. 'We'd need a patsy,' he said. 'Someone we can blame, punish and dispose of before I take you home. Someone who wouldn't be missed.'

She tilted her head to one side. 'Surely as the head of security, you know someone who has it coming?'

The Cruel tilted his head, mirroring her thoughtful pose.

'There's someone I know. Nasty little man. Mark Sage, a former TD. Ruby ruined him last year for accepting bribes to build on green land. He lost everything in the court case and moved to England to escape the shame. He lives in Kent, isolated from everyone. This kind of revenge would be something he'd try to pull. It would be easy enough to set him up.'

'Does he deserve to be set up?'

He nodded firmly. 'I've met him a few times. Once at an environmental summit Ruby held at the house and a second time when I was sourcing some tools. I only use mine in a professional capacity. Others use them for pleasure.'

'Why would Sage have your kind of tools?' she asked.

'Because he's a sick fuck who likes to hurt little girls.'

Eliza shuddered with disgust. 'He'll do,' she muttered darkly.

Cornelius sat down once more in front of the dressing table and rubbed his eyes.

'Why am I discussing this as if it's an option?'

'Because it is,' Eliza said. 'Think about it. We both benefit. If you drag me home, battered and bruised, I'll be locked away forever and you go back to being 'The Cruel', the monster in the shadows. You'll be married off to some Lesser Branch breeder and always remain on the outside. But if you bring me back, having rescued me from the clutches of a pervert who was trying to use me to get Family secrets, you become a hero. You go up in everyone's estimation, raised beyond Punisher to Saviour, someone who can be relied upon to take the initiative and do whatever it takes to defend the Family, even a dud like me. The damage to your reputation will be undone. They might even match you to a Greater Branch girl as a reward. Your own mother was from the Greater Branch, to reward your father for his good work. They'd give you no less.'

Cornelius sat back, his hands behind his head. 'It's tempting. Really tempting. The incident with the *Gnáth* girl was almost my undoing. But . . . What do you get out of it?'

'A little overdue respect. You bring me back frail and vulnerable, having never said a word. Which is even more impressive considering . . .' she paused dramatically, 'that I fully believed no one was coming for me. I was willing to die to protect the Family who are ashamed of me and left me to rot.'

The statement hung in the air like a heavy fog. Cornelius and Eliza held each other's gaze for a long moment before the torturer spoke.

'That is genius,' he breathed. 'Almost Machiavellian.'

'I wouldn't go that far. I just want to survive,' she replied. 'Do we have a deal, oh conquering hero?'

The Cruel leant forward on the stool. 'If I agree, what assurance can you give me you won't run off again?'

'Are you negotiating terms?'

'Indeed I am.'

'Fine,' she said. 'Name them.'

Cornelius smiled at this brave little thing. Devious and clever, both loyal and disloyal, trying to cope with the bad hand life had dealt her. He held up his index finger.

'Firstly, you do what I tell you when I tell you. Secondly, you make one move, even think about running and I will break you into a thousand tiny pieces like the filthy runaway you are. Thirdly, you make the Blood Promise. You make the Oath to bind you to your words.'

He watched Eliza's tongue push against her cheek and roll under the flesh of her bottom lip as she pushed down her annoyance.

'All right,' she said finally. 'Here are mine. Firstly, you do not turn against me. You do not sell me out. Secondly, you do not use any of your medieval shit on me. Thirdly, you also take the Blood Oath.'

She leaned forward, the ropes restricting her. Her breasts swelled distractingly against her t-shirt.

'Untie me, so we can agree on this properly.'

He hesitated. Was he really willing to do this? Join a disloyal bitch and betray everything? He played through his doubts. Despite being a dud, she was still the daughter of the Patriarch and he a son of the Bastard, Lesser Branch. She was offering something no one else would ever give him, something he couldn't get on his own; a chance to remove the blemish the encounter with the *Gnáth* girl had left on his character. The tiny blemish that had caused his father to doubt him, despite all he'd achieved and all he'd done since, even on his death bed.

Eliza swallowed nervously as she watched him considering. Once again, she was struck by his male beauty. Her eyes travelled along the line of his square jaw, over his face, his high cheekbones, his perfectly straight nose. And his lips. She remembered the feel of them on hers, the taste of his skin and his body pressing into her as he'd kissed her in front of the *Gnáth* witnesses. She took a steadying breath and made another decision.

'I have one other thing I can offer you,' she said.

'And what's that?'

She fought the blush that threatened to rise up from the base of her throat.

'My virginity,' she said, her voice steady and unwavering. 'It's the only other thing I have of worth.'

Chapter 5

THE WORDS HIT Cornelius like a freight train. Her
virginity. The virginity of the Patriarch's daughter.
Now that was a prize worth having, even if she was
Barren and powerless. The Cruel moved from the stool to the
bed in one fluid movement, half-kneeling.

'You would give it to me? To seal our bargain?'

She nodded, never breaking eye contact. Her green irises
were flecked with gold, her pupils wide with desire. She was
tempting in and of herself, never mind what else she offered.

'I know you want me,' she said. 'I felt it when you kissed
me.' She looked down, flushing scarlet. 'Yesterday I was kissed
for the first time. And I liked it. I'd like to experience what
comes next.' The red marks of embarrassment on her cheekbones added enough vulnerability to her desire to render her
irresistible. 'With you. I know I should be terrified of you but
I can't get you out of my head. I want you.'

The ropes instantly unravelled. He took her by the hand
and helped her to her feet.

'I do want you,' he admitted, drawing her close to him. 'I
have since the moment you decided to fight me on the train.
But once you give me this, that's it. It can never be undone.
There's no magic that can make you whole again. No,' he tried

to pull away, 'you're the Patriarch's daughter. It's not right. It's not acceptable.'

'I know,' she said. 'But the best way to bind a Blood Oath is with the blood of lost virginity. If I give it to you, neither of us will be able to break our bond, even if we wanted to.'

Cornelius felt himself weakening as she placed her hands on his chest. His arms wrapped automatically around her waist. She touched her nose to his.

'It felt so good when you kissed me. I want more. I want you. I want you to fuck me.'

She pressed her mouth to his and desire won out over reason. His hands travelled over her body as he kissed her, lingering on her backside while Eliza's fingers moved into his hair, twisting and pulling it. He broke away and pulled his jacket off, tearing at his shirt and spraying buttons everywhere.

Eliza gazed at him, her pupils huge and black with desire. He knew just how good he looked with his clothes off. His body was almost hairless and carefully honed, lean and muscular from years of training and hunting. His broad shoulders tapered down to narrow hips. He took her hands and guided them over his skin, hearing her breathing quicken as she touched him.

She pulled off her own t-shirt and black bra. Her pale breasts swung gently as she stood back up. Cornelius dropped to his knees and took a nipple in his mouth. Her back arched as she gasped. Steadying her with a firm hand at the base of her spine, he closed his teeth over the nipple. She let out a small cry.

Cornelius smiled against her skin, feeling her chest rise and fall as she grew more excited. He moved his mouth to the other breast, wrapping his tongue around the nub. He growled as she dug her nails into the skin of his shoulders, tightening his grip on her backside and burying his face into her chest.

Eliza gasped as his tongue danced across her skin. Oh, this felt good. To be skin to skin with him, have his hands on her. Feeling brave, she wove her fingers into his hair and pulled him away from her. He yelped, but he was smiling. He got to his feet and turned her around so she stood in front of him as he sat down on the bed.

'Take the rest of your clothes off,' he ordered.

She looked at the floor while her deft fingers undid the buttons on her jeans and slid them down, along with her underwear.

'You are beautiful,' he breathed as she stood naked before him. He trailed his fingers up and down her body, making her shiver in anticipation. Touching her neatly trimmed pubic hair, he smiled. 'Who are you keeping this tidy for?'

'Just myself,' she answered, her voice husky.

'It would have been such a pity to carve you up.' His fingers brushed past her nipples again.

He grabbed her hips and pulled her down onto the bed. He dipped his head to kiss her once more. She groaned and draped her arms around his neck as he pressed his arousal into her. He moved his lips to her neck and nipped her throat, sending a sharp twinge of desire down her spine. She squirmed beneath him, sighing and groaning. She wanted him. She wanted all of him, right now. Cornelius smiled as she writhed, as she absorbed all of these feelings for the first time. He gently dragged his nails down her body and along her inner thigh. He stroked the sensitive skin at the base of her belly, making her quiver and hiss at the contact. Slowly, he circled his index finger on her outer lips. She shuddered at the intensity of the small movement and tried to pull away. He pressed his other hand against her shoulder.

'Hold still,' he said. 'You'll like it.'

He pushed his fingers into her, and she gasped.

'You're so wet.' He laughed in wonder, touching her clit softly. She twitched against his hand, unable to help herself, hips shifting of their own accord as he thrust his finger rhythmically in and out of her.

She dragged her tongue across her teeth as he touched her. She was rising and rising, burning in the intense heat from her own body, fired by his touch. She was on the crest of a wave, about to crash down. At the critical moment, he withdrew and she mewled in outrage, grabbing his wrist, seeking that touch again. He kissed her, then sucked his index finger, groaning in pleasure.

'You taste *so* good.'

He moved down her body, licking and sucking, nipping at her skin as he travelled down until he reached the juncture of her thighs. He buried his face in her mound, kissing the sensitive skin there. He grazed her outer lips and she whimpered. He kissed the delicate skin over and over again, brushing his lips against her, making her tense with need. He licked the whole length of her vulva with the flat of his tongue, opening her up, teasing both her inner lips and her clit.

Slowly, painfully slowly, he began to move his tongue around her clit and dip it inside her. She pushed her feet against the bed. Cornelius wrapped his arm around her thigh, holding her in place and forcing her to open her legs wider. She was whispering to herself as she climbed upwards, nonsense words of lust and desire, a fervent plea to be released. She couldn't hold on much longer, not with his tongue playing across her like a little flame. Her sweet-hot pain could only be relieved if he let her come, and he knew it.

Eliza arched her back as the sweet agony built. This was heaven, this feeling, this lust. Her sobbing breath caught in her throat.

'Please,' she begged, 'please.' It was a prayer, although she wasn't sure what she was praying for.

He drew back and sucked on her clit, stabbing his tongue forward to tip her over the edge. She jerked and spasmed as the orgasm blossomed within her.

'Oh!'

He sucked hard on the little nub, extending and maintaining her climax, making her peak and fall even as she came.

I'm going to die. It's too much. It's too wonderful. I am going to die.

Cornelius released her and she collapsed on the bed, panting and gasping as the tremors faded away. The Cruel kissed his way back up her body, briefly teasing her nipples again. He pressed his mouth to hers, swallowing up the last ripples of her climax.

'See how good you taste?' he asked, his eyes black with hunger for her.

She nodded, dazed by the force of what she'd experienced.

'Are you okay?' he asked, his features creased with concern.

'It's like the Veil woke up inside me,' she breathed. 'Will it always feel that good?'

'I'll try.' He laughed, and kissed her. She ran her hand down his body and timidly stroked his erection through the fabric of his trousers.

'Wait,' he groaned, standing up.

He shucked off his remaining clothing. Eliza's eyes travelled over his erection, drinking him in.

'Come here.'

She scrambled across the bed, eager to touch him again. He took her hand in his and closed it over his penis, moving it up and down.

He groaned as she instinctively picked up the pace. 'Slow down. I don't want to come all over your hands.' He pulled away. 'I want to fuck you. Wait here a second.'

He moved across the room towards his bag of torture tools. She stiffened for a moment, but relaxed when he reached for his jacket and pulled out a box of condoms. Cheeky bastard must have been going to sneak off with some *Gnáth* girl. He wrestled with the cellophane wrapping, tearing it with his teeth. She tilted her head to one side, carnal need making her bold. She got off the bed.

'What are you at?' he asked throatily.

Without answering, she sank to her knees and kissed along his pelvis towards his penis. He exhaled shakily as her lips moved up his shaft, towards the tip. She lingered there a moment before opening her mouth.

'Shit,' he muttered. She bobbed her head back and forth slowly, using her tongue to tease him, mimicking as best she could what he had done to her, to make him feel as good as she had.

Cornelius gasped as her tongue darted out. Fuck, she was quick on the uptake. He wanted to hold her by the hair and thrust into her mouth until he came down her throat, but there was a sweeter prize to be had.

'Baby, stop.' He sighed, reluctantly pulling back.

'Am I doing it wrong?' she asked, a tremor of uncertainty in her question.

He helped her to her feet. 'No, baby. It felt really good. It makes me want to fuck you even more.'

'Oh.' She blushed. 'Well, that's okay then.'

Cornelius kissed her and pressed his body flush against hers. He guided her backwards, cupping her backside. She ran her hands over his back and shoulders. Together, they tumbled back onto the bed. Cornelius knelt and tore the foil off the condom with his teeth before rolling it on. He settled between her legs, cupping her head in his hands

'You ready?'

She nodded, her chest rapidly rising and falling. He grinned and kissed her.

With one swift thrust, he entered her.

'Fuck!' she growled through gritted teeth. She dug her nails into Cornelius' back. He lay still, giving her a moment to grow accustomed to the feel of him, despite every fibre of him screeching at him to move. He drew back a little and reached between her legs. She was bleeding, not a huge amount, but enough to make a Blood Oath with. He moved his hips gently and she made a little sound, halfway between a whimper and a moan. He moved again, a touch harder and faster. Eliza closed her eyes and groaned.

'Do I feel good?'

'Yes.'

'Does it hurt?'

'A little,' she admitted. 'I kind of like it.'

'Do you want more?'

'Yes.' Her voice came in a breathy whisper, loaded with need. 'Oh God, yes.'

'Then swear.' He brought up his fingers stained with her lost virginity and pressed the blood to her eager mouth.

He pulled back and slammed into her, making her wince.

'Swear,' he barked again.

'I, Eliza Ruby Marion, of the Greater Branch, daughter of Jacob the Patriarch,' she groaned, 'swear by the Veil, oh, by the bones of our ancestors, by the blood!' She gasped as he thrust into her again, harder this time.

'Keep going,' he ordered.

'By the blood in my body, by the blood on my lips, by Him who protects us, that I will keep the words I spoke, the promises I made. I will not betray my vow to Cornelius, son of Caolan!'

The words ended in a gasping shout as Cornelius lifted her up and they rolled into a sitting position. He held her by the hips.

'Move.'

'How?'

'Kind of back and forth and up and down.'

She writhed slowly on him.

'Like this?'

'Exactly.'

He pressed her forehead to hers, celebrating in the feeling of being inside her, the touch of his skin against hers, her scent mixing with his own.

Together, they increased the pace, breathing in and out as one. It felt so good to be inside her. The gorgeous heat was spreading through his body, and his breath came in short, shallow gasps. He felt her muscles contracting around his shaft, felt his own heart thunder in his chest.

'You feel so good,' she whispered, kissing him.

'So do you,' he answered. 'If I'd have known how good I'd have come up with the deal myself.'

'You owe me an Oath,' she breathed, lowering her mouth to his shoulder. She bared her teeth and bit him.

'Oh, you sexy bitch.' He laughed in shock as she pierced his skin.

When she pulled back, there was blood on her lips.

'That's so hot,' he panted.

She leant in to kiss him, transferring the blood to his mouth. 'Swear,' she demanded, mirroring his earlier tone.

Cornelius closed his eyes, enjoying the pain in his left shoulder. Eliza wound her hand into his hair and yanked his head back sharply.

'Oh!' he groaned. 'I like you. I like your fight.'

'Swear,' she snarled, tightening her grip.

'I, Cornelius Caolan James of the Bastard Lesser Branch, son of Caolan, swear by the Veil, by the bones of our ancestors, by the blood in my body, by Him who protects us, by the blood on my lips, that I will keep the words I spoke, the promises I made. I will not betray my vow to Eliza, daughter of Jacob.'

With the final words of his vow, Cornelius tipped Eliza back onto the bed. He gripped her wrists. He thrust into her again and again, faster and faster, grunting as his climax built.

He could feel hers rising once more beneath him. A thin sheen of sweat covered her skin. She smelt like oranges and cherry blossom. She was beautiful as she moaned beneath him and, for a little while, she was his.

'Come for me,' he begged. 'Come for me.'

With a wordless cry, she obliged. She locked her legs around him as he hurtled into orgasm. All the hair on his body prickled, his body on the edge of release. He came with a shout before collapsing against her.

They lay together, tangled in each other's limbs while their breathing slowed and their hearts stopped pounding. Cornelius withdrew and lay beside her on the bed. He licked the blood from his lips. She smiled shyly at him, her eyes sparkling. He rested his head in his hand and smiled back at her.

'Good?' he asked, wiping the last trace of blood from her mouth.

'Life-affirming. You?'

'Not bad, for a beginner.' Rolling off the bed, he artfully dodged the pillow she threw at him and retreated to the bathroom.

Eliza smiled as she watched him go, his lean body reflected in the bathroom mirror. She closed her eyes and sank down on the bed. Wow. So that was sex? It seemed more than a fair trade for her safety. A smile pulled at her lips and a giggle threatened to bubble out of her throat. She pressed her hand to her mouth, keeping the sound contained. Her whole body tingled. She pressed her knees together; her clitoris still pulsed, aftershocks of pleasure making her knees tremble. She was a little sore but she didn't care. She had no idea she could feel like that, that her body could give her pleasure like that. She sighed. She'd have run away years ago if she'd known this was her reward. Hopefully, this wasn't a one-time deal.

I fecking well hope not. I want more. I want him again.

She yawned and stretched, suddenly tired as the post-coital glow wrapped itself around her. She wrapped herself in the sheet, inhaling Cornelius' scent of salt and clean linen. God, he smelt good.

When Cornelius returned, Eliza was sound asleep. He gazed at her for a long moment before climbing in beside her. Momentary doubt flashed across his mind but the woman stirred and wrapped herself around him. Her gentle, even breathing soothed him and she was warm and he wanted to sleep . . .

Chapter 6

CORNELIUS WOKE WITH a start in an empty bed. He leapt to his feet, thinking Eliza had slipped away. It took him a moment to realise her clothes were still on the floor, and the shower was running. The roar in his blood hushed. He sagged with relief and rubbed his shoulder where Eliza had bitten him. Dull pain rippled through him, making him smile at the thought of the morning's activities.

Then his stomach dropped.

He'd fucked a Greater Branch girl. Shit, he'd fucked the Patriarch's daughter. He'd not merely crossed the line; he'd triple jumped over it. Sex had got him into trouble before but this was a whole other kettle of fish. And the fish were poisoned. Lesser Branchers did not breed with Greater Branchers except in exceptional circumstances. His dead parents, bless their bones, had been an exceptional circumstance. Caolan had circumvented a bomb threat to the Family during the Ulster Troubles. The entire tribe could have been wiped out if he hadn't been so vigilant. He'd saved everyone; his reward was just and fitting. His son remained in the Lesser Branch. A Greater Branch wife was thanks enough. After all, Lessers had a dishonourable heritage.

The Lesser Branch magic originated from a slave girl who stole blood from their sleeping god and shared it amongst the other slaves. As a punishment, all the descendants of those slaves were doomed to be servants of the Greater Branch for eternity. His family line, the Cruel family line, was descended from the Slave who stole the magic.

He had no right to have sex with Eliza. And he'd made a pact with a runaway, broken his vow to the Family, and his own personal code, and not inflicted punishment on her. He'd made a fucking Blood Oath to her so there was no way he could go back on his word. He was going to frame someone to cover their tracks, betraying everything he'd ever been taught for a dangerous thrill and a good lay.

And it had been a good lay. Eliza had been eager to please. She was a fighter. He liked that. A lot. On the bed sheets, the evidence of Eliza's lost virginity reminded him of his promise. She didn't deserve to be punished. There was nobility in her motivation for leaving.

He stripped the stained sheet off the bed. Despite his reservations about having fucked her, he wanted the trophy. She was an incredibly rare prize.

A tap at the door interrupted his musings. He opened it to a pretty member of the hotel staff, holding a tray.

'Your lunch, Mr MacCatháin.,' She stumbled over his surname, blushing, and Cornelius belatedly realised he was still naked. He took the tray from the girl and she scurried away gratefully. He stared at the cloche. Eliza had some gall to order from the expensive room service menu when he was footing the bill. He set it down on the dressing table, beside his phone. The screen flashed with a message from Kylie confirming their date. He ignored it and crossed to the bathroom.

Eliza was rinsing her hair. Her back was to him and he spent a long moment admiring her backside. His eyes travelled up her spine to her shoulders and the nape of her neck. He frowned. A faint crescent-shaped scar was etched into her fair skin. How had she got that? He stepped in behind her.

'Hello!' she said, laughing as he wrapped his arms around her waist and kissed her neck. 'Sleep well?'

'Hmmm. Are you sore?'

'Yes,' she said. 'But it's a good kind of sore.'

'Your lunch is here.'

'Our lunch,' she corrected. 'I ordered you something too.'

'How kind of you to order me food with my own money.'

'It's only a toasted sandwich and a cup of tea.' She turned in his arms and kissed him.

'You have doubts,' she said simply, when she pulled away.

'I do,' he said. 'What we did breaks all the rules. I'd be in massive trouble if anyone ever found out. I'm not sure about the plan, either. We need to discuss it properly . . . if you keep touching me like that, your lunch will go cold.' He moved her hand from his penis, returning it to the small of his back.

'I may have created a sex pest,' he teased, running his hands through her wet hair and sighing.

'There's no point having regrets now.' She smiled at him. 'The damage is done. We might as well have some fun.'

He licked his lips. 'Having slept on it, I'm not sure you're worth the trouble.'

She gasped in mock shock as she dug her fingers into his rib cage and tickled him.

'Stop it!' he cried. 'We'll fall!'

Eliza stood on tiptoe to kiss him, her hand brushing his rising erection.

'You are definitely a sex pest,' he growled. 'I'll have to make use of you while I can.'

Eliza's eyes glittered as she twisted her fingers in her hair. Cornelius frowned.

'I know, I need to turn it back,' she said. 'Can we get some bleach later?'

'No need. I can fix it.' He pressed his fingers against her scalp. She squealed as he cast the spell. 'Hold still,' he ordered, but he couldn't hide his amusement.

The dye slid off and ran down her body, restoring her natural white-blonde hair.

'You're even more beautiful now.'

'You're all charm, you. You already got into my knickers.'

'Watch your smart mouth,' he warned. 'Hurry up and get dry. I want this lunch I've paid for. And then I want you for afters.'

'There are some flaws in your plan.' Cornelius' lips moved against Eliza's back as they knelt panting against the dressing table.

'I know.' She groaned as he withdrew. 'I don't look like I've been held against my will for six months. We also have no proof your patsy took me,' she called after him, as he wandered into the bathroom to clean up. They'd knocked over the room's chess set in their ardour. Eliza gathered up the pieces and set them in their rightful place. She paused for a moment and moved a pawn forward.

'Luckily for you, I can help with both those things,' he called back. 'Fucking people over is my speciality, so at least you being a captive can be realistic.'

Eliza's skin chilled as he re-entered the room. 'You promised you wouldn't hurt me.'

'I won't, baby,' he said, casting his professional eye over her body. 'Bruises of varying age can be mimicked. I can make your flesh shrink to make you look starved.' He touched her rib cage. 'I'll crack a few ribs. Magically obviously. I'll dull your nerves so you don't feel too uncomfortable.' His hands moved to her cheeks. 'Your face will need to look as if you've gone ten rounds with a heavyweight.'

'I need rope burns or something like that, too,' she ventured.

Cornelius moved a pawn in answer to hers and crossed to his tools, still out from the morning.

'We can reproduce the wounds some of these make but we don't want to go overboard. Somebody will recognise my handiwork. And you aren't fucking anyone else to keep them quiet.'

Eliza pressed her lips together, hiding her smile. *Jealous type. Interesting.*

'What do we do about Julian?'

'He loves me,' she said. 'Like a big brother. He'll do anything to keep me from being hurt. Once he knows about Sage abusing children, he'll gladly help us.'

She turned her attention to his implements, gazing at them in fearful fascination. She picked up the thumbscrews and inspected the vice mechanism.

'Do you really use all of these?'

'Most of them. A few are purely for intimidation, like this one.' He picked up the choke pear. 'I would never, ever use this. It's too old and too brutal. But I've never needed to use it. The mere sight of it is enough to break most people. I use the whip most often against stupid bastards who try to muscle in on our territory.'

'I thought your job was to protect the seams?' Eliza asked, toying with the vice.

'It is. Those people aren't a direct threat to the seams but if they managed to gather information about us, they could find out about everything else. We'd have no end of people trying to get power from the seams and they'd be harder to get rid of than a few stinky hippies.'

She laughed. 'Stinky hippies?'

'Oh, you know,' he sighed, 'those New Agey people who believe all the old myths about being connected to the earth and spirit guides. They have this knack of knowing where the seams are. They leave flowers and sacrifices and weird little dolls. They think they can reach some kind of spiritual awakening by fucking near the magic sites. All they do is aggravate the seams and cause power spikes. They are the most fecking irritating people.'

Eliza turned her attention back to the thumbscrews.

'People really use these things for sex?'

'They do. The BDSM market is a godsend. Makes buying actual torture equipment far less suspicious.'

'And you don't use any for fun?'

'Not the ones I have here. Though I know where we can pick some up if you're feeling adventurous?' He gave her a wolfish grin and the heat rose in her face.

'I'll think I'll walk before I can run, thanks.'

He took the thumb screws from her and put each of his toys away in its allotted place.

'We need to come up with a really good story. When did you leave?'

'December sixteenth.'

'What was the weather like?'

'Pissing it down.'

'Perfect. Sage forced you off the road and kept you hidden. It was only your pain and desperation that strengthened your weak aura, enabling your mother to find you.'

Eliza nodded thoughtfully. Cornelius had switched into professional hunter mode, standing up straight, his shoulders back. It was a subtle change, but he was once more the menacing figure who'd confronted her on the train. She swallowed the lump in her throat; she was still afraid of him. He snapped the case shut and she flinched.

'Get dressed. We have a lot to prepare. I have a few days before I need to make contact with Jacob.'

He reached behind the television and unhooked a tiny camera Eliza hadn't seen before.

'Don't worry, it wasn't a live feed.' He laughed before her exclamation of pure rage. 'I'll destroy the recording.'

'You promise?'

'I promise. Although . . .' A roguish grin spread across his face. 'It would be really hot to watch the moment I took your innocence. May I keep it?' He tilted her chin up to make her look him in the eye. 'I promise I'll lock it down so tight. No one will ever find it, let alone be able to watch it.'

'All right,' she said. 'If you teach me about your tools.'

Cornelius frowned. 'Why do you want to know?'

'What if the Physician asks me details about my injuries?' She ran her hands up his arms. 'Please? Next time we fuck, you can put the video on.'

'You are so naughty. You have a deal. As much as I would like to take you up on your offer right now, we have to act quickly to pull off this plan.'

Eliza was dressed in a dirty shirt and ripped jeans, sitting on the bed in a bed and breakfast outside Folkestone. She inspected Cornelius' toolkit closely while the Cruel made the final preparations for their coup. Julian was half-watching television, although there was nothing on at this time of night, and the other half of his attention was taken up with her, his Eliza, with the horror of what was about to happen. Cornelius had corrupted Eliza, making her part with her soul to escape her punishment and ruining her innocence by making her complicit in the destruction of a toothless enemy of the Family just to cover his tracks. Something was happening to Eliza that he did not like. She was engrossed in Cornelius' profession, picking up his skills as easily as breathing. She was eager to try them out too. She'd shown particular delight in the cigar cutter, although even Cornelius winced when he demonstrated it on an unsuspecting root vegetable. She'd just laughed.

She picked up what looked like a police officer's truncheon. It was usually inserted in the anus or vagina and once a hidden button was pressed, a thousand jagged hooks shot out of it and could only be retracted once it was ripped from the victim's flesh. He shuddered as she viewed it dispassionately, oblivious to its past and potential crimes against human flesh.

He couldn't stay silent any longer. 'Do you really want to do this Eliza?'

Her head snapped up as if she'd just realised he was there. A frown wrinkled her brow.

'Cornelius is not a good man,' Julian pressed on. 'The moment you displease him, he'll turn on you.'

Eliza gave him a crooked, bitter smile. 'We made the Blood Oath.'

'He'll find a way to circumvent it,' the Hound insisted. 'He'll ruin you, turn you into something you're not. This plan is a prime example. What did Mark Sage ever do to you? Ruby already dealt with him.'

Eliza got put her arms around him and hugged him tight.

'Mark Sage hurts little girls for fun. He's a scumbag and he's escaped the law so far. This way a pervert dies and I get to come home in one piece. I'm not a traitor. I know my place is with the Family. I made one bad choice. A mistake. Should I be punished for that?'

Julian sighed. 'It's still murder, Eliza.'

'I know.' Guilt and worry danced across her face. 'But there's no other way for me to come home.' Her eyes were wet with tears, pleading for his help. 'Mark Sage is a bad man.'

'So's Cornelius MacCatháin. The only difference is you're sleeping with him.'

She blushed. 'It was the only way, Julian . . .'

'Was it though?' he interrupted. 'Or did you sleep with him because you wanted to, rather than because it was your only option?'

'Fuck you, Julian. I had no way out. It was either fuck him or get fucked over. And I am so tired of being fucked over.'

A tremor passed through her body; she was shaking and a thin layer of perspiration broke out across her forehead. Her flesh goose-pimpled and he saw her pulse racing under her skin. She covered her face, trying to stop her tears. Julian sat beside her and covered her hand with his as she composed herself.

'I'm really sorry, Pup,' she whispered. She squeezed his hands, giving him a watery smile. 'I was out of order. I just want to come home and Sage is a pervert . . .'

Julian snatched his hands away. 'No. Don't do that Eliza. Don't try to manipulate me. I'll help you, but don't treat me like an idiot.'

Eliza's nostrils flared and her face turned red. She opened her mouth to speak but the door burst open. Cornelius stood on the threshold, dressed in his black suit. Julian's stomach soured as all the rage left Eliza's face, replaced by lust. Cornelius' grin told him he'd also seen how she looked at him.

'Ready, baby?'

'Ready,' she said, her voice husky.

He took her by the hand and they left the room. Julian swallowed his disgust and followed.

Mark Sage opened another beer before resuming play of the punishment video. The sound of a belt on flesh, followed by the high-pitched yelps of the young girl, filled the dirty bungalow. He ran his fingers through his limp hair, following the motion of the belt on the computer screen. He wasn't even masturbating, just watching it to fill his evening. It was all he had to stop him thinking about the shit pile that was his life.

He tried to ignore his reflection on the screen; he knew he looked bad. He'd lost weight since he'd left Dublin. He smelt of sour sweat and old beer. Even in the mutating light of the computer screen, his skin looked puckered and sallow.

After Ruby MacTir had publically humiliated him for taking backhanders, his wife kicked him out of their Dublin home. His son, a member of half a dozen ecological groups, refused to speak to him. His sister in Kent was the only person who had any time for him. She had a spare house for rent that she let him use until he got back on his feet.

That would take a while. All his accounts were frozen until the investigation into his finances was completed. He was living off what he could sell on the Internet. That fucking woman had unearthed every shady deal he'd made from the year dot, which meant there were hundreds of thousands of Euros to be accounted for. He hadn't even tried to mount a defence and now he couldn't fathom why. He'd crawled under a rock to die quietly.

A knock at the front door disturbed him. He gazed at the clock. 12.32 am. Who the fuck called at this time of night? He ignored it. The knock came again, louder this time. Reluctantly, he got to his feet.

'Knock again, motherfucker, and I'll call the police!'

'Sage? It's Cornelius MacCatháin. Someone told me you might have a Judas Chair.'

Sage opened the door and blinked into yellow semi-darkness. He sneered in disbelief at Cornelius, who was accompanied by a hulking man he didn't know.

'You've got a fucking nerve, MacCatháin. Your employer ruined me.'

'That's nice.' Cornelius smirked, pushing past him.

'H-hey!' Sage stuttered, dropping his beer can. 'What the fuck? You can't just come into my house!'

The other man growled at him as he passed and Sage shut up. As drunk as he was, he knew there was something very wrong going on. He knew Cornelius from the circuit in the days when he used to buy torture devices like the Judas Chair. The young man unnerved him. Unlike everyone else he met at conventions and fairs, Cornelius didn't buy the devices to play with. Sage knew the stories about corporate types who'd gone missing or pulled out of deals when MacCatháin came calling. Even TDs had been known to fold their opposition to a MacTir motion after a meeting where Cornelius was present. He could be in serious trouble here.

'I sold my Judas Chair,' he said. 'To tide me over. They froze my pensions and accounts.'

Cornelius ignored him. The giant man-beast sniffed around the living room.

'I can smell her,' he growled. 'There's shit and rotting food and sweat but I can still smell her.'

Her? Who the fuck was he talking about? Cornelius turned towards the computer. The white glare from the screen lit him from below, casting half his face in shadow. He clicked the weeping girl off.

'Non-consenting.'

It was an accusation. Sage felt the blood drain from his face. He had no idea what was going on but he knew it would not end well.

'She's not in here,' the big man snarled. He looked like a bulldog, all squished face and broken teeth. 'She's up.'

Sage slammed against the wall. Cornelius had him by the throat. He hadn't even seen the other man move.

'Is there an attic?'

'Yes,' he croaked. 'But I don't use it.'

'Liar,' Cornelius snapped. 'Julian, find it.'

Julian searched the house, sniffing along the walls. He ran towards the back bedroom, howling with excitement. Sage jolted forward as Cornelius shoved him down the corridor.

Julian pulled on a cord, opening the hatch in the ceiling and bringing down the ladder.

Foul air wafted through the hatch. Cornelius stood stock still as if waiting for a missive from the abyss. Julian stepped on the ladder and inhaled deeply, while Sage's stomach roiled at the smell.

'She's up there.'

As if on cue, a sob floated down from the darkness.

'You're fucking lucky she's still alive,' Cornelius said darkly. 'Get up there.'

Sage stumbled up the steps. He fell at the top. The attic stank of mould, piss and vomit.

'Listen, MacCatháin, I've no idea what's going on here. I didn't do anything. I don't know who you're looking for . . . oof!' The air he was begging with was forced out of his lungs as Julian's boot connected with his stomach.

Cornelius took a small torch from his pocket, casting it around the attic while Sage tried to gain control of his breathing.

'Cornelius! Come quick!'

Behind the dusty boxes of old Christmas decorations, abandoned tools and detritus, hanging by her wrists from a hook and pulley on the exposed beam, was a woman. Cornelius passed the light over her. Her bare feet hung a few inches off the floor, her ragged clothes barely covering her modesty. Her ripped t-shirt revealed a bloated, malnourished stomach. Deep purple bruises marred her torso, interwoven with lacerations and burns. Her arms were covered in long gouges as if she'd been scored by a blade. Her hair hung dirty and matted in front of her eyes. There was a constant drip, drip, drip coming from her direction, a dark liquid slowly falling from her feet. The young man rushed forward.

'Shit! Julian, help me get her down.'

Sage watched, unable to move as the scene unfolded. Cornelius held his arms out to catch the girl as Julian searched for the rope. Gently, he unfurled it and lowered her down. There was a muffled sound from the woman as she descended into Cornelius' arms. He sank to the floor, holding her, and tilted her head back.

'Oh dear God. What did you do?'

Sage gagged. The girl had been torn to shreds. Her nose was caked with blood, her right eye was swollen shut and a smattering of cigarette burns decorated her neck and chest. A strip of duct tape sealed her mouth shut. She looked up at the man who held her. Clearly, she knew who he was; she began to cry against the tape, weeping something desperately. Slowly, Cornelius peeled the tape away.

'Please, please,' she sobbed. 'Don't hurt me. I didn't want to go. I didn't!'

'Shh. It's all right Eliza. I've come to take you home. It's all right.'

'I didn't say anything,' she gabbled. 'He wanted to know things but I didn't say anything.'

Cornelius brushed her matted hair out of her face.

'You're safe now, sweetheart. I've got you.'

He gazed around the room as he laid her against the wall. His face twisted in rage. Sage followed his line of sight and whimpered. A dozen blood-stained tools were scattered around the attic, lying in front of a camera on a tripod.

'You sick fuck.'

Sage realised, far too late, that it was a set up. He turned to run, tripping over a dusty box.

'Julian, stop him!'

Sage fell with a heavy thump as the huge man collided with him. He turned, flailing wildly, trying to break the other man's hold. He might as well have tried not to breathe.

'Tie him up.' Cornelius demanded. 'Then go down to the car and get my tool kit. She's bleeding internally.'

The girl whimpered, right on cue. MacCatháin knelt beside her.

'It's all right sweetheart. I'm going to take care of you.'

Julian vanished down the ladder. Sage struggled against his restraints but it was no good. The monster had tied him up too tight.

'Did you honestly think you could get away with this, you bastard?'

'Fuck you MacCatháin. I've never seen this bitch before.'

Cornelius' fist flew out, crunching against Sage's jaw.

'Mind your fucking filthy mouth!' he roared, grabbing Sage by the vest. 'If you had the tiniest clue who you were dealing with, you would never have taken her. What kind of idiot are you? Ruby tore you apart before. What did you think she'd do when you took her daughter?'

'I never touched her fucking daughter!' Sage howled. 'Why are you doing this? Wasn't it enough to ruin my life? Or does the whore want blood too?'

Cornelius pushed him backwards, smashing his head through the plasterboard. He groaned. Julian reappeared, carrying a black bag. Cornelius snatched it off his colleague and pulled a large brown bottle from its depths.

'Make sure she drinks all of it. I need to call Jacob.'

Julian held the girl against him, feeding her tiny sips of the formula. Cornelius pulled his phone out of his pocket and went over to the laptop as he dialled the number. Sage turned towards Eliza.

'Please darling. Don't let this happen. I never did anything to you. I don't deserve this.'

One cold green eye glared at him. 'You hurt little girls.' She coughed and turned away. Sage's heart hit the floor. He was doomed.

A scream filled the attic. Sage heard his own voice bellow over the heart wrenching sound.

'I know there's something going on! You MacTir fuckers aren't right! Tell me or I'll fucking skin you!'

'Fuck you,' came Eliza's rasping reply, over the tell-tale hum of a Taser warming up. Sage stared up at Cornelius. The young man was panting, his handsome face twisted in anger.

'No, no,' he whimpered. 'I never did! I swear, I never did!'

Cornelius' call connected and he turned from Sage.

'My apologies, Sir but we've found her . . . It's not that simple, Sir. Eliza didn't run away. She was taken. Mark Sage took her.'

Cornelius paced the attic, like a wild animal in a cage. 'I'm in his house in Folkestone. He's been torturing her for months and filming it . . . Yes, Sir. She's badly hurt but she's a fighter.'

He turned, knocking over a stack of paper. Sage shrieked as he saw endless newspaper cuttings of Ruby. His own handwriting scrawled all over them, screaming 'BITCH' and 'WHORE'. The eyes had been viciously scratched out of every single photo.

'That wasn't me!' he wailed.

Cornelius' foot lashed out viciously. Sage crumpled as it connected with his rib cage.

'Open your fucking mouth again and I'll tear your bastard throat out!' he snarled. 'Apologies Sir, he's got dozens of clippings of Ruby. Eliza too. All of the ones from around the crash. And her obituary. Oh, it's sticky.' He curled his lip in disgust. 'Sir, there's all kinds of shit here. A false passport, some other documents, photographs . . . oh shit.' He retched. 'He's got photographs of Eliza. Sir, permission to end this cunt?'

Cornelius' face softened and he glanced over at them. 'I'll see if she can.'

The young man knelt in front of Eliza. She appeared to be struggling to remain conscious. Sage wept. He was fucked. They'd really gone all out for this charade. Whatever their reason for targeting him, he was fucked. He watched through hot tears as MacCatháin put the phone next to the woman's ear.

'Eliza? Your dad wants to talk to you.'

'Daddy?' she mumbled.

'Eliza!' As close as Sage was, he could hear the reaction of the girl's parents at the end of the phone. He could even hear Ruby's sobs. He'd hoped they would be more satisfying, but not now.

'Daddy, why didn't you come? Was I bad?'

Her father's choked sob echoed through the attic. There was a fumbling at the other end of the phone.

'Eliza?' Ruby spoke now. 'Eliza, listen to me baby. Cornelius is going to bring you home to us. Everything's all right now. We love you and everything is going to be all right. Let me speak to Cornelius.'

Eliza held the phone out and Cornelius took it back.

'Ma'am? Yes Ma'am. I will.' Cornelius ended the call, his face set in grim determination.

'Julian, take her down to the car.'

As the giant man gently carried the semi-conscious Eliza down the stairs, Cornelius reached into his bag and pulled out a pair of black gloves. He removed his jacket and rolled up his sleeves before snapping them on.

'MacCatháin, please!' Sage begged, snot dripping from his nose. 'Don't kill me. I never touched her.'

Cornelius fixed him with a cold stare and then smiled viciously.

'I know,' he said, removing a butcher's hook from the bag. 'But there are plenty of little girls your perversion has damaged and you've evaded punishment for those crimes. Think of this as karma for all the times you've escaped detection.'

Sage uttered a fervent prayer as more and more tools for his demise were pulled from the bag.

'Your sister will be so sad when she finds your body,' Cornelius said. 'I mean, what a horrible way to die. Trussed up by a Dominatrix, dozing off as you wait for her to return and hanging yourself.' He removed the ball gag and forced it into

Sage's mouth. 'You being into all this torture stuff really *is* a godsend. Nothing I inflict on you will seem odd.'

Sage was dragged to his feet, his hands forced behind his back, under the rope. Cornelius cuffed them there, attaching the cuffs to the hook on the pulley. Sage was pulled up by the system before the ropes fell away, dropping him suddenly. He screamed against the gag as his own weight stretched his shoulders. Cornelius removed the cat-o-nine from his bag and shook it, before drawing it back and releasing it like a thunder-clap.

Chapter 7

ORNELIUS PRESSED A few more keys on his laptop and the machine whirred and chuntered as it burned data onto a disk. He stretched and rolled his neck, easing the cricks that formed while he was working. Eliza was stretched out on the bed, sketching in a notebook, as she had every night since they returned to their original hotel. The knee-splitter was propped up in front of her as she made notes on its application, force per pound, other possible uses for it, etc. She was a keen student, soaking up everything he taught her like a sponge. Their little plan B, in case she was closely questioned about her ordeal. He reached for his bishop on the board and moved it without considering the consequences.

'Six months of torture discs completed.' He yawned, flopping down beside her.

'Thank you,' she said absently, still drawing. 'Check-mate by the way. Your king's exposed.'

He brought his hand down hard on her backside.

'It's a lot of work making fake videos.'

'I said thank you,' Eliza snapped. 'I'm trying to do the homework my teacher set me last week. For some reason I keep getting distracted.'

Cornelius pulled the notebook away from her. He fished in his pocket for the red pen Eliza had bought him as a joke and flicked through the book, ticking the sketches.

'Stop it!' she cried, laughing and trying to take it off him.

He turned his back to her, blocking her access to the book. 'Overall, Miss MacTir, I'm very impressed with your progress,' he said. 'You've demonstrated real understanding of the subject matter as well as some insightful analysis.' He wrote a big 'A+' on her drawing of a breast ripper.

'You're such a brat,' she said.

He looked down his nose at her. 'That kind of lip will get you put in detention.' He wagged his index finger at her. 'As it is, I think you've done very well and it's time for break.' He threw her book on the dressing table.

'You'd better not have creased the pages.' Eliza tried to get off the bed to collect the book but Cornelius grabbed her waist and rolled her back on the bed, face down.

'Are you giving me cheek, missus?' he probed, striking her backside again.

'No.' Eliza giggled.

'I think you are,' he said.

'I'm not, Sir. I promise,' Eliza gasped, playing the innocent. She turned her head to bat her eyelashes and pout at him.

He leant in to kiss her. 'I think you are. And now I think you're flirting with me to get out of trouble.'

'Is it working?'

'No.' He brought his hand down hard, half a dozen times.

'Cornelius, stop!' Eliza laughed, trying to wriggle away.

He gave her one final, much harder, slap before releasing her. He sat against the head board, rubbing his eyes in exhaustion.

'I've worked non-stop all weekend to make those videos. You don't appreciate me.'

'I helped!' she said, crawling over and straddling him. 'I helped you with continuity. And the editing. I spotted Julian's shadow when you didn't. Not to mention I noticed my 'bruises' weren't consistent. I found the warehouse. And I helped match the attic to the videos we made.'

'All right madam,' he said. 'Don't get big-headed. Hang on.' He reached for the remote. 'Sage is on the news again.'

A stern-faced woman in her thirties stared at them from the screen.

'Police investigating the death of Mark Sage, the disgraced Irish TD, have said they are not looking for anyone else in connection with his death. The former politician was found hanged in the early afternoon on Friday. The coroner has recorded a verdict of death by misadventure. It is believed Sage was involved in some kind of sexual activity that had gone wrong.'

Cornelius clicked off the screen.

'Mission accomplished.' He looked down at her. 'Celebratory fuck?'

'Why not?'

Eliza held onto Cornelius as they came together.

'You're going to kill me,' she groaned as he rolled away.

'Hah! You're just using me while you can.'

She frowned at his words. 'Last night tonight.' She sighed. 'It won't be so bad.'

'Oh yeah, I'll be fussed over for a few weeks and then relegated once more to the shadows.' Her bitterness was palpable. 'I can do things, you know. Not having magic doesn't make me any less Fae. I can still be useful.'

She draped a hotel dressing gown over her shoulders, hiding her nakedness, and leant back against the dressing table. She gathered her hair over one shoulder and plucked at the ends as if trying to pull the sadness out. He touched her face, wiping away an escaping tear. A frisson flashed through him, deeper than sexual attraction and as fast as lightening. The intensity frightened him and he snatched his hand away.

She sniffed loudly, apparently oblivious to his reaction as she tried to hold back further tears. 'I'm sorry,' she said. 'It's just . . .' She fell silent.

'What?' he asked.

'You'll laugh at me.'

He put his arms around her waist. 'Try me.'

'I like being here with you. When we go back to the house, I'll go back to being a nothing.' She ran her hands up his arms. 'Here with you, I've been someone. Useful. And the sex is a nice perk.'

He chuckled.

'I knew you'd laugh at me.' She tried to wriggle out of his embrace.

'I'm not laughing at you. I'm laughing at what you said. And yes, the sex has been a pleasant perk of this mission.' He kissed her. 'Ideally, I'd like it to go on longer but if we want to sell this to Jacob fully, we have to act now.'

Eliza rested her head against his chest and took a deep breath.

'You smell so good,' she said. 'I wish I could bottle you up. As it is, I'll have to make do with memories.'

She gave him a half-smile. It was the same one she'd given him in the hospital; one of gratitude. It hit him like a thunder-bolt. She was grateful to him for giving her a little human contact.

Tears shone in her eyes. She shook her head as if trying to dispel unpleasant thoughts. He realised that she was trembling under his touch.

'I'm sorry,' she repeated. 'I don't mean to spoil the fun. I knew I'd have to go back eventually. That this,' she sighed, touching her chest, then his, 'would have to end.'

He frowned at her. Did she have feelings for him? Feck, did he have feelings for her? Double feck. No, no, he decided.

It was just the sex. They were a good match in bed and they'd worked well together in setting up Sage. She was observant and clever. Really clever. Her improvised 'Was I bad?' down the phone was a calculated move designed to ramp up her father's guilt. And at the same time, there was self-doubt, fear and uncertainty. It was that juxtaposition that made her so attractive. Like her, he didn't want things to end just yet.

'Do you want a job?'

'Pardon?'

'Do you want a job?' he repeated. 'On the security team. Think about it. You planned your escape meticulously, you avoided capture for six months, you got me on your side in a heartbeat and you planned every detail of setting up Sage. I need someone with that kind of vision and attention to detail on my team. Plus,' he breathed, turning on the charm he knew was irresistible, 'it means the sex doesn't have to end yet.'

Eliza laughed, the belly laugh of the highly entertained. 'I love it! But how are we going to get my dad to agree?'

'I'm sure you'll think of something, Madam Strategist.'

He pressed his mouth to hers. She wrapped herself around him.

'You rock my socks,' she murmured against his lips.

He drew away from her as her words sank in.

'Careful,' he warned. 'I am a very bad man.'

'Which is precisely why you rock my socks.' She yawned as she got into bed.

Cornelius curled himself around her, kissing her neck as she settled to sleep. His mouth brushed against the scar and he sat up.

'Eliza? How did you get that scar?'

She stiffened beneath his touch, and did not answer for a long time. 'My brothers were nasty when we were little. They used to pick on me for being Barren. One day it got out of hand, Alex threw a glass at me . . .' She trailed off and Cornelius pressed her no further.

She rolled over and rested her head on his chest.

'Goodnight, baby,' she said sleepily.

'Goodnight, Eliza.' He stroked her hair as she drifted off, and pulled up the blanket to cover her scar.

Chapter 8

ELIZA PUSHED DOWN her nerves as they reached Heathrow for the flight back to Dublin. As they walked through Departures, she felt the looks the *Gnáth* were giving her. Her split lip hurt like Hell but it was clearly effective, as was the false black eye Cornelius had given her. She cuddled up to him and did her best to look like someone aware she was attracting stares but trying to ignore it. Cornelius put his arm around her and kissed the top of her head; her bottom lip was too sore and swollen to kiss.

She had the opportunity to hone her acting skills when she popped to the toilet. An older woman leant over as she washed her hands.

'Are you all right, pet?' she asked, offering a look of concern over her glasses.

Eliza grinned brightly in response, inspecting her bruised face in the long mirror over the sinks.

'I'm grand. I know my face looks awful. We got side-swiped by a drunk driver last week. I smacked my face off the front passenger seat. Just my luck. Great end to my holiday!'

On the plane, there were a few glances and whispers as she took her seat. She forced a stony glare onto her features, flipped her hood up and slid her sunglasses on. Cornelius sat on one side of her, impassive and distant once again, while Julian sat on the other. Both were silent for most of the flight. Julian's silence was nothing new. Since they'd set up Sage he hadn't spoken to either her or Cornelius. The Hound was making it bloody obvious he did not approve of their illicit affair.

As they began their descent, Cornelius leant over to whisper in Eliza's ear.

'How did you get out of Ireland before?'

'I was booked to go to a conference in Edinburgh the weekend of the storm. A few of us from the library went together. I was driving to pick up a take-away as we prepared for our presentation, and I lost control of the car in the rain.'

Cornelius whistled in admiration. She was a clever girl.

As soon as they landed, she transformed into a meek, frightened being. Cornelius took her hand as she trembled.

'Julian, go to the baggage claim. We'll follow soon.' He sat back down beside her as the other passengers filed out.

'Sorry,' she whispered. Damn, she was good. He knew it was an act and he was still almost convinced.

A member of cabin crew approached them. 'Is everything all right, sir?'

'It will be soon.' He lowered his voice to speak confidentially to the woman. 'She was attacked. She finds large crowds difficult. When everyone's off, we'll follow.'

She nodded, smiling kindly, and retreated.

'Everyone's gone now, Eliza. I told you I'd get you home and I will. Take my hand.'

He led her to the front of the plane and down the steps. In the maze of baggage claim and passport control of Dublin airport he pulled her close, protecting her, shielding her from everyone else. At Immigration they separated briefly as a guard checked their passports. She ran to him on the other side of the barrier, and he jealously guarded his nervous charge while in front of them Julian provided another wall with the luggage.

Jacob had sent his favourite car to pick them up, a burgundy Aston Martin DB2. It gleamed in the rain. Diarmuid, Jacob's chauffeur and another member of the Lesser Branch, jumped out of the car.

'Welcome back Eliza,' he said warmly, although Cornelius saw the pain that flickered across his face at the sight of her. Her clothes gaped on her. Her jumper had ridden up, revealing deep purple bruises on her wrists.

'There you are Eliza. Diarmuid's going to take you home,' Cornelius said.

She span to him. Her sunglasses fell and her eyes were wide in panic.

'You're not coming with me?'

'It's not appropriate . . .' he began.

'Cornelius, you promised!'

'I can't,' he said. 'I'll be right behind you. You can trust Diarmuid. He's one of us.'

'Cornelius,' the chauffeur interceded, 'we're drawing attention to ourselves. It won't hurt this once. She's about to freak out.'

The Cruel gazed down at the frail little thing. Eliza looked on the verge of falling apart.

'All right.' He fished in his pocket for his car keys and ticket. 'Julian, can you follow in my car?' he asked, giving him a wad of notes to pay the ticket.

The Hound nodded and shuffled off towards the long stay car park. Diarmuid opened the rear passenger door.

'Will you sit beside me?' Eliza asked.

'If that makes you feel more comfortable.'

She nodded and climbed in. To Cornelius, the cream leather smelt like Ruby's perfume. He felt a sudden guilty pang and pushed it away. Eliza curled up on the seat, hugging her knees. 'I can put the partition up,' the chauffeur offered. 'She won't see as many people then.'

'Good plan,' Cornelius said.

As soon as the partition went up, he had his mouth on Eliza's. He hitched up her skirt and settled her on his lap as he pulled at his zip.

'You are incredible,' he whispered. 'If I didn't know better . . .'

She pressed her mouth over his and writhed on him.

'You can't fuck me,' she whispered. 'The Physician will notice when he checks me over.'

'On your knees then,' he ordered.

Eliza complied as the car pulled out of the airport. Soon they were moving away from the drab, grey outskirts of the city and heading north into the countryside.

Everything changes once you leave cities, Eliza reflected, even the motorway. It changed from being monotonous and grey to become an onyx black thoroughfare to anywhere. In the rain, the countryside was more vibrant and alive than the city. The violet thunderclouds hung low over pale green swathes of young wheat; the hedgerows, dark leaved guardians of the fallow fields, stood firm against the rain. Diarmuid turned off the motorway on to a dual carriageway and deeper into verdant countryside. Field after field of green filled Eliza's vision as they drew closer to the house.

She felt a flash of anxiety in her chest but Cornelius kissed her hand and it vanished. With him at her side, the Family would listen to her. In response to Diarmuid's unseen command a gate opened in the hedge farther up the road, leading onto the private mile long drive that led to house.

She tensed as she felt the crunch of tyres on gravel. Cornelius pulled her on to his lap to whisper in her ear.

'Do you remember the hydrangeas?' he asked, as if she were simple, or a child.

Eliza gritted her teeth. She *hated* those fucking awful old lady plants. There were thousands of them lining either side of the drive. Behind the deep rows of flowers were the Family's acres of land, forests where they'd hidden, lived, hunted and worshipped for millennia before a succession of big houses were built in the clearing. The current incarnation of the Big House was a Georgian build; beautiful and white, a fairy-tale house.

Finally, they came to the end of the hatred hydrangeas and the spectre of the house rose before them. Eliza felt trapped in a horror story. If the house had been one of horror, its Georgian exterior, once gleaming and white, would now be cracked and worn. Chunks of plaster would have fallen from the walls onto the ground. The grand door frame would be warped and rotten with damp, and its embellishments would no longer be the swirls and cornices of the era but dead ivy trailing over the building, boarded up windows and missing roof tiles.

But it was perfect. They even had cable television and fibre optic broadband. Her father was a clever man, aware that they needed to be up to speed with the outside world to better protect their secrets. When he became the Patriarch, he immediately hired builders to separate the first floor of the house into apartments for when his seven children needed their own space, as well as a place for the Cruel, his security team and the Physician. The rooms on the second floor and the old servant quarters on the top floor were only ever used during the Ritual when the entire clan, Greater and Lesser Branch, descended on the Big House.

Francis, the butler, waited at the door with a black golf umbrella. He wore a modern black suit, marking him as a member of the Lesser Branch. He ran down to the car door and held the umbrella over her and Cornelius as they made their way to the house.

Eliza paused in the half-light of the hallway, feeling the house embrace her. She knew this building like she knew her own face. The hall floor was a mix of Italian and Connemara marble, a combination of cream and emerald green diamonds across the huge space. The walls were half-panelled with dark walnut wood, contrasting with cream paint on the upper half. Portraits of the Family adorned every public wall of the house. Everyone had one painted when they were a baby and again when they were twenty one. There was no wall that wasn't covered in the faces of the Family.

Eliza closed her eyes, feeling the age of the place, hearing the sound of heels clicking on the marble. They stopped suddenly, followed by a crash of glass against the floor. Eliza turned towards the noise. Her mother stood in the grand hallway, white-faced and open-mouthed, her letters falling unheeded from her hand.

For a long moment they stood there, mother and daughter, staring at each other without saying a word. Then it happened. Simultaneously, they broke into a run, arms outstretched, towards each other. Ruby burst into sobs as she embraced her lost child. She clutched at her, as if afraid some spectre was going to rise up and snatch her away again. Eliza wept quietly in her mother's arms, holding on for dear life.

Cornelius shifted uncomfortably. He thought he knew Eliza well enough to guess when she was play-acting, but he couldn't tell if she was pretending now. Was she overcome with all her guilt, sadness and shame? He rubbed the back of his neck as an unpleasant thought occurred to him. Had it all been a trick? Had he been sold a lie?

A shout from the corridor that led to Jacob's study distracted him. The Patriarch charged down the passage. He scooped his wife and daughter up in his arms. Jacob towered over the women, as all the men did in this family. His broad shoulders seemed stooped, as if he had been aged by Eliza's disappearance, and there was a week's growth of blond beard on his face. His eyes filled with tears as he held Ruby and Eliza. Ruby turned her gaze to Cornelius. She untangled herself from the others.

'Thank you,' she gasped, throwing her arms around him.

Cornelius laughed, uneasy with this show of affection. His gaze fell on Ruby's deeply auburn hair for which she had been named, a genetic deviance that only came along once in a thousand years. It was shot through with white strands, only noticeable because he was close to her. They hadn't been there six months ago. Eliza had done this, with her selfishness.

He caught his lover's gaze. She looked down. She too had noticed the change in her mother.

Good, he thought viciously. *Let her be ashamed.*

Jacob kept Eliza close to him, extending his hand to shake Cornelius'. Ruby let him go.

'Thank you.' He turned back to Eliza and touched her cheek. 'Your poor face.'

'It's not as bad as it was,' Eliza said. 'Cornelius fixed it.'

'I did what I could,' he said stiffly. 'I'm no healer. Permission to be excused, Sir? I want to finish my report on this and get it to you before the end of the day.'

He saw Eliza stiffen at his cold tone, at the way he pulled away from her. She grabbed him, not caring that her parents were there. Her hands rested on his chest, and he felt his anger rising. His heart beat fast and angry under her fingers.

'I told you I'd get you home,' he said coldly.

'Thank you,' she said, never taking her eyes from his. He knew she was silently begging him not to be angry with her. His shoulders relaxed but he still stepped away from her.

'Sir? If it's all right with you, may I check on her later? I've never had to rescue someone before.'

'Of course!' Jacob agreed. 'You brought our light back to us.' He kissed Eliza's temple. 'Come on sweetheart, your uncle Matthew wants to see you.'

The three of them turned away from Cornelius, arm in arm. The Cruel stood in the hallway for a long moment, feeling sick. Julian entered, calling his name but there was no answer. Eventually, he had to shake Cornelius to get a response.

'It's done now,' he said. 'You have to make the best of it.'

The Cruel nodded, but the nausea still threatened.

What had he done?

The Physician's hands were warm as they passed over her body. Eliza felt a deep tingling in her side as her ribs knit back together. Her father's younger brother sighed at a job well done. All of Eliza's bruises were gone, her injured shoulders repaired, her bones reset and her face restored. She breathed a sigh of relief when he turned away to make notes in his book. Cornelius had done a good job on her injuries. Not even the doctor could tell they had been fabricated especially for him.

Matthew sat opposite her, his eyes kind.

'Cornelius did a brilliant job with your internal injuries. With a bit more training, he could have healed you completely.'

Eliza nodded but said nothing.

'You're a marvel, Eliza. I doubt any other member of the Family could have withstood what was done to you.' She heard Jacob and Ruby mumbling outside the privacy screen the Physician had put up in Jacob's office, around the mahogany desk he was using as a treatment table.

'I'm not going to patronise you. It will take a long time for you to recover and you won't forget it entirely. I'll design a rehabilitation programme for you. You'll need to discuss what happened to you and process it if you are to move on.'

Eliza winced. Matthew was another soul she was pulling into her web of deceit. She cursed herself for leaving. She had caused everyone so much grief and heartache. So what if no one spoke to her? She had a home and her health. And she had genuinely loved her job. Cornelius was right; she had been selfish.

'Do I have to?' she said. 'I'd rather just forget about it. Surely you can give me something to help me do that?'

'I understand that desire, but repressing the events will cause more damage in the long run. It will manifest itself in other ways. Chatting with me a few times a week is better for you than magically repressing your memories.' He leant in. Eliza shivered, looking down at her forearms where her skin had turned white. 'Do you need a breather?'

'Yes please.'

She slipped off the table and darted into the quiet of the hallway. She heard Matthew tell her parents to give her a moment. She was sweating and her heart raced, pounding so hard she felt like she was going to die. What was wrong with her? Why couldn't she stop it?

She ran her hands into her hair, pulling at the roots as she fought the panic. She was going to get caught. Eventually, someone would work out that it was all a lie. Cornelius wasn't going to help her anymore. She was damn sure of that.

Cornelius! He was angry with her again. She needed him on her side. She gazed up at the ceiling, where one of his hidden cameras whirred quietly. She recognised the tiny sound from when they made the films in the warehouse. She worked out its trajectory and moved away from the line of sight. A second camera picked her up but it became clear as the corridor swept round that there was an alcove the cameras couldn't see and couldn't track her to. A blind spot. She ducked into the niche to calm down.

Hugging her knees to her chest, Eliza breathed in and out, focusing on battling the heat and her panic. To take her mind off of what had happened under Matthew's touch, she ran through her options. The Blood Oath meant Cornelius couldn't betray their secret, but it didn't mean he had to keep helping her. She was on her own again. She would have to keep up the victim act with Matthew for a while, until she could convince him and her parents she was well again. For now, she needed to withstand the new scrutiny she would be under.

Approaching footsteps disturbed her. Cornelius walked down the corridor towards Jacob's office, carrying a manila folder, keeping out of the camera's line of sight.

I wonder if that's on purpose, she thought, getting to her feet.

She took a moment to appreciate his movements as he stalked up the corridor, remembering the feel of his muscular arms around her as they lay together after their ferocious sex. She could almost smell his skin, salt and clean linen. The thought of him was enough to soothe her. He was about to cross the corridor to knock on the study door when she let out a low wolf whistle. He jumped and dropped the folder. It landed with a heavy thud, and some of the contents spilled out, copies of the DVDs and photographs they'd made.

His eyes flashed with irritation.

'Eliza, what the fuck are you doing?'

'Hiding. And finding flaws in your security.'

'There are no flaws.' His words were clipped and his nostrils flared.

'Yes there are,' she replied, refusing to cower before him. 'Look at your cameras. Look at their trajectory. They only cover half of the corridor. If you approach just right, you can avoid being seen altogether.'

He looked up, following the direction in which she pointed.

'Ah feck,' he said.

'This alcove is completely hidden. Have a look later on. You won't see us talking. Anything could happen in here and there would be no evidence.'

She pulled him further into the niche and wrapped her arms around his neck.

'You could fuck me in here, if there was a curtain to hide us. No one would ever know.' She felt him stir, but sensed the tension in his shoulders as he tried to resist her. 'Are you angry with me?'

'Furious,' he said. 'You really hurt your parents.'

'I know. I didn't realise how much damage I'd do. I'm sorry for that.'

He tried to untangle himself from her. 'You should go back in.' He was trying to be distant with her, but she tightened her grip.

'Are you not my friend anymore?'

He half-laughed. 'Were we ever friends?'

'We were pretty friendly in the car. And this morning. And last night. Especially last night.'

His face broke into a grin as she reminded him.

'See? You like me. You like being with me. We are friends.'

'I know what you're doing.'

'Is it working?' She stood on tip toe to kiss him. She was right, he did like her. She knew it was more than the sex. He was affectionate with her, he laughed at her jokes and he openly admired her intelligence and cunning. He'd even called her 'incredible' this morning. 'Incredible'. You didn't say incredible the way he'd said it, breathless and awestruck, unless you meant it, unless you liked the person you were saying it to. He pushed her against the dark panelling. Using it to balance herself, she jumped up and wrapped her legs around his hips. They ground against each other, aware only of each other.

'I want you so much,' he said. 'It's not fair to tease me.'

'I thought 'fair' wasn't in your vocabulary.' She giggled breathlessly, nibbling his bottom lip. 'I thought I'd remind you why you didn't want this to end.'

The door to Jacob's study opened, forcing him to drop her. Eliza adjusted her skirt and hair, adopting her victim guise. Her shoulders drooped. She pulled her sleeves over her hands the way timid teenagers do to avoid making eye contact. The heat of sexual excitement left her face. She hugged her torso as if trying to hold herself together as she stepped out of the alcove into the corridor, and through the door of the study.

Cornelius closed his eyes and took a few steadying breaths.

She's in your head. He heard his father's voice criticising him. *Just like the Gnáth girl.*

He ignored the nagging doubt while he waited for his heart to stop racing. He fixed his rumpled shirt and picked up the folder, taking one more breath and exhaling slowly before knocking on the door.

'Come,' Jacob answered.

Eliza and Ruby were cuddled up on the sofa while Jacob sat in the winged armchair behind the huge desk. Matthew perched on a window seat. Cornelius loved the Patriarch's study. All the furniture was mahogany, covered in blood-red leather. The walls were lined with overflowing bookshelves. Scattered amongst the shelves and window ledges were artefacts from every generation of Eire's history as well as a few Greco-Roman, Etruscan and South American pieces. The windows looked down over the front lawn and on a clear day you could see for miles, almost into the next county. The study smelt of old books, freshly rolled cigars and good whiskey.

'Am I interrupting? I can come back.'

He avoided looking at Eliza. Just the thought of her panting and writhing was enough to send all the blood in his body flooding back to his penis.

Jacob waved him in. Cornelius closed the door behind him.

'I've brought my report.'

'Thank you. Sit down.'

'I have to say,' Matthew said, 'you have skills as a healer. If you ever want to practise them, you know where my office is.'

Cornelius gave him a polite smile. 'I was glad I was able to help.' He risked a glance at Eliza. 'How are you feeling?'

'Better now I'm home. I'd like to have a bath. And then I'd like to sleep.'

Ruby nodded, rubbing her daughter's back. Eliza flinched, genuine pain flashing across her eyes. What was going on?

The three men got to their feet as the women left the room. As soon as the door closed, Jacob sat back down, head in his hands, pinching the bridge of his nose with trembling fingers.

'Matthew . . .' he finally whispered, 'how damaged is she?'

The Physician rubbed his chin as he considered his answer. 'Physically, she's whole. Her emotional and mental wounds will take a long time to heal. There's no way to tell how she'll cope. She may shut down for a while, be unresponsive to questioning, refuse to talk. She could also be angry, violent, cry for no reason, be easily frustrated or frightened. We need to give her space when she asks for it and comfort when she comes for it.' He leant forward, his china blue eyes serious. 'At no point must she ever be allowed to feel as if this was her fault. She is dangerously close to believing that.'

Jacob bowed his head, gripping the back of his neck. Cornelius let out a long breath and Jacob's head snapped up.

'Do you have something to add?'

'Sir, I mean no disrespect but Matthew will have a hell of a job convincing her of that. She was kept by that pervert for six months and she believed no one was coming for her. Because she's Barren, she thought we'd left her to die. She has it in her head that no one wants her here.'

Matthew blew out his cheeks and Jacob's hands cracked. 'It's not her fault,' he rasped. 'She's not the first. She won't be the last.'

'Sir, what you say and what others say . . .' Cornelius sighed. 'I asked her why she thought no one would come for her and all this pain tumbled out of her. She sat on the floor and wept. It was like she'd kept it inside for years.' He paused and frowned, as if unwilling to say more.

'What else did she say?' Jacob prompted.

'That no one had spoken to her properly in four years. That her brothers were vicious towards her. She told me . . .' he swallowed, 'she told me she felt invisible. She said you were ashamed of her and that if she died, it would be no great loss to us.'

Jacob covered his mouth with his fist. His knuckles were white.

'Four years?'

'Yes, Sir.'

'Fuck.' Jacob slumped in the chair. 'Did you notice this despondency, Matthew?'

Matthew blushed and shifted in his seat. 'No, Jacob. To be honest, I had not. I don't really notice Eliza.'

His older brother laughed bitterly. 'You're not the only one. That needs to stop. She's one of us. She doesn't need magic to be a Fae-child. We are a fucking family and it's about time we acted like one.' He banged the table. It cracked and groaned under the impact, making Matthew and Cornelius jump. He was called Jacob the earth-cracker for good reason; his strength was legendary. 'How many times did I tell the boys? She isn't useless just because she has no magic!'

Matthew leaned forward once more, his index finger raised.

'You've given me an idea, Jacob. Eliza's recovery might be aided if she has a role within the Family.'

'Anything we give her is going to feel like a consolation prize.' Jacob shook his head. 'Here, Eliza, you were kidnapped but now you can play with us? Surely that would cause more damage?'

Cornelius pressed his lips together. This was his opportunity to put his plan into action. Did he really want to? It was so risky. He blinked and a vision of Eliza naked and smiling down at him flashed into his mind. His dick made up his mind.

'Not necessarily,' he said, 'if we pitch it right.'

'Go on,' Jacob said.

'Given Sage was able to track Eliza to her eco-conference in Edinburgh, security needs a serious overhaul. New protocols need to be put in place, new considerations to be made. Who better to help me with this than Eliza?'

The Patriarch steepled his hands in front of him as he digested the Cruel's words. 'I'm not suggesting I train her as a torturer,' Cornelius hurried on. 'But I could use her experiences to train my team, like a consultant coming up with strategies to prevent it happening again.'

He flipped open his folder and fished out Eliza's notebook, the pages he'd marked with red pen carefully removed. He passed it to Jacob.

'She's incredibly observant and her memory is unbelievable. These are drawings of Sage's tools. I found her making them three days after we rescued her. She wasn't able to sleep until she'd finished them. If you look closely you can see where she's matched the tools to the wounds he inflicted.'

Jacob nodded as he flicked through the book. He passed it to Matthew, who murmured appreciatively at the brutal beauty of her sketches, before putting it back on the desk.

'She's a good strategist as well. We played chess while the worst of her bruises were healing. She hammered me, every match. I could never see which way she was going. She's brilliant, Sir. If we could use this . . .'

Jacob held up his hand.

'Matthew, what do you think?'

'It's a good idea. Turning her negative experience into a positive one adds a sense of destiny to what happened to her, as if she needed to be taken to protect the Family better.'

His older brother pressed his fingers to his lips as he nodded. 'I'll have to think about it. It's an idea that has merit, but . . .' He reached for the notebook again. 'She was able to sleep after she drew these?'

Cornelius nodded, not trusting his voice.

'I'll need some time. I'll have to consult our laws to make sure it's permissible. After all, you are the direct descendant of the Slave.'

He took the folder which contained Cornelius's report, the discs and the photographs, slid the notebook into the folder and put the entire thing in the top drawer of his desk.

'Forgive me, Cornelius, but I'm not ready to read this yet. I will give your proposal serious thought. In the meantime, I have another job for you. I know it's not really what you do, but would you watch over Eliza a while longer? She seems to trust you and at the moment she needs to trust someone.'

Cornelius nodded his assent as he got to his feet.

'Do you need me at the moment, Sir?' he asked.

'No. No. What I need is a stiff drink. 'He got to his feet and clasped the man who had rescued his daughter in a bear hug. 'Justice was done?'

'No, Sir,' Cornelius answered. 'Vengeance.'

Jacob smiled grimly.

'Good.'

Chapter 9

Ruby passed the comb through Eliza's hair again. She sat watching her own reflection in the glass, her face pinched and tense. It was the last sign that she had been harmed. She didn't want to be touched, even by her mother. Ruby put down the comb and began braiding her daughter's hair.

'It's so good to have you home, darling.'

'Thanks, Mum.'

Ruby's fingers moved quickly, gathering up every strand of hair.

'The boys have missed you.'

Eliza snorted in derision. 'Whatever.'

'They have, pet. They feel dreadful about what happened to you.' She paused. 'And about what they did to you.'

'Mama, I'm not up to this discussion. If they felt dreadful, they'd have been here today. They feel guilty because their behaviour looks bad on them, not because they love me.' Eliza met her mother's gaze in the mirror. 'Please drop it Mum. Just for now?'

Ruby nodded and silence settled once more.

'I'd like to get Julian and Cornelius a gift, to say thank you,' Eliza said.

Ruby kissed the back of her head. Eliza winced, and saw the reflected flicker of pain in her mother's face.

'They did a wonderful job bringing you home, but it was still their job, my love. Your safety and happiness should be thanks enough.' She knelt in front of her daughter. 'Don't get too close to Cornelius, darling. It's not appropriate.'

Eliza grabbed her mother's arm as she tried to get up. Ruby stared, trying to pull away as Eliza's grip tightened.

'He saved me, Mother. He's a hero. My hero. If I want to give him a gift, I will.' Her voice came out in a low growl. She let her mother go as a wave of nausea swept over her. What the Hell was wrong with her? What was she doing? Ruby blinked a few times before a brilliant smile lit up her face.

'Of course, darling. Are you hungry?'

Eliza shook free of the sick feeling and forced herself to focus on her mother.

'The kitchen's still open,' Ruby prompted.

'I'd love some spaghetti and mince if Cook's got some going. But I don't want her to go to any trouble.'

Ruby smiled again at her daughter.

'I'll go down and see what she has. The phone in the kitchen is on the blink again. Will you be all right for a little while?'

There was a discreet cough in the doorway. Cornelius stood there, freshly showered and shaved. Eliza swallowed the lump in her throat.

'Jacob asked me to look after Eliza until she's had a chance to readjust. I'm happy to sit with her while you go down, or I could go for you?'

Ruby stepped into the hallway.

'I need a moment,' she said. 'Thank you. I'll be back soon, sweetheart,' she called to Eliza.

'Okay, Mum.'

Eliza stood up to meet Cornelius as he entered the room.

'Your parents are devastated.'

'I know. I did a terrible thing in leaving.'

'Yes you did. You have to live with that. No punishment I inflict on you could measure up to how you feel right now.'

She sat down on her bed, holding her head in her hands. Cornelius sat beside her and rubbed her shoulders. A faint tremor danced across her skin, but she did not wince like she had with Ruby. She sat up straight, and let him brush a strand of hair out of her face.

'So,' he said, 'where does your new guilt leave us?'

'I don't feel guilty about sleeping with you. I know I should, but I don't.'

'That's interesting.' He grinned. 'Do you want to finish what we started in the niche?'

'I thought you'd never ask.'

Ruby was gone almost an hour. They had time to play, tidy up and set up a game of chess. Cornelius had been pondering his third move for ten minutes, trying to avoid a quick checkmate. He'd lost the coin toss and Eliza had chosen to be black. He'd narrowly avoided losing after only two moves, seeing her move her King's pawn forward one. He wasn't bad enough at chess to fall for that move.

'Try any cheap nonsense like that again, Eliza and you won't sit down for a week,' he warned.

Ruby appeared at that point, carrying a tray. There were three bowls of spaghetti and mince, covered in ketchup and cheese.

'I thought I'd join you for dinner,' Ruby said, 'and it would be rude not to bring Cornelius something.'

Eliza grinned at her mother as she took the bowl. Ruby handed Cornelius his portion before settling down beside her daughter on the floor. The three of them ate in companionable silence. Eliza rested her head on her mother's shoulder as she chewed, and this time she didn't flinch.

'Is a dining table not good enough for you three?' Jacob stood at the entrance to Eliza's rooms, smiling at the scene of contentment. He sat on the other side of Eliza, who offered him the remains of her pasta.

'No darling, you eat that. I see you were in the middle of trouncing Cornelius at chess again.'

'Yup. He's rubbish.' Eliza laughed. The sound was like a tinkling bell. 'I beat him in five moves last time.'

The Cruel got to his feet.

'I didn't come here to be insulted,' he said good-naturedly. 'I'll take the dishes back to the kitchen. Eliza, I'll be outside the door if you need me. Goodnight, Ma'am, Sir.'

He gave Eliza a polite, professional smile as he collected the dishes, brushing his hand so subtly against hers that neither Jacob nor Ruby saw it. As he took her bowl, she slipped something into his hand.

When he got rid of the dishes, Cornelius ducked into a corner. She'd passed him a piece of paper. She'd sketched a little rock with a smiley face, on a sock. He laughed.

'You are going to get me killed.'

But he still folded up the paper and put it in his wallet.

'How are you feeling today?'

Matthew started every session with Eliza with the same question. It annoyed her. She was bored, frustrated, irritated as Hell and horny as fuck. She'd been home nearly a month and she'd only managed to have sex with Cornelius three times, partly because after the first week, Jacob ordered Julian to take over watching her at night. She'd also been having one of her horrific periods this week. She'd barely moved from the couch for the four days she was bleeding.

To add to her frustration, her father was wrapped up in business in the *Gnáth* world since she'd come home, dealing with a problem with one of the oil companies they were the 'ethical' advisers for. It meant he had been unable to come to a decision as to whether she could work with Cornelius. She wanted to scream out all of her irritation at her uncle, but instead she gave him a small smile.

'I slept through last night. That's the third night in a row. My appetite's back. I've gained another four pounds, so I've put back on all the weight I've lost. I'm not jumping at every little noise and I'm more comfortable being on my own. I was able to sit in the sun for an hour yesterday and read.'

And send dirty texts to Cornelius. He was ever so cross.

Stop it. You'll get us killed.

He hadn't even given her a smiley face. She was still fuming about that. She was just trying to stave off boredom. Her days consisted of her daily session with Matthew, jogging around the grounds as part of her recovery and scheming to get to Cornelius.

She dragged her attention back to Matthew, who scribbled more notes in his pad. There was genuinely something bothering her. She wasn't herself. At all. She took deep and perverse pleasure in winding Cornelius up and putting him in danger. Even her frustration at Matthew's innocent question was out of character.

'I'm angry all the time,' she confessed. 'There are moments I want to smash everything around me, or say something nasty to hurt someone. That's not like me at all. I don't know who that person is.'

'What do you do in those moments?'

'I try to play chess, go for a walk, find people. But Mum's busy with the *Dáil* and Dad's away. I can't keep bothering Julian and Cornelius. They have jobs to do. Everyone has jobs to do.

And it's all important. I know my job wasn't as important, but it was still a job . . .'

She pulled her knees up to her chest, shielding her vulnerability.

'We talked about this. Eliza,' Matthew said. 'You are valued and you are important. But you clearly aren't ready to go into the *Gnáth* world just yet. You almost had a panic attack last week just standing at the press conference.'

Eliza frowned and plucked at her jeans. That hadn't been put on; the flashing cameras, the size of the crowd and their questions made her fear the *Gnáth* would unravel the whole story they'd given the media a few weeks ago. They had to sell the idea that she'd suffered memory loss after the crash and after she was discharged she'd lived at a woman's refuge until someone recognised her from the news. Cornelius had been put to good work, falsifying all that information.

'I know. I'm sorry.'

Matthew patted her hand. 'It's not your fault. But you can't rush your recovery. You've made amazing progress since you've come home, but that can give you a false sense of security. We need to take baby steps. Being angry, feeling panicked and displaced are all normal in your situation. Listen, the whole Family will be here next week getting ready for the Ritual. Let's use that to get you used to large groups again.'

A knock at the door interrupted them. It was Jacob. Eliza grinned and jumped up to give him a brief hug. She was too afraid of the likelihood of another painful tremor. They'd been getting worse and more frequent in the last few days. She didn't want to touch anyone, apart from Cornelius. No amount of pain could stop her wanting to touch him.

'Hello, Daddy. Welcome home.'

'Hello, lovely girl. How are you doing? You look a little brighter.'

'I feel brighter. I need to take baby steps.'

Matthew nodded and got to his feet. 'I was just saying that the Family coming here for the Ritual would be good practise for getting Eliza used to crowds again.'

Jacob smiled at her. 'Sounds like a plan. Do you want to help me organise the opening banquet? Your mum will be swamped in Dublin this week.'

'I'd love to. Can I choose the menu?'

'You can choose whatever you want, petal.'

'Can I help Cornelius with the security arrangements?'

Jacob pressed his lips together. She gave him a small, hopeful smile. He sighed and gave in.

'All right. I promise we'll talk about you working on the security team soon.'

Flashes of a train. A girl with brown skin. The scream of panic. The girl, helpless, on a bed. A groan of pleasure. Lost bits of conversation. A gruesome spectre in the dark, holding Eliza above hellish flames. She screamed . . .

It was his own scream that woke him. Jacob sat bolt upright in bed, shivering and drenched in sweat. Ruby had snapped on the light and was pressed against the bedroom wall in panic. Blood welled up in the middle of her lip and dripped onto her chin.

'Did I do that?'

'Such a nightmare, my love. I tried to soothe you and you punched me. What did you see?'

Jacob shivered. His sweat was icy cold. He rose to change his clothes.

'Visions. Visions of Eliza. Something's wrong here. I feel like I'm going mad . . .'

Ruby crossed to her husband.

'I've felt it too. Eliza is hiding something from us.' She hesitated. 'She is very fond of Cornelius, even considering he rescued her. Maybe she was weak . . . ?' She tailed off, leaving the question unasked.

Jacob frowned as he considered the idea.

'After the debacle with the *Gnáth* girl? Would Cornelius risk it? I know he wants Eliza to be a consultant on her abduction to avoid it happening again. It makes sense from a security point of view. She's eager to help him. There's nothing in our laws which says she can't do that, it just wouldn't be acceptable given who she is.'

He rubbed his forehead as an ache began to form. 'There's something else.' He groaned in frustration. 'Something else is happening. I can feel it but it keeps escaping me, like a wisp of mist. Eliza is different. She's recovering so quickly from her ordeal . . . If I didn't know better, I'd say she'd blossomed, but it isn't possible so late. Not unless she has had sex. Even then . . .'

The Patriarch sat down beside his wife. Ruby rubbed the blood away from her chin. He began shaking violently from head to foot.

'Jacob, what's wrong?'

'I'm frightened, Ruby. There's something terribly wrong and I don't know what it is. With all my power I cannot discover it and that scares me. I have only been frightened once, and that was when she disappeared.'

The Blood-Red held her husband to her breast until his shaking stopped.

'In the morning, love, go to Him. See what He says. If anyone will know what's going on with Eliza, He will be able to discover it.'

Jacob emerged from his study the next morning, exhausted and aching. Ruby waited for him in the hallway.

'He told me He was, and I quote, "too tired to deal with the pointless bitch." If anyone else had said that, I'd have punched them.'

Ruby sighed and rubbed her husband's shoulders.

'Where is Eliza?'

Jacob frowned. 'In the garden, I think. I'll go find her. I need the air.'

His morning had left him exhausted. He felt older than his years. The Patriarch line bred its strongest and its best at a young age. He'd been a father of seven by the time he was twenty-five and Patriarch by thirty-two. He wasn't even fifty and his sons had made him a grandfather ten times over. Facts like that made him feel ancient.

The late August sun was splitting the stones as he wandered through the gardens. He heard some of his grandchildren playing in the adventure playground he'd built with his own hands for his beloved daughter. The younger ones chased each other through the maze. Their shrieks of laughter only served to remind him of his nightmares.

Eliza had fallen asleep in the warmth of the sun below the trees of the orchard. Her feet were bare, her sun hat covered her face and her book lay abandoned beside her, pages ruffling in the warm breeze. She looked so peaceful in the leafy shade. He didn't know how long he stood there and watched her but eventually, her subconscious became aware of his presence and she woke.

'Hello darling. Did you enjoy your nap?'

'I didn't mean to fall asleep, but it was so comfortable. I finally feel safe here again.' She yawned, sitting up. Her pale eyes narrowed in concern as she scanned his face. 'What's wrong, Daddy?' She patted the rug and Jacob gratefully took a seat.

They sat in silence for a while as Jacob gathered his thoughts. Eliza leant back and let the sun warm her limbs. Finally, her father spoke.

'I'm worried, Eliza.'

'About what?' she asked.

'About you, love.'

Eliza stared at her father. Before she could question him, he pushed on.

'I'm not sure how to phrase this but your mother and I feel there's something wrong. Since you've come home, we have been consistently . . . ill at ease. It's like you're hiding something from us.'

Eliza opened her mouth to protest but Jacob held up his hand to silence her.

'You are different since you've returned. If your tale of kidnap is true . . .'

'If? If it's true?'

Jacob ignored her outburst and continued.

'You are recovering at an amazing rate. But there's something else. The Cruel's behaviour has changed. He has never cared for anything other than his job. And now he's soppy over you, eager to do all he can to help you recover. I've seen how he looks at you; he worships you, Barren though you are.'

Jacob looked away from her. 'Your mother and I are making decisions we *never* would have made before you left. Cornelius is the direct descendant of the Slave, Eliza, and I've let him be alone with you in his rooms as well as yours. I've even given serious consideration to the idea of you joining the security team, which is ludicrous. The daughter of the Patriarch cannot serve the son of the Slave. And yet I'm considering it. What has changed here? And why can't I pinpoint it?'

It was only now he looked back at her.

'Did you do something rash?' he asked. 'Were you really taken? Or is something going on between you and Cornelius?'

'No!' she cried, her voice strained and unhappy.

Her hand lashed out, an involuntary gesture, and she grabbed his wrist. She dug her nails into the tender flesh and pulled him close to her. He tried to pull back but he discovered he couldn't.

'Daddy, please stop digging. Please. I've caused enough pain. Everything is fine, Daddy. Isn't it? You'll tell Mammy everything is fine, won't you? '

Jacob nodded, his mind foggy and his head heavy.

'Cornelius is above reproach, Daddy. He only wants to use me as a resource to better protect us. Let me help him.'

Her father nodded again, more slowly. What she was saying was perfectly reasonable.

'It's highly unusual, but there's nothing in our legislation that says you can't help him.'

'Jacob!' Ruby's voice cut through the air.

She ran down the path towards them, and snatched Jacob's hand away from her daughter.

'What have you done?' she demanded.

'Nothing, Mother.' Eliza smiled, taking Ruby's hand and holding it fast. 'Everything's fine. There's nothing to worry about. Everything's as it always was.'

'Everything sorted? Good. I need to get to Dublin and Cook wants you two to pop down to discuss the menu for the banquet.'

'I'll catch up,' Eliza promised. 'I just need to tidy this stuff away.'

Jacob kissed her cheek before accompanying his wife back to the house, holding her hand in his. When they were out of sight, Eliza fell to her knees, retching. A strong pair of hands helped her back to her feet.

'So you have blossomed. I knew it. You smelt different.' It was Julian. Her beloved, faithful Julian.

'Yes,' she admitted. 'Yes, but I can't control it.' She turned to him and put her hands on his shoulders. 'Promise me you won't tell anyone. If they knew the truth, they'd kill Cornelius. I have one death on my head. I don't want another. Julian, look at me.' She took hold of his head and forced him to look into her eyes. 'If they knew what I could do, it would frighten them to death. I've caused enough pain. Julian, you need to forget you saw this. If you let slip that you know, they'll punish you too. They'll say you were trying to help Cornelius usurp my father's place. I can fix this. I just need time.'

Julian pulled away from her, sadness and disappointment in his eyes.

'Are you trying to brainwash me too? Bend me to your will? I knew Cornelius would ruin you. You've become a liar and a manipulator. You're only interested in self-preservation.'

Eliza dropped her hands, twisting her fingers in shame.

'You tried to influence me before, didn't you?'

She nodded. He sighed. 'You can't fix this Eliza. It will come back to bite you.'

'Are you going to tell on us? Me and Cornelius?'

Pup shook his head. 'No. We need him. And you're right. He'd be killed for sleeping with you.' He took her hands in his, running his thumbs over her knuckles. 'I'll keep your secret, Eliza but you should leave him. He's ruining you. Soon you'll be a monster, like him.'

Julian turned and walked away, leaving Eliza alone with her guilt.

Chapter 10

THE NEXT FEW days flew by as Eliza helped her father prepare for the Ritual. It was the Fae version of Christmas, a massive celebration of their existence. The house was full to bursting as the entire clan, Greater and Lesser Branches, descended. All the lines were closely related after five thousand years of breeding within the tribe. The house was full of laughter and life once more. Old rooms were opened and the dozens of women now in residence set about cleaning, pressing and altering the cloaks for the ceremony.

As a child, Eliza had watched this bustle and activity with envy, deeply jealous that those who surrounded her had abilities she could never dream of. This year there was no jealousy. She was involved at the heart of it, organising everything from the sleeping arrangements to the extra security needs, working closely with both Cornelius and Julian. So far, Julian had kept his word; his love for her outweighed his disappointment at her behaviour. She tried over and over again to get a moment alone with him, to talk to him, to explain that she just wanted to keep hidden. But he dodged the conversation when she tried to bring it up. He wanted to avoid what she'd become, a manipulative little schemer. Eventually, she stopped trying.

The ballroom was reopened and decorated as if for a wedding. She'd even organised a band, made up of her cousins Eoin, Gregory and Thomas. The kitchen was hotter than Hell as the cooks prepared a feast to celebrate the Ritual. Eliza had written a menu with Cook: scallops with red pepper purée, wild mushroom risotto, venison, dauphinoise and roast potatoes, late summer vegetables from the garden and a dessert buffet.

Ball gowns were pulled out of wardrobes, pressed and steamed to perfection. Squabbles broke out amongst the younger girls over who got to wear which jewels. The boys complained about stiff collars and stuffy waistcoats, but on the whole the Family was happy to be all together once more.

Eliza retreated upstairs as the ballroom filled up. She was sitting in front of her mirror trying to hold back tears when her mother came to collect her. She took a deep breath as she added her blusher, afraid of what the evening would bring; in all her scheming, there was one thing she could not control. Ruby put her arms around her shoulders, but drew back as Eliza tensed.

'You have done a wonderful job, darling. Everyone is salivating over the menu. We're all here for you. Everyone is a well-wisher.'

'Thank you, Mum.'

There was an audible gasp from Eliza's relatives as she entered the room. The simple black cocktail dress showed off her slim shoulders and beautiful curves, her pale hair had been tied back to show off her diamond and pearl earrings and her great-grandmother's diamond necklace.

Murmurs flew around the room as she entered, touching on how beautiful she was, how strong to withstand her ordeal and what a pity it was she could not be used for the good of the Family. She was led up the dais by her mother and sat beside her father, in what would usually be Colum's place. Her eldest brother grabbed her hand before she settled in her seat.

'Welcome home. I missed you.' He smiled at her as he dragged her into a bear hug.

Anger flashed through her as he embraced her.

You fucking bastard. You fucking lying bastard. You were the worst of them.

Her six brothers had been mercilessly cruel to her when they discovered she was powerless; they'd beaten her up, locked her in cupboards or in the attic. And Colum had always been the one to start it. It was Colum who'd hacked at her hair with the letter opener, who'd abandoned a twelve year old Eliza in the middle of a run-down housing estate in Dublin and who had poured bleach on her Debs dress. He'd taken every opportunity to make her miserable. And now he hugged her as if he loved her? The hypocrisy burned the back of her throat.

A scream built within her as the hug went on. She tried to pull away but her other brothers leapt up to for a group hug; she was surrounded and could not escape. Her skin crawled as they touched her.

'Get the fuck away from me,' she breathed.

In unison the men stepped back and the ballroom burst into a round of applause. Eliza covered her mouth and swallowed her fury. Now was not the time for this.

Cornelius frowned at the display of affection. He knew how Eliza had been tortured by her brothers, seen the scars they left behind. He didn't understand that kind of cruelty. She'd been a little girl, her lack of magic was not her fault and yet they denied her any kind of sibling love. How could anyone not love her? He gasped at the intensity of that thought, trying to ignore the squirming in his stomach.

Jacob remained standing as the applause died away. He took a deep breath before addressing the Family.

'Brothers and sisters, I welcome you once more to our ancestral home as we prepare for the Ritual, which renews us, our power, the seals around the Veil and Him who protects us. This year is particularly special. Almost eight months ago, we lost our precious Eliza. We thought she was dead. It was not so, she was taken. Thankfully, she was returned to us. Cornelius and Julian brought her back and delivered vengeance on the man who took her. But she faced a terrible ordeal before then, worse than what the *Gnáth* did to her. She believed that because she was Barren, because she was different, we would not come for her.

'We did that. We created that feeling, that doubt and self-loathing. We behave in a disgusting manner towards those who are different. That needs to stop.' He looked directly at his eldest son.

He knew how they hurt her. Why the Hell didn't he stop it then?

'We are a Family, a tribe, the last of the Fae, with five thousand years of history, blood and love. Greater Branch, Lesser Branch, powerful, powerless, it does not matter. We are the same. We are the People. We do not treat each other badly. We stand strong together, all of us, regardless of ability, Branch line or appearance. We will not abuse each other anymore. We are one; it's about time we acted like it.'

There was a strange silence in the ballroom as Jacob raised his glass.

'To new beginnings and new promises.'

The hall erupted into applause once more as Jacob took his seat.

'Now that's out of the way, let's eat.'

Eliza clapped, but her smile was tight, as if something bothered her. Cornelius clapped along with the crowd, but his mind had snapped to attention. There was something wrong with his lover; she was growing more and more anxious in the crowd. By the time the plates were cleared away and the music started, Eliza looked ready to bolt. Her father leant over to her and they got up. There was applause as Jacob asked his daughter to dance.

Cornelius risked a long glance at the Patriarch and his daughter. As Eliza took her father's hand, there was a flicker across her face. Cornelius did what he did best; he blended into the shadows to hunt. He followed the movement of the Patriarch and Eliza. There it was again. A flicker. Blankness swallowed her face for a split second.

She swayed as she danced with her father, clumsy on her feet and unfocussed. She gazed around as if she saw nothing. Suddenly, she jerked away from Jacob. The music stopped and everyone turned to look at them. Eliza's chest rose and fell at an alarming rate as she hyperventilated. Cornelius took a step forward as his lover began to fall apart.

'I'm sorry,' she whispered. 'I'm sorry.'

She bolted through the crowd and out of the French windows. Ruby got to her feet to follow but Colum grabbed her hand, stopping her. Jacob stood in the middle of the dance floor, confused and forlorn. Matthew came towards him.

'She needs time Jacob. Love and time.'

The Patriarch nodded.

'Boys, start playing again,' he instructed the band. 'She'll feel worse if she thinks she's ruined the evening. Everybody should get up and dance. Cornelius? Go and find her. Take her to her rooms.' The Family hurried to follow his instructions and Cornelius followed the path of the fleeing girl.

It was easy to see where Eliza had gone; as she'd run down the garden, she'd cast off bits of her clothing as if trying to lighten her load. Her discarded shoes told him she'd run towards the orchard. Her diamond necklace glinted in the grass and Cornelius stooped to pick it up. One of the matching earrings lay beside it. He gazed around in the gathering gloom, looking for its twin. He found it underneath a pear tree. The hook was covered in blood; she must have ripped it out of her ear and thrown it as she ran.

She'd even taken her dress off. It was caught on the branches of one of the holly bushes that marked the entrance to the orchard. Cornelius untangled it, trying not to ruin the delicate silk.

What are you, her manservant? His father's voice snapped at him from the depths of his subconscious. *Whatever is happening to her, this bitch deserves it! You should let her suffer.*

Cornelius closed his eyes as he attempted to drown out the savage thoughts. Eliza was all that mattered now. Where was she? He shut out all distractions, the birds settling in the trees and the loud music from the house, and listened. He could hear her crying and retching but he couldn't pinpoint her location. There was a crash from the old summer house and he sprinted towards it.

Eliza knelt on the floor, semi-naked, sobbing and gasping as she vomited. Her stockings were torn and as he drew closer he saw the angry red trails of her own fingernails along her back. In some places, the nails had broken the skin, the welts dripping with blood.

'Eliza?' He stretched out his hand.

'Don't touch me!' she howled. 'Please, please don't touch me.'

Slowly, carefully, Cornelius knelt beside her.

Eliza's fingertips were torn to shreds, a bloody, pulpy mess. She'd been clawing at the floor, ripping gouges out of the wood. And still she was tearing at it.

'Baby, stop that!' He grabbed her hands and pulled her into a sitting position.

His lover howled again and fought against him, trying to escape. 'No!' she wailed. 'Please don't touch me! Cornelius, make it stop! Make it stop!'

A few weeks ago those screams for mercy would have made Cornelius delirious with glee. But now, hearing Eliza weep and beg for his help, he felt sick. He released her before taking off his dinner jacket. Careful to avoid touching her skin with his hands, he put it on her before drawing her back into his arms. He held her while she calmed and stopped crying. Eventually, they sat in silence, stunned in the aftermath of Eliza's pain.

Her hair was lank with sweat and she shuddered so violently he thought she was descending into shock. Slowly, that too faded away.

'Did anyone follow you?' she said. She sounded as if she was speaking from her deathbed.

'No. But someone is bound to check on you eventually. We should get you inside.'

Making sure he didn't touch her exposed flesh, he guided her to her feet before scooping her up. As quickly and quietly as he could, he carried her to his office on the east side of the house. He settled her on the sofa before dashing off to collect her things which he'd left in the summerhouse.

When he returned, Eliza was staring into space, silent tears running down her face.

'Does it still hurt?'

She shook her head, unable to look at him. 'It felt like someone set me on fire. They wouldn't stop touching me.'

Cornelius stared at her, confounded by this new mystery.

'I need to wash,' she said.

'I'll take you through the passages. We won't risk bumping into anyone then. There's one that leads straight from my living quarters to your bedroom.'

She didn't respond. She'd retreated into herself again but it wasn't shock. He saw from the movement of her eyes that she wasn't staring into nothing any more but was working something out, figuring out a solution to a puzzle. She did the same when they played chess.

She followed him towards the old escape passages. The house was riddled with them, a relic of a bygone era when they had feared an attack from the *Gnáth* world. It was a matter of minutes to travel from Cornelius' office to his living room and half that time again to reach Eliza's rooms. Below them, the music of the band had been replaced with the throb and hum of her father's massive sound system.

'You should let your parents know you're all right.'

She didn't answer, shrugging off his jacket as she entered the bathroom. The Cruel locked her front door and followed her.

The sink was filling with steaming water. In the light of the bathroom, the scratches on her arms and shoulders didn't seem so bad. As she rinsed away the congealing blood on her fingers, he saw that it was only the nail and not the digit itself that was damaged. He frowned.

'I don't know how you didn't hurt yourself further . . .' he began, but something in the sink caught his eye. 'What the fuck?'

He leant over the water, but he was met with a smash of watery blood and blackness rushed up to meet him.

Her hands were gentle as she ran her fingers through his hair. He stirred and rolled on to his side, trying to wrestle for another few minutes' sleep.

'Baby,' she called, 'wake up.'

He stretched and yawned. They were lying on her bed.

'What the fuck happened?' he groaned.

'I had another panic attack and you brought me inside. You left me to puke in private. When I came back, you'd conked out on my bed. I'd have let you sleep for longer if it was safe.'

She smiled at him. He grimaced at the pain in his head. There was something wrong here. Something missing . . .

'This is wrong,' he said. 'You don't have panic attacks.'

Eliza shifted uncomfortably. 'I've had a few. At the press conference . . .'

'No. This is different. Even if you had, I would never just fall asleep if there was danger. What's going on here?'

Eliza licked her lips and took a deep breath, but she did not speak. Cornelius ran his hands into his hair.

'I'm losing my mind here, Eliza. You've turned my whole world on its head. I don't know which way is up anymore. I've betrayed everything by joining you and now you're hiding things from me . . . and you've got to . . . got to be . . . And . . . and . . .' Language deserted him, and he broke down into choking, little boy sobs.

Eliza stared for a moment before she reached for him and pulled his head into her lap. Her heart twisted as he wept. She had caused this pain. She ran her fingers through his hair, soothing him, comforting him, taking away the hurt. Gently, lovingly, she began to remove this sadness from him.

'It's all right darling. It's all right. Calm down.'

He sat up, rubbing his right eye with the heel of his hand, sniffling and hiccupping. Oh God, she'd really messed him up.

'Everything's fine, I promise.'

She cradled his head in her hands and kissed him, tasting the salt of his tears. She wiped his face. His body relaxed as she touched him.

'Everything's fine,' she repeated, strengthening her spell. 'It's been a long day. I had a panic attack. You helped me and now you're tired.'

He nodded and yawned. 'Can you set an alarm for six? I want to sleep beside you.'

She smiled at him. 'All right baby.'

Silently, they fell against the sheets. He curled himself around her, resting his head against her breast. She wound her fingers into his hair, gently rubbing his scalp until he surrendered to sleep.

Chapter 11

CORNELIUS STRETCHED AND groaned. His back was stiff and his mouth was dry, as if he had a hangover. He rolled over, reaching for Eliza. She wasn't there and the sheets were cool to the touch. Where was she? He clambered out of bed, feeling gross and creased. Sleeping in a suit was always a bad idea.

'Zee?' he called, wandering around her rooms. She wasn't in the shower or watching TV, or in her kitchenette. Where the Hell was she?

He glanced at his watch; five past eight. He never slept this late. He was sure he told Eliza to set an alarm. He rubbed his forehead, a headache pulling at him. He needed a shower, clean clothes and coffee. He made his way down the passage to his rooms.

Clean, shaved and refreshed, Cornelius felt much better. Eliza had probably just let him sleep. Her panic attack had been stressful for both of them and a lie-in was a rare treat. At least he wouldn't be late for his rounds.

He started his patrol the same way every day, moving around the house, checking all the cameras were operational. He then turned his attention to the alarms, including the smoke detectors, before making a sweep of the grounds. It was a ritual, an ordinary but essential part of his duty. His father had instilled in him that this procedure was the most important of his duties. It was not the big shows of power or the threats that really mattered; it was providing safety and security for the Family on an everyday basis. It was here he needed to take most care.

His two-way radio crackled; a delivery was waiting for his approval. There had been a tiny shift in the weather over night. It was still dry but slightly cooler. A mild breeze blew, chasing a few errant leaves across the lawn. He stood still for a moment, eyes closed, letting it clear the last of the cobwebs away. He took a deep breath and strolled towards the gate, admiring the garden as he went. Daniel kept it looking beautiful all year round. It was still a riot of colour and perfume, even as summer was fleeing. The gardener knelt in a flower bed, tending to some yellow roses.

'It's looking well, Dan,' Cornelius called.

The other man looked up and smiled at the Cruel.

'Thanks, man.' He stood up and handed him a few of the roses. 'For your mammy's resting place. I hope you don't think I'm spying but I see you up by the graves sometimes. Thought you might like some.'

'Thanks. She loved these. I'll see you later.'

After giving the groceries the all clear, Cornelius patrolled the grounds, once again checking the cameras trained on the road and throughout the gardens, the orchard and the playground. Everything was fine, as it always was; he ran a tight ship. He went through the gate that separated the Family cemetery from the rest of the gardens, and stood at his parents' grave, as he did every day, as silent as they were. He laid the roses on his mother's side and kissed the headstone. He glanced at his watch. Half-past ten. He had a few minutes before he had to be in his office. There was time to check on Eliza.

She wasn't in her usual spot in the orchard, where she liked to sit outside and read on fine days. As they'd prepared for the

Ritual, she'd been working here, pouring over documents and order forms. It was odd she wasn't there. Maybe it was too cool to sit outside today? Maybe she was in the library?

She wasn't. He couldn't find her. She wasn't in the kitchen or with Matthew or her father. She still hadn't returned to her own rooms. His confusion became worry and eventually soured into anger. He went to the security offices, where his team was working on data, monitoring the seams and keeping an eye on the security cameras.

'Has anyone seen Eliza?' he asked, trying to keep the edge out of his voice. 'She's got some files I need,'

He was met with a chorus of 'No's.

'Maybe try Julian,' someone suggested as he span away.

Cornelius did not want to speak to Julian. The Hound was reproachful; every now and then he would look at Cornelius as if he were some kind of disgusting slug, and Cornelius felt castigated by his disapproval. As a result, he avoided his former henchman when he could. Still, he couldn't find Eliza and it would irritate him until he did. It was worth a shot.

The Hound was in the gym, lifting weights. 'Julian, may I have a word?'

'What do you want?' he grunted.

'Have you seen Eliza?'

'No.'

The shortness of Julian's reply stretched Cornelius' frayed temper to breaking point.

'Mind your fucking tone. I am still your superior.'

The Hound threw down his bar, narrowly missing Cornelius' feet. He stepped forward, squaring up to his boss.

'Maybe you should behave like a superior and then you could expect to be treated like one.'

'What the fuck is that supposed to mean?'

'Don't play coy. You and Eliza. You didn't act like a superior with her. You acted like a beast, listening only to your base instincts. You took advantage of her and you've ruined her. You've made her a snake. A snake like you.'

Cornelius laughed in disbelief.

'Are you *really* that dense? Are you so blind? She ran away, faked her death, created a false identity. She did all of that on her own. She was deceptive well before I got to her.'

Julian's tongue flicked across his lower lip. 'That's different. She left for good reason, because she thought she was hurting her parents. What she's doing now, that's all you. You made her that way.'

'Come on, that's not true. She made the bargain with me. She laid down the terms.'

'Because you gave her no other choice,' Julian growled. 'You have no pity or compassion. You could have listened to me and found another way. But you chose to hurt her. She had no option but to sink to your level.'

Cornelius stared at him, incredulous.

'Is she to bear no blame for her actions? I didn't force her. She chose her way out and she liked it . . . oh.' Realisation dawned on him. 'Are you jealous? Do you love her?' He laughed unkindly in the face of the misshapen Hound.

Julian's fist curled as Cornelius belittled him. 'My love for Eliza is pure. I love her like a sister. All I ever wanted to do was protect her, keep her safe. But she's stuck in the mire with you. She's turning into you, and you're so wrapped up in the sex you don't even see it. You call me dense but you can't see what's going on, what she's doing.'

'What the Hell are you talking about?'

'Check your cameras. Actually do your job. Look at Eliza, at what she's doing. Then come to me and tell me that isn't your influence.'

Julian barged past a confounded and angry Cruel. He clearly knew something Cornelius didn't and that made him furious. What on earth was Julian talking about?

He stormed back down to the offices. His team sensed his fury and wisely avoided eye contact. He tried to open the door to his private office and found it locked. Feck's sake, of course it was locked. Since he'd been sneaking around with Eliza, he'd moved the camera feed of his rooms, her rooms and a few other choice make-out spots to his private office. He pulled his keys out of his pocket; neither the key to the main office or this room were on the ring.

His breath whistled through his teeth as he realised exactly where Eliza was.

'Guys, I need to look at some top level stuff. You know the drill; clear the office. Tim, make sure you lock the door.'

They did so, gathering up their laptops to continue work elsewhere. As soon as Tim locked the door, Cornelius pressed his hand against the wood. A faint blue light travelled out from his palm, sealing the room, sound-proofing it.

'Eliza, open the door.'

There was no reply. Cornelius drummed his fingers against the door of his office.

'Eliza, open the fucking door.'

When she didn't answer, his temper snapped. He kicked the door. He heard her scrabbling at his equipment. He kicked the door again. With a shower of splinters, it burst open on Eliza, sitting at his desk, her eyes wide in panic.

'Whatcha doing, lover?'

Eliza blinked rapidly as he stood tall and menacing in the doorway. Her mouth was slack and she was panting.

'Hi baby.' Her voice shook. 'I'm looking at that footage, like you asked.'

'I didn't ask . . .' An image on the screen caught his attention, him and Eliza in her room. But something was wrong with the picture; it looked as if she was about to hit him but her hand . . . it was obscured by light.

'Move,' he ordered.

'Baby . . .'

'Now!'

She hesitated. He picked her up and threw her in the corner. She whimpered as she landed. She tried to get up, but he bound her with magic so she couldn't even twitch her fingers and handcuffed her to the radiator for good measure.

'Oh feck,' she whispered.

Content that she wasn't going anywhere, Cornelius sat down at his desk. She'd hacked his computer and had been trawling through security footage. Footage of her. She'd been deleting it. There were whole chunks of days missing. With a few clicks and taps, Cornelius managed to restore the lost material. He played it back, watching in mute horror as light flared in Eliza's hand, as she smashed it into his face, as he stumbled and fell. He paused and rewound it, watched it again. And again. He narrowed his eyes as he saw Eliza catch him and drag him to her bed. Her hands moved over him, running through his hair, over his chest, stroking him like a pet.

With mounting anger he viewed his tears upon regaining consciousness, tears he did not remember shedding. His stomach twisted as he saw how she touched him, stroked him, how the tension left his body as she wound her fingers into his hair. She'd erased the memory. Just taken it from him.

He sat back in his chair and viewed all the footage she'd tried to remove; Eliza with Ruby, Eliza with Jacob, with him again, with some of the Lesser cousins, hugging her brothers, hundreds of images, hundreds of touches. And the same expression on the faces of these people, confusion, anger or worry smoothed away in an instant. He saw it on his own face, again and again and again.

The realisation hit him so hard he felt dizzy. Eliza had blossomed and her power was a subtle one; she could influence people through touch and she'd been practising on him. She'd done it last night, the image on the screen was proof of that. But why? What had happened?

The entire evening rewound in his mind. He saw her run, saw her vomiting and clawing the floorboards of the summer-house. He carried her to her rooms and . . . and she'd been healing her hands as she cleaned the blood off them. When he noticed, she'd hit him, knocked him out, planted another idea in his head. How strong must she be to mess with his mind?

He covered his face with his hands, his head spinning. There was something else here, another piece he was missing. How was she able to heal her hands? Vomit surged up his throat as he put the puzzle together.

Eliza had shown a natural aptitude for his trade. He hadn't been as good as she was until he was twenty-one, after a lifetime of training. He thought she was a natural. But she wasn't a natural. She was a leech! She'd copied his gifts and his powers. She hadn't learnt them, she'd downloaded them. Illegally downloaded them at that. She'd stolen his gifts and he hadn't even noticed, hadn't been able to notice. Had she done that to everyone else? Stolen a copy of their talent and then made them forget?

A prickle travelled down his spine and he turned. Eliza stood behind him, her hand outstretched. He jumped up and kicked the chair at her, knocking her backwards.

'Ow.' She rubbed her shins. 'That hurt.'

'Ow? Ow? You've been stealing powers and brainwashing people and you're concerned about your shins? How did you get out? What the fuck am I saying? What's my binding spell and a pair of handcuffs compare to what you've nicked?'

'Could you not shout that?'

'I sound-proofed the room. No one's going to fucking hear us!'

She frowned. 'Why did you do that?'

He ran his hands through his hair. 'You stole my keys, locked yourself in my office, I had to break down the door. Do you honestly think there wouldn't be some kind of repercussion? I didn't think I'd find out you'd fucking blossomed! Fuck!'

He kicked the wall in frustration, and cursed again as the bones in his foot cracked.

'Why didn't you tell me?' He crossed the room and grabbed her. 'Answer me!'

'I didn't want to get into any more trouble.'

'Bullshit.' He let her go. 'You didn't tell me because you don't trust me.'

'It's not that simple . . .'

'It *is* that simple. You don't trust me, after all I've done for you. I turned my back on my duty, on my vows, I broke the rules, betrayed the Family, I put my life on the line for you and you don't fucking trust me!' He was shouting again. 'I made the Blood Oath, Eliza. I couldn't turn on you, even if I wanted to. That should be enough for you.'

'Well, it wasn't. I made a deal with the devil to save my skin,' she said. 'My power came on like a light switch the moment you entered me. I had no fucking clue what to do. I didn't know then if your Oath covered keeping this hidden. I can't control it . . .'

'You seem to be pretty good at manipulating people.'

'Fuck you, you bastard. I learnt that from you.'

Cornelius towered over her. He hoped he was scaring her. Fuck, she deserved to be scared. 'No you don't, MacTir. You were devious long before I met you. You brought sex into it.'

'You kissed me! You showed me how to get out of trouble. I played dirty because that's how you play. I appealed to your sex drive because it was the only option I had left.'

He recoiled as if he'd been slapped. It was all a game to her. It had always been a game; how can I outsmart my enemy? Well, she'd won. It made his heart hurt. She covered her mouth, as if ashamed of the words she'd thrown at him.

'Oh, baby, I didn't mean it like that,' she said. 'I'm so sorry.' He flinched as she neared him. She looked at the floor. 'You're right,' she said. 'I should have told you. I should have trusted you. But I was scared, Cornelius. I'm a leech and I can't control that side of it. I keep copying power until I have all of it. And it hurts, every time. Whenever someone touches me, a tiny copy of what they have slithers into my body and it burns. Last night was the worst. Everyone touched me and kept touching me. I felt like I was on fire.'

A tear trickled down her cheek. Cornelius watched it fall, fighting the urge to comfort her. She closed her eyes.

'When I found out I could . . .'

'Brainwash people,' he supplied viciously.

'Change their perceptions,' she said, 'it was a blessing. I could hide it and try to get it under control. If anyone found out, they'd ask questions and you'd get in trouble too and . . .' she paused, swallowing against her tears. 'I don't want anything to happen to you. I care about you.'

He snorted in derision. 'Pull the other one. It has bells.'

'It's true,' she insisted. 'I mean, that first time, it was just self-preservation and pure, filthy lust but afterwards . . . and since . . .' She trailed off.

They lapsed into silence. Cornelius sighed. He rubbed his forehead, trying to absorb all this new information.

'Hiding in plain sight. But you've used it for other things, haven't you?'

She shrugged and made a face. 'Maybe to get my own way once or twice. Like convincing my dad to put me on the security team.'

'Don't lie to me Eliza. You used it on me last night. I didn't remember crying until I saw this. You went inside my head . . .' He stopped as a horrible thought occurred to him. 'Did you make me want you? Is what I feel for you real?'

'Of course it bloody is! I didn't need magic to make you want me. I just had to take my clothes off.'

'I don't know, do I? You've been messing with my head for weeks. If you'd touched me just now you'd have made me forget again, wouldn't you?'

She sighed and nodded. He growled into his hands.

'Does anyone else know?'

'Only Julian.'

His anger surged again. At this rate she'd give him an aneurysm. 'So you trust him, but not the man you're sleeping with?'

'He worked it out.'

'You didn't try to brainwash him?'

She shrugged. 'I can't.'

'What do you mean you can't?'

'I tried, but it never worked. '

Oh, this rubbed salt into the wound. 'So you can manipulate me, your mother, your father, pretty much the whole clan, but the fucking runt is immune?'

'Don't call him that. It's not his fault.'

Silence fell over them again. Everything Cornelius had thought about Eliza, her abilities, even their relationship, had disintegrated in the last few minutes. The world had been revealed as an illusion. He looked at her; she seemed small and meek again. Who was the real Eliza? She sniffed and rubbed away a tear.

'Do you hate me?' she said.

'Don't do that.'

'Do what?'

'That,' he said. 'Fecking, emotional, girly nonsense. It just confirms that you're a manipulative bitch.'

Eliza's gasp made his guts twist but he was right. She was manipulative. She'd manipulated him sexually, emotionally and magically. Sexually and emotionally he could deal with, but magically? No way. She'd stolen his freedom, messed with his head and taken away his choice.

'I'm sorry,' she sobbed, her voice catching. 'I'm really sorry.'

She turned to leave. Cornelius grabbed her. If she ran out of here crying, someone would want to know why she was alone with him in a locked office, and that would only be the start of their questions. She didn't fight him or try to pull away.

Instead, she wrapped herself around him. Despite his rage and his mistrust, he gave in and hugged her.

'I really am sorry.' She sniffed.

'Shh,' he said, 'I am so, so angry with you.'

'I know.'

'But I don't hate you. It hurts like Hell but I don't hate you. You should have told me. We'd have come up with something.'

'I knew you'd be angry.' She nuzzled his neck. 'It was easier to keep it hidden.' She kissed the base of his throat and her lips moved up his neck. 'If it's any consolation, I don't trust anyone. You taught me that.'

'Oddly enough, that doesn't help. Neither does that.' He groaned as her hand slid down his chest, towards his crotch, his breath hissing as she touched him through his trousers. 'I know what you're doing, madam.'

'Is it working?'

'Nope.' He slid his hands under her shirt. 'I'm going to be mad for a while.'

'Give me an hour. You won't be mad when I'm done with you.'

Something in her tone made him freeze. He snatched her hands and pushed her against the wall.

'Eliza, you are never, ever, to get inside my head again. If I catch you, this will be over.'

'I wasn't going to. I was going to blow you. You're always so amenable after a blow job.'

Despite himself, he warmed to her smile. 'Ah well, sexual manipulation I do like. At least I know I'm being manipulated. It'll take more than a blow job though.'

She licked her lips and looked up at him, eyes shining. 'I'll do whatever you want,' she said.

He tilted his head to one side. 'If I'm going to trust you, if we're going to keep doing this, you need to make another Oath. You can't use your brainwashing shit on me again.'

'Okay,' she answered, without a moment's hesitation.

He opened a drawer and lifted out one of his knives. He held her right hand flat and nicked her palm, making her wince. Cornelius put her blood to her mouth.

'Making a second Oath needs slightly different wording. Repeat after me: I, Eliza Ruby Marion, wish to add to my Oath to Cornelius Caolan James.' Eliza carefully repeated the words.

'I hereby renew my previous pledge and add this promise. I will never again use my magic to manipulate Cornelius, son of Caolan. I swear this by the Veil, by the blood in my body, the blood on my lips, by the bones of our ancestors and by Him who protects us.'

She repeated the promise perfectly. He nodded in approval as she licked the blood from her lips.

'So what now?' she asked.

'I'm still angry with you.'

'I'd like to remind you that I offered a blow job.' She rubbed her nose against his. 'We could be really naughty and do it in here. You did say you'd like it.'

'You're incorrigible.' He laughed. 'You can't help yourself, can you?'

'You said you liked sexual manipulation. Come on, let me say sorry properly.'

He sighed and sat down. Eliza sank to her knees, eager to make things right.

Afterwards, Eliza sat on the desk while Cornelius leant back, sated and calm. 'You really are very good,' he said.

'That's because I have an excellent teacher,' she replied, getting up. She ruffled his hair as she went past. He grabbed her and pulled her over his lap. He slapped her backside hard and she squealed.

'You are a very wicked girl.'

'True, but then you are a very wicked boy.'

'I'm going to take the afternoon off,' he said, running his fingers across her backside. 'Go up to my rooms, strip down to your underwear and lie face down across my bed. I'll be up in ten minutes.'

'Yes, sir.' She grinned back at him.

As she hurried away, he mentally rolled his eyes, ignoring the niggling doubt. Had she coaxed him into forgiving her? No, no. She'd made the Oath again and nobody could break it, no matter how powerful, not even Him who protected them. He was still furious with her. Her forgiveness would be hard earned.

He looked back at his screens, at all the images of Eliza. He sighed and typed in a few commands; the footage vanished forever. What was one more secret? Besides, he smiled to himself, Eliza would find a creative way to thank him for deleting them.

He whistled jauntily as he made his way to his bedroom and his wicked Eliza.

The house was quiet. Everyone was out enjoying the gardens and the fine weather while it lasted. Julian was making his way outside when a throaty giggle stopped him dead.

'Stop. We need to go outside. They'll be looking for us.' It was Eliza.

'Just one more kiss?' Cornelius asked. 'It'll be hours before I can kiss you again.'

'One more.'

Anger clawed at Julian. Cornelius had no right to touch Eliza, and she should be running away from him, not willingly sharing his bed. He was an accomplice in their wickedness. He should never have promised to keep their secret. He should have gone straight to Jacob and told him everything. But they needed Cornelius and without him his beloved Eliza would be in danger again . . .

Eliza's laugh danced down the corridor, stoking his indignation. He needed to put a stop to this, before anything happened. What if Cornelius got her pregnant? He stormed down the passageway to confront them.

And then he saw her face.

It was the smile that did it; the grin from ear to ear as she looked at Cornelius that stopped him dead in his tracks. Julian had never seen her smile like that, not even as a child. She radiated joy. She was truly happy. And it was Cornelius who made her feel that way.

They didn't see him as they kissed each other, touched each other's faces, held on to each other for dear life. They broke apart as the shriek of his mobile phone interrupted them.

'Feck, your dad's looking for me.'

'I told you. You'd better go.'

He started down the corridor but turned, running back to kiss her once more. Eliza laughed as she pushed him away.

'Go! Or you'll get in trouble.'

Left alone, she sighed and leant against the wall, touching her mouth. She closed her eyes, still smiling, contentment personified.

Finally, she moved. She froze when she saw Julian, her guard flying back up. He could see it in her eyes, her defensive expression.

'Hello Julian,' she said, cautiously.

'Hello Eliza.'

'How are you?'

'I'm fine. You?'

God, this was weirdly formal.

'Grand.'

'Grand? Eliza, I saw how he kissed you. You're feeling more than grand.'

She laughed, her face colouring a little.

'He really makes you happy, doesn't he?'

The blush deepened.

'Why?'

She pressed her lips together. 'He saw me Julian. He saw me and he didn't pity me. Everyone pities me, even you, even though you love me. But Cornelius . . .' She even smiled when she said his name. 'Cornelius sees me; he sees my potential. I didn't need magic for him to want me.'

'He wanted what you could give him as the Patriarch's daughter.'

'Maybe at first. But I wanted to escape punishment. It's a fair trade, don't you think?'

Julian shook his head at her logic.

'He made you a murderer.'

'Sage deserved to die.'

Julian didn't entirely disagree. Sage had caused pain to Heaven-knew how many girls, but his death weighed heavy on the Hound's soul.

'Cornelius is an evil man, Eliza.'

'He does evil things. It's not the same thing. He does these things to keep us safe. That's why he likes me. I see him. Not just his title.'

Julian scoffed at that.

'All this seeing. Does he see you? The real you? The one with the powers?'

'Of course.'

'You told him?' Now that was surprising. 'Willingly?'

'Like you, he put the pieces together. It was easier to tell him everything. Including the brainwashing, before you ask.'

This wasn't the Eliza he knew. She took his hands in hers.

'I'm going to be honest with you, because I need you understand. It's not just that Cornelius will keep me safe or help me get a handle on my power. He's like me. He's an outsider, a creature in the shadows, somebody no one really sees or understands. Neither of us are angels and we understand each other. We protect each other, watch each other's backs. And I need him. It's that simple.'

The Hound felt his heart soften and his anger faded. Cornelius had given her everything a young woman her age should have. He had made her feel like a person, like she mattered. How could he deny her that?

'He really makes you happy?'

The grin came back. Bliss flooded her face, all the confirmation he needed.

'If he hurts you, I'll break his legs.'

Eliza laughed and hugged him.

'Thank you. I'm glad we talked, Julian. I'm glad we're still friends.'

'I'll always be your friend, pet. I don't approve but I'm not going to abandon you. Cornelius is not the only one on your side.'

'Thank you, Julian.'

'I'm serious, you know. I'll break his fecking legs.'

'I'll remember that. We should head outside. They'll be wondering where we are.'

'There you are!' Matthew was making his way down the corridor towards them. 'We need to have a talk about last night,' he said. 'You don't mind, do you, Julian?'

'Not at all,' he said, ignoring Eliza's filthy look.

'Good. Come on then.' Matthew took Eliza's arm.

She glanced back over her shoulder, mouthing 'Help me!' at him. Julian shook his head and made his way outside.

Matthew dragged Eliza to his office. She sighed, she wasn't in the mood for this. She just wanted to sit outside and eat. Cook had fired up a barbeque as the weather was so fine.

'You should have come to see me first thing. We need to analyse episodes like that quickly, to help you develop an effective way of dealing with them.' Matthew fussed around his small office, searching for his notebook as he expounded on various psychological and medical theories.

God, Matthew, shut the Hell up.

'So, how are you feeling?'

'Better than last night. Calm.'

'Good, good. And how did you feel last night?'

Eliza shrugged. Might as well go for honesty. 'Angry. Overwhelmed. Mostly angry. My brothers were horrific to me when we were growing up and they had the bare-faced gall to hug me.'

Matthew scribbled frantically in the notebook.

'Anything else you want to share?'

'Nothing else to share. I've never been the centre of attention so it was too much for me to handle. '

Her uncle put down the book and smiled at her. 'Let's work on your breathing exercises.'

Oh fucking Hell.

They made their way to the yoga mat in the middle of the floor. Eliza sat down, crossing her legs. Matthew groaned and puffed as he joined her.

'Right, you know the drill. Close your eyes.'

Eliza did not. Instead she stared at her uncle as he closed his.

'Deep breath in, hold, and out.'

She followed the instructions without enthusiasm. Her eyes travelled around the room, looking for something to rescue her from her boredom.

The world span and a wave of dizziness swept over her. She covered her face and closed her eyes. When she opened them she found herself staring down at Matthew, and at her own body. She shouted in surprise but no sound came out. She looked down at her hands; they were see-through. She could see the carpet through her palms. She realised what she was doing; she was projecting. She was walking in the astral plain.

This was incredible. Only a few of the Family could do this, including her mother.

She made to take a step forward but her legs felt oddly heavy and cumbersome. She looked down at her foot, which was slowly rising into the air. It was like wading through treacle. Matthew was still speaking, talking her through the exercises. Her body reacted instinctively, following his instructions because there was no one else to follow. Painfully slowly, she sank down to kneel beside her body, leaning in to inspect her own face. She frowned. Had she always had that scar under her bottom lip? Was her nose wonky or was it just the angle she was looking from? She was getting wrinkles, there was no doubt of it from this perspective. She definitely had crow's feet forming. She sat back, her movements already becoming more fluid, and considered herself.

Is this how Cornelius sees me? Does he see all these little flaws? Or does he just see the whole?

Staring at herself wasn't going to help her natural paranoia, so she stood up. It was getting easier to move. She smiled. Now this was a useful skill. She would have to hone this particular talent. She took one step and then another towards the desk, gradually speeding up as she grew more confident in her movements. She was halfway across the room when a cold gust flew through her. She turned around.

Matthew was getting to his feet.

'Eliza? Are you all right?'

He touched her but of course she did not respond. How could she? His frown deepened and he shook her.

'Eliza? Eliza!'

Matthew turned to grab his desk phone. Eliza swore and headed back to her body. Panic made her move faster. She reached out to her body and was absorbed into it just as Matthew began dialling. Her eyes snapped open and she jumped to her feet. She dashed across the room and snatched the phone from his hand. Matthew turned to her, eyes wide in fear. She grabbed his arm and dug her nails in.

'Everything's all right Matthew,' she said. 'Everything's all right. There's nothing to worry about. I think today's session is over, don't you?'

He nodded as she released him.

'Good. Come on, we don't want to miss out on the barbeque.'

Matthew smiled at her. 'Do you think Francesca's done the chimichuri sauce? I love that.'

'I hope so,' she said as he headed towards the door. She pulled her phone out of her pocket and fired off a text. Thirty seconds later, Cornelius replied.

Try to be more careful. I can't delete all the tape. :-p

She ignored his rudeness and headed out to the garden, her belly rumbling angrily.

Astral projection really makes you hungry.

Chapter 12

HE Ritual day dawned bright and clear, the final day of summer. The house was hushed with tension and excitement as the Family waited for evening to draw in. Finally, the clock struck the appointed hour and they gathered in the hallway. Children under the age of fifteen were placed in the living room. Ruby wove a spell over them so they would sleep until it was all over. Eliza wished she could curl up in that room with them. For the first time in her life, she was truly complicit in the cruelty that extended their magic, because now she needed it too. Without it, she could never hope to gain control of her terrible gift.

There were several cousins who were about to witness the 'glory' for the first time. There were fourteen initiates in total. They stood at the back of the crowd, whispering excitedly. The workings of the Ritual were kept secret until you were fifteen. Once they'd seen it, those fourteen children would come to loathe it. Though no one mentioned it, they knew they lived in a strange paradox. They loved Him who ruled them but they hated what they had to do, but the power . . . Well, wasn't the power enough to absolve their guilt?

Her father stood on the grand staircase in a crimson cloak, whilst those below him wore black. Ruby carried two white robes. Their appearance caused a murmur of curiosity amongst the new members of the Faithful; they had no idea what they were for. Eliza wished she could keep it hidden from them forever.

Jacob raised his hand and silence fell over the hundred people in the hall. He pulled his hood up and those assembled followed suit. Cornelius, Julian and Francis the butler handed out torches to guide them in the darkness that was coming. The Cruel grabbed Eliza's hand as he handed her a torch. Despite the awfulness of the situation, her heart fluttered. She was falling for him. She had been since that first kiss. She loved working with him every day in the build up to this night and that would continue once everyone had gone home. He'd found a way to make her useful; if she could do that and be his lover, at least for a little while until they matched him up, she could be happy with her new lot in Family life.

All six of the remaining Family lines, including the two of the slave-born Lesser Branch, waited in silence until the sun had set and the twilight settled around them. Jacob and Ruby raised their torches and the congregation mirrored them. The torches sparked into life and a thousand menacing shadows awoke. Jacob and his wife descended the staircase as the People watched in revered silence. They were making their way to Jacob's study.

The desk and the Persian rug had been removed to reveal the Family crest carved into the floor, a grinning skull surrounded by red roses. Jacob knelt to perform the necessary secret signs to open the entrance to the Ritual space. With a mighty crack, the floor opened. There was a rush of air and heat, followed by a foul stench which filled the study. One of the initiates whimpered.

Jacob and Ruby went through the hole in the study floor. The men from the Greater Branch went next, followed by the women. The men of the Lesser Branch were next to descend, then their women, followed by the initiates and finally those who had little or no power. Eliza's lies were compounded once more as she took her usual spot. Broken Joshua stood beside her, whimpering and panting.

'Don't want to go. Don't want to.'

Eliza reached out to him and took his hand. He settled instantly.

'Nice Eliza. Pretty girl.'

Joshua gave her one of his beautiful smiles. Broken, but still beautiful. Josh's curls meant he'd been popular with girls inside and outside the Family, before Cornelius' father laid into him.

'Do we have to, Liza?' Tears trickled down his face.

'Yes Josh. But if you're a good boy and stay quiet, I'll take you to the zoo next week.'

Josh nodded and put his finger to his lips. Hand in hand, they followed the others into the darkness.

Deep in the earth below the house, there were caves. For millennia the Family, no matter their number, had gathered to perform the Ritual which provided their power. Thousands of years of fear and trepidation filled the stale atmosphere of the caves. The torches did little to alleviate the darkness. It was a steep descent to the main cavern where the ceremony would be performed. The walls were slick with wet moss and the ground was uneven. A girl in front of them slipped and fell to her knees; her torch plunged down to her left, falling forever, until the darkness below swallowed the light.

Slowly, so slowly, they crept down into the limestone caverns. No one spoke, but the darkness sighed and whispered to the Faithful. It grew hot and close as they descended. The stench grew worse, sweet and hot like rotting flesh. Joshua began panting again. Eliza squeezed his hand to comfort him but he was frightened. They all were. They always were.

Down they went into the depths of the earth, their footsteps echoing endlessly in the blackness. All sense of time was lost here. They could have been walking for minutes or hours.

Finally, they reached the Grand Chasm, where the Ritual was performed.

It was an amphitheatre, with rows of seats carved out of the rock face. A Bacchanal could have stumbled across this ancient place and thought it the Dionysia in Athens. There was a stage and an altar in the middle. The Family placed their torches in the brackets some ancient Patriarch had installed and took their seats in order of their descent.

A throne stood in the middle of the stage, carved from the stone of the caverns. Antlers emerged from the top of the backrest, sharp and menacing in the gloom. The flickering torchlight illuminated the carvings which decorated it. One panel revealed a young woman lain across the altar, another showed a knife and a hooded figure, and yet another showed a cup running over with liquid that could have been wine, but wasn't. Eliza felt her stomach lurch. She knew what the liquid in the cup was supposed to be. The Family crest, the same gruesome skull nestled in a wreath of crimson, bleeding roses, grinned from the back of the room at those gathered in the theatre.

Ruby laid the white robes on the stone and retreated to her seat with the Faithful. Jacob stood at the plain altar, and removed a knife from his robes. Its blade was fashioned from blood red steel, its handle and hilt of silver. He placed it gently on the altar, alongside a silver chalice studded with rubies, and the virginal robes. It was time.

'Faithful, we gather here to perform the ancient rite, which has protected our power and strength since the Age of Heroes. We are the last of the Fae who once ruled this island. Eire is the gateway to the Otherworlds and along with our god, we protect her and the Veil which separates us from the horrors of the Lands Beyond. We have a duty to renew and restore our god every year with a sacrifice equal to his great gift of our magic. Welcome to our new initiates; today is the day you become a full member of our glorious clan. Stand!'

Eliza watched the stage closely for the person who would occupy the throne. Jacob raised his voice and began the chant:

'We are the true children of the earth.'

'We are the true children of the earth,' the Faithful repeated.

'We are the blessed, who carry the magic in our blood.'

The hoard echoed Jacob. Only Eliza did not speak.

'We know the true secrets and worship at the true altar.'

Her father was glaring at her as he spoke but her lips did not move.

'We acknowledge the First-Father as the true god and pro-genitor of our clan.'

She felt him willing her to speak but she would not. The chant would go on without her. She did not have the stomach for it this year. Her newfound need for this abhorrent spectacle left a bitter taste in her mouth.

'We come, First-Father, to repay your kindness with the sacrifice.

We beg you, First-Father; return to us and renew our power once more.

First-Father, our king, our god, protector of our clan,

Answer our prayer and accept our sacrifice,

Rebuild the seals around the Veil.

Make us strong to protect the paths to the Otherworlds.

First-Father, Faroust, we beg you, appear. '

As the last word left the Patriarch's lips, there was a bright flash of light and the cavern filled with smoke.

The smoke slowly cleared to reveal their god. He was tall but he stooped. His form was covered by a brilliant white cloak. He reached his hands out towards the Faithful, hands the colour of ash, gnarled as tree roots, with swollen knuckles and the flesh shrunken against the bones.

'My children, welcome.' His voice was the wind whistling through dry leaves, rustling and hissing. 'I have come to answer your prayers and accept your sacrifice.' He wheezed. He always wheezed at this point of the Ritual. Eliza felt her skin crawl, knowing what was about to happen.

The First-Father lowered his hood. There were muffled gasps from the newcomers. Like his hands, his skin was grey and the flesh had shrunk to his skull. A few wisps of hair clung to the top of his head. His lips were gone, revealing black and broken teeth. His eyes were milky with cataracts. Eliza shifted in her seat uncomfortably. Joshua whined and crouched on the floor, trying to hide.

'Do not be frightened, little ones. Once the Ritual is over, I will be restored to you.'

He turned and took a seat on his throne.

'Jacob, you may begin the sacrifice.'

Jacob returned to the altar. He raised the dagger in his right hand and the two cloaks in his left.

'A thousand years ago, the Church attacked us while we made our sacrifice to our god, while we did our duty to protect the earth from the horrors of the world behind the Veil. At great personal cost, our Lord drove back the attackers and sank us into these caverns to protect us. His magic was at its lowest ebb and as a result, he was reduced to this shell. He is condemned to return to it every year, a fine reward for his act of love for the Family.

'To preserve our power, and renew the magic, strength must be given and purity sacrificed. Those who are chosen are truly blessed. He who gives his blood is the most powerful of his peers. She who lays down her virginity will have strong children.'

The initiates began to murmur as generations of their ancestors had before them. They'd known nothing of the ceremony until this moment. The fear building amongst them since His arrival threatened to spill over into full hysteria.

'To repay the First-Father, we hand over our strongest son and daughter. Faroust, please name those you need.'

Cruelty

The spectre cast his gaze over the assembled crowd. His selection seemed to take forever. Finally he spoke: 'Thomas MacCraith and Sophie óBaoill.'

Two children from the Greater Family. It wasn't always like that; last year it had been twins from the Lesser Branch, the year before one sacrifice from each Branch. The mothers of Sophie and Thomas uttered cries of panic, swiftly muted. It was supposed to be an honour to be chosen. It meant their magic was the strongest of all the people gathered here. They could not afford to anger the First-Father by appearing ungrateful.

Thomas was nineteen and built like a brick wall; he would most likely survive the bloodletting. Even so, he was ashen as he climbed the stage, physically shaken by this 'honour'. He trembled as he changed into the white robe of sacrifice, and Eliza could see he was struggling to keep his composure.

Sophie sobbed silently as she climbed the stage.

It was her sixteenth birthday.

Last year, her birthday present had been her initiation. During her first Ritual both the sacrifices had died; the boy from his wounds, the girl when the First-Father, in his need, smashed her head off one of the altar's sharp corners with such force her brains spilt all over the floor.

Jacob tried to dry Sophie's face before handing over her robe.

Thomas was brought to the front. He knelt, trembling, as Jacob raised the dagger to his throat. He stared ahead of him at the wall, and didn't flinch as Jacob cut into the vein pulsing under his pale skin. He pressed the silver chalice to Tom's neck. Painfully slowly, the boy's blood drained into the cup. Jacob pressed a cloth to the boy's throat before handing the goblet to the decrepit god.

Faroust brought it to his nose, inhaling the aroma of the blood as if trying to capture the bouquet of a fine wine. He sighed audibly as he savoured the scent, brought the cup to his lips and took a sip. Eliza's stomach clenched as he swilled it around his mouth. An obscene pink tongue darted out from between his lips and leisurely licked the blood from his teeth.

'This is acceptable,' he croaked.

Tom got to his feet and removed his white robe and shirt. He stood in front of the altar, his hands curling into fists. He closed his eyes and inhaled deeply before he lay down on the stone. Jacob stood above him and slipped a rubber block into his mouth.

So he won't bite off his tongue.

Tom's eyes were closed as he lay still, waiting for the next step. Faroust took the blade from Jacob, who stepped back. The god looked up at the Faithful.

'*Téann an tSraith ar,*' he breathed.

'The Cycle goes on,' the crowd acknowledged.

He touched the tip of the blood-red blade to Tom's sternum. The boy, to his credit, did not flinch. Faroust dragged the blade down Tom's body. The boy grunted and convulsed as the god parted the flesh. Faroust put his fingers on either side of the cut he'd made.

There was a wet squelching sound, accompanied by Tom's high-pitched scream, as the god tore open his flesh. The initiates cried out in horror, some breaking into sobs, others retching and vomiting. Eliza could only watch, her eyes full of angry tears. Faroust ran his finger along Tom's breastbone as the sacrifice twitched beneath his hands. The spectre reached into Tom's chest and curled his fingers around the bones.

With a startling snap, he opened Tom's rib cage.

There were more tears, more cries of horror, not just from the initiates but from others among the Faithful. Faroust ignored them, licking Tom's blood from his fingers. He mounted the altar, crouching over the pale, sweating boy, whose blank eyes were fixed on the ceiling. Faroust picked up the blade once more. Carefully, he made a tiny incision in the heart. In the next moment his mouth was clamped on the beating organ.

Eliza felt dizzy as she watched the monster suckle on Tom's heart. She took a step backwards and was caught by a strong pair of hands. She looked up; it was Cornelius. She hadn't noticed his approach; his father had taught him well. He had moved to comfort her and no one had seen him. Their attention was fixed elsewhere. Cornelius pulled Eliza into his arms and kissed her cheek.

'It's so awful, Cornelius,' she breathed.

'Shh, Zee. If he hears you, he will hurt you.'

Faroust continued to drink, sometimes sucking and slurping, sometimes lapping like a cat. His appearance was changing before her eyes; his frame filled out, the pallor left his skin, his hair grew back, long, black curls so different from the pale colouring of the Family. Finally, he was sated. Finally, he sat back.

A young man knelt above Tom, where an old man had crouched only a few moments before. His lower jaw dripped with blood. Eliza felt vomit burn her throat as that vile pink tongue sailed over bloodstained lips and chin. Faroust took the cloth Jacob offered and wiped the excess away, before climbing down off the altar. He turned to his Faithful. He stood tall once more, well over six and a half feet, his deep navy eyes focused.

'Your blood is pure,' he announced, his voice warm and melodious. 'You are strong, Tom. You will live.'

The god touched his finger to Tom's heart. There was a soft sigh from the organ as it healed. Tom gasped against the bite block and kicked his heels. Eliza knew he was going deeply into shock. Faroust put his smooth hands on Tom's open ribcage and pushed. The bone protested and creaked as it was forced back into place. With a sickening click, it returned to its rightful position. Faroust pulled Tom's flesh back into place; it squelched and slurped as the god rearranged it. He dragged his finger along the incision and it was as if the wound had never been.

Julian approached the altar. Faroust nodded his assent and the Hound gathered Tom up and carried him to Matthew. The Physician scanned him with his ocular gifts. He whispered to Julian while Jacob mopped up, as best he could, the remnants of the blood. Julian carried Tom up the slope, the boy's parents hurrying behind. He would administer treatment in Matthew's office until he could join them to heal Tom properly.

It was Sophie's turn. The girl was so frightened she could barely stand. She sobbed uncontrollably, her panic and her fear choking their way out of her throat. Ruby got to her feet to support the child as she took her steps towards the altar. The Blood-Red had once been chosen for this 'honour'. Who better than the strongest of all the women gathered here to prepare her for what was to come?

Ruby led the younger woman to the altar. She kissed her forehead and whispered gently to her. Sophie nodded, her sobbing softening into frightened sniffs and whimpers. Faroust looked on coldly as Sophie was laid back. Eliza wanted to scream at them to stop. Sophie was only sixteen. How strong could her magic really be?

Faroust crouched over the young woman. A small scream escaped her as he moved her skirts up. She tried to push them down.

'Please, please don't,' she begged.

He ignored her. With one swift movement he removed her underwear. Sophie instinctively pressed her legs together, a futile attempt to protect herself. Faroust pulled her legs apart with little care. A pop echoed around the cavern and Sophie cried out; he'd dislocated her knee.

He reached out for her and she raised her arms to defend herself. Faroust growled with impatience and snatched at her hands, pushing them back. There was a snap of bone as he restrained her.

'Do not fight me,' he commanded. 'Remember that I honour you.'

Sophie closed her eyes and turned her head away from the congregation of the Faithful as Faroust pressed his body against hers.

Eliza was aware of Cornelius tightening his arms around her. Her chest rose and fell rapidly as Faroust prolonged the moment, prolonged the anticipation and his pleasure. The First-Father's eyes were closed and a smile tugged at his lips.

'Sick fuck,' Eliza spat.

Cornelius covered her mouth with his hand, stifling any further criticisms. If Faroust heard her, he would punish her.

But the god was lost in his own indulgence. He shifted his robes so they covered and concealed Sophie, a tiny, meaningless, act of compassion. He turned her head so she was looking at him. He touched her face, wiping away her tears like a lover.

'You are protecting the Family,' he said. 'You will join the other heroines of our line.'

He forced himself inside her. Sophie arched her back and howled, her sorrow echoed in the sobs of many in the crowd. Faroust was oblivious to them. His eyes were closed and his lip was bloody again, this time where he'd bitten it in his ardour. For a moment he lay still, savouring her. Finally, he began to move. He put his hand over Sophie's mouth, muffling her sobs. His own breathing grew ragged as he moved faster. His body tensed and he grunted, his climax reached. He licked his lips as he panted and gathered himself. Slowly, he withdrew from her and climbed off the altar. He pulled down the girl's skirts as her sobs erupted again.

Faroust stood with his back to the crowd. Jacob nodded to Sophie's parents who hurried forward. Between them, they lifted her from the altar.

'It hurts, Mammy,' she whimpered.

'I know, I know.' Her mother soothed her as her father picked her up. They too would go to Matthew's office where the Physician would ensure she had no injuries that would cause problems as she grew older.

When the sobbing girl was gone, Faroust turned to the crowd.

'The sacrifices were perfect, children, as proven by the survival of those you offered. The cycle goes on. I must rest now. You may return to the world above and keep it safe from the Otherworlds.'

The Faithful bowed to their god. They gathered up their torches and began to file out from the back.

'Stop!' the god shouted. 'Eliza, daughter of Jacob. You are to stay here. I would speak with you.'

Cornelius gripped her, a gasp bursting from his lips, as new terror engulfed the chamber. All eyes turned to Eliza. She looked down, avoiding their pity and their questions.

'My lord,' Jacob said, 'we've resolved our issue with Eliza. There's no need for . . .'

'Silence, Jacob,' Faroust ordered. 'What I want with your daughter is none of your concern.'

There was a frightened murmur amongst the Faithful. Ruby grabbed her husband's arm and glared at him.

'He'll kill her,' she hissed. 'Do something!'

Tears glittered in Jacob's eyes. 'There's nothing I can do,' he said.

Eliza came down the stairs, towards the dark haired man on the stage. She held his gaze and showed no sign of the fear rumbling in her belly.

'Sir, I am willing to speak with you on whatever topic you choose,' she said demurely, curtseying low. She turned to her parents. 'I'll be all right.'

'Out!' the First-Father demanded. His voice boomed, causing the walls to shake and evoking a few shrieks. The Faithful scurried out, leaving Eliza alone with their progenitor. She watched them go; Cornelius lingered for a moment. Her heart ached as their eyes met; pain and guilt danced in his eyes. A tear slid down his cheek and then he was gone.

Faroust walked around her, inspecting her.

'Take down your hood. I want to see what you look like.'

'Of course, Sir.'

Eliza managed to keep her hands from shaking as she pulled it down.

'You look normal enough. Pretty for an ordinary person.'

She didn't miss his loaded meaning. She was supposed to be magically Barren and those who were Barren caused no problems. They were not permitted to do so. So what had Eliza done to cause Jacob concern?

'Thank you, Sir.'

'Stop calling me 'Sir'. My name is Faroust. I would rather be called by my name during a private conversation.'

Eliza was taken aback by the invitation to be so personal and her brave front dropped for a moment.

'Why would you let me call you by your name? I'm a dud. A nobody. According to the rules, I'm not even worthy to be down here with you,' she said, her voice shaking.

'And despite that fact, you disapprove of me.' Faroust sighed, taking a seat on his throne. 'It's so potent, it's like heat. Ritual getting to you?'

He was so achingly smug that, despite her better judgement, Eliza lost the last drop of civility in her tongue. 'It's just ridiculous. If I wanted to see an over-dramatic, crappy vampire film, I'd watch one of the horror channels.'

Faroust's mouth fell open.

'Madam, I am wounded,' he said, putting his hand on his heart.

'Then you won't want to hear my opinion on what you did to Sophie.'

'Oh, I think I do.' His voice was soft, subtly threatening.

Eliza swallowed; she was in serious trouble here. She may never again see the light of day, but what the Hell? She'd never get the opportunity again.

'I know all blood gods need their virgins but I think publically raping a sixteen year old is fucking disgusting. If virginity really is so necessary to renewing the cycle, you could at least afford the child a little dignity. Do you need to humiliate her in front of her whole family? Do you need her virginity at all? Do you need so much blood? Or are you just lapping up the attention?'

Eliza was shouting. When had she started shouting? Faroust was standing over her. She raised her eyes to glare at him.

'It's a cycle, you brat. I feed your magic, it feeds mine, on and on into infinity. The rules are that I have to have the strongest and there have to be witnesses. That's how it works. It has been that way for five thousand years.'

'Did Sophie look strong to you? Were Anna-Beth and Jonathan óRuairc strong?'

The god frowned in confusion and a terrible realisation dawned on Eliza.

'You don't even remember them, do you? They're the twins you killed last year.'

He shrugged. 'Their magic was strong, but their flesh was weak.'

'They were their parents' only children. They went home and killed themselves after it was over and you don't even have the decency to remember them?'

At least he had the grace to look ashamed. Eliza snorted in disgust and turned away from him.

'Where are you going?' he asked.

'Home. I'm done speaking with you.'

He grabbed her arm and pulled her against him. 'I decide when you're done.' His voice stayed soft, but the threat made her tremble.

She tried to pull her arm away and he tightened his grip, making her buckle. She couldn't keep up the front any more, not this close to him. She trembled.

'So you are frightened of me.' He smiled.

'Terrified,' she admitted.

'And yet you talk to me like I'm dirt and you're the god. You think I'm a monster.' He sniffed her hair. 'I like you. I like your bare-faced cheek.'

'Does that mean I get to live?'

Faroust peered at her. 'Your father told me something had changed about you. He thought you might have blossomed.'

'That isn't possible, Sir,' she lied, managing to keep the tremor out of her voice despite the panic that threatened to take hold of her.

He leaned in to sniff her hair again. She suppressed a flinch. 'There is a flicker of change about you. A shift in your aura but . . .' he let her go, 'I cannot tell if it is magical. Give me your hands.'

Hesitantly, she held them out. The First-Father took them in his own. His were warm and strong and soft. He entwined his fingers with hers and closed his eyes. The rush of power from him stole her breath away. She forced her secrets to the darkest corner of her mind, where she prayed she could keep them.

As she struggled to keep him out, a thousand images from him flowed over her and filled her brain with information, too quickly for her to understand. The First-Father released her hands and she fell against him. He held her there while she recovered. She'd caught a glimpse of his true power and she was breathless and terrified.

'No, not magical,' he muttered into her hair. 'Sexual.' She felt his smile against the top of her head. He pushed her away from him. 'Naughty girl. Who have you been fucking?'

'C . . . C . . . Cornelius, Sir.' The stammer was not an affectation; she was shaking from his touch.

'The Cruel? How twisted are you if you choose to fuck the sadist? To lose your virginity to him?' He laughed.

'At least I chose who to lose my virginity to, Sir,' she snapped, despite herself.

He stopped laughing. He raised her head so she could look him in the eye. Fury burnt in those pale orbs.

'My, my, you are a fiery one. Cornelius clearly didn't break you. You must have similar perversities. Tell me, little Liza, why did you choose him? Come to that, how were you able to choose? Barren wombs don't usually get to have any fun.'

Eliza ignored his barbs. She could not afford to lose her temper again. She had to play his game.

'Well, despite his job, he is very sexy. That and he rescued me, Sir.'

He perfectly raised a perfect eyebrow. The perfect raising of a perfect eyebrow was clearly another Familial trait.

'I was abducted by a man called Mark Sage when I was in Scotland. Cornelius raged across the Irish Sea and saved me. I rewarded his brave endeavours with my virginity. And of course, once I started fucking him, it was difficult to stop. He has very clever fingers.'

The navy eyes flashed with amusement.

'Do you love him?'

She shrugged. 'Since when did sex and love correlate in this Family, Sir?'

He laughed again but didn't speak for a long moment. The way he gazed at her, the intensity of his stare, made her feel as if she was naked. He licked his lips as if he wanted to devour her.

'At least I'll be able to explain to Jacob what's happened to his daughter. Poor Cornelius. I'll have to tear him limb from limb. He is so very good at his job. I don't know how we'll replace him.'

Eliza's world span and she took a step backwards against the altar. She gripped it for support.

'What? Why?'

The god shrugged, mirroring her earlier apathy. 'Cornelius overstepped the mark. He had no right to have you, even if you offered your innocence freely. Virginity is sacred, even if you are Barren. You'll be punished, of course, but Cornelius is really to blame. He is the descendant of the Slave and you are the Patriarch's only daughter.'

She shook her head as her heart constricted.

'Please don't. Please don't kill him. It was my fault. Please, don't hurt him.'

Faroust continued to stare at her, a smirk on his lips. She felt her knees buckling as the horror descended on her.

'I'm the one who did wrong. He shouldn't pay for my weakness.'

The tears began to fall. The god shifted position. Eliza pushed away from the altar and moved to stand in front of him. She threw away her pride and knelt at his feet in supplication.

'Please, Sir. He shouldn't be punished for my mistake. I'll do anything.'

'That's a pretty wide promise. What if I decided to make you watch all of Sage's videos of you? Oh, yes. I know they exist. Or I could make you kill and eat a dog on this altar?'

Eliza blanched at his words. Was he a monster after all? Did she have any hope against him? She looked down at the ground and took a deep breath.

'Sir, nothing you could threaten me with could be worse than what Sage did to me. Or the thought of what Cornelius might suffer because of my weakness.' She raised her eyes, her gaze steady and unwavering. 'I will do anything you ask of me if it guarantees his protection.'

Faroust rubbed his chin and got to his feet. 'Even if I wanted you on the altar?' he asked.

Eliza glanced over her shoulder at the white stone, stained with Tom's blood and Sophie's humiliation. She swallowed the revulsion that threatened to become vomit. Slowly, she got to her feet. She took a deep breath and went to the altar.

The limestone was drinking the blood as hungrily as Faroust had done. She levered herself up on to the stone and sat on a section that was less stained. She regarded him coldly. 'What do you want me to do?'

Faroust tilted his head as he considered her. 'Oh, you're a strong one.' He smiled as he crossed to her and cupped her head in his hands. She looked up at him, her gaze unwavering.

'You really would, wouldn't you? To save him? You must love him.'

'I owe him my life. The least I can do is save his.'

Faroust touched her bottom lip with his thumb. 'You must be very passionate,' he murmured, tilting her backwards until she lay flat against the stone.

She didn't close her eyes. She wasn't going to give him the satisfaction of giving into her fear. Faroust frowned suddenly and stood up.

'You are not a sacrifice,' he said simply.

He pulled her to her feet and she felt his power wash over her once more. He pressed each of the roses in the Family crest. The back wall opened, revealing the passageway to his secret chamber.

Chapter 13

ELIZA WAS SURPRISED when she entered Faroust's home to find it a pleasant and thoroughly modern apartment.

She spotted the black leather lounger in the spacious living room, the fifty inch television and the game consoles, alongside a Blu-Ray player. She rolled her eyes. It was a thoroughly modern *man's* apartment.

'Shoes. Off,' Faroust ordered as they stepped onto the hardwood floor.

She bent to remove the heels, losing her balance and toppling against him. Faroust smiled down at her. She half-smiled back as a woozy light-headedness came over her. She shook herself as she realised what was happening; he was casting a spell, trying to lower her resistance. He wanted to fuck her and he wanted her to want him to. Did he only rape one woman a year?

As they made their way through his home, the effortless masculinity of the place struck her; it was decorated in strong shades of grey and cream. The sofa was the size of a bed; you could have napped happily there. They passed by the kitchen and the bathroom but he was clearly intent on taking her to the bedroom.

It was spotless. The wrought-iron bed was huge, made up with pure white sheets. It was so different from the Ritual room and a million miles from what she'd expected.

'And all this time we thought you lived in the Underworld,' she said coldly as he removed her sullied cloak, throwing it into a laundry hamper.

'Far too hot,' he said. 'I prefer to live in comfort. Stand there.'

She fidgeted on the thick carpet as he left the room. There was the sound of running water and the scent of soap. When he returned, he was naked. He lay down on the bed and Eliza felt her throat constrict with desire. He was beautiful. The body which barely an hour ago was little more than a walking corpse was now perfectly sculpted, as smooth as a statue. He looked as if he spent his life honing his muscles in the gym. That strange wooziness came over her again as he lay on his side, propping his head up on his hand. He smiled lazily at her. She shook her head, fighting the urge to give in.

'Take your clothes off. Do it slowly. Seduce me.'

Eliza blinked hard, taken aback. 'Excuse me?'

Faroust sat up and gathered her against him. Even sitting down, his head was at the same height as hers.

'You heard.' He smirked. 'You said you'd do anything. This is my price for Cornelius' safety. I want you to seduce me.'

Eliza crossed her arms. 'I want doesn't get. Besides, I didn't think rapists needed to be seduced. I thought it was all about power.'

The god's eyes turned hard and cold. He jaw tensed. Eliza's heart thumped hard as her fear gathered strength.

'I am not a rapist,' he said.

'Really? I think Sophie would disag..agh!'

Faroust grabbed her by the throat and rose to his feet, pushing her against the wall. She clutched at his hand, trying in vain to pull it away.

'I tried to make it easy on you, Eliza. It would have been much easier if you'd just given in.'

He dug his nails into her neck. She gasped as the veins pulsed and constricted in her throat. Her resistance was melting away and desire flared in her belly. Her rational mind, the angry soul that wanted to fight him, no longer had control. He lowered her to the floor. She looked into his eyes and felt herself wanting him. It was an odd sensation; a body on fire with need and a soul screaming in hatred, scratching at the wall, fighting to get control of the carnal, sexual body left to his mercy. No, this wasn't right! If he wanted to fuck her, he should fuck her while she gazed with hatred at him. But no matter how she tried she wasn't strong enough to fight the spell of a five thousand year old god. He'd locked her mind away and her body was firmly in control.

'Take your clothes off,' he ordered. So she did.

She was wearing a simple black dress. She pulled it over her head to reveal her lingerie, ornate black lace complete with silk stockings and suspenders. She wore it for Cornelius, who'd bought it for her only the day before.

No, no. This isn't for you. This isn't fair!

Faroust let out a long, low whistle.

'Turn around.'

She rotated slowly, so he could admire the expensive underwear.

'I wasn't expecting such a lovely gift today. Take the rest off.'

No! Resist him!

He wanted her to give him a show and so she did. She unfastened the stockings. Faroust groaned in appreciation as she put her foot on the bed and rolled them down. She turned her back on him and shimmied out of the suspender belt as she reached back to unfasten the bra. She slid it off and dropped it on the floor. Finally, she stepped out of the miniscule panties and stood naked before him. He was rock hard watching her.

Wow, he's big . . . Eliza, snap out of it!

He closed the gap between them pressing his body against hers.

'Once we've done this, you will want me,' he breathed. 'You needed persuading this time. Next time, you will give me all of you. Without coercion.'

He took her hand and guided it to his penis. She began to move back and forth, wanting to please him. Pleasing him meant she would be safe. Cornelius would be safe.

'I want you to take me in your mouth.'

She sank to her knees, reaching up and dragging her nails gently along his inner thigh, making him hiss softly. She kissed along his thigh towards his dick, giving him the tiniest lick at the base of the shaft. She left a trail of butterfly kisses and licks, working her way up to the head. She swirled her tongue around the tip.

The god groaned softly. Finally she gave him what he wanted; she took him in her mouth. Bobbing her head, she used her hands to work his shaft. She swirled her tongue around and around, teasing the tip.

'Oh fuck, that's good.' He grabbed her hair and began to thrust into her mouth. She ran her hands up the back of his legs and dug her nails into his backside.

'That's so good,' he muttered as she sucked hard on him.

What is wrong with you? Bite him! Do something. Don't be his whore. Come on!

She pulled back and blew gently on him, making him gasp. She flicked her tongue up and down along his penis before swallowing him again. She put her hand around the base of his penis and squeezed before moving it gently back and forth, teasing him, bringing him to the brink.

Eventually, her technique was too much for even the god to handle. He twisted his hands into her hair and held her still, grunting as he came down her throat. She almost choked as she swallowed down his semen. He pulled back and sat down on the bed. Eliza stayed kneeling on the carpet, licking the hand she used to wank him off into her mouth, catching the last few drops of him.

'You are very good.' He smiled.

She got to her feet, feeling her own grin spread across her aching jaw.

He tasted nice . . . No, stop it! Eliza, fight him. Get control back.

'Get over here,' he said.

She obliged him eagerly. She stood between his knees as he ran his hands over her body, murmuring in appreciation at the softness of her skin. He kneaded her backside gently and lowered his mouth to her nipple. She sighed as his tongue teased the nub. He bit down on her breast and she gasped in pleasure.

'Are you kinky?' he asked.

She shrugged. 'Maybe. A little. I like being spanked.'

Idiot! Don't tell him that!

He whimpered at her words, and rolled her down on to the bed.

'Would you like to explore other things?'

'Maybe.'

He nuzzled her neck as his erection swelled again. 'Touch yourself for me. I want to watch you masturbate.'

She blushed.

'Don't pretend you don't do it.' He sat back and took his penis in his hand. 'Don't pretend he didn't teach you.'

Free of her inhibitions and revelling in his voyeurism, she brushed the tips of her fingers over her neck and breasts. She lingered over her nipples, pulling and twisting them. She swept her hands down her body, moving in ever lowering circles, hissing when her feather light strokes moved across the sensitive skin between her belly and her vulva. Her right hand brushed the outer lips of her vagina. She moaned as she lingered there for a moment, teasing herself.

What am I doing? Ohhh.

She pushed her index finger inside her. Her scent, sweet like oranges, filled the room. Faroust growled as she began to fall apart under her own touch, letting out a small cry as she touched her clit. She moved her finger around her clit, in little circles. She bit her lip as she climbed, opening her eyes as she teetered on the edge of climax. Faroust moved his hand back and forth at ferocious speed as he watched her. She rubbed her clitoris faster, with more jagged movements.

'Yes. Yes. Yes,' she panted. She squeezed the little nub between her legs and exploded with a soft cry. She collapsed against the bed, panting hard.

God, that felt good.

Faroust crouched over her, his dick dripping semen onto her belly.

'I didn't tell you that you could come.' His pupils were so widely dilated in lust his eyes were black.

'Sorry Sir. You'll need to be more explicit in your instructions.' She leant up on her elbows as her breathing slowed. Feeling brave, she pressed her mouth to his. He forced his tongue into her mouth. His lips were soft against hers. Power rushed through her again. He tasted like life and death, ice and fire.

'I didn't say you could kiss me either,' he growled between kisses.

'I'm sorry, but you have a beautiful mouth. I couldn't help myself.'

And I liked it. He's a good kisser . . . So is Cornelius. Don't give in, don't forget.

Faroust lay down on top of her, cradling her body against his. She gasped as he pressed his erection into her.

Oh, oh, that feels good . . .

He kissed her deeply before moving down her body, nipping at the sensitive skin on her rib cage. She winced as the pain welled up, but she soon forgot about it as he thrust a finger inside her, his palm moving against her throbbing clit. She groaned as he massaged her. It felt good, really good. Cornelius didn't touch her like that.

Fuck, he's going to hate me . . . oh, shit. Yes, just like that. No, remember Cornelius; this is for him. Keep him safe. Oh, but that feels so good . . .

All at once Faroust withdrew, pulling his body away from her.

'I want all of you.'

Eliza frowned, confused by what he meant. The room span out of control as the wall he'd put between her body and mind crashed down. With her mind restored, trepidation returned but the desire was still there, burning hot. She could not escape it, could not over-ride her need. She wanted him, genuinely wanted him. His plan had worked beautifully. She was afraid and she didn't care. She just wanted him to fuck her. Even Cornelius had left her mind. The spell was cast. For now, she was Faroust's.

'Lie flat on your belly,' he said. 'Put your face down and reach your arms out in front.'

She obeyed, gasping as she felt the cold metal of a handcuff close around each wrist. He pulled her arms forward and cuffed her to the bed post. He pulled her down so the metal cut into her wrists, almost more painful than she could stand. He snapped a cuff around each ankle, stretching her tight over the bed.

He knelt behind her and tilted her hips up, causing the bonds at her wrists and ankles to dig even deeper into her flesh. Faroust bent to kiss her on her back before he slammed into her. She gasped, but he snaked his hand around her mouth and nose, silencing her and cutting off her air. He rode her hard, thrusting deep and swiftly into her. He pulled out completely and slammed into her again. And again. And again.

Fuck, oh fuck, that's good.

He released his hold on her mouth and grabbed her hips, forcing her backside higher into the air. She cried out as he quickened his pace.

'That's right, scream for me,' he panted.

He reached underneath her and rubbed his fingers against her clit. She closed her eyes as a second orgasm, more brutal than the first, built inside her. She wanted to press her knees together, she wanted to run, but she didn't want him to stop fucking her.

Behind her, Faroust groaned and panted. She could feel from his movements and pace that he was getting close. She squeezed her pelvic muscles. He cried out as she contracted around him.

'Do that again.' He laughed. 'Oh, fuck, that's good. I'm going to come.' He gasped, increasing the pressure on her clit.

Eliza cried out as he emptied himself into her. He collapsed against her back.

'Fuck,' he breathed, kissing her shoulders.

They lay there for a long time as they caught their breath. Eliza trembled when the god finally withdrew and crumpled beside her.

'I can see through time,' she gasped. *That was amazing.*

Faroust chuckled breathlessly as he undid her cuffs. Her wrists and ankles were red raw where the harsh metal rubbed against the skin. Her left wrist bled a little. The god pulled her against him, kissing her wrist where the skin was broken, groaning as he licked her blood.

'I told you you'd want me.' He laughed, pulling her to him. 'I like a feisty woman. You and I are going to have lots of fun. I like you Eliza. You are special.'

'I'm honoured you think so, Sir.' As the high from the climax faded, self-disgust began to creep in. She'd actually enjoyed herself. With their raping, blood-drinking, five thousand year old god. She'd had sex with a monster and liked it. She felt sick. Faroust laughed at her tone.

'You're a fighter. I like that. A lot.' He tilted his head as he looked at her. 'You really are very beautiful. I can see why Cornelius gave in to you.'

As she lay against him, she felt the swirl of images wash over her, as they had the first time he touched her.

'I wonder what your secrets are, Eliza.' He lowered his head to nuzzle her neck. 'What are you hiding from me?'

'Nothing, Sir. You know my only secrets.'

'Don't call me 'Sir'. What are your secrets?'

'That I've been sleeping with Cornelius. That I give a great blow job. And you were right; I do want you. Despite your actions.'

Faroust sighed deeply. 'Would it make it easier for you if I healed Sophie's soul? I don't want you constantly throwing that back at me.'

'It would certainly make it easier on Sophie.'

'Fine. I'll do that now. Go and have a shower, there's a good girl. I can still smell Cornelius on you.'

'Well, he is my boyfriend,' she answered sharply.

Faroust's eyes were hard as flint. 'Now mind yourself. I don't have to spare Cornelius and I do not have to help Sophie. Go and wash.'

She swallowed her reply and stormed away from him, into the bathroom.

Eliza closed the door and locked it. The room was more like a spa than an ordinary bathroom. The floor and walls were clad in blue-grey granite, the bath carved out of black marble. A mirrored cabinet at the far end of the room reflected her distress under the soft lighting. She turned on the shower, a steam monstrosity which shot water from every angle. She sat on the floor and let the scalding water fall on her shoulders. Her wrists and ankles burned with pain. Those marks would bruise later.

In the privacy of the bathroom, her strength crumbled away. Fear for Cornelius stabbed at her. Guilt crept in and she wept, heaving, choking sobs that shook her whole frame and revealing a depth of fear and grief no one, not even the god in the other room, could have imagined. Only the drumming of the water was louder.

Her body flushed with a heat that had nothing to do with the scalding water. The power and secrets from Faroust were breaking down her resistance. It never mattered how hard she fought, her body always gave in and guzzled down the power like a man dying of thirst in the desert.

'For fuck's sake!' she growled at herself. 'Hurry up and take it.'

The pain vanished and the magic seeped into her. Where the discomfort had been, there was peace. Eliza sobbed again. Had it been that simple? If she had just accepted that this was her power, could she have absorbed it far quicker? Or had contact with Faroust finally given her the control she sought?

The trembling faded away and her calm returned. She took a deep breath. She had to keep this hidden from Faroust. He would kill her and all those in the house above her if he knew what she was capable of. Slowly, her resolve returned. She'd managed to avoid capture for six months, she'd convinced everyone she'd been kidnapped, she'd kept her dreadful power hidden and so far she'd been able to hold her own against their god. She'd taken power and memories from him and he hadn't noticed. She was no ordinary witch.

Up until now, she'd been able to hide that her magical abilities had awoken. She knew exactly when it had happened; the morning she'd sacrificed her virginity to Cornelius. It wasn't unheard of, just extremely rare. Historically, few duds married and those that wed hadn't always developed their magical gifts. It would have been obvious that she'd been willingly sexually active and Cornelius would have borne the brunt of the punishment for that, despite the fact that she had seduced him.

As she sat under the water, she took stock. She hadn't been lying to Cornelius. When she touched someone, every time she touched them, their magic flooded her and a copy of it imprinted on her soul. And it hurt. Sometimes it hurt so much she wanted to rip off her skin. It only stopped once she had a copy of everything they had.

At first, it had been instant, a short, sharp, shock, like the static from a cheap jumper. Unpleasant but manageable, but then she'd only been touching Cornelius. Now, as she came into contact with more members of the Family, the pain was prolonged as she worked harder to absorb and hide all the magic she was stealing. It was why she had reacted so badly at the dinner a few nights ago. Everyone had touched her and not just once. She hadn't had time to absorb any magic before a new lot tried to invade her. It had got jammed and then flooded her all at once when she was dancing with her father. She wasn't able to cope with the pain when it finally hit her, so she ran to fight it. Seeing her in that level of distress would only hurt the ones she loved. Through the fog of pain and panic, her only clear thought had been 'Don't let them see you like this.'

She had been hugged by everyone again today and the transfer of power wasn't as painful. Sometimes there was no pain at all, as her body stole the last few drops of ability from another person. Maybe she finally had all they had to give? There was no power she didn't have now. She could see auras like her mother, follow trails like Julian, even heal herself like Matthew had done. She'd been floating above the bed when she woke up this morning.

She knew it wasn't the blossoming itself that was a problem. It was the fact she'd been twenty-three when it happened. In five thousand years, no dud had ever blossomed that late unless they were married. She could have argued that it was her plight against Sage that awakened it in her, but then she wouldn't have been his prisoner for six months. That lie, in the midst of all the others she'd told, would be the one to unravel her. Her parents would have discovered the truth and two souls innocent of her crime would have been punished.

Her gift was terrifying. In all the history of the Family, there was no one with this ability to copy and steal the magic of the others. There had never been one who could do it all. She was an abomination to every Family belief and sentiment. To be what she was would be to rival their god. That would throw everything they believed in, the very reason for their existence, into doubt. She had already damaged them enough. She would not do it again. That was why the other side to the magic was a blessing; she could weave a protective web around herself and prevent anyone from stumbling across her secret and causing mass panic. The song was right: sometimes the lie is the best thing.

She'd have to play it carefully to protect herself from Faroust. At the moment, Thomas' blood had given him the libido of a teenage boy, a libido he was all too willing to indulge. The idea made her shudder but she could use sex to protect herself from him. If she was willing to fuck on his terms, she could get through this relatively unscathed. She was nothing if not a survivor. She'd fucked herself out of trouble before; she could do it again.

It was odd that he wanted her to want him. Thanks to his spell, she did, but the reality of it also made her want to vomit at the same time. If she was to survive, she needed to ignore the disgust and feed the desire.

She lifted her head and the water sluiced over her face and chest as she got to her feet. There was a faint twinge between her legs. He was a big guy; she'd need time to adjust to him. It was a miracle she wasn't bleeding. She reached for the soap and scrubbed the last of him away. She fiddled with the buttons and there was a fresh rush of hot water. She rinsed out the shampoo and let herself float away for a moment.

A pair of hands clasped her breasts. She shrieked and her elbow flew back. As she was released, she span on her heel and charged her attacker. She caught him by surprise and they clattered to the floor. She clambered on top of him and raised the shampoo bottle in defence.

'Eliza, what the fuck? I surrender!'

A naked Faroust was pinned beneath her on the cold bathroom tiles. She dropped the bottle and, despite it all, began to giggle.

'You scared the shit out me!'

'Look who's talking! I only wanted a quick grope. Fuck,' he said, rubbing his head. He smiled indulgently at her as she continued to giggle, knowing it was only her nerves and anxiety escaping. When she stopped, he sat up and kissed her.

'You smell much better. Come back to bed. I have big plans for you. You're going to have to work really hard to keep Cornelius safe.'

She touched his chest shyly, spreading her hands.

I want it. The magic surged through his skin and into her, no pain, no fighting, no sickness.

Stop, she ordered. And it did. She sent out a silent prayer of thanks to the Veil.

'What are you smiling at?' Faroust asked.

Eliza didn't answer. Instead, she bent her head to kiss him and slid herself on to his erection. She would play the game. She would survive.

Chapter 14

ELIZA AND THE god lay in the living room, wrapped only in bed sheets, the remnants of their meal scattered over the coffee table. They'd spent the night screwing in every room of the apartment. Eliza was deliciously exhausted. Her body ached and her limbs were heavy. She hated to admit it but the sex was incredible. In fact, it was almost worth the danger of her predicament. Almost.

The god was dozing as she lay curled up beside him. If anyone had looked in on this scene, they would have thought them an ordinary couple enjoying a post-coital sleep. He was beautiful. He looked like one of the Elgin Marbles; his face could have graced the works of the old Masters or the Pre-Raphaelites. Lying here sleeping, naked and vulnerable, she could almost forget what he was, forget the things he did to recapture this youth and beauty. She felt a rush of love for him; a combination of years of Familial training and awe for his power.

She laid her head against his chest and closed her eyes, feeling better now she could control whether or not she took his power. But as she tried to sleep she was bombarded with images and memories rushing at her, all desperate to tell their story.

Stop it! she ordered, irritated by their intrusion. Immediately the images froze in her mind and she was able to see them clearly. She was surprised they did as she asked. What would they show her? Would she risk looking?

From the beginning, please.

The memories obeyed, ordering themselves as they filtered into her consciousness. They were the god's own memories of his existence, the truth behind their long line.

Like all the Faithful, she was well versed in the history of their tribe. Faroust was the son of Mebh, Faerie queen of Connaught and Angus Mac In Og, the god of youth and beauty. He was one of the *Tuatha Dé Danann*, the original deity-kings of Eire. These two had joined together to create a being that wouldn't be swayed by the wars of heroes and gods. He was charged with protecting the Veil and keeping the doors between worlds safe until the end of days. It was lovely. It was a beautiful story.

It was bullshit, a romanticised myth of his beginnings. Now Faroust's own memories revealed a little of him to her.

She felt his own awareness of his mother's womb. His father had lost a wager with Mebh. The payment was to impregnate her with a son. As soon as the deed was done she retreated to a place of safety, away from Connaught, to the small tribe who lived on the patch of soil the Family occupied even now. It had been a great forest then.

Fearing the consequences of the lost wager and the dark queen of Connacht's plans, Angus concocted a spell to cause her to miscarry their son. Eliza winced as she felt the foetus' pain and terror. There was a bright flash of light as he came into the world. Through the haze of blood and birth horror, she saw Mebh. She was beautiful, with hair the blood-red of the sunrise on snow, skin the colour of the moon. Her eyes were the black-green of the magpie's wing.

His mother fought hard to save him. She fed him a concoction of herbs, mixed with her milk and blood from the placenta to make him stronger. In that act, she ensured he was immortal, like his father.

'So that's it.'

'What's it?' Faroust yawned.

Eliza froze.

Oh feck. Oh feck. Oh feckity, feck, feck. Quick, Eliza think of something! Her brain shrieked.

'I thought it was the moon,' she mumbled.

Faroust sat up, dislodging her. She twitched as if she'd just woken up.

'What's wrong?' she sighed, stretching.

'You were talking in your sleep. At least, I think that's what you were doing.'

'Sorry, I do that sometimes.' She settled back down on him. He smiled at her.

'So if I want to know all your secrets, I should let you yak away in your sleep?'

'Pretty much. But you already know all my secrets.'

The First-Father rose, dislodging her again. She felt him trying to read her mind, still seeking for what she concealed. She threw up a wall and sent him the signal that she was brimming with lust for him. The power she had taken from the Family, and from him, enabled her to deflect his probe with ease.

Faroust must have found the image she wanted him to see. He grinned. There was little that was gentle in that smile.

'I'm going to have so much fun with you, but first I'm going to have a shower. Tidy up.' It wasn't a request but an order. Eliza snapped to attention and saluted him.

'Sir, yes Sir!'

'Stop calling me 'Sir'!'

'I will if you stop giving me orders.' She stuck her tongue out at him.

Faroust grinned again and cupped her chin. 'Careful now,' he warned. 'I haven't even got close to being rough with you yet.' He kissed her softly before retreating to the bathroom.

Eliza decided to get dressed before she tidied up. Faroust had dark desires. He'd taken pleasure in tying her up so she couldn't move as he fucked her. When she'd come, she'd been unable to close her legs and had to wait as the orgasm tore through her belly. He enjoyed pushing her pain-pleasure barriers, but not like a Dominant would with a Submissive. If a Submissive used a safe word, the Dominant had to stop. Faroust wouldn't have stopped unless he was on the point of killing her.

She caught sight of herself in the mirror and winced. Her body was covered in scratches and bites, some of which had broken the skin, and small bruises raised their dark colours against her pale flesh. There were five small puncture marks on her neck where his nails had pierced her skin, and a hand-shaped bruise, which was beginning to darken and turn purple. Her shoulders ached where he'd suspended her from the ceiling and taken her from behind. He'd made her wrap her legs backwards around him at the knees, so he could thrust deeply into her. Her hips hurt as well. She felt like she was limping.

Behind one of the cupboard fronts was a dishwasher; behind another was a washer-drier with a million functions. Eliza inspected the kitchen; there was a self-cleaning oven, a built in coffee grinder and maker, a fancy Swedish fridge with a separate cooler for wine, and the heartbreakingly expensive blender that Cook hankered for. The hob was halogen. How on earth had they got all this stuff down here and installed without anyone noticing? There had to be a second entrance somewhere.

She loaded the dishwasher and remade the bed. As she dried the copper bottomed pot that could not go in the dishwasher, she became aware of an odd noise above her. It was a keening, like a whine of agony.

Instinctively, she looked up. The sound was high above her head as if it was in . . . the house. Like her mother, she could sense and hear things outside of her immediate vicinity. It was a side effect of the astral projection skill. Curiosity called but she ignored the temptation to investigate.

The whine came again and her heart melted. There was so much pain in that noise, she had to find out what it was. She closed her eyes and strained to listen. Her spirit lifted out of her body. It made her feel sick and dizzy but in a few moments she had better control of her movements. She sent her spirit up towards the sound.

The noise came from her mother. Ruby lay sobbing, her head in Jacob's lap, while he tried to calm her.

'Please Ruby. Please stop crying,' he pleaded. 'It'll be all right.'

'How can it be all right?' she howled. 'He'll kill my little girl. He'll have his fun with her and then he'll kill her. He'll take her from us forever. I can't lose her again.'

Jacob's face entered her field of vision. Her father had been crying too. Eliza's heart snapped. Her guilt over leaving roared back to life. She was a selfish bitch. Her parents had never treated her badly; they'd just had no idea what to do with her. She was a dud and duds weren't important. The realisation dawned on her that everyone was trapped, not just her and Joshua, but everyone, her parents, her brothers, her cousins. They were all trapped by the magic.

Her physical body remained aware of her surroundings. The shower was still running, so she took a risk. Maybe she could influence her father from here? She had to let them know she was all right. She wanted to soothe their suffering and end their pain. Her soul crossed to the room and she put her astral hand into Jacob's heart.

'Call down, Daddy,' she said. 'Call down, Daddy. Be brave. Call down and ask if I'm all right. Be brave.'

Faroust turned the shower off and Eliza dragged herself back into her body. As she opened her eyes, Faroust appeared in the living room. He frowned and moved his hand through the air.

'What's wrong?'

'There's been a shift. Something's changed.'

Eliza stiffened. Oh shit. The phone rang distracting the god. He snatched it up.

'What?' he roared. 'Jacob, you'd better have a fucking good reason for calling me at four-thirty in the morning.'

Eliza wrapped her arms around his waist, willing him to be kinder. She could hear her father stutter at the end of the phone.

'F . . . First-Father, is . . . is . . . Eliza . . . ?'

'She's fine, Jacob,' he said, his voice irritated but his tone softer. 'She's a good girl. She knows how to follow orders.' He handed the phone to her. 'Do you want to talk to your father?'

Eliza hadn't expected that. Her eyes welled up at this small kindness.

'Hi, Daddy.'

'Eliza! Eliza, are you all right?'

She heard her mother babbling in the background.

'I'm fine, Daddy. His lordship has been very good to me this evening.'

Faroust vanished from sight. He trusted her. This was good. She filed that away to use later.

She sighed like a teenager in the throes of her first crush, more for Faroust's benefit than her father's. 'He's wonderful.'

Faroust put his head round the door and winked at her. She heard her father's sob of relief and she teared up again.

'Daddy, don't cry. I'm all right. I promise. Please don't cry.'

'I'm sorry. Will you be coming back tonight?'

She looked towards Faroust. He took the phone again.

'Jacob? I'm having a lot of fun with your daughter, so she won't be back tonight or the next night. Send down a month's worth of clothes and toiletries. Have Cornelius leave them on the altar. You have twenty minutes. Say goodbye, Eliza.'

'Goodbye Daddy,' she said weakly.

Faroust hung up and turned back to her. 'The thought of a month with me that bad?'

Eliza swiped at the tears, but they kept coming. 'No, of course not. I've . . . I've just never heard my dad cry . . . before. They were terrified . . .' She couldn't finish the sentence. She burst into guilty sobs, weeping for all the pain she'd caused them when she ran away. Faroust pulled her into a hug. He began to chant in her ear.

'Shh. It's all right, love.'

Eliza felt the calm wash over her. The people she influenced must feel like this. She was warm and safe and would have done anything he asked. Only the power she'd absorbed from him meant the spell didn't completely work. She did stop crying though, which is what Faroust wanted. Clearly crying women made him uncomfortable. Another piece of information she could store away for a later date.

'Feel better?'

'Yes. I'm sorry. I love my parents so much. I didn't think about the Hell they must have gone through last year when I went missing, until now . . .'

The god pulled away from her. 'Have I treated you badly tonight?'

'That's not the point . . .' she began.

He snarled and stalked away from her. He kicked the couch and it flew across the room towards her. She jumped out of the way and it cracked against the wall.

'Go fuck yourself!' he bellowed. 'They should know that I honour you!'

'In time, I'm sure they'll see that.' She tried to keep the edge out of her voice. 'But we've spent thousands of years being taught that you are our protective god, but you're also the son of Mebh, queen of the Morrigan. In order for us to survive, you drink blood from our sons and rape our daughters. They're only human. What are they supposed to think you're doing to me?'

Faroust snatched up a glass from the counter and hurled it at her. She stepped back and it smashed at her feet.

'Don't you throw things at me!' She grabbed the TV remote and hurled it at him. It cracked him on the shoulder and exploded into a thousand pieces. He rushed her. She slipped away from him and leapt over the couch, towards the bedroom. He swore as he cut his feet on the broken glass. She tried to lock the bedroom door but he crashed into it, knocking her to the floor. She scrambled to her feet, but she had nowhere to run.

'Who the fuck do you think you are?'

'I'm not someone who's going to tolerate you throwing a tantrum!' she retorted.

Faroust laughed at her and Eliza lost it. She had always been the butt of the joke upstairs and now their god was laughing at her. Before she realised what she was doing, she picked up the wastepaper basket and threw it at him. It smacked him in the chest and spilled its contents over the floor.

'Don't laugh at me!'

'Temper, temper.' She hadn't even fazed him.

'Look who's talking! You didn't even let me explain before you went off on one!'

'You're hot when you're angry.' He backed her against the wall and tried to kiss her. She pulled her head away from him.

'You can't treat me like that and expect me to bend over. I'm not your slave.'

'I'm a god. I get what I want.'

'Not this time.'

Faroust groaned, grinding his hips against her.

'I could pick you up and force you.'

'Wow. Big man.'

He slumped at her reply. He was unaccustomed to refusal. She knew he wanted her because she fought back. He wanted her because she was strong.

'I should bend you over and spank you.'

'No point. I'd enjoy it.'

He whimpered and pressed himself against her again. 'You can't say things like that when we're quarrelling. The thought of it makes it difficult to fight.'

'I thought we were about to make up.' She wanted to end the argument now. She didn't know how far she could push him before he snapped back, snapped her. 'I didn't mean to upset you. I love my parents so much.'

Faroust stared at her for a moment.

'Tell you what. If you're a good girl and do exactly as I say, you may go up on Sunday afternoons for a few hours.'

Again, she was taken aback. She couldn't get a handle on him. He was all over the place, kind and cruel in equal measure.

Remember Sophie. Remember Tom. Remember the twins. Play the game, but do not forget.

'Thank you,' she said, regaining her equilibrium.

'I can be a kind and understanding god. I just get lonely down here . . .' He trailed off, puzzled. 'Now why would I tell you that?'

Eliza shrugged, but her nonchalance did nothing to dispel his mistrust. Faroust pulled her dress off her. He gathered her to him and sat down on the bed.

'Hold on to me, sweetheart. This will hurt.'

'What are you doing?'

'You know my secrets,' he said.

'I won't tell anyone. I promise.'

Faroust kissed her cheek. 'Not intentionally, but someone may try to force them out you. It wouldn't be the first time. I can't allow that to happen. This will protect us both.'

He pressed his hand to the base of her spine. She screamed as burning pain spread across her back. She beat her fists on his chest and shoulders, struggling to get away from him.

'Hush, pet. It will be over soon. Trust me.'

He pulled her closer to him. She bit his shoulder in an attempt to stem her cries. She tasted blood, his blood, as he continued to cast the spell. Her mouth tingled and throbbed as she felt more of his magic slide into her. Eventually, it was over. The pain vanished as quickly as it had begun.

'What did you do?'

'I've made my mark on you. It means your tongue is sealed and you can never share my secrets.'

She caught a glimpse of her back in the mirrored wardrobe door. A letter F had been branded into her, like she was a piece of beef. He'd marked her as his property.

'No one can take your knowledge now,' he mumbled into her hair. 'You are my consort and no one will mess with you.'

She swallowed her white-hot rage at this further violation. It made sense for Faroust to protect himself. The mystery had to stay mysterious. If the Family knew he lived as an ordinary man, there would be chaos and fury at his betrayal. She appreciated the lengths one could go to in the name of self-preservation.

He rocked her back and forth, as if she were a child who needed soothing back to sleep after a nightmare.

'I'm sorry, sweetheart. It's the only way to protect myself. I have let you in and one day I will let you out. Your parents wear it too. No one can know what you three know; there would be uproar.' He spoke as if he had read her thoughts.

She nodded, unable to speak.

'Cornelius will be here soon. You should wash your face and comb your hair.'

'You're sending me out? Why be that cruel?' Anger flooded her again, leaving her shaking and weak. She was not used to feeling this way. It must be the magic. It was unbalancing her.

The phone shrieked in the living room before he could answer. Faroust placed her on the bed and left to answer the call. She jumped to her feet and rushed to his dresser, opening the drawers as quietly as she could, looking for the man drawer. Every man she knew had one, stuffed full of odds and ends that weren't useful anymore but were too good to throw away. Faroust's man drawer was well organised, divided up by little drawer separators. She located a tatty notebook and a half decent pen. Frantically, she scribbled a note to Cornelius before tucking it under the wire of her bra.

Faroust returned a split second after she closed the drawer. From his expression, she knew the conversation with her father hadn't been pleasant. She picked up her dress.

'What are you doing?'

'Getting dressed. I thought that . . .'

'No. You'll go out in your underwear. Only a man buys lingerie like that.'

'Like what?' It was the wrong time to challenge him but she couldn't help herself.

'It's slutty. Tastefully slutty, mind, but it's still tiny bits of lace hiding your . . . goods.'

'My goods?' If he continued in this vein, she'd lose her temper just to get away from him. Death might be an extreme way to escape his chauvinism but at this moment, angry and violated, she wasn't sure she could tolerate his ignorance. Upstairs the women were as important as the men.

'I'm wearing my dress. I'm not your property to be paraded around. Especially not in the underwear *he* bought me.'

Faroust snatched it out of her hands.

'I want him to see how lovely you look in the present he bought you.'

'What point are you trying to make? He's a mortal. You're a god. You win.'

There was a tentative knock on the wall.

'That'll be him. Out you go.'

'Not without my dress.'

The god shredded the garment like tissue paper. The lights in the room flickered and the ground trembled.

'Out. You. Go.' He snapped each word.

'I. Don't. Know. How. To. Open. The. Door,' she enunciated, mimicking him.

Faroust dragged her up the passageway to the door. He took her hand and put it over a small button hidden in the shadows.

'Push button, door opens. Easy. Out!'

He stormed back down towards the living room. She flipped a V at his retreating form before she pressed the button.

The door opened and a plume of smoke was released in the chamber. Coughing, she stumbled into the Ritual room. Cornelius leaned against the altar, his head down, his spirit broken. Her heart swelled at the sight of him. She saw a good man beneath his hideous occupation. She'd learned that torture made up only a small part of his existence. He spent most of his time on surveillance and protecting the children of the Family. She longed to rush to him, to hug him and tell him everything was all right but despite the fact the door was shut, she knew the creature inside would be watching them.

Cornelius had placed her belongings on the altar; a small suitcase with her clothes and her toiletry bag, overflowing with makeup and soaps. It looked like her mother had packed all the bottles and jars on Eliza's dresser. The overstuffed makeup bag provided the opportunity she needed to get the note to Cornelius. She hefted the suitcase off the altar, knocking the toiletry bag to the floor and spilling the contents. Both of them dropped to the ground to gather up the escaping cosmetics.

Deftly, Eliza reached under the wire of her bra and pressed the note into Cornelius' hand as they reached for the same jar of face cream. Just as swiftly, he tucked it out of sight; he was not the Family spy for nothing. They did not speak to each other as they collected the last of the bottles and jars. He didn't even raise his eyes to look at her, despite the provocative nature of her dress. She was no longer his.

Eliza offered him a ghost of a smile as they rose. He did not return it. He was as cold as he'd been on the night he caught her. His training served him well, but Eliza felt his pain and anger as his eyes flickered over the marks Faroust had left on her body. There was a glimmer of recognition in his eyes as he assessed her bruises. He would know she had been tied up, suspended and bitten. He would know she had been fucked.

She gathered her bags and turned her back. Cornelius broke the silence with an involuntary cry; he had seen the mark. She did not look back; if she did, she knew she would break.

He reached for her, but his hand fell back to his side without making contact. The door swung open, framing Faroust in shadow. Eliza felt the world spin as he took her bags from her; she had a horrible feeling she knew what he was about to do.

Faroust pressed a finger to his lips as he passed her, before she could utter some protest. He sat on his throne and passed his gaze over the Cruel.

'Well, you're not very nice. I thought you'd be pleased to see your girlfriend in one piece.'

Faroust had taken a deep and perverse pleasure watching the scene that unfolded between Eliza and Cornelius in the Ritual chamber. He could feel how much they cared for each other and yet they'd been too terrified even to touch or pass two words.

'At the very least, you could have asked how she is.'

Cornelius did not respond.

'You know, I ought to kill you,' Faroust said. 'You've broken our laws. But it all depends on how much Eliza values your life, on how low she's willing to stoop.'

The young man bristled, catching the meaning in his words. 'I would rather die than watch her be humiliated,' Cornelius spat.

Faroust waved a long index finger at the Cruel. 'It's not your choice. It's Eliza's. Whether you live or die depends on her. Eliza? What's your pleasure?'

Cornelius glanced across at her. 'Eliza, you don't have to . . .'

'We need you,' she interrupted.

'Wise girl.' Faroust held out his hand. Eliza crossed to him and knelt.

'Don't rush,' he whispered. 'If you want him to live, make it good.'

Eliza looked up at him and lifted his robe. Without breaking eye contact, she took him in her hand and began moving it slowly up and down his shaft. Faroust stared at Cornelius, daring him to react.

'You don't look away. Not even for a second,' he said.

She lowered her head and brushed her lips against his swelling penis, teasing it with the brief contact. Faroust sighed as she rubbed her warm mouth against his flesh. She slipped her hand up his shaft as she darted her tongue out in a feather-light touch against the head of his penis. He stared pointedly at the Cruel as Eliza swirled her tongue around the head and let him slip into her mouth, just for a second, before starting to kiss up and down his length. She returned to the tip, circling her tongue slowly around it, lingering on where it joined the shaft.

'Oh,' he groaned, 'she's so very, very good. You trained her well.'

Faroust took as much pleasure watching Cornelius fight his anger as he did from Eliza servicing him. She licked him rhythmically now, building the anticipation of when she would next take him fully in her mouth, making him twitch. She would bring her lips up every so often but would only kiss the head, rather than take him in completely. When she finally let him slide into her mouth, the god almost broke eye contact with Cornelius at the sensation. She squeezed his shaft tighter, making him gasp as she bobbed her head. When she unsheathed her teeth to gently drag them along his hard length he almost lost it altogether.

'Oh my, Cornelius. You are definitely safe. She must love you.'

Eliza moved her hand away from the shaft and fondled his testicles. She squeezed them gently and Faroust's breath quickened, but he made no sound. Eliza returned her hand to the shaft and took him deeper into her mouth. He came down her throat with a quiet gasp, his eyes never once leaving Cornelius's face.

'Good girl, Eliza,' he sighed, holding her in place with his hand as she swallowed. 'You are safe, Cornelius. Now get the fuck out.'

Cornelius turned and walked away. Only when the door to Jacob's study slammed shut did Faroust withdraw from her mouth. Eliza got to her feet, wiping her lips and regarding him coldly as he stood up.

Faroust felt odd, as if he was ashamed by what had just happened. He couldn't look her in the eye. He shook the feeling off; it was absurd for *him* to be ashamed. He wasn't the one who'd broken the rules.

'Come back inside,' he said, picking up her bags and taking them to his room. 'I cleared some space for your things. You have a few drawers in here and some space in the bathroom. Make sure you put it all away neatly.'

Eliza hugged herself as Faroust walked out, fighting the urge to weep. Instead she pulled on her dressing gown and tidied away her things. The absurdity of unpacking her belongings burned within her. Her stomach churned and her hands itched as her power raged, beating at the door of logic and howling to be let out. She wanted to kill him. She wanted to end his unnatural, depraved life, to bring it all crashing down. The power roared in her belly.

Let me end him. Don't submit to the humiliation. Let me end him.

It was tempting but the part of her still ruled by reason whispered against it.

You're not on a kamikaze mission. This is the way of things. It will always be the way of things. Survive his lust and you can go home to Cornelius.

She took a deep breath and restrained her fury. That wasn't who she was. It had never been who she was. Now was not the time for rash actions, otherwise everything she had worked for, everyone she loved, including her darling Cornelius, would be lost. She had to play his game. Eventually he would get bored of her and she could go home.

She finished unpacking and went to Faroust, who was watching TV.

'Tell me. Do you really want a lover, or do you just want a sex toy?'

At her voice Faroust's head snapped up. He stared at her for a long moment.

'I want a lover,' he said at length.

'Then never ask me to do that again. I will be your lover. I will adore and worship you. I will do anything you want. I consent to everything but I am begging you, 'she crossed to him and knelt in front of him, 'do not make me do that again.' She put her head in his lap. He stroked her hair.

'I think that's fair, my pretty dud.'

She sat back and smiled at him. He touched her face, and the marks and abrasions healed, leaving her less battered and sore.

'What do you want to do?' she asked.

'I want to sleep, like lovers do. Curled around each other.'

Eliza stood up and held out her hand. He took it and they went to his bed.

In his rooms far above Eliza and the god, Cornelius paced furiously. Fucking bastard! He kicked over his table and ran his hands into his hair. Was having her not enough? Was humiliating her necessary? No, no it wasn't, but Faroust wanted to demonstrate his power, to prove Eliza was his and she would do what he wanted. Cornelius wanted to scream.

He unfolded the note and read it for the hundredth time. He felt himself tear up; she'd put herself in such danger to get this to him.

Cornelius,

He doesn't know. I'll be all right. You rock my socks.

Your Eliza xx

Though it broke his heart, the Cruel took out his lighter and burned the note in the fireplace. He couldn't risk anyone finding it. It would bring catastrophe for Eliza. Cornelius lay down on his bed. The pillow still smelt of her from the previous afternoon, before the Ritual began. They'd just laid together, nothing sexual, just laid there and spent the afternoon talking. Had it really only been yesterday?

They had something special. In this festering, incestuous hole they'd found each other and fallen for each other. He'd do anything for her, now there were no secrets between them. Eliza hadn't needed magic to keep him under control. She was special without magic. She'd captured him with sex, but it was her soul and her intelligence he had fallen for.

He needed to do something; he was winding himself up sitting here worrying about her. He ran down to his office where he monitored the comings and goings of the house. There was no hiding from him in this building.

Cruelty

It was six am and the house was waking up. He poured a large coffee and sat in silence, examining the monitors. He watched as Ruby and Jacob hugged in their bedroom. If they lost Eliza again, it might kill them. He turned the volume up.

'She's Barren. How can she survive his lust without magic?' Ruby sighed.

'We have to hope, love.'

Eliza was a survivor by nature; she could survive a nuclear holocaust. She'd be queen of the cockroaches. He wished he could read the note again, to reassure himself that she was all right. That she wouldn't do anything stupid, that somehow she'd be able to stop herself from leeching power from their god. Surely, as old as he was, *he'd* notice her siphoning his power eventually? If she was very, lucky and didn't do anything foolish, she'd be all right.

The alarm on his phone went off. He had a prisoner to take care of, a hacker who'd attempted to break into the company files in a vain attempt to dig up dirt on Ruby and where she was getting the money for her environmental programmes. The Patriarch caught the little snot tracking him while he'd been working away. Jacob was convinced the prat had seen something but he was refusing to talk. Now it was Cornelius' turn to work the spy over. He was looking forward to it. A good work out would help him with his anxiety over Eliza.

He picked up his bag and headed towards the kitchens. When his father had been the Cruel, the former Patriarch gifted him an interrogation room made from an ancient storeroom, a dark, soundproof place, with no access to sunlight or fresh air. Cornelius rarely used it, priding himself on being able to break a prisoner in the outside world and never get caught. His father had always been proud that his son didn't want or need the security blanket of the interrogation room.

Today, Cornelius was glad of its existence. He could take all the time he wanted to break this man, get really creative. He rolled his shoulders, limbering himself up before he unlocked the door and flicked on the light. The bare bulb cast the room in a greasy yellow light. His prey knelt in the centre of the room, shirtless and barefoot. His arms were extended above him, his head bowed. He'd only been here a few days but he looked like he'd been imprisoned for years.

He was skinny, with a rounded, undefined stomach. His chest fluttered in and out as he breathed. His head snapped up when the light went on. He blinked in its harsh glare as Cornelius stepped towards him. His hair was plastered to his scalp with grease and sweat.

'Hello, Andy,' Cornelius said, pulling a chair over. 'I understand you did something stupid.'

Andy shook his head. 'I was doing my job,' he croaked. 'I'm a reporter.'

'Really?' Cornelius feigned interest. 'What do you report on?'

'Political scandal. People need to know how the government uses their money.'

The Cruel pulled on the rope suspending the young man, forcing him upright and further, until his feet were three inches off the ground. He panted under the strain. Cornelius knelt beside him and locked a cuff around each ankle, pulling the young man taut.

The Cruel stood in front of Andy, who whimpered as he tried to breathe through the discomfort.

'Ruby MacTir is an exemplary TD. She spends her time trying to create eco-policies which are affordable and practical, to protect Ireland's countryside and reduce our carbon footprint. Is that a poor use of the taxpayer's money?'

'She's her husband's pawn. She blocks housing developments in the name of protecting the green belt, but they are also areas which could have reserves of natural gas or oil. Jacob MacTir has shares in some of the world's largest energy companies. He's using his wife to line his pockets.'

What was this kid on?

'Jacob is an ethical adviser to those companies, helping them find ways to produce power without fucking over the planet. He consults with oil companies to try and limit the environmental damage they cause. He travels all around the world, investing in alternative power sources because he wants to protect the environment. How do you fucking figure he is tapping Ireland's green land for oil and gas reserves?' He laughed. 'Which paper do you work for?'

Andy looked down, his mouth set in a firm line. Cornelius pushed him down by his shoulders, making him kneel and giving the rope plenty of slack. He released him suddenly and Andy flew upwards, yelling in agony as the cuffs on his ankles jerked him to a stop.

'Which paper?'

'The UCD student paper.'

Cornelius blinked incredulously at the younger man. He sat down on the chair and covered his eyes with his hand, dissolving into full blown sobs of laughter.

'Fuck, dude, you're a fecking *student?* You're not even a real reporter?'

'The truth can be reported by anyone!'

'I'm sure it can be,' Cornelius sighed, wiping away a tear, 'but you are barking up the wrong tree. How old are you?'

'Nineteen.'

'Nineteen? Holy shit, you're an idiot kid, poking his nose in where it doesn't belong. I'll speak to my boss and send you home.'

Andy glared in outrage as Cornelius pulled out his phone.

'Fuck you, you cunt.' The boy spat. 'You can do what you want, but I won't just go away. I know about the Ritual.'

Cornelius dropped the phone and turned on the prisoner. 'Really?'

'Yeah.' Andy smirked. 'I know all about it. I know what the plan is.'

Cornelius made a mental note to clean out Jacob's laptop.

'I'm not going to stay silent,' Andy pressed on. 'I'm going to let everyone know what shit your boss is trying to pull.'

Cornelius reached inside his black bag and drew out a set of knuckle dusters.

'You have two choices. You either tell me what you found out and I'll let you go. Or you try to be the big man and I fuck you up.'

The boy swallowed and paled. But he held to his mission. 'The people deserve to know the truth.' His voice wavered.

'You're an idiot.' Cornelius sighed. He drew back his fist and cracked the boy across the face.

After he punched him, Cornelius pulled out his pliers and snapped every single one of the kid's toes. Andy screamed and wept, but he didn't reveal what he'd learnt about the Ritual. Cornelius turned to the whip next and lashed the living shit out Andy's back. There was a pool of blood under his broken feet.

'What the fuck is your problem?' Andy howled.

'You're a stupid prick who won't save his own skin. Tell me what you know and this ends. You can go home.'

Andy shook his head vehemently. 'No. If you're willing to kill me, it must be important.'

Cornelius rubbed his forehead in frustration. The boy was stronger than he looked.

'You're getting off on this. You're a sick fuck. I bet you can't even get it up.'

Cornelius laughed at the boy's pitiful attempt to wound him. He pulled out his knee splitter.

He released one of Andy's legs and pulled his jeans down, sliding the device up his skinny leg. Slowly, so slowly, he tightened the vice mechanism. The jagged jaws of the instrument cut into the flesh. Andy threw his head back and screamed as the machine crushed his kneecap.

Cornelius got to his feet. He grabbed Andy's chin and forced him to look at him. The boy screamed.

'What's that?' he demanded, staring at Cornelius' empty hand.

'Just a little friend of mine.'

Andy shrieked and tried to jerk backwards as Cornelius forced him to perceive it moving toward him. He shuddered and sobbed as the imaginary creature slithered around his neck and down his wounded back.

'Oh my God!' Andy screeched, pulling frantically at his restraints. 'It's trying to burrow into my back! Make it stop! Make it stop!'

'Tell me what you know.'

The boy sobbed, snot dripping down his chin. He was broken. It had taken only an hour.

'Make it stop. I want to go home.' His voice came out in a low keen.

Cornelius took the boy's head in his hands. 'Tell me what you know and I can let you go home.'

'You promise?'

'Cross my heart. Look, I'll even get rid of the monster so you can tell me.'

Andy took a deep breath and Cornelius released the spell.

'I was in a bar in Belfast last week and I saw Jacob huddled in the corner with his laptop. He was on the phone to someone, saying things like 'I know how important the Ritual is. I'm working on it now. Yes, I'll be back soon. Yes, I saw. How is she? Where's this new piece of land we're saving?' He was trying to keep his voice down and glancing around the room. I thought the Ritual had to be important. I saw the opportunity for a good story.

'I hacked the Wi-Fi using my phone and used it to get into MacTir's laptop. It's not hard when you know how. I planted a virus to copy all his documents onto to my device. I had just opened his day planner when he burst into my room. It said . . . it said Ruby's attack, Ritual with three exclamation marks on the same day. I thought it was code for something but that's all I saw. I don't really know what it is. Can I go home now?'

Cornelius screwed his eyes closed as Andy's words sank in. He had to make sure the boy was telling the truth. He shook his left hand and pressed it against Andy's forehead. The boy wailed as Cornelius' hand sank into his head. The Cruel ignored his cries and focused on finding his memories. He was soon satisfied he'd told the truth.

He released his captive, who sank to the floor, whimpering and shivering in fear. He called Jacob.

'Sir? I know it's not the best time, but that idiot boy has been taken care of. He doesn't know anything. I'll get Julian to dump him at a hospital.'

'Thank you, Cornelius. Can you come up to my study once you're done?'

'Yes, Sir.'

Andy had passed out by the time Julian appeared. Cornelius cleaned his tools, ignoring the comatose human on the floor.

'You love your work don't you?' The Hound wrapped the student in a tarpaulin sheet. 'You should have been born during the Spanish Inquisition.'

'There are dirty jobs to be done while we carry out our great mission. Would you rather there was no one to protect us?'

Julian looked down at the broken Andy.

'Bit much though, wasn't it?' he said. 'Not this poor bastard's fault our Lord has Eliza. It's yours.'

Cornelius stomach dropped at Julian's vitriol. But he was right. If he hadn't given in to his groin, Eliza wouldn't have come to Faroust's attention. He was left speechless as the Hound hauled the boy over his shoulder and left.

It wasn't even lunch time. Despite Julian's unpleasant honesty, the hour he'd spent dealing with Andy had left him invigorated. He loved his job. It raised him above the rest of the Lesser Branch. He was the secret defender in the shadows, keeping them protected from the *Gnáth* so the rest of them could carry on with their mission in peace. And Eliza had been right; returning her as a victim had impressed the Greater Branch and he was treated with open respect. The respect a hero deserved.

His heart tightened as he thought of Eliza once more. She'd looked a mess when she met him to collect her things. Her skin was sore in several places where she'd been bound, and around her scalp it was red where he'd pulled her hair. He'd seen bite marks, scratches and bruises and knew Faroust would push her to breaking point. Cornelius just enjoyed tying her hands, spanking her and whispering dirty things in her ear, stuff that was acceptably kinky. Like what he'd planned for the previous night. Shit, there was a punnet of strawberries he needed to eat . . .

He reached Jacob's office and took a moment to compose himself before he knocked on the door. Jacob was sitting with his head in his hands, glaring at something on his desk. Cornelius guessed it was his report on Eliza.

'Did she really survive all this?' The Patriarch sighed. 'I never thought she would be so strong.' He looked up at the Cruel with red, tired eyes. 'Do you think she'll be able to survive him?'

Cornelius closed the folder and pulled it away from Jacob.

'When I saw her downstairs, she was calm. She was in one piece. Eliza is a survivor and she adapts quickly. She'll do whatever she needs to in order to endure.'

Just like she did with me.

'It's like losing her again.' Jacob slammed his fist down on the table. This time the desk snapped in half. 'We're not his playthings!' he bellowed, leaping to his feet. 'He needs us as much as we need him. He can't just use us however he feels like.'

Cornelius stared, speechless at his leader's outburst.

'Hasn't she suffered enough? Haven't we suffered enough? Every year we complete our duty, give him the sacrifice, protect the seals!'

'Sir, it is our duty. We are his People, descended from those warriors he rewarded with his magic after the *Tuathane* tried to rip open . . .'

'It doesn't mean he can abuse us. It doesn't mean he can use my child as his plaything. That makes our god no better than the cunt who abducted her. How can I live with that paradox? That I serve a man who rapes our children and drinks their blood? That I handed my daughter over for his pleasure without complaint?'

The Patriarch tipped the remains of his desk over and pummelled his fists against it, smashing it into splinters. He fell to his knees, gripping his head and bursting into angry tears. Cornelius knelt beside him and put his arm around his shoulders.

'What can I do, Cornelius?'

The Cruel opened the folder and pulled out one of the DVDs.

'What are you doing? I don't want to see that shit.'

'I want to show you something. Something that will give you hope.'

He picked up the laptop, which had been balanced on the window seat, and pushed the disk in. Eliza filled the small screen. The date on the bottom right of the picture indicated this was taken towards the end of her time as Sage's prisoner. Her face was badly bruised and she was painfully thin. She sat cross-legged on the floor, but she didn't look cowed or broken. Her back was straight and she looked up at the camera.

Sage stumbled into view and grabbed her by the hair, dragging her to her feet and attaching her to the pulley. She didn't flinch, didn't jerk away as he began to work her torso over with a cat-o'-nine-tails. She didn't even cry out.

'Tell me what you're hiding!' Sage screamed at her.

'Fuck you.' Her voice was steady. Sage stumbled away, panting with exhaustion and physical weakness. He let Eliza fall to the ground before he left the attic. Slowly, she sat back up and massaged her shoulders. Not a single tear fell.

Cornelius clicked the film off. Jacob sat silently in the splintered remains of his desk.

'That was four days before I found her. Sir, she is strong. She survived Sage. She will survive Faroust too. He doesn't want to fuck her up, just f . . .' He stopped, embarrassed by his near slip of the tongue.

'Just fuck her,' Jacob finished. He got to his feet, rubbing his face. 'Thank you Cornelius. Eliza's right; you're a good man.'

Cornelius blinked hard, taken aback.

'I spoke to her on the phone. She seemed fine. And he is very taken with her.' The Patriarch was speaking to himself now. 'She'll be fine,' he decided. He looked at the Cruel. 'Don't say anything about this conversation to anyone.'

Cornelius nodded and left the study, knowing he was dismissed. Like Jacob, he felt optimistic. Eliza had managed to get around him after all; who was to say she couldn't get round Faroust?

Chapter 15

ELIZA MADE GOOD work on getting around Faroust. She made an effort to please him and he rewarded her by treating her like his lover, rather than a plaything. He'd even eased off a little on the bondage and suspension. He was much gentler with her and, despite her doubts, Eliza was beginning to see his charm. He was clever and sharp-witted. He was a good cook and he was good in bed. Though she could not forget what he had done to Sophie, knowing he was going out of his way to please her made her position as concubine easier to bear. And he liked the fact she wasn't completely meek, that she acted with greater bravery as each day passed. She often made him laugh with a sarcastic rejoinder. The fear was still there, but it wasn't so powerful. She hadn't lowered her guard completely, but things were easier between them.

The first week with him was almost identical to her first night; they fucked, ate, watched television and fucked some more. The only real difference was that they hadn't fought. Every day, Eliza grew stronger. She felt him probing her psyche, trying to find her secrets. To protect herself, she'd carefully siphoned power from him, tiny sips, so small he wouldn't notice, weaving them around her soul to keep him away from the truth.

She could now control when she took his power, but she did not have the same access to his memories. They only came when he was sated and sleeping, when his guard was truly down. When the memories came, they whispered to her in broken fragments, sometimes showing their secrets to her and other times making her live them. The first twenty-one years of his life passed by in a blur. Mebh left her precious son with the people of the village. His duty was to guard the Veil, the opening to the paths to the Otherworlds which kept the Universe from collapsing in on itself and gave Mebh a way home if she needed it. The villagers were her gift to him. They served his every whim and he ruled them with love and kindness.

Things only became interesting when the *Tuathane* came to the village in the forest . . .

The Tuathane, loyal only to their own morals. They did not aid the Heroes, gods or Fae in their endeavours. They tried to tear the Veil apart to get to the Otherworlds, driven by tales of wealth, adventure and beautiful women. She felt his anger as he stood in front of the Veil, the invisible doorway only he could see. The Tuathane had come to his home, asking for hospitality and rest. But he caught them trying to force the Veil open with their false magic and blood sacrifices. He gathered the leaders in front of his hall and laid their crimes before them. He executed them with his own sword.

There was a scream from the forest, and a thousand Tuathane flooded the clearing. The warriors of his tribe surrounded him as the women and children vanished into the trees. One of the insane Tuathane released an arrow at the god, scraping his face. He ignored the welling blood but she was aware of his panic as he realised his people could not withstand the onslaught of this army. She felt sick, as he had felt sick. A stinging pain ran up her arm. It emanated from her wrist, his wrist. He was calling to the People, telling them to drink his blood, passing his magic to them. His mother needed the Veil. She needed this land. The Tuathane were god killers, they knew ways to end immortality. He could not stand alone.

In a heartbeat, he was flanked by his warrior men and women. Together they drove back the Tuathane. The earth ran red with their blood, reflecting the moon as it rose above them. That night, the Ritual was born. In gratitude for his gift, they offered up the virginity of their most beautiful girls and the power of their strongest boys. He was elevated beyond protector to god.

Faroust stirred and the memories scattered. Eliza panted for breath. Each time she caught a glimpse, it became more intense. That was the most she had seen in three days. She felt sick. The god was still sleeping, so she crept out of the bedroom to the living room. She opened the tatty notebook and tried to write down what she had witnessed. She hadn't even pressed the pen against the paper before her body was wracked with pain. Her skin felt as if it was on fire. She doubled up and lay on the couch until the pain passed. The spell Faroust had put on her when he branded her back was a powerful one. She couldn't even write it down.

After a while, the pain faded and she was able to stand. She stumbled into the kitchen and put the kettle on. She closed her eyes and tried to stop the trembling that suffused her whole body. She was so lost in concentration she didn't hear Faroust calling her, wasn't even aware of him, until he put his arms around her waist. She jumped, but it stopped the trembling.

'Morning,' he said. 'How long have you been awake?'

'About half an hour. I thought I'd make you breakfast.'

He gazed around the kitchen. 'I notice that breakfast is seriously lacking.' He picked her up and settled her on the breakfast bar.

'I couldn't decide what to make you. You have a disgusting amount of tasty food in your fridge. How do you get it down here? Does my dad bring it?'

'Something like that.' He stretched and yawned. 'Do you fancy going out today?'

She frowned. 'Bored of me already?'

'No, you bimbo. I thought we might have a day out.'

'I didn't think you could leave here.'

He laughed. 'Of course I can. Sometimes I leave for months at a time. I forward my calls; your dad would go insane if . . . he . . . knew . . .'

'I see.' Her voice was cold as stone.

'I have to be here in August, and for the Ritual of course, because that's when the magic is weakest and you need the most protection . . .' His voice trailed away to nothing.

'Uh-huh.' She leant forward in challenge. 'We were told that if you left here, we would all perish and die.'

He shrugged. 'That only really applies in August and September, but time warps the truth. Mythology. Whatcha gonna do?'

His offhand confession was typical. Eliza often found herself slipping under his spell. She knew she should be outraged that he was free to get away from them, that he'd been lying to them, but her desire for fresh air and his feckless charm made her forget it for the moment. He made her laugh again and he kissed her. He could be gentle and affectionate. She struggled to believe this man was the same person as their god.

'So do you fancy going out or not?'

'Yeah, that'd be nice.'

'Hey! Let's be really wicked. Let's take off for the rest of the week. I'll book us a flight and we'll go anywhere you want. London, maybe? Or Paris or Venice or . . .'

She kissed him, interrupting his train of thought. 'How about the zoo? Phoenix Park is far more appropriate for an official first date.'

'All right. Zoo it is then.'

Eliza made a move to get off the breakfast bar but Faroust stopped her. She looked up at him and smiled. He was hard against her.

'Do you think the breakfast bar could take it?' She laughed.

199

'Only one way to find out.'

The breakfast bar stood up remarkably well to their experiment. There wasn't even a scratch. After a late breakfast and a long shower, they were finally ready to go. Faroust took her hand and led her to his study.

'For future reference, if I am not here, you are not allowed in this office. It is out of bounds and it will be locked.'

'Why?'

'Because I say so.'

Like the rest of the apartment, it was immaculate. Unlike her father's study, it was soulless; there were no books or knick-knacks or anything to give it personality. There was a desk, a computer, a phone and shelves and shelves of the Family's financial records, all carefully labelled.

Why aren't I allowed in here? I know all about this shit. What's in here that I can't see?

'That's interesting.'

'I like to keep up to speed on where the Family's money is going. Sometimes Jacob comes to me for advice.'

'Is that what you do all day? When you're not occupied with concubines?'

He shook his head. 'I monitor the seams and seals. They give off a faint signature, like gamma-rays.'

He opened the laptop on his desk and clicked on an icon. The screen filled with electronic meters, all of which were level.

'In times gone by, we could only sense when a seam was aggravated when it was about to split open. That would open another pathway to the Otherworlds and unbalance the Veil so it was always a rush job to fix. By placing detection meters at the sites of the seams, I can intervene much sooner and send out people to deal with the problem.'

He tapped a few keys and clicked on an icon. A map of Europe sprang up on the screen. He zoomed in on Ireland. There were lines cutting across the whole island; some were razor thin, some, like the one at the Giant's Causeway, were thick and glowing.

Just like the ones on Dad's computer.

'These are the seams in Ireland, where the wall is thinnest between our reality and the Otherworlds.' He pointed to a few lines on the screen. 'The thin ones are thin bands of power and usually manifest in a bumper crop or similar. The thick ones are where the real power is, where the strange things happen. People can't cross into the Otherworlds like they used to, but things sometimes get through, and the power can be manipulated by idiots who don't know better. It is our job to monitor these and keep them under control. There are other seams in Britain and in Europe which are less volatile than the ones here, but it doesn't hurt to keep an eye on them.'

I know all this. There has to be something in here he doesn't want me to see. We'll see about that. Her eyes flicked to the certificates on the wall.

'What are those?'

'I am a qualified solicitor, specialising in property law, which enables us to fend off developers building near the seams. I prepare all the bills we propose to the *Dáil* and the *Seanad*, making sure they are watertight. I am also the Family archivist. I have information on every single member of our clan, Higher and Lesser born, for the last five thousand years.'

Eliza laughed in surprise. 'You're a busy boy then?'

'I don't spend all my time playing video games and having sex. You wanted to know how I got my groceries, right?' He steered her to the middle bookshelf. It looked just like the other four. 'Try to take a file off the shelf.'

She did as he asked but she couldn't pull the file down. It was an empty box, glued to the shelf. They all were. He pressed on the third shelf and the door opened, revealing a passageway to the surface.

'If we need to get out in a hurry, we can go this way.'

'Where does it go?'

'You'll see.'

The climb upwards only took a few minutes, unlike the descent from her father's study. They came to a small door above their heads which Faroust opened with a flourish.

'Oh my God, it's the lodge! You live underneath the groundkeeper's lodge?'

'Let me give you the tour.'

The lodge was down by the back gate, as far away as you could get from the main house while still being on the property. It was modestly furnished with the rejects from the Big House; things that were no longer fashionable but still had use. The living room had a small faded sofa and matching armchair. The kitchen was a galley, just large enough for a person to avoid burning their arse on the gas stove as they reached into the cupboard. The mattress of the bedroom's double bed sagged in the middle but the timber frame looked solid. The bath was a little rusty and instead of a shower, there was an ancient rubber hose attached to the taps. Two pairs of wellington boots were neatly lined up at the back door, speckled with mud, but there was not a spot to be found on the floor.

Her curiosity sated, Eliza felt guilty for poking around.

'We shouldn't really be snooping. It's Daniel's home, after all.'

'Oh, I don't mind.'

The comment almost passed her by as she made her way to the front door. She paused mid-step.

'You're the groundskeeper? You're Daniel the dishy gardener?'

Faroust bowed deeply. 'Guilty as charged. Dishy, am I?'

'We've been ogling him for years. Susan is especially bad. But he's kind of tanned, well, as tanned as we get, and green-eyed.'

The god clicked his fingers and he was transformed into the gardener. His green eyes sparkled with amusement as Eliza blushed.

'Oh Lord. So you can change shape as well. Anything else you're hiding?'

'What? I need fresh air and sunlight and I've lived on this land for five thousand years. Why shouldn't I care for my home? I couldn't exactly do it as myself, could I?'

Eliza understood his need for a disguise. He'd be mobbed if he tried to walk freely amongst the Family. He wouldn't get a moment's peace, so he'd made rules to protect himself. She admired his ingenuity, despite her soul shrieking warnings.

Careful Eliza. If you fall for him, it won't end well.

Still, it was impressive. The lodge was far enough away from the house to escape notice. Even Cornelius didn't consider it worth spying on and the disguise of Daniel meant he had extra protection.

'Hang on. What about the Ritual? No one's ever complained about Daniel missing the Ritual.'

'That's part of the magic. No one notices when Daniel's not around. Come on, I've got a jeep in the garage. You'll have to hide as we go through the gate. I can't hide you magically. Even I have limits.'

The jeep, like everything else he owned, was perfectly clean. She lay down in the boot and Faroust covered her with a picnic blanket. As they trundled along the gravel drive, a gurgle of nervous laughter bubbled up Eliza's throat. She covered her mouth and held her breath. They stopped by the gate and she heard muffled voices exchanging pleasantries. It was a few moments before they were on their way again.

'Stay in the back until we're a safe distance from the house.'

When he pulled into a service station, she clambered over the seats to get to the front.

'I hope you didn't make a mess of my car,' he sniffed, looking back.

'I didn't. You are a little OCD about cleanliness.'

Faroust changed out the guise of Daniel and gave her a lazy, lopsided grin.

'Being a god isn't what it used to be. In the old days it was endless sacrifices, loads of women, the day to day running of the tribe, healing the sick and so on. These days, with the advent of technology, modern medicine, blah de blah blah, I pretty much sit around playing video games and keeping my house clean.' He made a sad little face at her.

Eliza raised an eyebrow. 'Sounds dreadful. Living in luxury, being free to come and go as you please, not having to live with our rules and regulations, only being consulted occasionally. Life of Reilly. Besides, you *just* said that you don't spend all your time in front of the box. Make up your mind.'

Faroust reached across to tickle her. 'Do I not get any sympathy? I've been side-lined in my own story.'

Eliza wriggled away from him. 'Nope. You get none. You are free. You could probably go away all year, if you wanted, and we'd be fine. I wish I had that level of freedom. I'm not even useful and I'm practically on lock down.' She sighed sadly, the jovial atmosphere evaporating with her words. They drove in silence for a while.

'Is life so awful in the house?' he asked finally.

Eliza lowered her eyes. 'There is a lot of love and happiness in the house but we live in fear. Fear of failing, of not protecting the magic, of letting down the Family, of the Rit . . .' She stopped mid-sentence and covered her mouth, realising what she'd almost said. She risked a look at Faroust. His jaw tightened and a cold look flashed in his eyes.

'I'm sorry,' she said. 'I spoke out of turn.'

'It's all right,' he answered, in the same soft tone. 'I asked the question. Thank you for giving me an honest answer.'

He looked at her and smiled. It was oddly sad, as if her words had wounded him. She didn't know what to do.

'What's your favourite exhibit at the zoo?' he asked and just like that the tense atmosphere was dispersed.

Away from the confines of the house, Faroust relaxed even more. He laughed and joked with Eliza, told her old stories about the Family and asked about her life, delicately avoiding her feelings about her Family and its role. She laughed when she was supposed to and answered his questions, but all the while she pondered the mystery of him. The god of the Ritual was terrible and cruel, quick to rage and eager to punish. She'd attended the Ritual since she was fifteen. She had seen what had happened to those sacrifices, sacrifices he chose, that he deemed imperfect after he had consumed them. She was under no illusion as to what the god was; he was a beast sustained by blood and rape.

The man was a different thing altogether. The man who walked around the zoo with her, who held her close to him at night, the man who took her hand in his and gladly missed the insect exhibit because she hated spiders, he was sweet and kind, understanding and interested in her. She could almost give into him, almost trust him . . .

The truth revealed itself all it once. It couldn't have been more obvious if it had announced itself with trumpets and a parade float. He knew she was hiding something from him. Using his power to read her soul hadn't worked and being threatening hadn't worked, so he'd changed tack. He was trying to get round her defences by being cute and charming. It made her blood boil and now she itched for a fight.

Faroust felt Eliza's sudden, inexplicable coolness towards him as they wandered around the gift shop. She refused his offer of a cuddly toy with a curt 'No thanks.' A few seconds ago she'd been doe-eyed over the baby seal. What the Hell had happened? Why was she suddenly in a foul mood? He had planned to take her to dinner but there was no point now. He was not sitting across from a sulky bitch all night.

'Come on, we're going.'

'Yes, Sir.'

He ground his teeth at her sullen tone.

They drove home in furious silence, Faroust growing angrier and angrier at Eliza's rudeness. How dare she treat him like this? After all he'd done for her and the Family, after all they'd shared these past few days, after all the secrets he'd shown her? Well, fuck her. She wasn't going up on Sunday. In fact, he'd chain her to the bed like they'd done with whores in the Old East. She'd spend the whole month, and longer, on her back. He'd go back to treating her as his living sex doll. He shot a few livid glances at her but she was looking at the floor, making it clear, without even opening her mouth, that she was ignoring him.

When they got to the house Eliza climbed over the seats once more, leaving a small trail of dirt and Faroust lost it. He sped back to the lodge house, tearing up the lawn in his annoyance. He slammed the garage door behind them, and heard Eliza give a satisfying squeak of alarm. Faroust paced in the small room, muttering to himself.

'Fucking, ungrateful bitch!' he snarled. 'What the fuck did I do? She should be hanging on my every word, worshipping at my feet. She's fucking lucky I chose her. Her life is in my hands. She should be terrified of me. Fucking whore!'

Being called a whore must have touched a raw nerve. Eliza kicked the boot open and jumped out of the car.

'Did I tell you could get out?'

'I don't need your permission.' She kicked her feet against the back tyre, knocking mud onto the immaculate floor. 'Oops! I made a mess.'

'Clean that up!' he ordered.

'It's only mud. It'll take two minutes to sweep up.' She reached into her bag and pulled a bright pink lipstick out. She twisted the tube. 'This will be far harder to clean up.' She broke the coloured cylinder and dropped it into the car.

'Eliza, don't you dare . . .'

She looked at him coldly, as she squished the oily colour under her thumb into the carpet fibres of the boot.

'You cunt!' Faroust shouted, pushing her out of the way to survey the damage. 'What the fuck?' He twisted towards Eliza but she'd slipped out of the side door. It banged against the wall, knocking flakes of paint on to the floor. He growled and took off after her. Dusk was gathering and the darkness would serve Eliza well. He sniffed the air, trying to catch her scent, spinning in all directions. Finally he caught a trace of her. She'd run off towards the orchards and the summerhouse.

He strode across the grass at a leisurely pace. He had no need to rush. He knew where she was and if she moved, her panic would help him relocate her.

There was a chill in the September air, a precursor of autumn to come. Faroust often walked the grounds at night, visiting those places which had been sacred to the tribe for millennia. It was self-indulgence, a quick wallow in the past before he went back to his modern apartment and his restricted role. He knew this place like his own soul. There was nowhere Eliza could hide.

His prey sheltered amongst the peach trees. The air was heavy with the scent of fermenting fruit, but it was not strong enough to hide her. The god stood on the crest of the hill in the half-light of the evening, his angry shadow stretching its malevolence over the trees below. Power and anger radiated from him like heat. His height and his colouring painted him as an avenging spirit; he knew he was terrifying.

'Eliza!' he called. 'Come out, come out, wherever you are!'

He was answered by a volley of half-rotten peaches smacking him in the chest.

'Eliza! Stop fucking about!'

Another peach flew towards him. It exploded on impact, splashing his face with putrid flesh.

'Bitch!' he howled. 'I'm going to rip your head off!'

Eliza laughed in the gathering gloom. The sound echoed eerily in the orchard, like she was a wicked ghost toying with an unwary soul. 'You'll have to catch me first!'

She stepped out from the trees, holding another peach. She flicked it up in the air and caught it deftly in her other hand. There was a fire in her eyes, a recklessness and a hunger.

'Throw another peach at me and it will be the last thing you do.' Faroust was aware that his voice was quivering, not just with anger but with a hint of fear. She couldn't possibly be sane to challenge him like this. And god or not, she could be dangerous to him.

The fruit left her hand. Faroust charged her. She stood her ground until the last moment before ducking out of the way. Faroust turned to chase her but his foot slipped on the mush of foul peaches. He fell on his face and Eliza seized the chance to dash up the hill towards the lodge. As she reached the top, a strong pair of hands grabbed her from behind. She was yanked off her feet and thrown over his shoulder.

'Did you really think you could outrun me?'

Faroust's voice boomed in her ear, the voice of a god. It echoed through the grounds and rumbled like thunder.

'Put me down, you great lumbering fuckhead!' she shrieked, beating his back and kicking wildly.

He jolted her on his shoulder in an attempt to subdue her, but the action only inflamed her rage. She dug her nails into his back and bit him, drawing blood. It welled up under his shirt but he didn't let her go. She tried to scream, but when she opened her mouth, nothing came out. Faroust had silenced her. She kicked at him again but her limbs wouldn't move. He'd bound her too.

She was in huge trouble.

Back in his rooms, Faroust dumped her on the couch, before stripping off his clothes, sticky with peach juice. He turned back to her and released the spells that bound her. She rubbed her head where he had smashed it on the roof of the passageway.

'You could have given me concussion, you twat.'

'What the fuck was that about?' he demanded. 'Are you insane?'

Eliza did not answer him. She crossed her arms and looked away.

'I'm talking to you!'

'No you're not,' she said. 'You're screaming at me.'

'Only because you've been a complete bitch all afternoon. It's like someone flicked a switch and you lost your brain!'

Eliza raised an eyebrow but said nothing. Faroust's hands twitched as if he fought back the urge to strangle her.

'Where'd the sweet Eliza go? The compliant, fun Eliza?'

'Go fuck yourself,' she muttered.

'What did you say?' He snatched her arm and dragged her to her feet.

'I said. Go. *Fuck*. Your. Self.'

'You're nuts. There's at least two Elizas living in your head.'

She laughed at him, right in his face. 'That's rich coming from you, First-Father!' she spat. 'One minute you're a great and powerful god, the next you're a simpering lovesick child! Do you think I'm stupid? Do you think I don't know what you're doing?'

Faroust dropped her on to the couch.

'You're trying to get inside my head. For all your power, and your magic, you can't get in there. So you switch how you act, hoping I'll drop my guard and tell you all my secrets. Well, the joke's on you. I have no more secrets!'

Faroust glared at her. 'Maybe I just like being with you.'

'Bullshit! You're the First-Father, the font, the magic source, killer of men and raper of women, and a hard-ass son-of-a-bitch.

I'm here because you threatened Cornelius. You had to coerce me into sleeping with you, trick me into desiring you. Do you honestly expect me to believe that you actually want us to be lovers? I'm just your concubine!' Eliza got to her feet, trying not to grin. She'd won this fight. She could see it written all over his face; she'd pinned him down with her accusations and won the argument. She channelled that anger into tears, crocodile tears for Faroust's benefit. They worked. His gaze softened.

'You're right. I still think you're hiding something. I know there's something wrong here. Some shift in balance, but I can't put my finger on it. Every time I get close, I'm directed off course and forget about it for a while. How can you make me forget it, Eliza?'

She shrugged and a tear fell. Faroust tracked its course down her face with a forefinger.

'Maybe you're spending too long listening to your cock,' she snapped. He didn't reply. They stood at an impasse for a while.

'Get it over with then,' she said.

'Get what over with?'

'Kill me. Rip my head off.' Her tone remained caustic, despite the tears running down her face. 'You're already pretty good at hurting me.'

He turned away from her.

'I'm going for a shower,' he said, his voice thick with a sadness that nearly broke her heart. She had seen the hurt on his face. Had she overstepped the mark? Even though she wasn't entirely happy about it, she knew that in the eyes of Faroust and the Family he showed her great favour in choosing her as a consort. She'd thrown it back at him in the vilest way possible. She needed to make it right. Cornelius might bear the brunt of his anger if she didn't.

She picked his clothes off of the floor, before stripping off her own and throwing them into the machine. She cleaned the smears of mud and peach juice off the floor.

The god rubbed the bridge of his nose as he let the water in the shower wash over him. Why had he let her talk to him like that? It wasn't the sex. He could creep out anytime he wanted for sex, with whoever he liked. So what was it? Did he genuinely have feelings for this girl? No, surely not? This little Barren thing, this bad-tempered, sharp-tongued slut? It was ludicrous. But when she'd cried, he wanted to hold her and kiss her and tell her it was all right. What was wrong with him? When he came out of the shower, the washing machine was trundling away in the corner and Eliza was cooking steak for dinner. He took a beer from the fridge and watched her as she moved around his kitchen, cooking and cleaning as she went. His stomach rumbled.

'You like it rare, don't you?'

He nodded. She bent over to pull a tray out of the oven. She'd baked wedges of sweet potato with garlic and rosemary.

'I love sweet potato,' he said.

'I know.' She risked a smile at him. 'Blue cheese or peppercorn?'

'Blue cheese.' He looked in one of the other pans. 'Did you make crispy onions?'

'I did. Go and sit down. I'll bring it when it's ready.'

'I'll set the table.'

Eliza knew how to please. She'd rustled up a rocket salad, another one of his favourites. He groaned when he took a bite of the steak.

'You, madam, are an excellent cook.'

'Thank you. Francesca taught me.'

They ate the meal in a strange, strained silence, half-way between forgiveness and anger.

Afterwards, as Eliza gathered the plates without a word and stacked the dishwasher, Faroust watched her through narrowed eyes.

'What's your game?'

'I'm tidying up.'

He barked a short laugh. 'I think you're trying to avoid being sent away so you can keep Cornelius safe.'

'I am, but that's not the only reason,' she said. 'I already have enough pity and ridicule to deal with, being the dud that got abducted. Can you imagine the gossip if I go up now?' She turned to him and laid her hand on her chest, putting on a scandalised voice. 'He took her after the Ritual and then told Jacob he wanted her for a month. But do you know what happened? He sent her back after a week. A week! Poor Eliza. She's not even any good at being a plaything.'

Faroust wrapped his arms around her waist. 'You can stay, as long as you don't throw anymore peaches at me.'

Eliza giggled as he nipped her ear. 'Deal.'

'You realise that this isn't the end of your apology, right?' He slid his hands under her t-shirt and pinched her nipples.

'Why do I feel scared when you say that?'

He chuckled and moved away from her. She reached for the tea-towel to dry the copper pots as he rooted around in one of the cupboards.

The washing machine signalled that it was finished with a high pitched beep. Eliza walked to the bathroom to collect the drying rack. Soundlessly, Faroust followed her. She had just opened the cupboard door when he pounced.

'Holy shit!' she screamed, as the sticky liquid, full of squishy lumps of fruit, landed on her.

'Not so much fun when it's you, is it?'

She span to face him. He waved the empty can that had once contained peach slices. She dragged her tongue over her teeth as he laughed at her, and picked a lump of the soft fruit out of her hair.

'You got me,' she said, taking a step towards him. He was bent over laughing. She leapt on him, smashing the sticky mess into his face.

'That's not fair!' He tried to protest but he was roaring with laughter as she squished more fruit into his hair. 'I just got clean!'

She hopped off his back and scrambled back towards the kitchen, presumably to find more fruit to throw at him. He grabbed her under her arms, hauling her backwards. He bundled her into the shower and turned it on. She shrieked as the water hit her.

'Are you done?'

'Yes!' she yelled.

'Really?'

'Yes! I promise! Stop!'

Satisfied, Faroust turned the hot water on. He pulled her out of her soaking wet clothes before stripping from his own. He threw the wet clothes on to the bathroom floor.

'I thought you didn't like mess.'

'The bathroom's easy to clean.' He turned her away from him. 'I think we need to get to work on the rest of your apology. I've got a paddle with your name on it.'

She whimpered a protest against this development.

'No complaining! You were naughty, so over the knee you'll go. Besides,' he groaned, pushing her against the wall, 'you love it.'

Eliza's cheeky reply was cut off as he covered her mouth with his hand and slid into her.

The alarm shrieked and Faroust groaned. He tried to roll over but his arm was caught. His eyes snapped open. He was cuffed to the bed. He tried to sit up but his feet were bound too.

'What the bloody Hell?'

He laughed. She'd used his special cuffs, which could only be opened by the one who'd fastened them. Even he couldn't break them; he'd enchanted them to ensure there was no escape once they'd been locked. If he pulled too hard, he'd break the bed.

'Eliza?' he called. 'Why am I cuffed to the bed? What are you up to?'

She appeared in the doorway wearing her bathrobe, munching a piece of toast. A few crumbs fell onto the floor. Faroust shifted on the bed as his initial excitement faded.

'Why don't you have a plate?'

She chewed slowly and swallowed before putting the toast down on the bedside table. It was laden with butter and jam. He grit his teeth as a sticky splodge landed on the wood.

She clambered onto him, brushing his bare side with sticky fingers. He yelped. She straddled him, licking her fingers, with that familiar wicked glint in her eye. He was simultaneously uncomfortable and aroused. What was she playing at? The key for the cuffs glinted on its chain around her neck.

'I don't think it's fair we've only been pushing *my* boundaries,' she said. 'I'm beginning to worry that you can only get off if you hurt me. And I don't like that you won't stop when I ask you.' Her face was serious. He pushed down his discomfort to focus on her words. 'You were too rough with me last night. I don't mind rough. Rough is fun, but there's a limit.'

She untied her robe and it fluttered down from her shoulders. His breath whistled through his teeth. Her body was covered in marks, marks he'd caused. Her wrists were chaffed and red from the cuffs which now bit into his skin. There were welts on her shoulders. She turned her back and he saw the angry marks of his nails. He knew that on her lower body there were teeth marks and scabs where he'd broken her delicate skin.

'You said you wanted to try new things,' he said. 'You like being spanked.'

'I do. But you'll end up killing me.' She leaned forward. 'You take it too far and I'm scared. It's close to what Sage did to me.'

He gasped as the pain of those words hit him. 'Really? That's how you feel?'

She nodded. 'I like rough,' she repeated, 'but look at this way. You hate mess. It makes you feel panicky and uncomfortable.' She leaned over the bed and picked something up. It was a squeezy bottle of honey. He whimpered and pulled on his restraints.

'What are you doing?'

'Making a point.' She flipped the lid open. 'Imagine if every time I made toast, I didn't use a plate. Imagine if every time we made dinner, I spread scraps all over the kitchen. Imagine if every time we had sex, I covered you in something sticky, forced you to endure it, even though I know you hate mess.'

She squeezed the bottle. A single drop of sticky nectar landed on his stomach. Using the tip of her finger, she spread it around his belly.

'How do you feel?'

'Turned on, but I hate the feeling. You've made your point.'

'Have I?' She gave him a wicked smile and squeezed more honey onto his skin.

'Yes!' He laughed nervously. 'Eliza, don't get any on the sheets.'

She put the bottle down, and picked up the toast, tearing off a small piece. Jam splattered onto his chest.

'Eliza, stop it.'

She held the toast against his lips and forced it in. He laughed through a mouthful of bread as she fed him the toast, bite by bite. When it was gone, she shifted into a kneeling position. She licked up the drip of jam before biting down on his nipple. He exhaled in pleasure.

'I kind of like you being in control,' he murmured as she lapped up the honey from his stomach.

She reached over the side of the bed once more. He froze, but all she brought up was a pack of make-up remover wipes. She wiped his torso tenderly, getting rid of the last traces of food.

'Thank you. Un-cuff me now? I really want to fuck you.'

'Not so fast.' She straddled him once more. 'What was my point?'

'You are not my plaything. I can't use you however I want, whenever I want.' He groaned. 'We need to strike a balance. You're so fucking sexy.'

'I know.' She smiled. 'I want you to make love to me.'

'There's no need for coy euphemisms.'

'I'm not being coy. I want to slow things down a bit. No toys, no videos, no bondage. Just you and me, enjoying each other for who we are. You want a lover. So let's make love.'

'That sounds like the sexiest thing in the world.'

She un-cuffed his ankles first, before moving to his wrists. He rubbed the irritated skin as she sat on the bed beside him.

'These really sting,' he said, pulling her close to him, taking hold of her right wrist and kissing the mark there. The skin healed, gradually returning to its natural paleness. He moved his lips to her left wrist, ran his hands over her skin and the marks and bruises slowly vanished. He cupped the back of her head and pulled her mouth to his, kissing her deeply. She wound herself around him as he brushed his hands down her back and cupped her rear.

He lowered her onto the bed, moving his mouth to her neck and shoulders, tenderly kissing the places he'd abused. He brushed his fingers down her stomach and she whimpered. She closed her hand around his erection and gently stroked it back and forth. He groaned at the tenderness of her touch.

He pressed his forehead to hers as new sensations flooded him. He liked this, this slowness, this tenderness. All his senses were filled only with her. He moved his hand and slipped two fingers inside her. He mirrored her pace, revelling in the feeling of being truly intimate with another person.

He felt her heartbeat quicken as he touched her. She closed her eyes and bit her lip, trembling lightly under his touch. He withdrew his hand and kissed her.

'Why don't I go down on you? To say sorry properly?'

'You can if you want.'

He was reluctant to admit it, but she really knew how to handle him.

'I do want.'

He kissed her again, pressing her into the mattress. He slid a thigh between her legs and ground against her, moving up and down. He kissed her until she was breathless, pushed hard against her until she panted with need. He kissed along her collar bone, moving down her body, brushing his fingertips over her skin. She gasped when he touched her below her navel. He slid down the bed, kissing the sensitive skin there, dragging his unshaven chin along her pelvis, making her twitch and writhe in anticipation.

He blew on her sex, rubbing his mouth against her, moving down. Her scent, citrus-sweet, made his mouth water. He wanted to taste her, he wanted to please her. He ran his tongue along her outer lips, drawing large circles with the tip. She whimpered, her nails curling into the mattress. He drew his tongue upwards, slow and teasing, using the tip to open her up. He stopped just short of her clitoris, before repeating the move, this time using his whole tongue.

She tasted as good as her scent had promised, like honey and oranges. He groaned as he licked her. This was good, feeling her tremble, hearing her gasp and sigh as he worshipped her. He did again, this time pausing to flick the tip of his tongue against her nub. She twitched and groaned as he did it again.

'That's so good,' she whispered.

He moved to focus on her clit, using the tip of his tongue to trace a circular pattern in one direction and then the other, before jabbing forward with it. He swept the nub from bottom to top and side to side, circled it once more before driving the tip of his tongue against her again. She panted beneath his ministrations, and he knew she was peaking. He kept licking, kept the same rhythm as her toes curled. She ground her hips, rising against his face, his eager tongue, shifting into the best position for her pleasure. Why hadn't he done this earlier? She was so responsive, so eager for his touch. She'd probably do anything he asked of her after this . . .

That's not the point. She wants more from you, she wants a lover too. So be one.

'I feel it. I'm almost there.'

He sucked on her clit, his tongue still working over it. She froze in position, her hips raised, her abdomen tight. Faroust slipped two fingers into her, stimulating her further. He rubbed his palm against her, adding more friction to the rhythm of his tongue. She liked it when he did that.

'Oh God, oh God, oh God, oh God.'

Eliza's whole body went rigid as she teetered on the edge of climax. Faroust sucked harder on her clitoris and she tumbled, crashing into orgasm. Her whole body shook and shuddered as she came. She wound her hands into his hair.

She wants me. She needs me.

Faroust kept moving his tongue, kept the pleasure going, until the shuddering stopped and she went limp. He crouched over her and kissed her.

'Was that good?'

'You know it was, you smug git,' she gasped. 'Did you like it?'

'Yeah; you taste wonderful.' He rubbed his nose against hers. 'I like pleasing you. Am I forgiven?'

She smiled at him, her eyes twinkling. 'Apology accepted. In future when you mess up, just do that and we'll be golden.'

He laughed. 'I'll keep that in mind. My turn, I think.'

He took her hands in his and eased himself into her. He lay still for a long moment, enjoying her and her heat. He should take more time with her, spend more time making love. He should enjoy her, all of her, connect with her. She sighed as he moved his hips slowly back and forth.

He released her hands and she wound her arms around his neck, pulling him closer. He kissed her, fighting the urge to pick up the pace. Her little sighs and whimpers made it very hard to keep things slow. His stomach was drawing tighter and tighter as they moved, like a slow fire spreading through his limbs.

'You feel so good,' she moaned, wrapping her legs around him.

She pressed her mouth to his and tilted her hips upwards. He circled his hips clockwise, paused and then moved in the opposite direction. He drew back and sank forward into her embrace, taking care to be gentle, taking time to appreciate her. He cradled her face in his hands, planting tiny kisses on her cheeks and lips.

'You are wonderful,' he murmured. 'I want to try something.'

She pouted as he withdrew. 'What are you doing?'

He reached for a pillow and placed it under her lower back, then sat back on his heels, between her thighs.

'Put your heels on my shoulders and push your hips up. If you don't like it we can stop.' He took hold of her hips and sank into her. She gasped. 'Too deep?'

'No, it's perfect.'

'Touch yourself for me. I want you to come when I'm inside you. I love feeling it.'

As her fingers danced over her clit, Faroust began to move, alternating long strokes and short ones, sometimes moving slowly, sometimes quickly. He loved the feel of Eliza's muscles contracting around him. He closed his eyes as his climax built, his heart racing. A rush of heat flooded his body as his stomach contracted. His chest tightened and his breath came in shallow gasps. A cold shiver shot down his spine.

'Eliza, come with me,' he breathed.

She obliged, calling for him as he came. He lay still for a long moment, his eyes closed, lost in the intense pleasure of their lovemaking. When he opened his eyes, he was trembling.

'Wow.'

He lay down beside her, woozy and a little disorientated. She didn't move for a moment.

'You okay?'

She answered him with a sobbing breath. She was crying.

'Hey, hey.' He gathered in his arms. 'Don't cry. It's okay. Shh.'

'It's a good cry. That was just . . . mind-blowing. Incredible.' She wiped her face. 'See? Slow can be good too.' She rested her head on his chest and sighed contentedly. He kissed her forehead.

They lay there for a while, quietly basking in the afterglow. Eliza entwined her fingers in his and brought them to her lips. His heart swelled and a lump formed in his throat as he realised he was happy, for the first time in a long time. Eliza made him happy.

'Get dressed. I'm taking you out to lunch. How does Restaurant Patrick Guilbaud strike you?'

'Expensive.'

'Only the best for you. Wear something fancy.'

'You shredded the only fancy thing I have. My mother didn't pack anything else.'

He felt a slow smile stretch across his face. 'I'll take you shopping. Wear something sexy.'

Chapter 16

HERE WERE FEW occasions when the Family gathered en masse as it did for the Ritual, and on the following Sunday, the house was practically empty. Ruby and Jacob sat in the Jade dining room with their sons, their wives and children, trying to get through Sunday lunch.

Ruby usually adored being a host. Her duel role as wife of the Patriarch and a TD meant she often got to hold functions. She loved the Jade dining room, where the bay windows brought in masses of light and provided a wonderful view of the grounds; you could see the orchards and the maze, down to the boat house and the lake. All the furniture in the room was original, and tastefully accented with jade statues from China. The silver candelabras were older even than the Victorians, but they fitted in beautifully with the feel of the room. It was Ruby's favourite space. But not today.

The table was set for twenty-four. One place missing. Eliza's absence was rammed home, and Ruby fell apart. Matthew gave her a sedative but it only kept her from sobbing out loud. She sat and ate with tears streaming down her face. The rest of the family sat in silence, even the youngest children. Alexander, the youngest of Ruby and Jacob's sons, tried haltingly to start a conversation about the benefits of electric cars. When he attempted it a third time, Colum kicked him. He swallowed a curse and went back to his roast beef. His wife, Jennifer, leaned across and whispered in his ear, loud enough for everyone to hear.

'Just leave it Alex. You're not helping.'

Jacob tried to eat but the silence weighed heavily on him and his appetite failed. Since Faroust had taken Eliza every meal was like this; they sat in the dining room, saying nothing, letting their food go cold. In less than a week, their marriage had crumbled. Ruby blamed him for not protecting their only daughter. It was his fault they'd lost her again.

The tension was broken by the sound of the handle turning. The door swung open and a smiling Eliza stood on the threshold. Time stood still as her family tried to work out if she was really there. Finally, she spoke.

'Any spuds left?'

Immediately, a clamour of questions erupted as they surged forth to meet her. Her nieces and nephews grabbed at her, unsure why she'd been missing but happy as only children can be that she was there. Only Ruby stayed in her seat, unable to believe her eyes.

'She's not really there,' she slurred.

Eliza went to her mother and put her arms around her.

'I am Mum. I really am here.'

Jacob's heart soared as Ruby looked up into Eliza's smiling face and burst into happy tears. Eliza kissed her mother's forehead, rocking her as she cried.

'Are you back then?' Ruby sniffed.

'Only for the afternoon,' Eliza said, 'but his lordship says I can come up on Sundays until six.'

'That's very generous of him,' Jacob murmured.

Eliza didn't look like a girl who'd been held for a week against her will. Her eyes sparkled as she took a seat between her parents. She didn't show any signs of abuse or mal-treatment. She looked like a young woman in love. The idea of his daughter being used as the god's plaything made Jacob feel sick. He had feared that she would return broken and bruised, or not at all, but Eliza seemed gloriously, suspiciously happy.

As if she read his mind, Eliza reached across and took her father's hand.

'It's all right Daddy,' she whispered. 'Everything will be all right.'

Jacob nodded and although he didn't quite know why, he believed her.

They spent the afternoon in the garden, lapping up the last rays of the summer sun. They chatted and laughed and drank white wine as the children played amongst the trees. All the while, they carefully avoided mentioning the First-Father and Eliza's relationship with him.

At five o'clock, while the boys gathered their children, Eliza slipped off to her bedroom to collect a few books. She took the long way so she could pass Cornelius' rooms. He was in his living room, watching TV. She tapped on the door frame. He looked up and his face broke into an ecstatic grin.

'You're alive then?' he joked, half-heartedly.

She dashed into the room and closed the door. In a heartbeat, they were in each other's arms, kissing and pulling their clothes off.

'I've missed you,' she whispered, pushing him back on the couch and straddling him. 'I have ten minutes before they notice I'm gone.'

'That's more than I need.'

'Shit,' Cornelius groaned. 'It's twenty-past.'

Eliza raised her head from his chest. 'I'll need a quick shower before I go down. He'll be able to smell you on me.'

The colour drained from the Cruel's face at the thought.

'It's okay, baby,' Eliza laughed, kissing him.

'Maybe we shouldn't be together anymore?' he said as she got up.

She span to face him. 'Are you dumping me?'

He shrugged. 'You're his now.'

Eliza knelt in front of him and touched his face. 'I'm not his. I'll *never* be his. What I do down there, I do to protect you, protect us. He'll get bored of me in time and then we can be together again.'

Cornelius grabbed her hand. 'Are you willing to risk it? Being with me behind his back might get us both killed.'

She pulled away from him. The pain in her eyes made his heart ache.

'If you want to end things, I'll walk away and not bother you anymore.'

'I . . . I *can't*.' He sighed. 'I don't want to lose you. The thought of not being with you, not being yours, makes me feel sick. Will he be waiting for you?'

Eliza glanced at her new Cartier watch. An expensive gift from her god lover. Cornelius' jealousy twisted in his gut.

'No. Not yet.'

Cornelius moved away from her and picked up a small black box. Two of his tiny cameras glinted inside. Eliza stared at him in confusion.

'Place these somewhere he won't see. Not in the bedroom,' he added quickly. 'I'll sleep a lot better knowing you're safe.'

'I'll sleep better knowing you're watching over me. Have a look at the screens in about five minutes.'

She kissed him again before dashing down the corridor. Cornelius stood in his living room, missing her already, even though her scent lingered in the room.

As Eliza headed downstairs, her arms full of books, she caught sight of Colum in the hallway. He smiled at her. She swallowed her sneer and moved past him. He grabbed her hand and pulled her to him.

'Hey kiddo. Are you all right?'

'Like you give a flying fuck how I am.' Eliza snatched her hand away.

Colum backed away at the fury in her voice. 'Ah now, Eliza . . .'

'Ah nothing, Colum. Stop pretending you care.'

'Of course I care. You're my baby sister.'

Eliza laughed at him, loud and sharp. 'You're going to use that line, after all you did to me?'

He looked away from her, taking a few deep breaths, and shrugged.

'I'm sorry for all that crap, but . . .'

'Sorry? You're sorry? You bullied me, you attacked me, assaulted me, put my job at risk and you're sorry? Do have any idea what you did to me, all of you? You're my big brother; it's your job to protect me when others attack. Instead you led the fucking charge.'

He took a step towards her, his arms outstretched, and she stepped back.

'Don't be like that. I made a mistake. We all did. I want to make it right.'

'Why? Because you feel sorry for me? Because Sage took me and abused me?' She took a step towards him. 'Or is one of your brood like me? Does looking at your own little dud make your gut twist because you're frightened others will do to her what you and our brothers did to me?' Now they were face to face, inches away from each other. 'Or is it because I'm the god's whore now? Are you frightened I'll tell on you and he'll hurt you? That's why they've sent you out here; to assess if I'm a threat?'

Colum swallowed as Eliza smirked at him. Fear radiated off of him. She could almost smell it.

'Don't worry. I'm not like you,' she said coldly, turning to walk away.

Her movement jolted Colum out of his paralysis. He ran after her. 'Eliza, please, we need to . . .'

'I don't need to do anything. I need nothing from you or the others lurking in the corridor. I don't need your consolation, your love or your pity. If you want to play happy families, play with them.'

Colum was not to be dissuaded. 'But we are family, Eliza. For Mum and Dad's sake we should try to get along.'

'Why? We never did before.' She paused and smiled deliberately slowly. 'Ah, yes. I was never a threat before.'

'It's not like that,' Colum protested. 'Eliza, you're our sister and what we did to you was wrong. We want to make it better.'

'You really want to? All of you?'

He nodded.

'Then I do not absolve you of your guilt. You should feel it and wallow in it. It should cling to you, like your hatred clings to me. I spent twenty-three years as your punching bag. I carry the scars. You don't get away with eight months of wretchedness.'

Eliza turned and marched into the study, leaving a speechless Colum behind her. Ruby and Jacob waited for her. Her mother held out her arms and Eliza buried herself in her embrace.

'Next week we'll go out for the day. We'll go wherever you want.'

'Thanks Mum, but I'm happy just being with you and Dad.'

Ruby gave her another tight squeeze as Jacob opened the trap door.

'I love you.'

'I love you too, Mum.'

Jacob stood up and turned to Eliza.

'Bye, Daddy,' she said, hugging him. 'I'll see you next week.'

'If he hurts you Eliza, I'll kill him. I swear I will.' She heard the barely restrained hatred and fury in her father's tightly controlled voice. It wouldn't take much for him to rebel against the First-Father.

Eliza patted his back. 'Don't feel like that Daddy. You'll give the game away,' she whispered. 'Everything must be as it has always been. There can be no crack in the façade. Business as usual. It is an honour being bestowed upon me.'

Eliza ran down to the apartment. She had fifteen minutes before Faroust was due to return from his day's work as Daniel. She carefully placed the cameras in the kitchen and the living room, the rooms they had the least amount of sex in. She stared into the camera and slowly stripped her clothes off, re-minding Cornelius that she wasn't really Faroust's. She jammed them into the washing machine, jumped into the shower and scrubbed vigorously at her skin, washing her lover from her body.

She was finishing up as Faroust came in through the back door.

'Why are you in the shower?' he called, his voice full of suspicion.

'Baby Anna-Lise was sick on me.'

'Ewww. Good call.' He shuddered shucking out of his clothes and getting into the stall with her. 'Good afternoon? Everything all right?'

Eliza shrugged, trying to affect nonchalance but her fingers fluttered to the scar on her neck, the subconscious gesture betraying her. She felt his lips against the marked skin.

'I could take it away, if you want me to?'

'No thank you.'

'Do you want to talk about it?'

'No. Thank you.'

She raised her head and let the water sluice over her face, washing away the tears that were threatening. She hadn't wept over her brothers in years. She was not going to do it now.

Faroust's arms tightened around her and she allowed herself to relax into his embrace. For a moment, just a moment, she toyed with the idea of telling him in graphic detail what her brothers had done. She was already on the verge of tears and, with a little help from her stolen magic, she was sure she could make him angry enough to punish them on her behalf. She shook her head; that wasn't fair. They all had wives and children who needed them.

'Did you see Cornelius?' Faroust asked, jolting her out of her musings.

'No.'

'Good.' He turned her to face him. 'What do you want to do tomorrow?'

'Whatever my lord and master wants to do.'

Faroust smiled down at her. 'Are you sure you don't want to talk about it?'

'I'm sure. It's just sibling stuff, old issues that never got resolved.'

He raised an eyebrow, clearly unimpressed. 'That scar is more that sibling rivalry.'

'How do you know? Do you have any siblings?'

He opened his mouth to answer, but closed it as he considered the question. 'I don't know. Probably. You know what gods and witch-queens are like. Randy bunch.'

'Explains a lot.'

Faroust's mouth quirked in amusement. 'What are you insinuating?'

'I'm not insinuating anything. I'm flat out saying it; you're a horny bastard.'

He laughed, unable to contain his amusement. 'That I am. With that in mind, why don't we get out of the shower and into bed?'

Can't breathe. Can't breathe. Get me out. Get me out! So much mud. Screaming. Who's screaming? Blood. Blood everywhere! Where is everyone? Oh no! Mother? Mother! No, no, no, no!

Eliza woke with a start, shaking and covered in sweat. She threw herself out of bed and crawled to the bathroom. She barely made it to the toilet before vomiting. What the fuck had she just seen? Whatever it was, Faroust had been terrified when it happened. She wiped her mouth, but her stomach wasn't finished. She puked until her throat was sore.

She pressed her superheated body against the cool marble of the wall, panting for breath as her heart pounded. She could take his power as and when she wanted, she needed to hide her secrets, but the memories were a different matter. His guard had to be truly gone for her to get them. She hadn't seen any since the previous week, since the day they'd gone to the zoo. But now, as they'd slept, she'd been flooded with this terrible one.

The light flicked on. She threw her arms up to cover her face from the sudden brightness. Faroust turned it off again and she heard him move to the kitchen. He returned with a glass of water, and handed her a wet washcloth to clean her face.

He cleaned up the few stray drops of vomit with an anti-bacterial wipe before flushing the toilet. He sat down beside her.

'You all right?' She heard the strain in his voice. He hated all mess but vomit was particularly bad for him. She knew it had taken every ounce of his self-control to clean it up.

'I am now,' she croaked. 'Thank you.'

'That must have been one hell of a nightmare.'

'I saw Sage again,' Eliza lied. 'He was burning me.' She took a jagged breath. 'I hadn't dreamed of him for weeks. I thought I was getting better. I'm sorry.'

Faroust put his arm around her. She felt him shudder at the touch of her clammy skin.

'It's not your fault, baby. What happened to you was horrific. Flashbacks after trauma are normal.' He paused, sighing deeply. 'Nightmares are tough. They spring from the darkest part of your psyche and distort the facts, sharpening the worst parts until you feel like you're going to die.' In the diffused light of the hallway his face looked dark and sad, a tortured soul.

'You sound like you're speaking from experience,' she said.

'I'm five thousand years old. You think I haven't had a nightmare or two in my time? Or faced my fair share of trauma?'

She shook her head.

'I was there when my mother was killed by Cúchulainn. I was trying to help her war against the Heroes. I'd brought the warriors who helped me defend the Veil. I saw her fall from her chariot. I rode in to help but the Heroes had laid a trap. Scanthta drove her spear into the earth. It cracked and churned upwards as she pulled the weapon from the ground. It knocked me off my horse and buried me, along with several of my men. I had to dig my way out with my bare hands.'

Eliza raised her eyebrows as realisation dawned, the darkness giving her the safety to do so. No wonder she'd reacted so violently to that memory.

'I tore my hands to shreds. By the time I got out, my mother was tied to a stake and that fucking Hound was declaring her death sentence.

'I tried to get to her, but my leg was broken. The bone was sticking out of the flesh. I was twenty-one and my magic was new and green. I couldn't heal myself to rush to her rescue.

'I know Mebh was not a good woman. We disagreed on many things, but she was still my mother. With all my soul, I wanted to save her. I howled and begged him to spare her. But it was no use. Without taking his eyes off me, he drove his sword through her chest. He ripped her heart out. And he ate it.'

Eliza covered her mouth as tears filled her eyes.

'You saw that?'

He nodded. 'My remaining warriors carried me off the field and then returned for my mother. He'd left her body on the battlefield for the crows. My men cut her down and brought her back here. That bastard had left a tiny piece of her heart in her body, so her soul wasn't lost. I could feel it trapped in her body. I took the shell of my mother to the Veil.

'As she lay there, the doorway opened up, like a great ball of golden light. Tendrils came out and wrapped around her. The Veil picked her up and took her into itself. There was a flare and my body was filled with this rush of power. It was the last gift she gave me; her magic to make me stronger. And then she was gone.'

Eliza reached up to touch his face. There were tears on his cheeks. Her heart tightened with a rush of love and compassion for him.

'Afterwards, even though I was able to reset my bones and was twice as strong as before, I still had nightmares. I dreamt of her death, again and again. I couldn't even keep Bridgit in my bed with me because I lashed out in my sleep. I needed time and rest, and the nightmares went away after a while. You're crying again,' he said softly.

Faroust pulled her on to his lap. 'You're crying too,' she said. She gently dried his face and her heart twisted again.

He's not so bad.

'You need to give yourself time, Liza. I have literally all the time in the world. She heals all things.' He choked out a bitter laugh. 'Almost. Some things never go away.'

Eliza's head snapped up, sensing a revelation.

'Sorry?' she ventured, eager to keep him talking.

'It's nothing. My problem, not yours. Shall I run a bath?' It wasn't really a question, but a statement. He was ending the conversation.

'What time is it?'

'One-thirty.'

'Perfect time for a bath.'

'It'll make you feel better.' His voice was terse.

'No, it'll make *you* feel better,' she teased, tickling him. 'Because I'm all gross and sticky.'

He grabbed her hands as he laughed.

'Behave yourself. Be a good girl and brush your teeth while I run the bath.'

The bath was a huge affair, to compensate for Faroust's height. It was round, with a Jacuzzi function. 'Do you magically get stuff down here?' Eliza asked, as she sank into the rose-scented bubbles.

'No. It gets delivered to the lodge and I install it myself. With my own hands. What kind of pampered baby do you take me for?'

Eliza shrank against the side of the bath. 'Sorry. It's just if I was an almighty, powerful god, I'd do everything magically.'

Faroust's eyes narrowed and a wicked smile tugged at his lips.

'Do you doubt my ability, madam?' His voice was low and dangerous.

She shook her head as he climbed into the bath beside her.

'I think you do.'

'No I don't.' Oh shit, what had she got herself into now?

He clicked his fingers and her body spasmed as she exploded into orgasm.

'Holy Hell,' she gasped. 'That hurt!'

She splashed him angrily. He turned on the jets and settled into a nook.

'As with sex, there is something infinitely satisfying about completing something with your own hands,' he said. 'Doesn't mean I can't do it magically if I want.'

Eliza pressed her knees together and winced. He clicked his fingers again and the pain vanished. He moved closer to her and waved his hand over the water. She yelped as it went ice cold before flashing boiling hot and back to the perfect temperature he'd originally poured.

'I get it!'

'Do you?'

Eliza shot out of the water, and floated towards the ceiling. She shrieked as she was spun in a full circle twice before she was turned upside down.

'This is not dignified!' she howled. 'Put me down!'

'As you wish.'

Before she realised what was happening, she was plunging down towards the bath. She raised her arms to protect her head, but she never hit the water. She looked up to see Faroust laughing at her. She was upside down and spread-eagled, in mid-air.

'I quite like you like this.'

'All the blood's rushing to my head,' she whimpered. 'Please, I'll be sick again.'

Faroust blanched, set her upright and lowered her into the bath. She pressed the heels of her hands into her eyes and took a few deep breaths to recover her composure. How the fuck had she managed to hold her own against him so far? How much power had she really taken, if she hadn't even had a hint of this level of strength?

'Point made,' she said finally. 'You could probably bend the laws of time and space if you wanted.'

'I wouldn't go that far. There are some things I can't do.'

She kept her hands pressed to her eyes as she heard him move towards her. He pulled down her arms and kissed her. The dizziness vanished.

'That'll teach you to be cheeky. Think of every power you know: your mother's telepathy, your father's strength, Julian's sense of smell, Cornelius' ability to physically reach into someone's head. I have them all. There is no power that has ever existed or will exist that I don't have.'

A desire to question him about her own gifts tugged at her.

'What do you want to know? I can see you want to ask me something.'

'Has there ever been a power we had first, before you had it?'

Faroust frowned. 'A few times,' he admitted, 'but in those cases, I'm able to sense it and choose the owner of that power as my next sacrifice. Sometimes new magic doesn't pass on so if I take a copy of it into myself, it isn't lost.'

Eliza made a face at the mention of the Ritual.

'Couldn't you just take it through touch? There must be another way to renew the magic.'

He laughed. 'If it were only that simple. No one can do that, baby. It doesn't work like that.'

Eliza pressed her lips together in an attempt to hide her surprise. Her ability to copy other people's magic was a version of what Faroust did at the Ritual. And she did it so cleanly in comparison. That was a talent he didn't have and wasn't aware of.

Faroust tilted her head up to make her look at him.

'Why do you ask?' His eyes narrowed in suspicion.

'Just curious.'

'You haven't blossomed, have you, little Liza?'

She blinked a few times, affecting confusion.

'No. At least, I don't think so. How would I know?'

'If you had, you'd know. It's like . . .' He searched for the words, 'a light switch coming on.'

That's what it was like.

'I don't feel any different.'

'Good.' He reached for the soap. 'Turn around. I want to wash you.'

Eliza pursed her lips. 'Don't you think I do a good enough job?'

'I do. I just enjoy touching you.' He kissed her shoulder. 'It's nice to be so intimate.'

Eliza closed her eyes and groaned as his strong hands massaged the soap into her shoulders and back. She leant back against him. He was very attentive. Only the black cloud of the Ritual spoiled her contentment.

'I know I haven't, but would things change if I had blossomed?' she asked. 'Even if you caused it?'

He froze behind her.

'Yes.' His voice was hoarse.

'Why?'

He didn't answer her, but his anger was palpable. It seeped into the water, which began to steam.

'Baby, you're going to burn me.' She twisted around, reaching out to him and touching his chest. The water stopped steaming. He jumped out of the bath. Eliza scrambled out after him and pulled her robe on.

'Baby, what's wrong?'

'If you blossomed, I'd have to send you away. Like all the whores who came before, you'd want more. You'd try to persuade me to make you more powerful, lie and cheat and flirt and do whatever you could to make yourself stronger. You'd try to make yourself my queen. You'd try to take what's mine. If you had blossomed . . .' He turned towards her. She screamed as he pounced, grabbing her by the throat and pushing her against the wall. 'You'd need to die because you lied to me!'

She clawed desperately at his hands, tried to beg him to let her go but her voice was stuck in her throat. She pleaded with her eyes.

Let me go.

It was no good. Faroust was lost, his face twisted with rage. As his fury gathered pace, his Fae form emerged: great horns, like a stag's, burst out of his temples, his skin glowed green and gold, his eyes dissolved into blackness and his teeth grew sharp and jagged. The earth trembled beneath them as he changed.

Swirls and whorls of green and blue carved themselves into his skin. His shoulders widened, jagged spikes of bone pushing out of the flesh. She caught the reflection of his back in the mirror. A pair of wings, black like a raven's, tore their way out of his body, ripping the skin as they grew. Green-black blood poured from the wounds, pooling on the floor. His grip tightened on her neck as the wings spread out, blocking out the meagre light from the hall.

I'm going to die. He's going to kill me.

He lifted her up, scraping her back against the slate of the wall. The horns glinted menacingly at her and his black eyes burned in fury. She tried to kick him but the effort was wasted. She didn't even make contact with him.

'Is this what you wanted, Eliza?' he roared, as if with the voices of thousands. 'Is this the power you seek?'

She managed to shake her head.

He brought his other hand up. Talons, long and black as onyx, grazed her cheek. He pressed one to her forehead.

'I'll cut your head open and see what secrets you're hiding. And then I'm going to go upstairs and eat your Cornelius' heart.'

Eliza tried to fight, tried to get away but she couldn't breathe. She was fading. As her vision dimmed, she became aware of the magic inside her, of the power of the Family, her own gifts and the ones she'd stolen. For the first time, she really connected with it and from it she garnered the strength to fight back. It flowed from her belly, throughout her whole body and up her arms. With one great effort, she dug her nails of both hands into his wrist. His fingers loosened and she dragged air into her lungs.

'Let me go!' she barked. 'Faroust, stop this. Stop it now!'

Faroust's head snapped back like he'd been slapped. The rage vanished from his face and he dropped her. He stumbled backwards as she lay gasping on the bathroom floor. He closed his eyes and leaned against the wall. His Fae form faded, slowly receding. The horns and wings retreated back into his body. His skin recovered its human hue and his jagged teeth vanished.

Eliza staggered to her feet. Her breath came in ragged gasps. She took a few faltering steps towards him. His eyes were still liquid black.

'Eliza . . .'he began. 'Eliza, I'm . . .'

'Fuck you,' she rasped, wheeling away toward the bedroom.

When Faroust eventually followed her, ten minutes later, she was dressed and had packed her case. She snatched up her toiletry bag and pushed past him. He grabbed her arm and pulled her towards him.

'Let me go.' Her voice was cold. 'I want to go home.'

'I'm sorry.'

'You're sorry? You nearly killed me! Just for asking a question.' Her voice was low and gravelly. Her throat burned in agony. 'I'm not staying here anymore. This isn't like rough sex or when I threw peaches at you. You lost it and you tried to kill me. I don't know what stopped you but I'm getting out now. I'm not staying here.'

'What about being a figure of pity?' he asked quietly.

'I'd rather be pitied and alive! I'm sorry you're lonely. I'm sorry others have treated you badly. I'm sorry you have no concept how to treat people but none of that excuses what just happened. I am not your punching bag for when you go Fae-nuclear!'

'That's not me. Please don't go. I like you being here.'

'You like me being here? You blackmailed me into sleeping with you, you treat me like a blow up doll and now you've tried to kill me. You're a bully.'

The fury in her voice made him take a step back. She stormed into the bathroom and began throwing her toiletries into the bag.

'You're right,' he said. 'I am a bully. It doesn't mean I'm not sorry.'

'That's all well and good, but I can't stay.'

He nodded and stood aside from her, holding on to the door frame for support. The episode had clearly left him weak. Otherwise he would have been able to stop her.

'Goodbye, Eliza.'

'What about Cornelius?' she demanded.

'I keep my promises. He's safe.'

She picked up her bags and stalked to the front door. She stabbed at the release button. She didn't look back as she walked out.

Unclicking the handle of her wheelie suitcase, she made her way towards the path back to the house. The Ritual space was even more unnerving when it had no people in it, full of shadows and strange noises. There was an odd buzzing sound and she assumed Faroust was turning on the lights, like he had when she'd gone up on Sunday. The buzzing got louder, but no light came on.

Eliza fell to her knees as an electric shock of pain rocketed through her head. She clutched her ears as the buzzing grew louder. Was Faroust doing that? The sound reached a high pitched whine and then abruptly cut out. Towards the back of the cavern, a small flickering caught her eye, not where Faroust's door was but in an alcove she hadn't noticed before. The flickering light grew stronger and brighter.

Every fibre of her being screamed at her to run, to get out of the cavern, to get back to Cornelius and safety. But despite herself, she walked towards the light.

As she drew closer, she heard faint music, like a harp being played in the distance. She rounded the corner and gasped. She stood in front of the Veil, the golden doorway to the Otherworlds.

Chapter 17

ELIZA STARED INTO the doorway, frozen in place. The Veil was more beautiful than she had ever imagined. It was like looking through a rainbow, sparkling and shifting as if blown by a soft breeze.

The Veil seemed to sigh and something on the far side of the doorway moved. A tiny creature, no bigger than a child, but she could see its pointed ears and sharp claws. It was a *Ghillé*, a flesh-eating water pixie. She retreated as it turned towards her and took a step towards the Veil, sniffing and snuffling. She recoiled at its squashed fish face, its gills and piranha teeth. It snarled at the doorway but scuttled away without advancing further.

Eliza released her breath, relieved it hadn't seen her. The Veil was a delicate thing. If she upset it, Faroust would kill her. He'd kill her if he knew she was able to see it. She lingered one long moment before turning away. Something soft and warm touched her hand. She jumped. A tendril from the Veil reached out to her.

'Oh no.' She tried to step away.

There was no escape from it. Three more tendrils shot out, touching her. She stiffened as the power of the gate to the Otherworlds flowed through her. A thousand pictures of

Faroust filled her head; him as a child, standing in front of the People, falling in the fight with the *Tuathane*, the first Ritual, driving back the Vikings from the clearing, the Slave stealing his blood, on and on throughout his personal history. She watched him protect the village as the forest shrunk and the modern world encroached. She even saw his recent time with her and their fight of a few minutes ago.

The tendrils let her go. She looked into the glow of the Veil and screamed. Stretching out for miles and miles on the other side of the doorway were the dead members of her family. Thousands and thousands of them. Front and centre were Jonathan and Anna-Beth, the previous year's sacrifices, holding hands with their parents.

She pressed her hand to her mouth, tears streaming down her face as they glared at her with their dead eyes.

Anna-Beth's mouth moved but her words were so quiet Eliza could barely hear them. She took a step towards the dead girl to catch what was being said. The Veil quivered and shook as the spectre tried to make itself heard. Anna-Beth looked left and right. The dead around her closed their eyes as she stretched her arms out. One by one the souls, for what else could they be, were absorbed by the girl. She put her hands against the Veil and pushed. With a tremendous effort, one hand burst through the dimensions and grabbed hold of the living woman.

Anna-Beth pulled herself towards Eliza.

'Help us!' she cried, with the voice of twenty thousand lost souls. 'Set us free!'

'How?'

The girl grimaced as the Veil began to pull her back in. Her youth was heart-breaking; she'd only been nineteen when Faroust had taken her and her brother.

'Uncover the truth. Set us free.'

The Veil pulsed and contracted, dragging the soul of Anna-Beth away before flickering out.

Eliza stood still for an instant.

What are you doing, you fool? Run!

She bolted like a frightened rabbit, stumbling to collect her things. Even though her suitcase was unwieldy and her toiletry bag heavy, she didn't stop running until she reached the entrance to her father's study.

She opened it quietly, mindful of the fact that it was nearly three in the morning. Creeping up to her rooms, she deposited her bags in the hallway before collapsing on the sofa, head in her hands as she tried to think. Why had the Veil reached out to her? What had Anna-Beth meant? The little she knew about the Veil told her it was a dangerous thing, fickle and untrustworthy. It guarded the Otherworlds where all manner of strange and evil things lurked. Her vision could have been a trick of the Veil. But on the other hand, everything she knew about the Veil came from Faroust. What if he was lying?

She struggled with her vision. It didn't matter how she tried to rationalise it, in her heart she knew the ghost that had spoken to her had been her cousin, that all those ghosts had been her relatives and not a trick. And they were trapped, trapped in the Veil. But why? What truth had Anna-Beth meant? Was it part of the magic? Were the souls of the Family the fuel that kept the Veil balanced? If so, why did no one know about it?

She couldn't ask anybody what it meant. Jacob would feel duty bound to tell their god and Faroust would kill her, slowly and painfully. Only the especially magically gifted were able to see the Veil. Only the god was allowed to have contact with it. She was dead if she told anyone what she had seen.

She looked at her watch. Three-fifteen.

'Oh fuck,' she sighed, realising she'd automatically put on the gift Faroust had given her. She'd have to give it back. Her head was splitting. It was too much to take in. Was there something else going on? Why did the Veil contain all the souls of the Family?

Cruelty

The panic crawled up from her belly, clawing at her throat. She had stumbled onto something huge, too big for her to handle alone. On impulse, she grabbed her torch and ran to her bedroom. She pressed the brick which opened the door into the secret passage and ran down the corridor towards Cornelius' bedroom.

She pushed hard on the door handle, expecting it to be stiff with age. It gave easily, and she stumbled forward as the door opened. There was no movement in Cornelius' rooms. She pushed the door closed as quietly as she could. If he set off the alarm for his security team, she'd have a hell of a time explaining why she was here in the wee hours of the morning. She didn't know if she had the strength or power to soothe away that revelation from a whole group of people.

Eliza kicked off her shoes and crept to Cornelius' bedroom. There were three monitors in here. One cast an eerie blue-white light over his room. The others quietly spied on Faroust's apartment. As she drew close to the desk, she saw labels on the monitors: Ellie-1 and Ellie-2. Her heart twisted. Had he been watching her, unable to help, while she'd stumbled through Faroust's home? No. He'd have met her in the study if that was the case. He was lying with his back to her, sound asleep. He hadn't seen her plight.

Eliza sat on the bed beside him. She touched his shoulder.

'Baby?' she whispered.

He stirred and rolled over but did not wake. She ran her fingers through his hair.

'Baby?' she tried again.

Cornelius slowly came to. He sat up when his sleepy eyes focused on her.

'Eliza?' He rubbed his eyes. 'Eliza? What are you doing here? Does he know you've left?' He pulled her into his arms and tucked her under the duvet with him, as if trying to hide her.

She snuggled into him, feeling safe for the first time in weeks.

'We had a fight.' The mark on her back tingled. 'I need you to hold me tight. This is going to hurt as I tell you. I had a nightmare. I was him. I saw the death of his mother.' She winced, curling her toes against the pain. 'I threw up. Afterwards, he showed me some of his powers and we got talking about the gifts of the Family.'

She scrunched up her face and pressed her forehead against his shoulder as the pain built.

'Baby, stop. It'll kill you.'

'No!' Even to her own ears her voice didn't sound like it belonged to her. 'I have to tell you. He tried to kill me. He suspects I've blossomed.' Her voice cracked.

Cornelius rubbed her back as she sobbed into his shoulder.

'It's okay, baby. You're here now. He can't hurt you anymore. You're safe.'

'That's not the worst of it.'

The pain still burned but she could manage it if she put every ounce of stolen magic into fighting the spell.

'When I was leaving, I saw the Veil.'

'What? How?'

'It spoke to me.' She panted, her heart beating so fast she thought it would burst out of her chest. 'The Veil spoke to me. It showed me all this stuff about Faroust, about his life and then, and then . . . I saw . . . I saw Anna-Beth and Jonathan and all of us who have passed on. They're trapped, Cornelius, every one of them in the Veil, stretching back to the first of us. Anna-Beth asked me to free them.' The pain dulled a little. That was odd. Why didn't it hurt as much now?

She opened her mouth to tell him something new about Faroust, but it woke the spell up again. She collapsed against Cornelius as Faroust's magic finally took over, digging her nails into his back as the agony flowed over her. Her skin burned as her body tried to deal with the pain.

Eventually, she released her grip on his back and slumped against him. She was trembling and panting, but she had survived.

'Do you want some water?'

She nodded. Her body was on fire. She wasn't going to risk that again unless it was life or death.

'Sip it slowly,' he ordered.

She giggled. She'd been taken care of by two sexy men this evening. She could get used to this.

Behave yourself, her brain scolded. *Faroust tried to kill you.*

Cornelius raised an eyebrow. 'Hysteria setting in?' He took the empty glass and got back under the duvet. She shook her head as he wrapped himself around her.

'What am I going to do?'

'First of all, you are going to sleep, which you should really do in your own bed. Then you are going to have a good breakfast. Afterwards, you will tell your dad his lordship no longer requires you and then get back to being the newest member of my security team.' He kissed her softly and she felt herself melt against him.

'That sounds wonderful. You know I can't do that, right? I can't ignore what I saw.'

Cornelius sighed. 'I know. But it's four in the morning. Can we deal with this in daylight and after breakfast? You need a clear head.' He kissed her once more and she smiled against his lips.

'I missed you.'

'I missed you too,' he answered. 'You really should sleep in your own bed.'

But Eliza was too exhausted to move, tipping over the edge of sleep even as he spoke.

245

When the alarm went off at seven, Cornelius threw the clock into the bin, where it smashed. He rolled over and smiled at Eliza sleeping beside him. She seemed not to have suffered too many ill effects of breaking the spell. She stirred, and he lightly touched the purpling handprint around her neck.

Her eyes snapped open as if her subconscious was aware he'd been staring at her.

'Hi,' he said. 'Did you sleep well?'

'Beautifully. This is a very comfy bed.' She stretched. 'I should go back to my room. Freshen up, then go see my dad. I need to think about how I'm going to deal with what I saw in the Veil.'

Cornelius scratched his stubble. 'Any thoughts?'

Eliza made a face. 'There's so many possibilities. First of all, it could be the Veil keeping them. It could just be the price for keeping the Otherworlds away. But if that's true, why didn't we know that?'

Cornelius nodded thoughtfully. 'Maybe he doesn't know?'

Eliza raised an eyebrow. Cornelius held up his hands in defeat.

'You're thinking he's hiding something?' She nodded. He blew out his cheeks. 'This is dangerous ground you're on. This is blasphemy, treason.'

'I know,' she said. 'But I just can't leave them there. They're so lost, so sad.' She looked down and pulled at the bedclothes. 'Nobody knows our fate, that our souls are trapped in the Veil when we die. If we knew, it would be different. We are the People and we have a duty to protect the Veil whatever the cost, but there must be a reason he hid this from us and it can't be good. I can't ignore it. It's not just about protecting you and me. It's about protecting everyone.'

'What are you going to do?'

'I have to go back down there. I've been gleaning secrets and power from him.' Cornelius swore. Eliza didn't react. 'If I'm careful, and take my time, I can find out what he's hiding.'

'You're never going to let this go are you?'

'No.'

'Are you so sure you can do this? What if you get caught?'

'Baby, I don't have a choice.'

He lay back against his pillows, his hands in his hair. 'I liked it better when you were being selfish.'

She smacked him gently with the back of her hand.

'How are you going to worm your way back into his affections?'

'You know me. I can be pretty manipulative when I need to be.' She smiled, kissing his neck.

'That's true, but you need a reason to go back down there.'

She held up her wrist. The watch twinkled in the half-light.

'I need to return this gift. It's not right to keep it.'

He sighed. 'When are you going?'

She pursed her lips. 'In a few days. Let him stew. I want to spend some time with my boyfriend.'

Cornelius grinned at her. 'Boyfriend, huh?'

She blushed. 'Yup.'

'I like the sound of that.' He rolled her onto her back. 'Last night, you said you missed me. Why don't you show me how much?'

Jacob sat in his study, pouring over printouts. A few nights ago, there had been a massive disturbance in the seams all over Ireland. Faroust couldn't find a magical reason, so he ordered Jacob to find out what caused it. He was looking at CO_2 levels, greenhouse gases, light pollution, recent road works, everything he could think of, but he couldn't find anything. A soft knock on the door disturbed him.

'Come!'

Eliza opened the door. He'd been surprised when she'd been sent back up. She avoided questions about her time with Faroust and shook her head when the idea of her blossoming came up. She had simply returned to her duties on the security team. He didn't know why she'd returned, but he guessed the mark on her neck that she was trying to conceal had something to do with it. His daughter never ceased to amaze him. To withstand Faroust's passion, his violence, and be able to walk away . . . Her internal strength must be incredible.

'What's up, petal?'

'I found something his lordship gave me.' She held up a watch. 'I must have packed it by mistake. I should give it back.'

'I can take it.'

Eliza clutched the watch. 'I should take it back. It would seem . . .' she hesitated, 'ungrateful, if I didn't.'

'He may not want to see you,' Jacob warned.

Eliza swallowed, blinked and nodded, sadness clouding her features.

'I know, but I need to give this back. And I need to do it in person.'

'Okay, sweetheart. I'll ring down first. It's never a good idea to surprise him.'

Eliza fidgeted as her father made the call. It all came down to this. If Faroust didn't want to see her, there was nothing she could do to help her trapped kinsmen.

'Sir? Eliza would like to see you . . . oh? Of course. Yes. Right away.' He hung up and turned to her, surprised. 'He sounded happy. He never sounds happy. Be careful darling.'

'Yes, Daddy.'

Jacob hugged her tight as she passed him.

'I shouldn't let you go down there alone, but if he's in a good mood, you should be fine.'

He pressed the symbols and the floor opened. The electric lights which were never used during the Ritual flickered on, lighting her path.

Eliza paced herself carefully. She must arrive quickly, but not appear desperate. When she arrived in the cavern, Faroust was waiting in front of his open door, wearing dark jeans and a black t-shirt. His feet were bare. Even lounging around in the house, the man had style.

'Hi,' she said.

'Hi yourself.' He smiled at her. She'd gone all out for this visit; she was wearing navy jeans and a white shirt, unbuttoned to display a hint of her cleavage. Her hair was curled and gently tousled. The only thing that marred her image was the black scarf she wore to hide the injury he'd caused.

He took a step towards her and she retreated instinctively.

'How have you been?' he asked, as if it had been weeks rather than four short days since he saw her last.

'Fine. You?' She felt oddly formal with him.

'I've been better,' he said.

She crossed the distance between them, holding the watch.

'I wanted to return this. It didn't seem right to keep it.'

'I bought it for you . . .' but she had already pressed it into his hand.

'Thank you,' she said, 'but I can no longer accept this.'

She kissed his cheek and turned to walk away. Faroust let the watch fall to the floor with the tinkle of breaking glass. He caught her hand and drew her back to him. Without speaking, he unfurled the scarf from her throat. His handprint, so huge around her slender neck, pulsed purple, green and brown.

'I'm so sorry.' There was a sob in his voice. He dipped his head to kiss her neck and she sighed as a warm rush flowed over her skin. He pulled back from her and brought his right thumb to his mouth. He bit down on the digit until his blood, maroon now, no longer the green-black of his Fae body, welled up. He smeared the blood on his lips.

'I, Faroust, son of Mebh and Angus, swear by every drop of blood in my body, by the Veil and the blood on my lips, that

I will *never* raise my hands against Eliza, daughter of Jacob, in anger again.'

Eliza was giddy with triumph. It had been far easier that she'd thought. Faroust licked his lips before pushing his mouth to hers. She tasted the iron-rich remnants of his blood. She held back from absorbing power from him. She needed to seduce him. Once she had accomplished that, she had all the time she needed to siphon his secrets. He picked her up and carried her to his bedroom.

Eliza twisted her fingers in Faroust's dark hair as he rested his head against her breast. When he'd brought her back to his bed, he'd worshipped her like a zealot. As he'd made love to her, he'd lowered his guard and his power, unbidden, seeped through her skin, into her soul. And still he had not noticed.

She looked down at him with a flutter in her belly. He was so beautiful. That familiar rush of Family loyalty came over her. She closed her eyes against it, resisting the temptation it brought, forcing herself to remember Anna-Beth's face. She would discover the truth, but that didn't mean she couldn't enjoy the perks of the mission.

'I completely understand why Cornelius was willing to risk everything for you,' Faroust muttered against her skin. 'You are an incredible woman.'

You have no idea, she mused, with a pang of disgust at her own smug satisfaction. She slapped down the self-congratulation. That wasn't who she was. She needed to catch a grip of herself. If she got carried away, she risked the lives of everyone upstairs.

Faroust sat up. She reached for her underwear and pulled on her blouse.

'I should go back up.'

His face fell. 'You don't want to stay?'

'I've been down here for hours. My dad will be worried.'

'You can use my phone and let him know you're fine. I don't want you to go.'

Eliza twisted her hands, feigning anxiousness.

'Nor do I,' she said quietly. 'But I don't think it's healthy to spend every moment of my day with you. You're so intense and bad tempered, and scary when you revert to your Fae-self.' Faroust raised an eyebrow but said nothing. Eliza hurried on. 'You've promised never to attack me again, but you shouldn't have done it in the first place. And there will be other arguments . . .' She trailed off, leaving the rest unsaid.

Faroust took her face in his hands and forced her to look up at him.

'Forget about the future for the moment. What do you want right now?'

'To be here with you. But it's going to ruin me.'

He sighed deeply and touched his forehead to hers. 'So we need a compromise?'

'I may have one.' she said. 'During the day, I'm upstairs, working as part of the security team. At night, I come down here, but if I need space from you, you give it to me. No questions. No accusations.'

Faroust rolled his shoulders in annoyance and Eliza tightened her hold on him.

'It's not unreasonable, is it?'

'Oh no,' he said, sarcasm dripping. 'A mortal making demands of a god is perfectly acceptable.'

'Don't be like that.'

'You're holding me to ransom.'

'No I'm not. I'm trying to fix this. I want to be with you, to be your lover, but not the way we've been doing it. It will kill me.'

They glared at each other, neither one willing to back down. Finally, Faroust relaxed and took a deep breath.

'That could work,' he said. 'I could keep busy in the garden during the day.'

She pressed her mouth to his.

'Thank you.'

'I can't promise I won't lose my temper,' he warned. 'And you can't be with Cornelius anymore.'

'Not a problem.'

'Good. Call your dad. I'm going to make dinner.'

Jacob answered on the first ring.

'Hello, Sir,' he said.

'Hello, Daddy,' Eliza said brightly, settling herself on Faroust's desk.

'Hello, sweetheart.' His relief was tangible. 'Everything all right?'

'Better than all right. I'm going to stay down here tonight.'

Her father spluttered on the other end of the line. 'Are you sure?'

'Yes. I'll be up in the morning. Good night, Daddy. Tell Mam not to worry.'

'I will. Be careful, Eliza. I love you.'

'Love you too, Daddy. Good night.'

Faroust had poured her a glass of Rioja while she was on the phone. She sipped it as she watched him work in the kitchen. Every movement was fluid and graceful. The smells coming from the stove made her mouth water: ginger, garlic, soy sauce and sesame oil. He opened a bamboo steamer on the hob and checked whatever was inside.

'That smells amazing.'

He laughed. 'I've been feeding and taking care of myself my whole life. Sit down. I'll bring it to you.'

Eliza took her glass of wine and wandered around the living room. It wasn't so different from her rooms upstairs. There were books, mostly Irish poetry and James Joyce, CDs and DVDs, film posters and little knick-knacks. He seemed fond of little silver elephants, but there were no photographs. Not even of himself in Prague, which he'd told her was his favourite European city. There was no sign this man actually existed. Her heart ached. How lonely must he be? She couldn't imagine it, even from her position of exile.

She glanced over her shoulder. Faroust was putting the finishing touches to their dinner. She crossed to the bookshelf behind the couch to subtly check her camera was still where she'd left it.

'Ready!' Faroust called.

She got comfortable at the table, carefully positioning her wine glass on a coaster. Faroust handed her a pair of chopsticks and put down two plates of dumplings.

'Chicken and vegetable gyoza,' he said as he sat down. 'Duck in these ones. Soy and chilli dipping sauce.'

'Gyoza? You, sir, are full of surprises.'

'I do a mean sushi.' He laughed as she pulled a face. 'It's not all raw fish. I'll get prawns and avocado in next week and make you something spectacular. Now open up.'

He picked up a dumpling and popped it into her mouth.

'That's incredible,' she groaned. 'Can you teach me how to make it?'

He nodded, giving her a small smile, openly pleased at her praise. 'I've always loved to cook. Eat up. There's ramen to follow.'

Eliza took another sip of wine.

'I could get used to this.'

Careful! We're in this for the long haul. Remember the bigger picture.

After they had eaten, they lingered in the kitchen, drinking yet another glass of wine. There was a buzzing excitement between them now, a tension as intoxicating as it was painful.

'Say it,' Faroust said suddenly. 'Something's bothering you. It's written all over your face.'

'You're so different to how I'd thought you'd be,' she said. 'Don't get me wrong, there are parts I expected; your power, your authority, deviant sexuality, your mood swings. But there are other things about you that never would have occurred to me. You can be so gentle, so intimate and loving. It's knocked me off kilter.'

Faroust took her empty wine glass and washed it as he contemplated her words.

'I don't need to be the god all the time,' he said. 'I don't parade around in my own house with a big hood. Unless I'm in my official capacity as an idol, I'm a normal man. Well,' he laughed, 'as normal as I can be. It's difficult for me, Eliza. There's not a drop of human blood in me, once I've digested the sacrifice. For all intents and purposes, I'm an Otherworlder. My mother was Fae and my father was a god. I've had to learn how to be human and I find it hard sometimes.

'I don't spend a lot of time with people. Even as Daniel, I'm a bit of a loner. When I go out to find a playmate, it's over in one night. I travel, but I don't spend time with others. I stopped being free with my heart eons ago.'

He ran his hands through his hair, apparently unnerved by his own confession.

'I'm not a good man Eliza. The things I've done in the name of duty don't bear thinking about. I've had to be selfish and self-obsessed but then, I am a god, with a massive responsibility. You can't always think of others.'

Eliza nodded, trying to understand. He'd said it himself; he wasn't human.

'So most of the time I have to harden my heart and get on with the task in hand, which is protecting the Veil. But every now and then,' he smiled and drew her close to him, 'I can be a man and not the Fae-god.'

'I like the man,' Eliza said. 'The god scares me.'

'As he should.' Faroust laughed darkly as he wrapped his arms around her waist. She rested her head against his chest. 'I am born of dark gifts. So, what happened between you and Cornelius?'

The quick change of subject knocked her for six.

'We decided to end things,' she said stiffly.

'We?' Faroust asked, his tone more than a little cynical.

Eliza licked her lips. 'Yes, we. Considering he is technically my superior and I had recently been your playmate, we decided it would be inappropriate to continue our affair.'

'And it wasn't inappropriate before?' He chuckled.

'Not as inappropriate,' she said.

The god tucked a curled strand of hair behind her ear. 'So you're all mine?' His grin was infectious. Despite her plans and reservations, it made her knees weak.

'All yours.'

'Good. I'm taking you away this weekend. Make sure you get your passport tomorrow.'

'Okay.'

He kissed her, deeply, passionately. She stretched up on her toes to press her whole body against the length of his.

'Deviant sexuality, huh?'

'Yup.' She gave him a shy smile.

He picked her up by the waist and threw her over his shoulder. She shrieked with laughter as he carried her to the bedroom.

Chapter 18

ELIZA'S RETURN TO the house met far less excitement than when she'd appeared three days previously. She'd slept in because she and Faroust had been up until the small hours. When she finally woke up, Faroust had made her breakfast and eaten it off her stomach before scrubbing her in the shower. All of this meant she wasn't up until eleven o'clock, when everyone in the Family was at work.

Joshua was the only one who showed any excitement. He bounded down the stairs and lifted her up, laughing and spinning her around. He squeezed her ribs so tightly she squealed.

'Put me down!' she wheezed. 'You'll squeeze me to death.'

Josh put her down and hugged her more appropriately.

'I missed you, Eliza,' he said. He grabbed her hand and they bounded up towards her rooms. She chuckled. It had been a while since she had hung out with Joshua, and she was looking forward to spending the day with him. As they reached her rooms Joshua shut the front door firmly.

'Did you speak to the god for me?' he asked.

Eliza was instantly on edge. Joshua's voice was clear and his sentence coherent.

'I don't understand . . .'

Joshua grabbed her shoulders. 'I'm myself again. For the first time since I was sixteen, I am myself.' There was life in his deep blue eyes. Life and joy.

'Thank you for your petition . . .' He broke off. 'You didn't ask him anything,' he said slowly. 'You didn't ask him to cure me . . .'

'Josh . . .'

'It wasn't the god. It was you. From the day you first went down, I've been myself. You've blossomed.' He backed towards the door, panic and horror mixed on his face. 'I have to tell Jacob. You've been lying, Eliza. You blossomed and you've hidden it from us. We're supposed to work together.'

Eliza threw herself in front of the door as he turned from her. She grabbed his arm and dug her nails into his wrist.

'Eliza, that hurts!'

'Joshua, if you tell anyone, I'll get into big trouble. It'll be worse than what they did to you when you ran away. Faroust will kill me. And then he'll punish the rest of you. You don't want to get me into trouble, Joshua? Do you?' He tried to pull away but she twisted his wrist, pressing him to the floor. He let out a small cry as she forced more of her magic into him.

'Stop Eliza, please. It hurts!'

'You don't want to get me in trouble, do you?' she repeated. 'Not after all I've done for you. I *healed* you. I made you better.'

He looked up at her, his eyes full of sudden realisation. The realisation she wanted him to have. 'Yes. Yes, you did. I should thank you. You saved me.'

She let him go and he stumbled against the door, eyes closed, breath ragged and shallow. She cursed herself, guilt and vomit welling up inside her. Poor Joshua had been through so much and she'd inflicted her magic on him. She couldn't leave him like this, frightened and confused.

She knelt in front of him and brushed away his tears.

'Don't cry, Josh. I'm sorry, I didn't mean to scare you.' She rubbed his arm where she'd broken the skin. 'Or hurt you. I don't want you to have any pain.' She kissed his wrist softly.

'It doesn't hurt so much,' he answered, with a gasp.

She looked up at him and kissed his wrist again. 'I am sorry,' she said, her voice soft, low, melodic. She felt her cousin relax against the door. 'Let me make it up to you.'

'How?'

'I'm going to take the memory away from you.'

She put her hand on his head and brushed his hair, brushed away all the memories, brushed away his knowledge of her magic.

By the time she was done, the spell was as strong as steel. He trotted cheerfully out of her rooms, passing Cornelius on the stairs. The Family protector stood in the doorway, watching her adjust her clothing.

'I see you've met the new and improved Joshua. They already have him matched up. You're alive then?'

'It would appear that way.'

Cornelius stepped inside and locked the door.

'The house is practically empty,' he whispered.

'What happened to "We'll get caught"?'

'You weren't so worried about that when you were "fixing" Joshua. With your little kisses on his wrist, your little sexual inferences.' He sniffed. He must have seen the whole thing on his monitors.

'Are you jealous?'

'Not really.'

'Make sure you delete that tape.'

He grabbed her by the arm and dragged him to her. 'Are you giving me orders, missus?' he growled. 'I don't think I like your cheeky tone. We may have to punish you for that.'

Afterwards, as they lay on Eliza's bed, Cornelius traced the scar on her spine.

'I still can't believe he did that.'

'Why wouldn't he? He's the First-Father. His secrets must be protected. Christ, the things I know, Cornelius. The truths I've witnessed. And there's still so much to take from him.'

'You sound like you like that idea.' He sniffed his disapproval.

They lay in silence for a while. It was mid-afternoon; they still had time before they'd have to get dressed.

'Who's better?' Cornelius asked, shattering the comfortable quiet.

Eliza looked down at him, an eyebrow raised. 'You are,' she said. 'You rock my socks. Faroust uses me like a sex toy. I might as well be a blow up doll. I'd be easier to clean up.'

'I'll fucking kill him!' Cornelius snarled, tightening his fierce grip on her.

'I appreciate the gesture, love, but I'm fine. I'm in for the long game and that means doing what he wants. I need to be compliant to his needs.'

'Be careful, Eliza. No matter how strong you get, you might not be able to beat him if he finds out.'

Eliza smiled at him. 'I will be, baby. Now, by my watch, we have half an hour before we really have to get up.'

The rest of September flew by and soon it was October. The relationship between Faroust and Eliza continued steadily, within the set boundaries. She spent her days at Cornelius' side, coming up with new ways to protect the Family that did not rely on telepathy: personal alarms, tracking devices, computerised versions of phylacteries. In the evenings, she returned to her god-lover and their strange domesticity. She rather enjoyed it. When Faroust was in a good mood, he was a pleasure to be with, funny and generous, eager to show her a wonderful time.

He took her to London on their first weekend trip because she wanted to see the Elgin Marbles again, as well as the dinosaur exhibit at the Natural History Museum. He even surprised her with tickets for 'The Taming of the Shrew.'

'Is that supposed to be a hint?' She laughed.

'Depends on my mood,' he said. 'Today I rather enjoyed the tempestuous woman I woke up with.'

This weekend, however, there was to be no fun. Eliza curled up on the bed, her body wracked with period pain. It felt as if her womb was trying to crawl out of her body. She had a hot water bottle strapped to her and popped the co-codamol Matthew prescribed like sweets. She'd been grumpy and unable to focus while patrolling the grounds with Cornelius the day before, snapping at him when he tried to take her hand when they came to a blind spot. She apologised later, but he had been mournful and distant for the rest of the day.

Now she would give anything for his affection, to feel his cool hands brush her hair from her eyes or rub her distended stomach. Given her mood, she decided it was best not to go down to Faroust until the worst of the bleeding had passed. She left him a note and even signed it with a kiss. That should keep him warm for her.

There was a soft knock on her door and it creaked open. Eliza assumed it was her mother, bringing lunch and a fresh hot water bottle. Through the fog of drugs and pain, it took her a moment to realise Faroust was in her bedroom, growing more visible by the second.

'That's a neat trick. I thought you couldn't hide physical form?'

'Not other people's. Just my own. How are you feeling, *mo ghrá*?'

'Like my body is trying to kill me. The pills Matthew gave me barely touched the sides.'

Faroust winced as a cramp made Eliza jolt and shudder. She pulled her legs up under her and bit down on her fist to stifle her scream. 'My poor Eliza. I can help.'

'How?'

'I can stop the muscles causing you pain from contracting. You'll still bleed, but your pain will pass.'

Gently, he lifted her t-shirt. Her belly was swollen and red. He touched his finger tips to her stomach, above her navel. He closed his eyes and began to chant softly, and the crippling pain began to subside. She was so engrossed, it took a moment for her to register Cornelius, glowering in jealousy by the door. The instant he caught her eye, he span and left, silent as a ghost. Her heart sank.

Faroust finished his spell and opened his eyes. 'Better?'

'Wow. I might actually be able to function like a normal person! Thank you.' She sat up and kissed him.

'That's all right, baby,' he said. 'I'll see you tonight.' It was not a request. She nodded, although all she really wanted to do was curl up with Cornelius and watch a crappy film like a normal couple.

Shit. He'll be furious when I cancel our plans.

Faroust kissed her and faded into invisibility. The door swung to and clicked shut.

That's something else I need to be wary of. He could follow me at any time.

She waited until she was sure Faroust was gone before slipping into her black suit. Cornelius was heading out to test the range of the tracker he'd been developing, and she wanted to go with him. It would give them a rare opportunity to speak in total privacy.

He gave her a stony stare as she approached him.

'Can I come?' she whispered.

'If you must,' he replied curtly. 'I'll clear it with your dad.'

It only took a moment and Cornelius was storming past her.

'Come,' he ordered. The tone of his voice made her shudder, desire pooling in her belly. She trotted to keep up with him as he headed towards his car.

She shivered as she waited in the passenger seat of the Mercedes as he installed the tracking device. He was working on a spell that any member of the Family could chant to get help, but it would take time to perfect and to teach. The device would do for now.

He got in, shook off the rain and started the car without speaking. Faroust, in Daniel's skin, was leaving the lodge as they drove towards the gate. Eliza unbuckled herself and sank into the foot well. Cornelius glanced at her in confusion. She pressed her finger to her lips and he nodded. As he drove past Daniel, the gardener raised his hand and waved. Cornelius smiled, and waved back.

Eliza didn't squirm up from the foot well until they were on the road.

'What the fuck was that about? It was only Daniel.'

'Was it?' she said.

The seal on her back tingled. Since she'd been back with their god, the seal had strengthened as she gained more of his power. It made a weird kind of sense; it was his spell, his power she was taking. She winced as the spell took hold.

'I thought he took care of your pain.'

'It's in my back.' She struggled to get the words out. The pain spread, bringing with it a strange paralysis. Her chest tightened and her jaw clamped shut against her wishes.

'The seal? But I thought . . .'

'His magic makes it stronger - motherfucker!' She yelped as her muscles contracted. The Cruel pulled the car over as she convulsed, and sweat broke out on her brow. The spell, violent and powerful once more, punished Eliza mercilessly for her tiny infringement.

It was over in a matter of minutes, but it felt like an eternity. The convulsing and twitching stopped and Eliza sat back, whimpering and damp with sweat.

'Why did that happen?'

'Think. Think carefully.'

Cornelius covered his eyes and swore. 'It was Daniel, wasn't it? We saw him, and you had this reaction. You were hiding from him.'

She nodded, lips pressed tight against a fresh twinge of pain.

'Daniel has some connection to Faroust. What is he, a spy? Is he watching what you do and reporting back to Faroust?'

An almost imperceptible shake of her head, but Cornelius noticed it, and the light of realisation dawned in his eyes.

'Shit. He *is* Faroust isn't he? That's why you had to hide!'

Eliza's little whimper confirmed it.

'We have to be extra careful. He could be anywhere, at any time. He was in your bedroom. How did he get there without being seen . . . ?' His hands tightened on the steering wheel. 'Motherfucker! That bastard gave me roses for my mother's grave, knowing she's stuck in the Veil!'

His knuckles whitened as the anger grew. Eliza, chilled and shaking though she was, unbuckled and climbed across to hug him.

'Oh baby, I'm so sorry. That was a cruel thing to do.'

She held him until he calmed down, feeling him relax against her as his arms crept around her.

'I wish I could stay here forever,' she said.

'Why would you want to, when you've got the god's attention?'

'Oh, that's not fair!' She thumped him as she moved away. 'He threatened to tell my dad about us if I didn't sleep with him. They'd have killed you.'

The Cruel shrugged the way teenagers do when confronted with their wrong doing.

'You got away from him.'

'That's even more unfair! You know why I had to go back down.'

'Do I?' He was actually sulking, like a child.

Eliza sucked her teeth in annoyance. She didn't need his jealousy on top of all Faroust's shit. She reached over and flicked him in the ear twice.

'Ow!' he cried. 'What the actual fuck?' He grabbed her hands as she moved in to flick him again. 'Stop it!'

'Then snap out of it! You're not a child. Stop acting like one. You accused me of being selfish when I left, but you're the second most selfish person I know. I'm not risking everything to flatter my own vanity. I'm trying to protect the Family. Our god has been lying to us for five thousand years.'

'You don't know that.'

'Yes I do! What I saw is proof he's been lying to us. Is there anything in our lore that says our fate is to be trapped in the Veil forever?'

Cornelius shook his head. 'We're in too deep. We need to get out. We need to stop.'

Eliza stared at him in incredulous silence, swallowing her accusation of cowardice. He was clinging to the world he knew and the religion that had guided his life. He had always been sure of his role, sure of the Family and sure of his god. Until she stumbled into his life and messed it all up.

'Maybe if you'd seen what I've seen, you'd understand. If you can't do this with me, I'll understand.'

'I don't think you should do it at all. Ah feck, Eliza. I know there's something going on but we're Fae. It's our duty to serve the god and protect the Veil. What we're doing is blasphemy.'

They sat in awkward silence, unsure what to do next. Eliza was aware that her back hadn't hurt when she'd been talking about Faroust. The rule must not apply when discussing things the other person knew. Cornelius stared out of the windscreen, rubbing his hairline with his index finger. Eliza reached for him and he flinched. She dropped her hand.

'I wasn't going to do anything.'

'How do I know? You were casting spells on me for weeks to keep me under control.'

'Only to make sure you wouldn't tell on me.'

'I made the Blood Oath!'

Eliza's frayed temper finally snapped.

'My God, we already had this fight! You need to find your balls again. Because this person,' she poked him in the chest, 'is not the man who took me on the train. This person is not the intelligent, hard-nosed, sexy as all fuck man I am falling for. This person is a little bitch!'

Cornelius glared at her. Eliza sat back, folding her arms. She looked up at him from under lowered lashes, seeing the hurt on his face. She'd gone too far . . .

'A little bitch?' His voice was dangerously quiet. 'So you're calling me a coward?'

She said nothing. Saying anything would make it worse.

When another minute passed without her answering him, he threw the car into gear and pulled out into the road. He slammed his foot down on the accelerator. Eliza flew forward as she scrambled for her seat belt. They sped through the wet Irish countryside, away from the house towards Dublin. Cornelius pushed the car as fast as it would go as they travelled on the M50 towards the toll bridge and the West Link to Lucan. Eliza winced as they cut a corner speeding into a cul-de-sac.

'Careful!' she shrieked.

Without speaking to her, Cornelius slowed the car. They pulled into the drive of a small detached house, away from the neighbours. Eliza didn't need to be told what it was. Cornelius had a safe-house, a place to hide if the *Gnáth* latched onto him, somewhere he could disguise his connection to the Family if he needed to.

They sat in the driveway for a moment before Cornelius leapt out of the car, slamming the door behind him. Eliza gave him a minute before getting out. As she approached him, his phone rang.

'Yes?' he demanded sharply.

She overheard the voice of someone from the Big House. It sounded tinny through the phone.

'It's Tim, Cornelius. Are you in Lucan?'

'Yes. The tracker kept up with me then?'

'It just died. If we want any real range, we'll have to . . .'

'Fine. I'll be back soon. Start working on that.'

The Cruel clicked the phone off before Tim had a chance to answer.

'Fucking trinket just died. Not even in the next sodding county.'

'We can track via GPS on smart phones. They're reliable,' she said. 'A lot of cars come with tracking devices.'

'That puts us on the *Gnáth* map. Nobody's tried to get to us in a while, but that doesn't mean people have forgotten about the Fae. Or that they wouldn't try to get to us for our connections with the energy companies. Get in the house.'

The thunderous expression on his face left no room for argument. Eliza did as she was told. As soon as he closed the door, Cornelius grabbed her and dragged her into the living room. The safe-house was sparsely decorated; a television, bed and fridge, all in the one room. The thick layer of dust told her the house hadn't been used for some time. Cornelius pushed her against the wall.

'I am not a coward. And I am not a little bitch. I am the Cruel, the enforcer of the rules. You made me break them.'

'I prefer to think I made you aware of the truth.'

'You made me a traitor.'

'This is the opposite of treachery. It's protecting the Family.'

He exhaled through his nose. 'I wish you'd never seen the fucking Veil.'

'Don't you think I wish that too, so we could go back to fucking on the quiet?'

'That's how you made me a traitor. You made me swear a Blood Oath and now, no matter what you do, I can't tell anyone because I can't break my bond by using stolen magic.'

It took every ounce of Eliza's self-restraint not to hit him. 'I don't remember forcing you.'

'But you did manipulate me.'

'Into having sex with me, to save my skin. But now it's more than that. So much more. Baby,' she put her hands on his chest, 'I want to be with you, not for the protection you offer, but because we have something worth fighting for.'

He averted his eyes.

'Baby, look at me,' she coaxed. 'I never started out on a mission to turn our world upside down, but that's what's happened. If I hadn't seen it, I'd have crawled back into your bed and been your girl. But I saw the Veil and I saw our Family. I can't leave it alone. It would be wrong.'

They stood facing each other in tense silence. If there was only a way she could circumvent the spell . . . Maybe there was a way.

'The things I saw in the Veil don't technically have anything to do with Faroust, which is why I could tell you about them,' she said, half to herself. 'Reach in to my head.'

'What?'

'Reach into my head. See what I saw.'

Cornelius swallowed. 'I don't know,' he said. 'The spell is designed to stop even my kind of magic from accessing information.'

'But I'm not showing you anything to do with Faroust. I'm showing you the things I saw in the Veil, which are to do with the Family.'

He hesitated.

'This is the only way I can convince you we're doing the right thing. We can't just leave this be. This is the only way I can make you understand why I can't leave it alone. Please? I need you. I can't do this alone.'

He tipped his head back and sighed. 'You don't even have to take your clothes off now, do you? Fine. Let's get this over with.'

He positioned her on the small bed, tilting her backwards.

'I'll have to bind you,' he said. 'If you move during this, I could really fuck up your brain. Close your eyes.'

She felt him paralysing her. She focused on keeping her breathing slow and measured, aware all the while of an uncomfortable pinching sensation on her forehead. A silent scream bubbled up inside her as Cornelius' hand pushed into her head.

In a heartbeat, she was reliving her vision of the Veil. She watched Faroust strangle her before she'd raged out of his apartment. She witnessed once more the swirl of images of their god the Veil had revealed, and the horror of the truth. All these souls lost, Anna-Beth's lips begging for release for all of them. She felt Cornelius' distress as he saw what she had witnessed, as his world crumbled.

He withdrew and unbound her. Slowly, she came back to herself and was able to move again. He knelt in front of her with his head in her lap. She ran her fingers through his hair and he looked up at her, his eyes full of tears.

'I'll help you,' he said. 'Oh baby, what he did to you. I'd kill him if I could.'

'Shh,' she soothed. 'It's all right, love. We can't be rash. We'll take it slow and reveal the truth. We'll fix this.'

He nodded and laid his head down once more.

'I'm sorry I was jealous,' he said. 'I see now jealousy isn't the right emotion. Anger is.'

'Oh, I don't know, I quite like you jealous. Means you'll work that wee bit harder to keep my interest.'

'Hah!' Cornelius got to his feet. 'I've bet you've learnt all kinds of new things with our god. Surely you should be using them to please me, as I have to share you with him?'

'I might have learnt a few tricks.'

'Maybe when you stop bleeding, we'll go away on a 'mission' for the afternoon and you can show me some of them?'

'Sounds good to me. I'm sorry I was rude to you. You're not a coward.'

'You're forgiven.'

The alarm went off on her phone. Eliza looked at it, and swore. 'We have to get back to the house. This fucking journalist is coming to interview me about my six months of amnesia.'

'That should be easy enough. Just tell them you don't remember anything.'

Eliza groaned at his terrible joke. 'You, sir, have a dreadful sense of humour.'

'Would explain a lot of things. Like why I'm going out with you, for example.'

'Keep on saying things like that and you'll be having solo 'missions' from now on.'

He laughed and wrapped his arm around her as they left the safe-house to return to the Family.

Chapter 19

'ELIZA! IT'S HERE!'

Eliza laughed as Ruby snatched the paper from Francis. Not only was Eliza's interview in the glossy magazine, but there was also a piece on her mother and her annual winter charity ball. Pages scattered as she ripped the plastic sack containing the Sunday extras out of the paper. Eliza sat opposite her mother, chuckling at her excitement.

'Look, you're the cover girl!'

Eliza had captured the look of a strong victim well. To the whole world, this woman had survived a horrific ordeal and was stronger for having gone through it. The photographer had positioned the light beautifully. Her hair glowed, golden around her shoulders. She looked like an angel. Her eyes were huge and her lips slightly parted. The way she pulled her ring finger with her right hand added just enough vulnerability to the shot, without making her a figure of pity.

When the daughter of Ruby and Jacob MacTir had been involved in an accident and her body was never found, it had been international news. It meant Eliza couldn't just slip quietly back into Family life. And as Sage was dead, they had to come up with a new story to explain her absence. Her eyes flicked down to the headline: 'I was lost for six months.'

It had been her mother's clever rouse. In the press conference in July, they hinted at the reason for her disappearance. But all things need to be explained. They decided Eliza had suffered from trauma-induced amnesia. She washed up along the river and was brought to a local hospital. Once discharged, she was directed towards a homeless shelter in Edinburgh. She was only found because an Irishman on holiday recognised her as she was begging at the train station. Cornelius played that role well for the paper. He wasn't the Family spy for nothing. He'd also hacked the hospital database and created a file on a patient who had never darkened its doors.

It was a touching story, full of hope, tears and rehabilitation. The journalist had done a marvellous job.

'It looks good,' Eliza said. 'The story reads well. Good job, Mum.'

She flicked the pages and Ruby's russet beauty blazed into focus. She handed the magazine over. Her mother scanned the article.

'Celebrating its twenty-fifth year, Ruby MacTir's Eco-Ball is the highlight of the social calendar. Taking place on the 20th of December, this year the celebrations will be even bigger considering the return of her daughter Eliza,' Ruby read aloud. 'We need to get our costumes sorted.'

Eliza grinned at her mother, shaking off the unwelcome prickle of shame which travelled up her spine. She was back now and things were better. Everyone spoke to her and was respectful of her. Even po-faced Susan MacBride, her mother's assistant, was pleasant to her. People better understood the effect their accidental cruelty had on her.

Maybe they're just being nice because you're the god's whore.

She pushed away the self-doubt, the self-loathing. None of that mattered any more. All that mattered was the safety and happiness of the people she loved. Besides, if she hadn't left, she would never have discovered what lurked in the Veil. How many more would have been lost to it without that discovery?

'Have you thought of what you're going to dress up as?' Eliza asked, to distract herself from her own thoughts.

'I haven't even thought about decorations! We'll have to have a Christmas tree.'

'I think you should have lots of white and candles. Like German Christmas markets. It would fit in better with the Solstice,' Eliza said.

'That's a wonderful idea. Do you want to help me organise it? You did such a beautiful job at the Ritual.'

'Can I see your costume yet?' Faroust sat outside his bathroom with his back pressed against the door, listening to Eliza clattering about as she finished getting ready.

'No!' she called back. 'You have to wait. You could always come to the party, you know.'

'No thanks,' he snorted.

'Worried you might enjoy yourself?'

The bathroom door swung open unexpectedly, and he had to catch hold of the door frame to keep himself from sprawling on the tiles. He jumped up to inspect her.

'How do I look?'

Eliza wore an emerald green mini-dress which gathered in straps over her shoulders and showed a tempting hint of cleavage. Her hair was teased and curled with little flowers woven into her locks. She'd dusted her skin with a greeny-gold powder and highlighted her eyes with green kohl, making her irises dance and sparkle. Her slim legs were encased in green fishnet stockings, and on her feet, she wore a pair of golden sandals. A skull dangled from a bracelet of glass beads on her wrist. To top her outfit off, she had a huge pair of green wings made from wire, chiffon and sequins.

'Wow. You look like the absinthe fairy.'

'Do you like it?'

He grabbed her hand and put it against his crotch. She wiggled her fingers delightfully against his hardness.

'You'll make a mess.' She giggled. 'Besides, I have to go now.'

'We'll play later,' he said. 'Do your best to keep this nice. I want you to wear it more often.'

'Are you sure you don't want to come up?'

He nodded. 'You have fun. Enjoy the fruits of your labour. You'd only spend the whole night worrying about whether or not I'm having a good time. And you could hardly hang onto me, could you? People would notice.'

'You're an unsociable git.'

'That too,' he admitted. 'Up you go.'

Eliza danced away from him, like the sprite she was pretending to be. She was a vibrant little thing, full of life and joy. As they'd spent more time together, she'd gradually relaxed in his company. She was funny and clever, affectionate and hot-tempered. She brought light and joy into his lonely world. She was strong too. The previous week when he'd lost his temper with his computer and almost smashed it, she'd taken it away and quietly fixed the problem. She didn't even flinch when he shouted now. She was a special woman.

He followed her out to the cavern, and when she was halfway across he put his fingers in his mouth and wolf-whistled. She bent over and flipped up her skirt, revealing her tiny panties and the tops of her stockings and suspender belt.

'You'd best go, woman, before I lose control of myself! The altar isn't reserved for the Ritual, you know.'

She turned back to him and winked before skipping up the slope.

The house hummed with activity. Ireland's great and good milled in the hallway, waiting for Ruby to open the ballroom. A few TDs familiar to Eliza said hello and smiled as she moved through the crowd. Her father greeted people at the door, dressed as a pirate. When he saw her, he raised an eyebrow at the shortness of her skirt. She stuck her tongue out at him and span into the crowd, waiting for her mother to reveal her costume and start the party.

Amongst the guests, she spotted some of Cornelius' security guards. They were in costume, but they moved stiffly. The waiters carrying the champagne took pains to avoid them. She spotted Cornelius, dressed in an eighteenth century military coat and a cravat. He'd slicked his hair back. It suited him. As he spotted her his jaw dropped. She curtsied to him and he replied with a bow.

A commotion on the stair interrupted their flirtation. Ruby was coming out. Eliza turned with the rest of the crowd, stiffening as a familiar pair of arms wrapped around her waist and pulled her backwards. Cornelius pressed his erection into her and she stifled a giggle.

'You are going to find some time to sneak off,' he whispered.

'Yes, Sir,' she replied, never taking her eyes from the staircase.

Ruby entered and Cornelius stepped back. Eliza's mother was dressed as Abheaog, the Irish goddess of Fire. Her dress was all the colours of the flame, starting with a deep blue at the centre, radiating out to red, yellow and orange. The silk fluttered and moved like flames as she walked. The room burst into applause as the hostess came down the stairs.

'Welcome, friends, to our twenty-fifth Eco-Ball. Every year we hold a charity auction to raise money towards research into reducing Ireland's carbon footprint, as well as community recycling projects, funding education projects and continuing the upkeep of places of outstanding natural beauty. Even in these times of deep recession, I know we can rely on you to help our cause. Last year we raised €1.2 million. That was all down to you.'

The crowd applauded once more, full of satisfaction at their good work. Ruby raised her hands and the noise died away.

'Ladies and gentlemen, the ballroom is now open. Please join me for dinner.'

It was midnight before Eliza could slip away with Cornelius. She was intent of being the perfect hostess, ensuring everyone was happy and their drinks were topped up. She moved amongst the tables to speak to the more important guests, graciously accepting compliments on the white and silver winter decorations. She even called taxis for a few guests who had over-indulged in the free-flowing booze. The auction went off without a hitch, as did the raffle. Now the swing band was playing so people could gently warm up to dancing before the DJ started.

Eliza went to her parents, who were slowly circling in the middle of the floor.

'Hello, darling!' Ruby cried. Her bright eyes gave away that she'd had a drink or two now the formal part of the evening was over. 'Once again, you've done a fabulous job. Jacob, you should make Eliza our official party planner!'

'Thanks, Mum. I'm just popping to my room. I need a moment.'

Ruby's smiling face faltered and Eliza kissed her cheek.

'I'm all right. I just need a breather. I'll be back soon.'

As she left the room, she caught Cornelius' eye. He nodded and discreetly followed her upstairs. The music from the band floated up after them. Eliza stood in her living room, beautiful and otherworldly. The Cruel gathered her to him and kissed her hard.

'You're going to get covered in makeup.'

'Don't care,' he breathed. 'I've been dying to touch you all night. You are so, so beautiful.'

They rocked back and forth in time with the music, and slowly, almost unconsciously, began to dance.

'I wish we didn't have to sneak around,' Cornelius said, pressing his forehead against hers. 'Did you hear they're trying to pair me up with Susan?' He made a face. 'I know she's a Greater Brancher but she's so . . . so . . .'

'Prudish? Prim? Rude? Po-faced!'

Cornelius laughed at her adjectives.

'She's a snob. She thinks she's better than everyone and she's such an awful flirt. She flirts with everyone. And she's bad at it!'

'Could you imagine? She'd lie rigid the whole time with her eyes closed. It'd be like breaking into Fort Knox!'

'Don't give me that image, you brat! You'll kill my erection.'

She grabbed his crotch. 'You still feel rock hard to me,' she said.

'Oh, you are a bad girl.' She took his hand and led him to the bed. He lay down and she straddled him. Her opulent chiffon wings spread out behind her, making her every inch the dangerous and tempting fairy. He moved to roll her onto her back. She pushed down on his shoulders and shook her head.

'You want to be in control?'

Her eyes lit up with wickedness and lust. He lay back, putting his hands behind his head.

'I am yours, to use as you wish.'

With nimble fingers, she unbuttoned the trousers of his military costume. He propped himself up on his elbows as she slipped him into her mouth. He loved watching her suck him. She peeped up at him through her false lashes and groaned, the sound vibrating through his dick, making him gasp. She pulled away and kissed the head of his penis before pressing herself against him, kissing him deeply. He could taste himself on her lips and tongue, a sexy little trick she'd learned from him.

She ran her hand down his body and gripped his erection, moving her hand back and forth so fast he gasped and tried to jerk away, not wanting to come yet. She brought her hand up and slipped a finger between his lips. He groaned and sucked hard, more aroused than ever at her boldness.

She sat back and rooted in his pockets for the condom. They needed to be quick; someone would soon notice they were missing. She slid the condom onto him and crouched over him, keeping the prize he wanted tantalisingly out of reach. He curled one hand in her hair and pulled her head down to kiss her. In one swift movement, she slid on to him. He groaned into her mouth as she began to fuck him. She moved her hips slowly, using long strokes to draw out his pleasure.

'Oh, you're so good. You feel amazing.' He sighed.

She pulled away from him and pushed him flat on the bed. She increased the speed of her movement, grinding against him. Cornelius gasped as Eliza threw her head back and moaned. She guided his hands to her hips, using him to balance her. He moved his thumb until it pressed against her clit, drawing circles around it. She growled, moving faster, using her own momentum to add to his motions. Below them the band swelled to a crescendo.

'Come with me,' Eliza ordered. 'Come with me now. Oh yes!' She shrieked, throwing her arms out in triumph as Cornelius climaxed beneath her.

Eliza fell forward, balancing herself on her hands, her heavy panting mirroring her lover's ragged breathing. She kissed him deeply as she came down.

'I love you,' she breathed, without thinking.

Cornelius froze. Eliza's stomach dropped. Had she spoken too soon? They had feelings for each other, there was no doubt of that, and given time it would have been something more. She'd ruined things, put pressure on him and soured their fun. And then he smiled.

'I love you too.'

She rested her head against his chest.

'Will you wait for me?' she asked. 'Until all this is over?'

'I will wait for you as long as it takes,' he said. 'We'd best get cleaned up.' He kissed her once more. It was a tender kiss, full of promise, desire and affection.

She broke away from him and scurried to her bathroom, returning with a pack of makeup wipes. He spluttered as she rubbed the wipe over his face.

'That tastes vile!' He pushed his tongue out of his mouth in disgust.

'You're not supposed to taste it!' she said. 'There, you're done.'

She grinned up at him as took her hands and kissed them again knowing everything would eventually be all right.

Reluctantly, he returned to the party. Eliza followed about ten minutes later, having fixed her hair and makeup. He sighed as he watched her; her beauty was breath-taking. She caught him staring and winked, before she was absorbed by the crowd.

'Hi, Cornelius!' a high-pitched voice slurred. It was Susan. He groaned inwardly. The girl was pretty, but Eliza had hit the nail on the head. She had an ugly personality. She was rude and snobbish and skin-crawlingly insincere.

'We should talk.' She swayed slightly.

'I'm working, Susan,' he said.

'But you're going to be my husband.'

'No one's decided that yet, Susan.'

She giggle-snorted into her martini glass. The alcohol slopped over the sides and down her dress.

'Yes, they have. Jacob told me.'

Cornelius felt his temper rising. No one had discussed it with him. Usually matches were organised with the consent of the people involved.

'I wouldn't marry you,' he snarled, 'if you were the last . . .'

'Hello!' Eliza's cheerful greeting interrupted him. 'Everything okay? Susan, you don't look so good.'

He saw his lover grab the other woman's arm. This was risky, with all these people here.

'I don't feel so good,' Susan whimpered, turning green around the gills.

'Come with me, honey,' Eliza said. 'We'll get you some water.'

Cornelius watched as Eliza shepherded Susan away to a quiet corner. Trying not to appear obvious, he stood guard as she pushed the obnoxious woman's hair out of her face.

'Susan,' Eliza's voice took on its quiet chanting quality, 'you don't want to marry Cornelius.'

'I don't?'

'No, you don't. He's a Lesser Brancher. He's the direct descendant of the Slave. He's a bad man. He'll hurt you. You don't want to marry him.'

The spell washed over the drunk girl.

'I don't want to marry Cornelius,' she mumbled. She turned to Eliza with bright eyes full of tears. 'I don't want to, Eliza. Please help me.'

Eliza put her arm around her and kissed the top of her head.

'It's okay, sweetie. You won't have to.' She beckoned to one of the security guards. 'Hi Tim. Could you take Susan up to one of the guest bedrooms, please? She may need a bowl. You're a star, sweetheart.'

Cornelius and Eliza watched them until they were out of sight. Eliza's whole body was stiff. She looked livid.

And jealous. He couldn't help but smile. *Good. I like her jealous.*

'How fucking dare she?'

'Eliza . . .'

'No, she can't pull shit like this while you're working. I need to find my dad.'

Cornelius reached for her but she was on her feet and charging towards the French doors where Jacob was trying to sneak off for a cigar. Cornelius sighed and followed, ready to break up a scene.

'Daddy!' Eliza grabbed his arm.

'Hello!' Jacob laughed. The flush in his skin suggested he was very drunk by now.

Eliza snapped her fingers and he stiffened.

'Look at me,' she ordered. 'Do not match Susan with Cornelius. She isn't worthy to tie his shoe laces.'

'Cornelius needs someone better,' Jacob said, nodding. 'He needs better recognition of his services to us.'

'You're damn right,' she spat, releasing his arm.

Great. More footage I need to delete.

Jacob came to, blinking hard. 'Hello darling. Have you seen Niall? I need to talk to him about Susan. She and Cornelius won't be a good match.'

'He's out by the cigar bar.'

Eliza huffed as her father tottered off. A waiter passed her, carrying a tray of full champagne glasses. She snatched two of them and downed them. She was clearly agitated and annoyed at her behaviour. Jealousy had got the better of her. Cornelius laughed. That was rich given how she was behaving in the name of her mission.

He stared at her, saying nothing. She glared back at him.

'What?'

'Nothing. Good to know you get jealous too.'

'Shut up, Cornelius.'

He grabbed her as she tried to spin away. 'You were jealous. It's kind of cute.'

She sucked her teeth and exhaled. 'All right,' she admitted. 'I am jealous. I couldn't stand the thought of her near you. It must be a thousand times worse for you.'

He gave her a small, sad smile and nodded. Without speaking, they moved back into the shadows. She wrapped her arms around his neck and laid her head on his shoulder as his arms closed around her waist.

'It makes it easier knowing you love me,' he whispered. 'It makes it easier knowing the only reason you're down there is because of what you saw in the Veil. But sometimes I get so jealous, I feel sick.'

Eliza tightened her arms around him. Tears gathered in her eyes. He kissed her forehead.

'As soon as I can leave him, I will,' she promised. She stood on tiptoe to kiss him on the mouth. He curled his hands into her hair and deepened the kiss.

Eventually, he broke away from her.

'You'd best get back to the party. I wish I could magic you away and keep you to myself forever.'

'Don't tempt me. I still have all my credit cards in my runaway name.'

He laughed and wiped away a tear that trickled down her cheek. A movement across the hall caught his attention; Ruby had entered the ballroom. Eliza's shoulders slumped as circumstances forced them apart once again. She wiped away a smudge of make-up from his face and stepped backwards into the ballroom, holding on to his hand until the last moment.

When she finally broke contact, he felt bereft as she span away from him. He turned and slammed into Julian. The other man glared at him.

'You're still sleeping together.' It was a statement, not a question or an accusation.

'Yes.'

'Cornelius, he'll kill her if he finds out. You have to stop.'

'I can't, Julian.'

'Why not?'

He sighed. 'I love her. I can't let her go.'

The Hound grabbed him by the shirt front. 'If she dies, I'm coming after you. Your trade will seem like a dream compared to what I'll do to you.'

He threw Cornelius away with such force the Cruel cracked his shoulder on the wall. He knew Julian was right, but it wasn't as straightforward as all that. His train of thought was interrupted by two rowdy guests shoving and yelling at each other. Duty called, and he could push everything else away.

It was four in the morning by the time the last guest departed. Eliza was exhausted. She desperately wanted to crash in her own bed, but she knew Faroust would have stayed awake waiting for her. Drunk and unsteady on her feet, she made her way down to the cavern. Faroust was sitting on his throne when she arrived, toying with a half full tumbler of whiskey. Several empty bottles were scattered around the chamber. The look on his face could have curdled milk. Eliza squared her shoulders, ready for a fight.

'Hi lover.' She hoped she could jolly him out of his mood. 'Did you miss me?'

'Nice party?'

'It was lovely. Everybody had a wonderful time.'

He grunted and shifted in his seat, his navy eyes flicking over her. The angry silence stretched on.

'Did you fuck him?' he finally demanded.

Ah, so he's suffering at the hands of the jealousy monster too.

'Yes, Faroust. At a charity ball I was hosting, in front of my parents, I fucked Cornelius.' She glared at him, daring him to accuse her again.

'I can smell him on you.'

She shrugged. 'One of the guests was getting a bit handsy towards the end of the party. Cornelius did his fucking job and got the dickhead off me. To do that, he had to get between me and the man trying to grope me. We didn't have sex in that brief moment either.'

She watched him as he digested her lie. He got out of his chair and stumbled over an empty bottle.

'How much did you have? It must be nearly impossible for you to get drunk.'

'Hah!' He scoffed. 'I had all the booze in the house. Including my supply of thirty year old whiskies. Was the only thing that could stop me imagining you were fucking him.'

Eliza frowned as he staggered towards her. She grabbed him and held him steady.

'So you drank €50,000 worth of booze because you were jealous?' She wasn't in the mood for this. She was tired and drunk and her feet hurt from her stupid shoes. She put her hands on his chest and willed him to be calm. 'I didn't do anything with him, love,' she chanted. Faroust nodded in time to her voice. 'You're the only one I want. The only one I need. Let's forget you said that.'

She felt him relax as her voice wound its magic around him. He smiled down at her, his rage gone.

'Sorry pet. Let's forget I said it, yeah?'

Eliza fought the grin that tugged at her lips. She'd done it! She'd completely influenced him. Before, he would lean to her way of thinking, but this time she'd planted an idea in his head and he'd accepted it as his own.

He blinked hard and slumped forward. 'You'd . . . never cheat . . . on me,' he mumbled, his words leaden, as if he was repeating them against his will.

Eliza released the spell. In her own drunkenness, she had risked going too far. He still had reserves of power she was nowhere near tapping. Fortune may favour the brave, but she abandons the dumb fucks who push their luck. Faroust came back to himself. He blinked twice and doubled over, clutching at his skull.

'Fuck!'

'What's wrong?'

'My head feels like it's splitting open.'

He tried to stand up straight but crashed to the floor, gripping his head. He lay there, whimpering in agony, tears streaming down his face.

Panic seized Eliza. He'd know she'd done this to him. She knelt beside him and turned him on his back, lowering his head into her lap.

'Help me, Eliza,' he whispered.

She wiped the tears from his face. 'Shh, sweetheart. I'm here. It'll be all right.' She put her hands on either side of his head and massaged his temples. She closed her eyes, trying to find the damage.

Faroust's mind was carefully protected by his magic. Hers was so similar to his now that it had slipped through almost unnoticed. When his subconscious finally registered the intruder, it was so outraged by how late it had noticed her, it rebelled and attacked with everything it had, despite the fact that the idea had already part-fused with Faroust's brain. That was where the pain was coming from. She couldn't remove the idea now, it was too deeply embedded. She'd do more damage or reveal herself if she tried.

'We need to get you inside.' *Fuck*. She hadn't wanted to hurt him, just avoid a fight.

She held him tight, helping him to his feet. He could barely shuffle towards the apartment. She struggled to balance him and open the door but she managed it. She led him to the bedroom and put him in the bed. She had some super strength painkillers in her toiletry bag, but she had to cradle his head and stroke his throat to help him swallow the pills. He immediately collapsed into sleep.

As he slept, Eliza paced the living room. She was fucked. Royally fucked. She could take the jeep and flee. She still had her secret accounts and credit cards, she could just go. But things would be bad for the Family if she did. Faroust would destroy all of them if need be before he came after her. She would not abandon them. She'd done this, and she would accept the consequences.

Faroust slept through the morning. She was eating lunch and watching a talk show when he finally woke. He looked awful: his complexion was grey, there were dark circles under his eyes and his lips were cracked and dry.

'Hey baby,' she said. 'How are you feeling?'

'Pain's not so bad. I feel as rough as a badger's arse.' His stomach growled. 'And I'm famished.'

Eliza took his hand and led him to the couch.

'Stay here. I'll fix you something nice.'

He ate the chicken soup so slowly it went cold, but he finished it. Some colour returned to his face. She gave him two more pills and he curled up on the couch, his head in her lap. She stroked his hair softly and hummed to him.

'That's nice.' He sighed. 'You're the best, Li-Li.'

'I'm glad you're feeling better. You scared me.'

'I scared me. I've not had a headache like that in a long time.'

'You've had one before?' she asked, struggling to keep her voice light.

'Mm-mm,' he mumbled. 'All the magic in my head gets too much and my brain can't deal with it.' He shifted on the couch and gazed up at Eliza. 'You are so beautiful.' He reached up to take a tendril of pale hair. 'Beautiful Eliza, provider of sex, food and co . . . co . . . cothingumyol.' He chuckled. 'Wow! I feel floaty.'

'Are you a little high?'

'What's in these pills?'

'Magic,' she answered fondly. *Why are you hiding something? Why can't you just be our god, without the Ritual and the horrible secret?*

They sat in companionable silence while the TV shrieked about DNA tests and child support.

'I could stay here forever,' he said happily. 'We need grapes. A god's concubine should feed him grapes.'

'Concubine? So I am your whore?' She could have wept with relief. By the time Faroust stopped buzzing from the painkillers he'd never realise she'd caused his pain.

'Ah, but you're not a whore.' His words slurred.

'Really? How so?'

'You . . . you don't get paid!' Faroust howled with laughter at his own joke. Eliza dug her fingers under his armpit and tickled him mercilessly. He shrieked as her fingers tortured him.

'No! Stop!' He rolled away from her and landed on the floor with a thud.

'No more of those pills for you, lightweight.'

Faroust climbed back up the furniture to her. 'You're mean,' he slurred. 'Wow! Those are strong.' He kissed her sloppily. 'Come to bed.'

'Drugged and horny. Should be interesting.'

Faroust got to his feet and attempted to pull Eliza up. He lost his balance and they tumbled back to the sofa.

Faroust kissed her again. Half-cut and hard, his guard was down and the stream of images returned. Each time she caught a glimpse, they left her more confused and she learned nothing of those trapped in the Veil. The god they revealed was a kind and gentle god, so far removed from the beast of the Ritual.

Through his memories, she watched him protect his people. Wars broke out around them, again and again over the centuries. Their god used the mist to protect them. He never spilt a drop of blood in anger. He was loved and adored by the tribe. He healed their animals, made their children strong and brave, taught them how to control their magic, gave them rules for how to interact with the *Gnáth*, protected their crops and ensured that they were safe. He loved these people. He'd do anything for them. Even the Ritual was different. It was only ever the blood of a willing sacrifice. He extended this kindness to the Slave who stole his essence, welcomed the slaves as members of the Family and eased their transition into the fold.

She was torn by these images. He had been so kind and loving. The way he was with her was the way he'd always been with his people. When had that changed? When did he become the cruel beast that thrived on rape and blood? When had love stopped being his sustenance? She knew the stories well and she could take a guess at when it happened. It would have been when the Church attacked them, nearly a thousand years ago . . .

The Church was taking control of Ireland. The pockets of the old religions were dying out and the Fae returning to the Otherworld. Their old magic and charm could not stand up to the promises of the man from Galilee. Only Faroust and the Family remained, shrouded in the mist. As the centuries passed, other people came closer and closer to the tribe. They began to draw attention as they went about their daily business. The decision was made that they would assimilate themselves with the ordinary people of the world around them. They sold produce in the market, drank in the taverns and attended the local church. They were well behaved and kept to themselves; they were even baptised.

For years no one took much notice of them. It was only when pestilence, famine and war came that things changed. These people were never ill, they never lost a mother or infant in childbirth, in times of need they prospered when all else failed. They were generous with their good fortune, but their generosity only brought more suspicion. Finally, they were accused of consorting with the Devil.

The First-Father dealt with it quickly, making those who suspected them of evil forget the Family had ever existed. They retreated to their own village and did not risk more contact than was necessary. But one day, missionaries followed the men home after a hunt. They wanted to build a church and allocate a priest to the village. The elders pointed to the altar in a hut and said a priest visited them to enable their worship and the missionaries went on their way.

Thinking they were safe, the Family prepared for the Ritual. Faroust, forever young and strong, stood in front of his children, said the words and selected his sacrifice. How were they to know that the Bishop, determined these people would have a 'proper' church, saw the fires burning in the hills and marched towards them with his guard? That he would reach the village just as Faroust performed the bloodletting?

The Bishop ordered his men to attack, to slaughter these devil worshippers. Their magic was powerful, but they were unprepared, and they were no match for the steel. Half of them were cut down before anyone could cast a spell. Faroust leapt forward to save them. The Ritual was not complete, but he was still stronger than any demon the Bishop could imagine. He threw his hands on the ground and the earth plunged down, taking everyone with it, Bishop, soldiers and all. Faroust sealed the hole, creating the cavern where the Ritual was performed now. No one came for the lost bishop and it was not long before the Family could return to the world above.

But their god was different. His rescue of them, before the ceremony had been completed, had drained him of his power. It was why he diminished to a corpse every year and why he needed more from them. Why more blood was needed. Why virginity was needed.

Even as a child, Eliza had felt this story was a lie. She did not believe a god who could hide his people at will and kill armies with a wave of his hand would have been so damaged by this relatively minor act of magic. It was not a myth or an exaggeration, but an outright lie. It was a clumsy story and she knew something was hidden. It *had* to be linked to what was happening in the Veil . . .

'Liza! You're miles away. Pay attention to me.'

She snapped back to the god. Faroust sat back on his heels and pouted. He lost his balance and toppled over on the floor.

'Seriously, no more drugs for you.' She helped him to his feet. 'You have to drink gallons of booze to get pissed, but two tiny pills and you're anyone's.'

He smiled and gathered her against him. 'You are incredible.'

'All right,' she said. 'Back to bed for you I think.'

She pulled away from him but he grabbed her and held her tight. 'You are!' he insisted, his voice suddenly serious and sober. 'You are the most incredible woman I have ever met.' He kissed her hard and she felt his heart beating so hard and fast she knew that his feelings for her went far beyond desire.

'What are you smiling about?'

'You have feelings for me. I'm not just a sex toy,' she teased.

'Maybe. But don't tell anyone.'

'I can't. You sealed me.'

'Oh yeah,' he chuckled.

Eliza took his hand and firmly led him back to bed. He passed out as soon as his head hit the pillow. She could spend the rest of the day with Cornelius now. Well, what Faroust didn't know wasn't going to hurt him, was it?

She crept through the apartment, taking care not to disturb him. If he woke, she couldn't go upstairs. She took off her house slippers and popped them in the box by the study. She hesitated. It irritated her that she wasn't allowed in there. If it was only financial stuff, stuff she already knew, then there was no reason to lock her out. She tried the door. The handle didn't turn. Where were his keys?

They weren't in the kitchen or the living room, which meant they were in the bedroom somewhere. She cursed under her breath. Maybe she could pick the lock? Cornelius had given her a set of picks; it would be a good opportunity to practise. She knelt and wiggled the first pick in. It snapped and pinged across the carpet. Fuck. It had seemed so easy when she'd stolen the skill from Cornelius. Maybe she needed to practise the practical skills a little more? The second pick broke, slicing her finger.

'Son of a bitch.'

Faroust stirred in the bedroom and she gave it up. Today was not the day she would get the study to give up its secrets. She frowned at the door as if she could intimidate it into opening. It stayed defiantly closed.

'You win this round, door,' she muttered, sucking her bleeding finger. She turned and caught her reflection in the mirror. Slowly, a thought began to unfurl in her mind. *That could work. If I'm careful, that could work.*

She sat cross-legged, opposite the door, ready to project through it. After the last time, she didn't like to risk powerful magic in the apartment, but the situation called for it. She had to find out what he was hiding. She closed her eyes and focused on her breathing. In moments, her soul was standing in front of the door. She pushed her fingers through the door and waited. Nothing happened. The room wasn't alarmed. She made her way in to the study.

She floated over to the computer. Cornelius believed electronics were always the best place to start. She put her hand on the mouse and it went through the desk. She tried again and the same thing happened. She tried to pick up a pen but her fingers slipped through it. Bollocks.

'Okay, so I can't pick things up. What can I do?' She walked around the room, searching for inspiration. She winced and reeled as she circled, feeling uncomfortable. What was that? An aura? She moved forwards, searching it out. It was growing worse, deepening from discomfort into grief and sadness. She reached out, trying to work out where it was coming from. Suddenly, red filled her vision and she flew backwards. Her soul reconnected with her body and she slammed back onto the floor.

'Ow,' she whimpered. 'What the fuck was that?'

She sat up, rubbing the back of her head. Her stomach roiled and acid burned the back of her throat. Whatever it was, there was definitely something Faroust was hiding in there. And it was big. That level of pain, that kind of violence as it pushed her away, confirmed it. She got to her feet. She needed to get into that study. Maybe Cornelius could . . . the seal on her back tingled and she slapped the thought down. She needed his help but she'd have to be careful in how she explained it to him. One way or another, she was getting in.

Chapter 20

AFTER FAROUST'S HEADACHE, Eliza refrained from trying to influence him so brazenly. The incident made her aware of a change in her that she didn't like; she was easily aggravated, smug, self-important and arrogant. Even now, as Cornelius explained how to avoid detection when taking photographs, she could feel herself sneering. Did he never shut up? She fucking got it. Find cover and use the long lens.

'Eliza, are you listening?'

'Nope.'

He frowned at her. 'Don't be rude.'

'Don't be rude,' she mimicked. *What is wrong with you? Stop it.*

Cornelius tilted his head to one side. 'Mind yourself.'

'What are you going to do if I don't?'

His nostrils flared as he tried to stare her out. She refused to back down. Suddenly, he lunged for her. She shrieked in protest as he dragged her across his knee.

'What the fuck are you . . . ow!' she squawked as his hand connected with her bottom. 'Cornelius, stop it! They'll hear you.'

She tried to wiggle away but he gripped her waist tighter, throwing one leg over hers to keep her in place. His hand came down again and again, the slaps echoing around his office. She dug her nails into his leg, a futile attempt to force him to let her go; he just hit her harder.

'Stop! You're hurting me.'

This wasn't a little rough foreplay. She'd really pissed him off, and he was punishing her.

Finally, he released her. She scrambled up and away from him. Her face burned as hot as her backside. Anger boiled in her belly, her fingers curling into fists.

'You are to stay away from me until you remember your manners.'

'Fuck you. You're not my Dom,' she snapped, turning on her heel. His new laptop whirred happily on the desk by the door. Before she realised what she was doing, she picked it up and smashed it on the floor. It disintegrated into shards of plastic.

'Oh shit!' Cornelius leapt to his feet. She darted away in terror. Luckily, Tim was working in the main office and Cornelius wouldn't be able to chase her. She was safe. For now.

Embarrassed by her behaviour, she drove straight to Dublin to buy him a replacement. She groaned when the sales assistant told her it was going to be €6000 but she swallowed the cost. It was the least she could do. She waited until lunchtime, when the main office would be empty, tied it up with a bow and brought it to his office. The door was locked. She knocked but there was no answer.

'Cornelius? I brought you a present.'

She was met by silence. She knocked again. No answer. She sighed and rang him. His phone went straight to voicemail. He was ignoring her and she didn't blame her. She fired off a text and left him alone.

It was nearly four o'clock before her phone finally went off.

Help me set it up.

No kiss. Oh dear. She stopped by the kitchen on her way down. Maybe a cooler full of beer and his favourite food would earn his forgiveness?

She made her way through the office, which was unusually empty. Where was everyone? How much trouble was she in if he'd sent everyone away? She knocked on Cornelius' door.

'Hello madam.'

'I bring a peace-offering.' She held up the cooler, and Cornelius took it. He put it down on his desk but did not open it. Instead, he closed the door behind her

'I'm sorry,' she said, twisting her fingers.

'Hmm-hmm.'

'I am. I'm really sorry.'

She stood on tiptoe and he lowered his cheek to her lips.

'What's wrong with you?' he asked, opening the computer box with a flick-knife. 'I've never seen you act like that.'

Eliza took a deep breath and rubbed the back of her neck. 'I think I'm absorbing his personality too. I've been too eager to guzzle down what I can steal. I need to slow down, be more discerning in what I take and when I take it. Because I was able to take from everyone else and remain myself most of the time, I was fooled into thinking it would be the same with him.'

She waited for his reaction, but he didn't give one. 'Aren't you worried about me?'

'Of course I am, but my worry isn't going to help you. I don't fucking understand your magic.'

She crossed the room to him, pressing her chest to his back.

'I think I still have a long way to go to apologise.' She kissed his neck, and her hands slid into the waistband of his trousers. She turned him around and pushed him onto his armchair, scrambling on top of him and holding him down by his arms. He struggled beneath her, his eyes widening as he realised he couldn't move.

'That's new. And very sexy.'

She kissed him, ripping open his shirt.

Cruelty

As Cornelius rubbed his wrists where she'd held him down, he felt his anxiety ease a little. Eliza was getting stronger all the time. She was very good at subterfuge. Faroust hadn't guessed she was taking power from him and nobody was aware of the affair between them. He had trained her well, or at least he was so good at what he did that when she copied his talents from him, she became instantly good at hiding in plain sight. Thinking about it made his head hurt.

'You really will be all right, won't you?'

She smiled at him. 'I should be. I need time to work it out, that's all.' She pulled her jacket back on and frowned. 'Do you know something? Faroust isn't such a bad person. He's not a monster all the time. It's like he's two different people: the god and the man. Part of me wants all this, everything we saw in the Veil, to be wrong.'

Cornelius grabbed her and spun her to face him, his teeth clenched in jealousy.

'Do you have feelings for him?'

'No. Not the way I have feelings for you. I *love* you, body and soul. I . . . I . . .' She struggled for the words, 'I feel compassion for him. I understand how lonely he must be because, despite everything he is to us, he's an outsider. He can't be part of our everyday life because he would never get a moment's peace and eventually, no matter how careful we were, someone would notice him. Spending all that time alone has to affect you, even if you are a god. Maybe that loneliness drove him to terrible cruelty?'

'Maybe,' Cornelius conceded. 'What will you do when you find out what's going on?'

'I have no idea. We'll cross that bridge when we come to it.'

Cornelius snorted. 'I like this "we". "We'll" have to cross that bridge, "we" are breaking all the rules, "we" are blaspheming.

Seems to me *you're* doing all of these things and I have no choice.'

She raised her shoulders and gave him a massive, over bright grin, like a cartoon character pretending to be innocent.

'I have to go soon, baby. I have a prisoner to interrogate.'

As she pulled away he saw in her in a new light. She had a purpose now and that purpose made her strong. Her existence was no longer about survival; it was about protection, protecting everyone she loved from a hideous fate, from an afterlife trapped in limbo. She was a warrior defending them against the dark god who had been abusing them.

He drew her back to him.

'You're going to be in this for the long haul.'

'Are you going to dump me again?'

'No. I'm trying to tell you that I'll stand beside you, whatever happens. I have something for you. Close your eyes.'

Eliza smiled, covering her eyes with her hands as he twisted away.

'You can open them now.'

He held out a delicate silver chain with a twisting infinity symbol in the middle. It looped like a figure of eight, with no end and no beginning.

'I saw it last week,' he said, as she took it from his fingers. 'I've been waiting for the right time to give it to you. It's not as fancy as your watch . . .'

'I love it!' Her voice caught as she pulled off the watch and replaced it with the bracelet. She kissed him hard, wrapping her arms around him and holding him tight.

'I'm never taking it off,' she promised when they came up for air.

'I am yours forever,' he said. 'I will walk with you on this path, no matter how long it takes.'

'I love you,' she said. 'To the end of time and space. Is there anything you need me to do while you take care of your prisoner?'

'You could check how well the phylacteries are working. I've coded the spell into the computer but I'm not sure how effective it is compared to telepathy. Make notes on the results, compare them to the telepathy notes and enter it into the database.'

She grinned. 'That's a big job. You'll be done with your chore long before I finish.'

'Well, you'll just have to stay here until it gets finished. It's essential work. I'll be back later to supervise you.'

'How on earth do you make data input sound sexy?'

'Just talented, I guess. You'd best get started; it really is a big job.'

At midnight, Eliza stumbled down to Faroust. The programme Cornelius had created to track the Family phylacteries was a brilliant idea, but translating a telepathic spell to a computerised algorithm was hard going. Eventually, she finished her analysis on the test subjects and was able to help Cornelius negate the minor flaws in the programme. Traditionally, those capable of telepathy would be used to track Family members if necessary, but it was an exhausting process for the sensitive and could easily be disrupted. The computer programme would be far more efficient, but all those tests and numbers hurt her head.

She raised her left arm to open the door and realised she wasn't wearing her watch. She fumbled in her pocket and snapped it on, hiding Cornelius' infinity bracelet. She needn't have worried; Faroust was asleep on the sofa. She breathed a sigh of relief. If he'd been awake he'd have wanted sex and she was too tired to play with him properly. He'd pout if she refused him, and she wasn't in the mood for pouting gods. She tip-toed to the study and tried the door. It was still locked.

She got ready for bed. Faroust was out for the count. Not even the toilet flushing disturbed him. Eliza took off all her jewellery, apart from the bracelet, and settled in the bed. She was exhausted and within a few moments she was asleep.

When Faroust woke, it took him a moment to realise he was in the living room. He yawned and stretched as he headed to the bedroom. The sight of Eliza peacefully sleeping in his bed made him smile. Weeks had passed without her having a nightmare. She seemed brighter and happier. He flattered himself that he was aiding her recovery.

His heart swelled as he contemplated her. A man, or a god for that matter, could easily lose himself in her. He loved having her here, having a life with her, loved waking up beside her every morning. She was truly special, more than a bed mate, more than a consort. She was his lover in every sense of the word. She brought colour and laughter with her, understanding and compassion, passion and joy. In the few months she'd been down here, she'd made him happy.

Taking care not to wake her, he got into bed. He wrapped himself around her and she rolled over in her sleep, snuggling against him. He kissed her forehead and ran his hand up her left arm, concerned as he felt the bracelet. This was something different, something new. His probing fingers felt the looping infinity symbol, and anger swelled in his breast. He sat up abruptly, dislodging and waking her.

'What's wrong?' She yawned, rubbing her eyes.

'Who bought you that bracelet?' he demanded.

'I did,' she said. 'It made me think of you and the Family, how we are all bound together in a never-ending loop.'

'That's all right then.'

'Who did you think bought it?'

He said nothing, but his face grew hot.

'For fuck's sake, Faroust! I've had enough of this. There's only so many times I can tell you Cornelius and I are over. You either trust me or you don't!'

'Mind your mouth,' he warned. 'I am still your god.'

'Yes Sir, no Sir, three bags fucking full, Sir,' Eliza muttered, rolling away from him and wrapping herself up in the duvet.

Faroust leapt on her, digging his fingers into her sides. She screamed and kicked as he tickled her.

'Stop it! Stop it!' she howled. 'I'll wet myself!'

'Then you can clean it up!' He rolled her onto her back, still tickling her. She snatched at his hands but he pulled them away to continue his assault.

'Please stop!' she half-sobbed, half-laughed.

He released her. She groaned and rolled over, holding her sides.

'You're mean.'

'And you're cheeky. We're going to Prague this weekend.'

'Won't it be cold?'

'It's nearly spring.'

'It's the third of February!'

'So dress warm.'

Faroust pulled her into his arms and she pressed herself against him, her hands flat on his chest. He always felt so warm and calm when she touched him, as if she could touch his soul. He yawned and surrendered to sleep.

Spring gave way to a wet summer and Eliza grew impatient with her mission. No matter how she probed and searched, the truth about the Church eluded her. Faroust's memories revealed his kindness or his brutality, but there was nothing showing the transition. It was as if there was a gap where the memory should be. What could be so awful that he'd put a barrier around it, even in his own head? What had he done? What was he hiding?

'Eliza! Toast!' Faroust snapped, charging across the kitchen.

'Shit, sorry. I was daydreaming.'

'I can see that.' He frowned as she threw the blackened toast in the bin. 'The place is going to stink for days.'

'It's only toast. Put the extractor fan on and it'll be grand. The smell will be gone before you know it.'

Faroust grumbled to himself as she set about making more breakfast. She turned too quickly and knocked his coffee cup with her elbow. It fell and smashed, splashing hot liquid on him.

'For fuck's sake Eliza. What is wrong with you today?'

'I'm sorry.' She sighed as she sank to the floor to pick up the pieces. 'Pass me a cloth.'

He threw it down at her. The toast popped up and he snatched it, not even bothering to butter it before he made his way to the back. She chased him.

'Wait.'

He turned and slammed into her. The toast fell from his hand and landed on the carpet. He glared at her.

'What?' he asked through gritted teeth.

'You gardening today?'

'Yeah, I've got a tonne to do. Roses need sorting, and the hydrangeas. Don't make that face.'

'What face?'

'The 'I fucking hate hydrangeas' face. I grew those from seed a hundred and fifty years ago.'

She wished she'd never said anything about the damn hydrangeas. He was so protective of them.

'You going to be out all day?'

'As long as the rain holds off. I've got to go to the garden centre in Coolock later for a few bits and pieces. Make sure you clean up. Properly. I don't want any coffee stains on my cabinets. Or crumbs on the carpet.'

'Yes, boss.'

A few moments later, the door of the lodge slammed. She stuck her tongue out and flipped a V at the study door.

As Eliza loaded the dishwasher, she heard a loud click, and a creaking sound behind her. She turned, expecting to see Faroust in the doorway of his study. But he wasn't. He'd left the door unlocked and hadn't shut it properly.

Eliza's heart leapt. This was it. She could find the source of that pain. She could find out what he was hiding.

Hold your horses. He might realise and come back. Give him five minutes. She forced herself to be patient.

It was closer to ten minutes, and he had not returned, when she sprang from her seat and pushed open the door to the study. Faroust's neatness would help her; she could quickly discard the precisely labelled shelves of read-outs, stock portfolios and contracts. Personal stuff had to be in the desk. She sat down and pulled open the top drawer.

Her phone rang in her pocket, shattering the silence.

'What are you doing?' Cornelius hissed.

'You scared me.'

'What are you doing? I can see you on my screen.'

She looked through the open door and waved at the camera in the kitchen.

'Behave.'

'He never leaves the door open. There's something in here that carries a lot of emotion. It might be useful. I'm trying to find it.' She winced as the seal burned. She hadn't even said it was connected to Faroust. Bloody thing was getting stronger and she couldn't always override it.

'Have you?'

'No.'

'Then get out.'

She opened another drawer. Nothing but plant care instructions. She sat back in the chair.

'Help me.'

'Check the computer. There might be something on it.'

She wiggled the mouse and the unit woke up. 'I don't even know what I'm looking for,' she said.

'Yes you do. Internet history, photos, porn.'

'Gross.' She switched him to speaker and clicked through Faroust's files. 'Nothing jumps out at me.'

'Does he have any filing cabinets?'

She rifled through the unlocked drawers. More documents, but the bottom drawer was locked. *A locked drawer in a locked room.*

'Eliza?'

'I found something. I need a key. Do you have eyes on the back gate?'

'You're clear. Check under the desk, look for envelopes. He might have stuck it under something.'

She opened each drawer, checking top and bottom for a hidden key. She crawled under the desk and felt around, but there was nothing.

'Eliza, it's started raining.

He'd be back in soon. Where else would be hide a key?

'He's walking across the grass. Coming your way.'

She needed to get into that drawer. Where the Hell would he put the key? She closed her eyes, put herself in Faroust's shoes. He'd have put it somewhere he thought was really clever. She felt the grin stretch across her face. The broken mug. In the kitchen. At the back of the cupboard.

'Eliza?'

'Two minutes. I know where the key is.'

She raced to the kitchen. The mug was a little chintzy thing, a cheap souvenir, but he refused to throw it out. She lifted it out of the cupboard and turned it over; the key was stuck to the bottom. She rushed back to the cabinet.

'Where is he?'

'I can't see him!'

A door slammed above her, followed by heavy footsteps.

'He's inside,' she whispered.

'Eliza, leave it.'

'No.'

She knelt by the drawer. The key fitted but the lock was stiff. She swore as it caught, wriggling and twisting the key until the drawer burst open.

A mahogany box, like a treasure chest, lay in the bottom of the drawer. A breeze curled around her and she gasped. Faroust had opened the door. She lifted the box from the drawer, wiggled the key out of the lock and grabbed her phone.

'I got it. I'm coming up.'

She switched off the monitor and closed the study door behind her, moving as quietly as she could. She sprinted through the apartment and out into the Ritual room, clutching the box to her chest, her heart thumping.

Cornelius sat at his desk, his leg jiggling anxiously.

'That was too close. What did you find?'

Eliza held out her prize triumphantly and Cornelius took it from her.

'What is it?'

'No fucking idea.'

It rattled when he shook it. Eliza took it from him and put it down on his desk. It was a beautiful thing, a seamless piece of carpentry. It didn't even have a lock.

'Isn't this going to hurt you?'

'Technically, I'm not telling you anything. We're discovering it together.'

'You clever thing. How do we open it?'

'There has to be a trick.' She ran her fingers over it, trying to find a release or a button. She picked it up and turned it over, running her fingers over the engraving of the Family crest.

'It was upside down?' Cornelius chuckled.

'Shut up. I wonder . . .' She pressed each of the roses in the order she would to open Faroust's front door. The lid opened with a soft sigh.

Her phone shrieked in her pocket, making them both jump. It was Faroust.

'Eliza, were you in my study?'

'No.'

'Are you sure?'

'I know where I've been. I wasn't in your study. Why? What's wrong?'

'It was unlocked.'

'I didn't go in your study. I'm not an idiot. I know what out of bounds means.'

She heard him suck his teeth as he pondered the puzzle. 'I must have forgotten to lock it. I'm going to the garden centre. I'll see you later.'

'Bye.' She switched the phone to silent, ignoring Cornelius' look of disbelief. 'Do you have gloves?'

He handed them to her. She pulled them on and sat down at his desk. She took hold of the lid and opened the box.

She reeled as a rush of pain came over her, like the time she'd projected into the study. Her head hurt and her heart grew heavy.

'Shit. Can you feel that aura?' Cornelius said. 'There's a lot of pain in this box.'

Eliza shook her head to clear the bad feelings. There were envelopes inside the box, all carefully labelled and numbered.

'We have to put these back *exactly* as we found them. If he looks at this box, he'll know instantly if anything is out of place.' She lifted the first envelope. 'Are those dates?'

Cornelius shook his head. 'I don't know.'

She opened the packet and delicately slipped the contents out. Dozens of letters landed in her hands.

'Holy shit,' she breathed. 'Cornelius, look at the date.'

'1563? It can't be that old.'

'Look at the signature.'

Cornelius' eyes widened as he focused on the bottom of the page.

'No way. That isn't . . .'

'It is. That's Elizabeth the First's signature. The Virgin Queen was writing to Faroust. She even called him by his name.'

'She wasn't a virgin. Not according to this.'

'There are loads of them. Oh, my word. Some of these are really graphic . . .'

Eliza handed the letters to Cornelius who carefully placed them back in order.

'More love letters. Oh . . .' She laughed.

'What?'

'Lizzy wasn't the only one getting hot and heavy with our Faroust. Look.'

Cornelius' eyebrows shot up. 'Oh, oh my. The Earl of Oxford. That was more than I needed to know.'

They sorted through the other envelopes. There were literally hundreds of love letters, a few portraits and love tokens from men and women.

'Busy boy. You might want to get yourself checked out,' Cornelius said. Eliza elbowed him. 'What? Is there anything else?'

'We're on the last packet. It's a big one.'

'What's the date?' he asked.

'1845-1852'

'Oh joy. Potato famine.'

The last packet was thick and heavy. Eliza's fingers hurt as she picked it up. Her heart tightened and her throat stung.

'You all right?'

'I want to cry. It's this packet. All the pain is in this one.' She reached inside the envelope and pulled out a bundle of papers.

Unlike all the others, these had not been sorted through. Grief clung to them like ivy to an ancient building. They were tied with a tattered blue ribbon. Eliza hesitated. None of the others had any information on what she was looking for. This one wasn't likely to have anything either. Still, it might provide a clue. There was no point going back now. She took a deep breath and untied the ribbon.

Papers, letters and photographs scattered across the table. Cornelius searched through the pile.

'Death certificates?'

'Oh, Cornelius. This is awful. Look.' She handed him the letter she was holding.

'*Mr Laverty, I write this missive with a heavy heart. It is my sad duty to inform you that your wife, Mary, and your children, Aoife and Stephen have died. There was an accident, a fire . . .* oh God.'

Eliza picked up a photograph. It was Faroust, with a woman and two small children, as dark as he was. A family. He had married and had a family. She picked up another letter.

'*My darling husband, how we miss you. Aoife loves the hydrangea (is that how you spell it?) although of course she can't say it.*' She threw down the paper and took the certificates off Cornelius. 'Six and four. His children were six and four. And all those hydrangeas are for them. Oh God, and I said I hated them.'

Cornelius gathered up the letters and documents, tied them up and put them away.

'We should take these back. They're not helpful to us. Eliza, he's still the monster of the Ritual. These letters don't prove anything. Other than that he betrayed us again. Come on, we'll take it back. I'll have a look at his computer.'

Eliza nodded. Cornelius was right. These letters were proof he had not been their faithful god. Still, her heart twisted for those young lives cut short.

They waited until Cornelius' monitors showed Jacob's office was empty. They hastened down the path to the apartment. Eliza opened the door.

'Faroust? Are you there?'

There was no answer. She searched the apartment to make sure he was gone. She knocked on the study and tried the door. It was locked. She waved Cornelius in.

'Can you pick the lock?'

'What kind of assassin would I be if I couldn't pick a lock?'

He crouched, pulling out a set of picks. In a few moments the door swung open.

'He needs a better lock,' he said.

'You sound like you want it to be difficult.'

'A man can want a challenge.'

'Maybe his computer will offer you one?'

Eliza wiggled the key in the lock of the filing cabinet and sealed the box of memories away as Cornelius tapped away on the computer.

'Come on.'

'Two ticks. I just need to upload this . . . done. I now have access to everything he has, and everything he will ever create or look at on this machine. I'll have a look later.'

He turned off the monitor and moved the seat back to where he'd found it. They left the study and Cornelius fiddled with the lock as Eliza returned the keys to the broken mug. She turned but Cornelius was no longer by the study door.

'Cornelius? What the fuck are you doing? Where are you?'

'In the bathroom. It's nice down here. But it's all so sterile. I have a weird desire to touch everything.'

'Well don't. Come on.'

'Oh dear Lord. It's all alphabetised. Even his shampoo.'

Eliza charged down the corridor and grabbed his arm. 'You're such a messer. Come on.' She dragged him through the apartment. He stopped when they reached the kitchen.

'Please let me move something. Or let me lick the fridge.'

'Lick the fridge? What is wrong with you?'

'Ah come on. Let me mess with something. We could screw in his bed.'

She slapped him on the chest. 'No.'

'Well, I'm desecrating something.' He pulled away from her and opened one of the cupboards.

'What are you doing?'

'Turning a spice jar. Just one. And I'm taking an elephant.'

'Don't. He'll go spare.'

'It's not like I stole his girlfriend.'

Eliza fought the laugh bubbling in her throat and lost.

'You're an idiot.'

'I'm your idiot.'

She wrapped her arm around his waist and pulled him out of the door.

'That missing elephant will drive him bonkers.'

'Good.' Cornelius sucked his teeth. 'I'm going to put it on my desk and throw things at it.'

Chapter 21

ELIZA TURNED OVER and pulled the pillow over her head. What was that noise? It buzzed at the bottom of her skull, disrupting her sleep. She pushed the pillow against her ear but it didn't muffle the sound.

'What's that noise?' she asked Faroust. But there was no answer. He wasn't in bed with her.

The clock told her it was one-thirty. She swore; her alarm was set for half-past four. The security team, split into two, was scheduled for a week of training days and she was helping Cornelius run them. It meant a pre-dawn trip to Connemara to make the most of their training time. Faroust had been furious when she told him. They'd argued for hours before he gave in. Was he waking her up on purpose?

The apartment was in darkness. She swept through each room, irritation giving way to confusion. Faroust wasn't in the apartment, and nothing was turned on that could be making that infuriating noise. She even checked the phones were properly in their cradles.

She walked towards the entrance to the Ritual chamber. The buzzing grew louder as she made her way up the passage. What the Hell was going on? She pressed the release button, but the door stayed shut. She pressed it again and kicked the stubborn door, yelping as her big toe cracked against the stone.

Eliza limped back down the passageway and settled on the sofa. What was Faroust doing? The buzzing continued; there was no way she'd get back to sleep now. Once the pain in her toe eased, she headed to the study. It was locked, as it always was.

'Oh for fuck's sake! What if there was a fire?' *Think, Eliza. What could he be hiding?*

There was nothing in the Ritual chamber . . . Nothing but the Veil. What else could it be? He had never locked her in before. He had to be accessing the Veil. This was the perfect opportunity to investigate further. Luckily, being locked in wasn't a problem, not with Eliza's particular set of skills.

She hurried back into the bedroom and jumped into bed. She might need to drag her soul back to her body in a hurry. She closed her eyes and forced herself to slow her breathing.

She felt her body drift towards sleep and managed to pull her mind away from the offer of oblivion. There was a faint pop as her mind separated from her body, and she was projecting.

Eliza looked down at her sleeping form. She leaned over the body, which was apparently lost in sleep. She looked so innocent, but that was a lie. When had she last been truly innocent? When she'd been fifteen? Twelve? Younger?

She needed to move. Faroust could return at any moment.

Eliza swept soundlessly through the apartment, moving as easily in her astral form as she could in her physical one. She floated up the passage to the Ritual Chamber, passing through the doorway to the worship space like a ghost. The buzzing that had irritated her when she was in her body mellowed to a babble of voices. Turning the corner, she saw the glow of the Veil. She retreated to the shadows, edging around the cavern under cover of darkness. She hadn't seen Faroust yet, and she certainly didn't want him to see her.

She didn't have to look far to find him. He sat in front of the doorway, hugging his knees, staring into the golden light. Eliza frowned. Was he crying? She darted to another dark alcove to get a better look at him, and realised he wept soundlessly, plump tears rolling unheeded down his cheeks.

Even with her soul so far from her body, she felt her world spin. Had she been wrong? Had the Veil played a trick on her? Was Faroust pained by the fate of his faithful? If so, why inflict the Ritual? It didn't make any sense. She crept closer to the sad god, to see what he was staring at.

Through the warm glow of the gate, a multi-hued forest sparkled. Amongst the livid purples, blues and acid greens, Fae fluttered, terrifying in their savage beauty. A woman with long green hair flittered across the canopy. Her huge wings were white and powdery, like a moth's. A creature made entirely of black down, like the fur on a bat's belly, lounged against a violently yellow tree, its feathery wings swaying gently in the breeze. It yawned and stretched before standing up. The creature flapped his wings twice before taking off across an azure sky.

There was a giggle and a couple of bare-breasted women danced into view. They looked as if they'd been carved from the wood itself, their skin dappled copper, green and gold. They were being chased by a young, turquoise-haired boy, also naked and carrying a slingshot. He laughed as he shot clumps of mud at the retreating girls.

A pretty woman paused in front of the opening. Her hair was all the colours of autumn, her eyes as onyx black as Faroust's had been the night he lost control. Her skin was pale blue, like the sky before dawn. She seemed aware that someone was watching them, smiling as she realised it was one of their own. She reached out towards him, as if to say 'How did you get out there?'

Faroust rose, discarding his human form. This gentler transformation into his Fae form made him beautiful, rather than terrifying. In the glow from the Veil, Eliza noticed tiny details she'd not seen before. His horns were made from thousands of tiny branches intertwining with each other. Dotted amongst the slender twigs were hundreds of little white flowers. Green-gold skin covered his frame, blooming with green and blue whorls and swirls.

She watched as he extended that long hand with its jet claws towards the woman who beckoned him. But it all changed in a split second. The woman's face fell. She'd spotted something over Faroust's shoulder. Eliza realised it was her. The woman snarled and pulled away from the doorway with a screech. The others heard her panic and followed her.

'Wait!' Faroust called. 'Wait!'

But it was too late. The Faerie folk on the other side were gone. He spun around in frustration, staring into the cavern. Eliza retreated deeper into the shadows, hiding from his searching gaze.

The Veil shifted and pulsed and the light changed. Faroust turned back towards it. Eliza craned to see which Otherworld had opened up. She knew she should return to the safety of her sleeping body but when Anna-Beth's sad, beautiful face came into view she was rooted to the spot. Faroust merely sneered and turned away. Eliza pressed against the wall of the cavern as he swept past. Forgetting she was nothing but spirit, she sank back into the stone of the wall. She launched herself forward, scrabbling from the darkness as she heard the main door of the apartment open and shut. She had only a few minutes before he might get into bed. She hurried over to the Veil, eager to study it while she had the chance.

The Veil pulsed and sparkled in the gloom of the cavern, wordlessly promising answers to her unspoken questions. Tendrils floated out to her, coaxing her forward. They were tempting but reassuring, like the hands of a mother to a stumbling child. Eliza laughed as the tendrils touched her face and hands. She expected the Veil to flow over her again but instead the tendrils tightened about her wrists and throat, grabbing her and jerking her forward, then abruptly shoving her away, so hard she stumbled and fell to the floor. She pushed herself upright and brushed the dust off her hands, cursing softly.

Her second curse was louder, when she realised she was no longer looking *through* the Veil into another world, but instead was *in* the Otherworld, looking back into the cavern. She'd landed in a washed out world fashioned of hard grey dust. The air was stale and fetid, even to her spiritual senses. She felt her body shudder against it.

There was a presence behind her. She looked around, gasping as Anna-Beth's ghostly face appeared, like a reflection of the damned.

'Eliza? Eliza is that you?' The dead girl's face twisted in horror. 'Are you dead? Did he kill you?'

'No. I'm projecting.'

Anna-Beth's grimace deepened. 'You're still alive?' The panic in that plaintive cry chilled Eliza's soul. 'Oh God. Oh God! You can't be here. You have to get away. Only the dead can be here. You need to get out before it realises you're here.'

'Before *what* realises I'm here? Anna-Beth . . .' Eliza stepped forward to take the dead girl's hands.

'No!' Her cousin screamed, snatching them away. 'You can't touch me. You need to get out, now!'

'Anna-Beth, I will leave. Just answer my questions.'

'No time. It's coming. Run. Run!'

'Anna *please!* I need to know what secret you meant.'

'The Church. It's all to do with the Church, Eliza! Go!'

Eliza opened her mouth to ask another question but then she felt it, a deep chill spreading through her. The washed-out world went dark.

'It's too late. It's coming for you.'

In the distance, a shadowy figure moved towards them, towards the gate. Eliza felt her strength drain away from her. Terror rooted her to the spot. It was a creature of great length and size. It raised its head as it moved towards her. Yellow eyes glowed and an evil smile spread across its pointed face. A thousand jagged teeth glinted in the gloom. Eliza knew exactly what it was. Lig-na-Biste, the last great serpent of Ireland, a fire-eating wyrm, guardian of this land of doomed souls.

Deep inside her, she found the strength to turn away and seek escape. She could see the cavern; safety was so close. She tried to run, but she bounced back against an invisible barrier and fell again. Anna-Beth shrieked and crouched on the floor, clutching her head.

She felt rather than heard the laughter of the beast, resonating in her breastbone. She gazed back at the approaching serpent. Its black tongue slipped out and licked its lipless mouth.

'Oh, no fucking way.'

She pushed against the doorway, feeling it stretch and weaken under her touch.

'Come on. Come *on*.' She prayed through gritted teeth.

She could feel Lig-na-Biste getting closer. Suddenly, one hand pushed through the invisible barrier. She took two steps back and ran at the doorway. The beast roared with rage as it realised she was passing through, out of its domain. It charged towards her, snapping at her heels. Eliza crashed through the barrier and tumbled towards the shadows.

Lig-na-Biste's head followed, snarling and biting. Eliza crouched in the gloom, covering her head as the serpent reared to strike. There was a rush of air and a mighty crash, like a storm. Faroust stood in front of the wyrm, his arm raised, blocking a long fang. He was in his Fae form, deadly and beautiful. Eliza felt her stomach contract and her pulse increase despite the danger she was in.

Focus, Eliza!

'Explain yourself.' His voice was so quiet and cold, it caused Eliza's sleeping body, as far away as it was, to goose-pimple.

'Máistir. Bhí cailín. Tá cailín beo. Bhí sí ag caint le ceann de na anamacha!'

Faroust leaned in, scorn written all over his face. 'A girl broke in through the Veil and was speaking to a soul? You think I wouldn't have noticed?'

'Tá sé fíor. Chonaic mó léi . . . aaaaaaaah!' The serpent cried out as the god punched the top of its head.

'Shut up!'

'Tá sí taobh thiar duit!'

'Behind me?'

Eliza's heart faltered. There was no way she could make it back before he saw her.

'Master!' Anna-Beth's voice rang out through the open doorway. Faroust whipped round to face the girl.

'You dare speak to me?'

'Sorry, Master,' the girl mumbled. She was obviously stalling for time as Eliza got up. 'I just wanted . . .'

'Yes?' Faroust growled.

'I just wanted to tell you that we love you, Master.'

Faroust chuckled. 'Of course you do. Now be a good girl and tell me something. Was there a girl here? A living girl?'

Anna-Beth frowned and shook her head. Faroust glared at the cowering serpent.

'Thought not. Off you go.'

The spirit curtseyed and moved away.

Eliza fled.

Chapter 22

ELIZA STIFLED A yawn as she and Cornelius sat in the field where the security team training was taking place.

'I told you to get some rest,' he said, as she poured another cup of coffee. 'Caffeine is no replacement for rest. Jack,' he broke off to yell at one of his team, 'I can see you! You should have gone to bed at a decent time.'

'I did. Faroust woke me in the wee hours. And he made me this flask of coffee in the morning.'

Cornelius spat out the mouthful he'd taken and handed back the cup.

'What's wrong with you?'

'This is sex-coffee. I do not wish to drink Faroust's sex-coffee.'

'It is not sex-coffee. There was a . . .' she hesitated, 'a disturbance in the force last night and he woke me up as he was sorting it out. This is apology-coffee.'

The Cruel smiled, that toe curling smile she loved so much. 'I can drink apology-coffee.'

They sat in companionable silence for a while, watching the security team hone their ability to hide in plain sight.

'What caused the disturbance?' he asked.

Eliza stared into the middle distance, avoiding eye contact.

'Well,' she said, 'I'm pretty sure I did.'

Cornelius went still, his knuckles white as he clutched the plastic mug. Eliza was suddenly nervous in a way she had not been around him in a long time.

'What?' That one word, uttered so soft and low, made Eliza's skin goose-pimple and her mouth go dry. She couldn't answer him.

His sudden movement made her flinch.

'Guys!' he called. 'We're done for the day!'

A dozen members of the security team popped into view.

'Go back to the hotel and wait for your next instructions.' He turned to Eliza. 'You, get in my car.'

Eliza's heart sank. He'd finished three hours early. Normally she could jolly him out of his bad humour, like she'd done with the computer. But she hadn't broken something as trivial as a laptop. She'd played with the most dangerous object in the universe. Cornelius watched the others drive off before he got into the car beside her. She opened her mouth to speak but he held up a finger.

'Not one word.'

They drove in silence for half an hour until Cornelius pulled up outside a tiny whitewashed cottage, pretty as a postcard. He indicated for her to get out and she obliged, fear growing in her stomach. What was he going to do? He opened the door and dragged her inside. Unlike the safe house in Lucan, this place was immaculate. The rough walls were a brilliant white while the wooden floors gleamed. Cornelius steered her through the tiny hallway into the living room.

There was fireplace in the centre of the back wall where a blackened kettle hung. A dresser stood beside it, full to the brim with books and ornaments, rather than the dishes the original inhabitants of the cottage would have used it for.

She wandered towards the back window while he fussed with locking the front door. She gasped at the view. The cottage was close to a body of water so navy blue that all other blues seemed washed out and faded in comparison. In the distance, mountains gently rolled up and sank back down like the curves of a woman. It was almost like the Faerie world she had seen through the Veil, lush and alive and vibrant, despite the purple thunder clouds in the distance.

And yet it was so still, like a painting or a photograph. She felt its haunting loneliness. The blues, greys and purples of the mountains, the sky and the water reminded her of bruises. It was rugged. It was beautiful. And utterly remote from all civilisation. She understood why Cornelius had brought them here. The remote and savage beauty of Connemara would protect them while they trained, but also challenge their current skills.

'It's beautiful, isn't it?'

Cornelius' interruption into her reverie made her jump. He took her hand and led her to the sofa, comfortable and soft. She noticed there was no television in here. No phone either that she could see. He lit the fire. Even though it was June, it was an Irish June and she imagined this little cottage could get very cold.

Cornelius sat on the coffee table opposite her, his face deadly serious.

'I need you to tell me what happened,' he said.

The words tumbled out in a rush as she told her tale, leaving no room for him to interrupt her. The words filled the void left by his unresponsive rage, at least for a short while, but now her tale was done and the void was back, huge and silent and terrifying.

Cornelius stared at her for a long time, immobilised by terror. Eliza scooted off the couch and knelt in front of him.

'Don't look at me like that,' she said.

'Like what?'

'Like I'm a creature from a different world and you're trying to work out if killing me is a good idea or not.'

'Do you have any idea how fucking stupid that was? Anything could have happened to you. You could have been killed or trapped, or discovered. Then what would we do? All of us who love you? What would happen to us if we lost you again? What would I do if I lost you?'

'I . . . didn't think . . .' she stuttered.

The Cruel stood up abruptly, knocking her backwards.

'No, you didn't. That's your bloody problem, isn't it?' He covered his face with his shaking hands, gathering his strength. 'You're not on a solo mission here. I'm well aware you're the one facing the immediate danger but if it all goes wrong and you get found out, everyone pays the price. What you did was not a risk worth taking. Despite all your stolen magic, you have no idea how to control, or protect yourself from, the Veil. You went for the glory. That was selfish. Utterly selfish.'

He spat that last word at her as he sat back down.

'I'm sorry,' she began. 'I . . . I just . . . just . . .' Tears slid down her face, and then all at once she gave way and collapsed on the sofa, sobbing uncontrollably.

Cornelius watched dispassionately, letting the crying fit run its course before he offered her a box of tissues. He nudged her arm with it and sat down beside her. She was calming down, taking little gulps of air, rather than actually crying. He pulled down her hands and shoved a tissue into her face.

'Blow.'

She shot him an indignant look before she threw the used tissue into the fire, ripped another from the box and dried her face with it. She took a deep breath and sniffed as her equilibrium returned.

'You're an arsehole,' she said, pulling away from him.

'Ah now, there's no need to call me names. My job is to protect the Family, from all threats. Let me finish,' he said, seeing her open her mouth to protest. 'You have amassed a great amount of power in a short time. And due to our secret and incredibly dangerous mission, there's no way to adequately train you. Nevertheless, you have a responsibility to the rest of us not to get caught out. If you slip up, everyone suffers for your mistake.' He took told of her hands, which were shredding the damp tissue. 'Look at me, baby. I need to protect you as best I can during your mission, because that way I protect everyone. It's my responsibility as the Cruel, as a member of the Family, as your lover and the man who made you blossom.'

Eliza looked away from him as fresh tears began to well up.

'I thought it was too good an opportunity to miss,' she whispered.

'I don't doubt your intentions, just your method. It was reckless.'

'Not selfish?'

He chuckled and pulled her into his arms.

'You really don't like that word, do you? No, not selfish exactly. Reckless, which is pretty damn close.'

He wiped a smudge of mascara from her cheek.

'You're mean.' She sniffed. 'Did you have to shout? You couldn't speak to me like a human being? '

'Some would say I'm cruel. But in the long run you'll understand I did it to be kind.' He whistled a few bars of 'Cruel to be Kind'. She glared at him.

'You're not funny.'

'Pretty sure I am.' He leaned in to whisper in her ear. 'Means that I love you. Come on, stop sulking.'

'Women don't sulk. They contemplate.'

'Do you want to contemplate going to bed?'

She pushed him away, crossing her arms. 'No.'

He scooted closer and poked her. She narrowed her eyes. 'Stop it.' Her voice was scolding but a smile pulled at her lips.

He dove for her, pinning her to the sofa. She wriggled away, getting on top of him and digging her fingers into his rib cage.

He flipped her and pressed his body against her, holding her down. He kissed her, winding his fingers into her hair.

'I love your laugh. I'm sorry I made you cry, but do you understand *why* I had to be so hard on you?

She sighed and nodded. 'I get it. I do. Now you've been hard on me, do you want to be hard in me? After that telling off, I need a really good seeing to.'

He gasped in feigned shock. 'You are a bad girl. I know exactly what to do with you.'

Eliza stretched out in the sleigh bed, revelling in the crisp white sheets. From where she lay she could see out of the window that ran the length of the attic conversion, revealing panoramic views of the landscape under the brooding mass of cloud. Cornelius left the blinds open as they made love so they were lit by the setting sun. It had been weeks since they had last been together so he'd taken his time. She was so utterly satisfied and deliciously tired that moving seemed ludicrous.

Cornelius dozed beside her. She rolled over to gaze at him, struck by how beautiful he was and how much she loved him.

Who'd have thought it? she mused, running her fingers through his hair. *That I can't bear the thought of living without this man I once feared.*

His eyes fluttered open and he stretched. 'Hello.'

'Hello.' She smiled. 'You need a haircut but you're amazing.'

He sat up, rubbing his eyes. Eliza felt her throat constrict.

'Thank you. Do you enjoy sex with him?'

Why did he have to ruin the moment? She huffed at him and got out of the bed, snatching at her clothes.

'Why ask me that now?'

'Because I'm jealous, and it bothers me.'

She dropped her clothing and stood between his knees, wrapping her arms around his shoulders, resting his head against her breast. She wondered how to answer him. All those months ago, when she had first been taken by Faroust, the sex compensated for the danger, but now . . .

She tilted his head up. 'Physically, it's good but, but emotionally I hate it. I don't want him touching me. I don't even want to sleep in the same bed with him. I want to sleep in the same bed as you. Forever.'

'So you *do* enjoy it?' He frowned.

'Good sex is good sex. It's human nature. But it's better with you.' She sighed as she saw the sadness in his eyes and tried once more to soothe him. 'With you,' she kissed him, 'I'm free. I can tell you what I want, when I want it. I can lose myself in you. In your mouth, in your arms, in your scent and never have to worry about thinking the wrong thing or not reacting perfectly.

'I know that when we're together, you genuinely care about satisfying me and not just your ego. You want to make me come the way I like to come, not just the way you prefer, and I want the same for you. That's what makes us so good together. We know each other, know each other's rhythms and needs. And that makes it *so* much better.'

Cornelius pulled her down into the bed.

'You are so sexy,' he moaned.

'Only because you make me feel it. I wish we didn't have to go back to the hotel.'

He smiled down at her. 'Technically, we don't.'

'Really?'

'First of all, this is my cottage . . .'

'Your cottage?' Eliza interrupted. 'You own this place? I thought it was a holiday rental.'

'It's *my* cottage. Even I have to take leave, so I bought this place and did it up with my own hands. Took me four years.

Every weekend I had off, I was down here sanding the floors or fixing the roof . . . why are you blushing?'

'I got distracted by the thought of you shirtless and sweaty.'

'You are such a nympho,' he teased. 'And rude. You interrupted me.'

'Sorry.'

'As I was saying, I own the cottage, so we can stay as long as we like. And secondly, I've set up a search and rescue exercise for the others. We've essentially disappeared and in the morning, they have to come looking for us. I've set up a billion red herrings and false trails. And I have sensors all around the property which will go off when anyone gets within two miles of here. So we can spend all tomorrow in bed. Or on the sofa. Or in front of the fire. Or in the bath.'

Eliza wrapped her legs around his hips and pulled him closer to her.

'Sounds wonderful. I hope all our training days are like this.'

An angry shriek disturbed them. Cornelius looked up, confused.

'That's not one of my sensors.'

Eliza stiffened, the blood draining from her face as she realised what it was.

'Get up!' she said, pushing him away. 'It's my phone.'

'Ignore it and come back to bed.'

'I *can't*,' she said, pulling on her underwear. 'It's the phone Faroust calls me on.'

She tumbled downstairs, looking for where she'd dumped her jacket and that goddamn phone. If she missed the call, there'd be Hell to pay. She pulled it out of the pocket and swiped her finger across the screen.

'Hi baby!' she cried, with a joy she did not feel.

'You're not at the hotel.' Faroust's voice was so cold and hard it sent her stomach plummeting.

'No,' she admitted, her brain cobbling together an excuse. 'I'm sorry, honey. Did you call the hotel?'

'No.' She felt his rage burning at the end of the line. 'I drove to the hotel to see you.'

Eliza nearly dropped the phone. 'Oh sweetie. I'm sorry. I'm still out training.'

A noise on the stairs made her turn. It was Cornelius, carrying her clothes.

'Thank you,' she mouthed as she took them.

'Really?' He snarled down the phone. Cornelius winced. 'Because I've been here since midday and at three the entire security team came back. Apart from you and your fucking Cruel!'

Eliza swallowed, her heart racing. 'We're out setting up the training exercise for tomorrow.'

'And that's taken you six hours?'

'We want to test the digital phylacteries. It takes time to set up and run simulations. As I'm a dud, I'm the perfect test subject. We're out at a cottage where there are lots of things that could disrupt a signal.'

There was silence at the end of the line. Eliza cradled the phone between her ear and shoulder and pulled her shirt on.

'Baby, are you still there?'

'I don't want you alone with him.'

Eliza sighed and sat down on the sofa. She swiped the phone to speaker while deftly pulling on her trousers, one handed.

'Faroust, he could hardly leave me on my own in the middle of nowhere, could he?' When he didn't answer, she tried a different tack.

'Baby, we talked about this. You said you weren't going to interfere with my job. I'm finally making myself useful, and you promised I could do this.'

Before he could answer, a shrill wail filled the air. Eliza jumped. Cornelius held up a finger and moved to the kitchen. The wailing stopped.

'What was that?' Faroust growled.

'I'm not sure,' Eliza said, as Cornelius returned. He was white. Eliza frowned at him. With a look of horror on his face he shoved his phone into her hand and walked away. On the screen, in perfect detail, was Faroust's jeep, his face just visible through the windscreen. He'd crossed Cornelius' sensors. He'd followed her.

'How fucking dare you?'

'What?'

'You're at the cottage.'

There was a pregnant silence at the end of the line.

'What?' he repeated, far more quietly.

'You tripped one of Cornelius' sensors. That's what the noise was. A photo went to his phone. I can see you!'

'Did he see it?'

Eliza frowned as Cornelius returned, carrying the bed sheets.

'No, he didn't. He left it in the living room. Your face just flashed up on the screen. You're lucky I saw it first. Do you have any idea how fucking stupid you are? Do you have any concept of what could have happened if he'd seen you?'

'You watch your tone!'

'Fuck you!'

The sound of a car pulling up brought Eliza back from the brink of her fury. Cornelius was trying to conceal the signs of their fornication as best he could; there was every chance the god would just force his way inside. He kicked the sofa bed open and made it up as Eliza and Faroust's argument escalated. She could still smell him on her as she talked to her god. They needed to shower, but there was no time.

'Get outside!' Faroust roared. 'You're coming home!'

'No! You promised you'd let me do my job.'

'That was before you sneaked off with your ex!'

'I didn't sneak off anywhere. I'm following orders from my boss. I'm helping make us safe. Something you've undermined by coming here!'

'Lower your voice.' the god ordered. 'He might hear you.'

'He's in the shower,' Eliza said. 'He can't hear shit.'

'Eliza, you come out right now. Or I come in. And he dies.'

'Fine.' She was trembling as she ended the call. She wanted Cornelius to hold her and tell her it would be all right. She wanted him to run outside and tell their god to piss off. But he couldn't. Eliza had to do this on her own.

'You'll smell like sex,' he warned.

Idly, she clicked her fingers. 'Now I won't. I have to go. I'm not allowed to play with you anymore.' There was a catch in her voice.

Cornelius' eyes were moist. 'Wait a sec,' he called, as she turned away. He opened his laptop bag and pulled out a pendant.

'It's a microphone,' he said. 'In case you need me. Codeword: daybreak. I'll come out.'

Eliza quickly attached it before pulling on her shoes and stalking out to Faroust. She crossed her arms against the cold as she headed towards his jeep. The god eased himself out of the car. Swallowing her fear, she adopted a defiant pose.

'Where's your stuff?' he demanded.

'Inside.'

'I thought I said you were coming home.'

'You told me I could do this training week.'

Faroust glared at her, but she refused to buckle.

'Get in the car.'

'No.'

'Get in the car,' he repeated, his voice venomous.

'No.'

He lunged for her and she darted out of the way, avoiding his grasp.

'Eliza, you are getting in the car right now or so help me, you won't be able to sit down for a month when I'm done with you.'

'I don't want to get in the car. I want to stay here and finish my work.'

Faroust pressed his lips together so tightly, his mouth vanished. 'I won't say it again. Get in the car.'

Eliza threw her arms up in exasperation.

'I have work to do. You agreed to this weeks ago.'

Her god-lover crossed the distance between them. 'I did. But never once did you mention that you would be alone, in a cottage in the arse end of nowhere, with your illicit ex-boyfriend.'

'We're setting up an essential training exercise. It would be easy enough to take a child or a dud. Sage already did it. Faroust, please. I'm finally useful to my Family. Let me be useful.'

Faroust's nostrils flared at her continued defiance.

'You are useful. To me and my sexual needs.'

'You fucking buck eejit! Do you have any idea how fucking stupid you sound? How stupid you're being? We're trying to keep the Family, you and our terrifying, and highly illegal religion safe! And you, in a jealous fit of pique, almost reveal yourself and shake the foundations of everything we believe in!

'Do you have any concept what could have happened? Your image was captured by the sensors and sent to Cornelius' phone. Within thirty seconds, it gets sent to his laptop and then stored in a database, where any member of Security can see it. If I hadn't intercepted it, everything we know as truth would be uprooted and destroyed. What would you do then? Kill us all? Bind us? Wipe our memories? Or just fuck off and leave me and my parents to deal with the fallout?'

'Eliza . . .' he began, surprise making his voice weak.

'I haven't finished! If it hadn't been me who saw the photo but Cornelius, what would have happened to him? You'd have killed him. And how do I explain that? How is the Family supposed to feel safe if our head of Security is brutally murdered? Because don't pretend you wouldn't! And . . .'

'You are so beautiful.'

Faroust pushed her against the door of the jeep, pressing his mouth to hers. She curled her fingers and dug her nails into the palms of her hands as she tried to gain purchase to push him off.

Before she realised what she was doing, her hand lashed out and she smacked him around the face. He stumbled backwards as Eliza felt the world collapse around her.

They stood in horrified tableaux for an eternity. Finally, Faroust turned his head back to Eliza, his mouth slack in shock and his eyes wide.

'You hit me.'

'I hit you.' She couldn't keep the squeak out of her voice.

'You hit me,' he said again, as if so stunned by her actions, he could process no other thought.

'I know.' She was panting in fear. 'I hit you.'

'I know. My face hurts.'

'My hand hurts.'

'I imagine it would. My face hurts.'

'I'm not surprised. There's a really angry handprint on it.'

Faroust half-laughed at her odd little joke, but it was more an expulsion of air than actual laughter. He touched his cheek where she'd belted him and winced. He seemed totally at a loss. She'd done the unthinkable and neither of them had any idea what came next.

Eliza swallowed as she watched him process what she'd done. With the rage gone from his face, he looked young and oddly vulnerable. He moved towards her, taking her chin in his fingers and raising her head to make her look at him. Her breath caught as he offered her a slow, lazy smile.

'I doubt I look as good as you when I lose my temper.'

He lowered his mouth to hers and kissed her. She did not resist him this time. His arms slipped around her waist and he lifted her up. She felt his heart racing as they kissed.

'You are very sexy when you take charge,' he said. 'I like being told off by you. When we get home could you . . .' He faltered. '. . . tell me what to do a little more often? In bed? And in the same tone? I like you bossy.'

'Like a Dominatrix?'

Faroust grinned, his white teeth wolfish in the dark. 'I don't want you to hit me again. But I'd like you to be bossy with me. Tell me what to do. Be on top.'

Eliza felt her face twist into a smile. 'I can do that. Do you want to start now?'

'In the back of the car?'

She shook her head and stepped away from him.

'No. You're going to go home. I'm going back to work and I will deal with you when I return.'

Faroust swallowed, clearly aroused by her take-charge persona. 'Okay.'

'Okay? Is that how you answer me when I give you an instruction?'

'Sorry. Yes, Ma'am.'

'Very good. You can go now.'

He turned to return to the car, but a thought occurred to Eliza.

'Wait! How did you track me here?'

'GPS,' he said, 'on your new phone.'

'Mine's switched off. It drains the battery. And tracking the IP of a Smartphone is complicated.'

Faroust shook his head. 'I installed a chip in the back.'

'You installed a chip? To keep tabs on me?'

The god shrugged.

'You don't trust me?' Her throat was tight.

'I do. I just want to know where you are all the time. Keeps me sane.'

Eliza pulled the phone out of her pocket. He'd bought this for her as an apology for the fight about this training week. And the bastard had used it to plant a tracking device on her! It was tainted now, as much as she loved it.

She threw the device on the ground and stomped on it, over and over again until it was smashed into glittering pieces.

'Eliza! What the fuck? That was expensive!'

'Give me your phone and your Sat-Nav,' she ordered.

When he froze, she smiled at him

'We're still playing,' she clarified.

'Oh. Right.' He fumbled in his pocket for his phone.

While he pulled the Sat-Nav out of the car, Eliza scrolled through his phone; she deleted her number for her regular phone as well as the information in the Maps application. Faroust eagerly put the Sat-Nav into Eliza's outstretched hand. She erased the history and fiddled with the settings so it wouldn't be able to lead Faroust back to Cornelius' retreat.

'Off you go,' she prompted, handing it back to him.

'You didn't need to smash the phone.' He regarded the destruction Eliza's foot had wrought. 'I could have taken the chip out. Hey, you deleted your other number.'

'That's right. You abused the privilege to contact me so now you don't get to communicate with me at all until I get home.'

Faroust pouted in pretend dismay and hung his head. Eliza did her best to swallow her laughter.

'Now get out of my sight before I decide you can't jerk off until I get home.'

He glared at her. 'You wouldn't.'

Eliza shrugged. 'You wanted me to be bossy.'

Her god-lover bowed and got into his car. Eliza watched as he drove out of sight. She waited for ten minutes and then returned to the cottage.

Cornelius stood up to greet her. His face was ashen, the strain of listening to their conversation written all over his face, but his eyes were kind. He opened his arms and she buried herself in his embrace.

They held each other for a long time, saying nothing.

'You handled that well.' Cornelius said at length. He sounded as if he was proud of her.

'I've been practising,' Eliza replied. Her throat was sore and her eyes stung with unshed tears.

'You look exhausted. Let's go to bed. There's that smile again.'

'What smile?'

'The little grateful one. The one just for me.'

As they lay together, Eliza wrapped herself around him and laid her head on his chest.

'I love you,' she said quietly.

'I love you too.'

'Thank you. For sticking by me. And not saying anything about him.'

'That's all right. It was very entertaining when you smashed the phone to bits. And when you punched him. I particularly enjoyed the part where you punched him. I almost cheered.'

Eliza tried to laugh but her heart wasn't in it.

'My hand hurts.'

'It will do.'

There was a moment of uncomfortable silence.

'I don't punch people. I don't like that I punched him.'

Cornelius shifted in bed so she could see him properly. He took her right hand and kissed it. The pain vanished as his lips brushed her skin, and warmth spread through her body.

'Better?'

'A little. The pain's gone. But I still shouldn't have punched him.'

'Zee, you have a funny morality. We killed Sage, for fuck's sake. I torture people for a living. Punching Faroust isn't even on the same scale.' A mischievous smile played on his lips. 'As an outsider can I inform you that it was incredibly funny? I wish I could have seen it or recorded it. I could watch it over and over again to cheer me up when I feel down.'

His silliness made her smile.

'Whatever happened to "this is blasphemy, we shouldn't be doing this, he's our god"?'

'That was before he started fucking my woman.'

'So you're all right with the lying, the murdering and the rape then?'

His bottom lip jutted out and his tongue skated across it as he considered the question.

'No, but there was a distance before. Now I can't pretend it isn't there.' He brushed a lock of hair out her eyes. The nearness of him made her skin prickle. 'What are you planning to do when you find out the truth?' he asked

'Whatever's necessary to make it stop. I get that there's a circle and if we want the power, we have to give something back, but there has to be another way.'

Chapter 23

OR SIX BLISSFUL days, Faroust left Eliza alone. There wasn't a text or phone call, or even an email from him. She helped Cornelius train both halves of the Security team during the day and slept beside him at night. For a little while they were able to forget their reality and drown in each other.

But now it was over.

They packed up the car in the afternoon and made their way back to the East Coast of Eire. They took a long detour, racing down country lanes, looking for a quiet spot to enjoy each other one last time before she became Faroust's again. But no matter how long they tried to stay away, the road home beckoned.

Cornelius pulled the car over at a lonely petrol station. The sun was setting and darkness was approaching fast.

'I'm going to fill her up. We've an hour to go before we get back.' He frowned as he said it, as if it sounded weak, another attempt to delay the inevitable.

As he walked to the pumps, she slipped out of the car and pulled her phone from her pocket. She dialled a familiar number and waited for the answer.

'Hello?' Faroust's voice, low and warm, flooded her ears.

'Hello.' The catch in her voice surprised her. She cleared her throat and tried again. 'Faroust? It's Eliza.'

'Hello, Ma'am.' She could visualise his grin. Six days away from her and he still wanted to play this game. 'I hope you had a pleasant trip.'

'I did, thank you.' She stepped back into her role. 'We're about an hour from home. There's the gear to unpack, and a debriefing, and then I suspect Mum and Dad will want some time with me. I should be downstairs around eight.'

She turned, aware of a noise behind her. Cornelius had finished at the pumps and was heading in to pay. She watched him go and swallowed a sigh. The ripple of muscle under his shirt made her weak. She blinked and brought herself back to Faroust.

'Can I do anything for you?' he was asking.

'Dinner and a show wouldn't go amiss. And a bath.'

'As you wish, Ma'am. I'll see you at eight o'clock.' Something in his voice made her shudder.

'Just how much trouble am I in?' she asked.

She felt his chuckle reverberate in her breastbone before the sound reached her ears.

'You might want to clear you schedule. You won't be able to do much for a while.'

He ended the call and Eliza tried to ignore her mounting trepidation. Hopefully, he was just winding her up.

The walk that took the Faithful an hour during the Ritual took only seven minutes when running alone. Eliza chose not to run, but instead walked down the tunnel, as if she couldn't care less that she'd be late. At eight-fifteen, she knocked on the door that led to his apartment. The grinning skulls with the red roses leered at her as the door opened, smoke and all. Faroust was not there to greet her. Apprehension prickled the base of her neck as she made her way in. What she saw made her cover her mouth and gasp. The apartment was gently lit with tea lights. Edith Piaf sang mournfully in the background. A bottle of Asti waited in an ice bucket on the coffee table. An arrangement of cream roses sat behind the wine. She laughed; they were the ones that looked as if they'd been briefly dipped in blush, another of her favourite things.

She slipped her bag from her shoulder, untied her shoes and lined them up with his. She crossed to the coffee table to inspect the roses. They'd been obscuring her view of a small black box. A white card was propped open on it. *Open me*, it commanded in Faroust's ornate handwriting. Glinting inside was a replacement for the Smartphone she'd smashed in Connemara. It pinged in her hand and she almost dropped it. It was a message.

im not bugged. ;-p cum in2 ktchn. bring wine xx

Eliza grabbed the bucket and her new phone, her worry replaced with anticipation.

He'd set the dining table with perfect elegance; from the bright white table cloth to the silver candelabra casting a soft glow over the room. It was an understated, yet significant show of affection.

Faroust stirred a bubbling pot. He turned when she put the bucket down. He bounded over to her and lifted her off the floor. She wrapped her arms around his neck as his mouth found hers.

'You did all this for me?' she asked when he broke away.

'I missed you. I wanted to show you how much.' He pulled her legs so they wrapped around his waist.

'I can feel how much,' she teased. 'I'm surprised you haven't lost control and whisked me off to bed yet.'

'You didn't say I could.'

She giggled as he flexed his hips. 'You still want to play this game?'

'Are you kidding? What do you think has got me through the week? I love it when you get bossy. Like the time with the jam.'

He put her down and ran his fingers into her hair.

'I really did miss you,' he said. 'It wasn't just the sex, or having another person around. I missed you. The touch of you. The smell of you. The sound of you. Even your bad habits.'

'What bad habits?'

'Wet towels on the floor.'

'Fair enough.' She laughed, wrapping her arms around his waist.

Faroust looked down at her. He couldn't keep the grin off of his face. He really was ecstatic to have her back.

'Did you miss me?'

'Yes, 'she said. 'But I would have missed you a whole lot more if you hadn't tried to drag me home. Eejit.'

'I overreacted,' he admitted. 'But does having all your favourite things waiting for you when you come home make up for it?'

Eliza pretended to think about it. She squeezed her thumb and index finger together to indicate a tiny amount.

'Sit down and open the wine. Maybe dinner will help you forgive me completely.'

He brought her a pasta bowl brimming with spaghetti, mince, tomato ketchup and cheddar cheese. Unexpected tears stung her eyes and she pressed her hand to her mouth to stem them.

'Hey.' Faroust crouched beside her. 'What's wrong?

'It's just . . . I didn't think you'd noticed all this stuff I love. It's overwhelming to know how much you care.'

And you feel guilty, you power stealing slut! her Familial conscience spat.

'Of course I care about you.' His voice was soft; there was no recrimination in it. 'Do you think if it was just sex I was

336

looking for you'd be as free as you are, or that I'd spoil you the way I do?'

He gently pulled her hands apart as she plucked the fleshy pad of her thumb. 'Look at me?'

She obliged, although all she wanted was for the ground to swallow her up. His face was so loving she nearly confessed everything, there and then.

'It's like I said before, I'm not the god all the time. I'm the man for most of it. And the man cares deeply about you. And if I may say so, I'm a pretty good man most of the time. Until the god half of me forgets I'm supposed to be a man and tries to inflict my authority on my independent and very bad-tempered sex-toy.'

Caught off guard, Eliza began to laugh. He pulled his dining chair so it was beside hers.

'Eat up. It'll go cold.'

She grabbed his hand and kissed it.

'Thank you.'

'No problem. Now, after this we are going to have a bath and after that, if we can contain ourselves that long, we are going to bed.'

'I thought you said you wanted me to be in charge?'

'So I did. Do you object to my suggestion, Ma'am?'

Eliza raised her glass with a smile.

'Not at all.'

They didn't make it to the bed. Moments after they climbed into the tub, Faroust lost the last of his self-restraint. He pulled Eliza over to him and positioned her on his lap. She'd barely caught her breath before he was inside her.

'Ride me,' he begged.

In that moment, he surrendered to her completely. She pressed her hands against the wall for balance as he grabbed her hips. Water splashed over the side of the bath, extinguishing the candles and plunging them into darkness. They came together, growling and panting like big cats.

'Wow!' Faroust breathed.

'Isn't that my line?'

'Not this time. Bed?' He raised his eyebrows suggestively.

'What about the mess?'

'Who gives a shit?'

Eliza pressed a hand to her chest and gasped for air.

'Oh dear Lord. Who are you and what have you done with my anal-retentive lover?'

'Sex is more enjoyable than cleaning. I don't want to spoil the mood. I'm still hard, boss-lady.'

'Then we'd best get into bed. Dry me.'

'Gladly, but you realise your arse is mine when we finish this little game?'

'In for a penny, in for a pound. Or should that be a pounding?'

Faroust reached for a towel and wrapped it around her. He closed one eye as he pretended to think about it.

'Maybe just a thorough spanking? But then again, you'd enjoy that.' He picked her up and hefted her over his shoulder. 'Come on, bed. You said something about anal?'

'No!' she shrieked. 'I called you anal. I did not offer anal sex.'

'You might like it.'

'I very much doubt it.'

He threw her down on the bed. She bounced and landed provocatively, legs splayed wide.

'Not even a discussion about it?'

'No.' She shook her head emphatically.

He shrugged and pulled her down by the ankles so her bottom rested on the edge of the bed. He sank to his knees in front of her. She propped herself up on her elbows to watch him.

'I'll just have to work on changing your mind.' He blew on her sex and she lay back on the bed, revelling in his worship of her. He must have *really* missed her.

A few hours and a dozen or so different positions later, Faroust and Eliza lay panting on the bedroom floor. He lay on his back, while she sprawled on her front beside him. He laughed throatily, an expulsion of exhaustion, and filthy, unadulterated desire. Eliza echoed his tone, a breathy giggle of disbelief at her own wantonness.

'That was incredible,' he sighed, extending the adjective.

'Beyond. That was existential. Celestial.'

'You're quite the poet,' he said as she laid her head on his chest.

She idly traced patterns on his chest with her index finger as he twirled his fingers in her hair.

'I wish I could always be like this,' she said.

'What do you mean? It is. We argue. We make up. We have glorious sex.'

She half sat up, resting her head on her hand.

'No, I wish you could be like this more often . . .'

'Naked?'

'Would you let me finish?' she said. 'What I mean is, I wish Faroust the man would keep Faroust the god in check a little more often. I wish I could share this person with everyone else. It doesn't seem fair I'm the only one who gets to see this version of you.'

Faroust frowned as he digested her words.

'The Ritual is the Ritual, *mo ghrá*. It is what it is. If it isn't performed, everything and everyone you love is lost.' He got to his feet and pulled her up. 'The god of the Ritual cannot be your lover. Just as your lover cannot be the god of the Ritual. Wait here. I have another gift for you.'

'Faroust, you don't have to keep buying me things.'

He gave her a shy smile and retreated to his study. When he returned, he held a black box in his hands. It was beautifully lacquered and gleamed in the candle light.

'This was my mother's,' he said. 'She . . . she gave me everything. Even when she was gone . . . the gift she gave to me . . . I owe her everything.'

She took the box from his outstretched hand and prised open the lid. Inside was a gold necklace, ancient and glorious. It was diamond shaped, set with the deepest rubies and sapphires. A large emerald glowed in the centre. She stared at it for a long moment, rendered speechless by its beauty as it sparkled and flashed in the apartment lights.

He took the necklace from the box and slipped it around her neck, turning her towards the mirror. The ancient gold glowed against her milk-pale skin, the stones burning with their own light. Her nakedness only enhanced the ornate nature of the necklace. She looked different. She stood straighter, as if the jewellery had imbued some kind of royal grace upon her.

Faroust combed her hair with his fingers and artfully arranged it over her shoulders. She gazed at her reflection in wonder. It wasn't a woman who stared back at her but a Gaelic goddess, lost in time, who had stumbled into the modern world. A goddess for her god. Ah, if only he knew.

'It could have been made for you,' he said. 'People think gold tarnishes and falls apart, but not if you take care of it.'

She shook her head, shattering the illusion the necklace created. This was too much. His mother's necklace was a gift for a loyal heart, a heart that had no other agenda.

'I . . . I . . .'she stuttered. 'I can't accept this. It's too precious. Too special. I'm not worthy of it.'

The mirror reflected a new image of her now: a silly girl with ideas above her station, terrible sex hair and a necklace that no longer glittered with promise and beauty but seemed to burn with anger that it had been put on this upstart's skin.

Faroust frowned and turned her to face him. 'Don't be silly. I give it to you, not because you're worthy of it, but because it is worthy of you.'

'But . . . but . . .'

He kissed her again. 'But nothing. I want you to have it because . . . Well, because I love you.'

Eliza swallowed the lump in her throat. That wasn't part of the plan. She didn't love him, couldn't love him. What kind of person was she to do this to somebody else? Even if they were a monster?

But he isn't completely monstrous, is he? He is capable of great love and kindness, especially to you. He's waiting for you to say it back. How good a liar have you become, Eliza?

She composed herself and without a flicker of shame, she looked him in the eye.

'I love you too.'

His face broke into a beautiful grin. 'Come back to bed. You look like a goddess. Goddesses should be worshipped.'

Eliza got no sleep that night. Faroust's words rattled around in her head, keeping her awake. She didn't love him. This was bad, and there was no way out. Even if she discovered what Faroust was hiding, what could she do? She'd played this whole thing by ear, hoping she'd discover it quickly and then . . . well, then what? Release the souls? End a religion and destroy her family? Convince Faroust to fuck off?

Cornelius was right: she never bloody thought things through. She did everything on impulse. She was a good strategist, but only when it came to short term plans to get out of her immediate fix. Her long term plans were, to put it mildly, a bit shit.

She needed to talk to Cornelius. But if she told him, if she could tell him, that Faroust had declared his love for her, her poor Cruel would freak out. It didn't matter how many times she told him that it was him she loved, he wouldn't believe her now. She could understand his position: how could he compare to Faroust, with his strength, his power, his wealth?

She didn't want any of those things. She wanted Cornelius. But what would happen when Faroust ended things? Would he let her go back to her old life? Branded as she was, she would never be able to share his secrets so she wasn't a threat. What if he never ended it? She couldn't expect Cornelius to wait for her. He was entitled to live his own life. Holding onto him would be selfish.

Her head hurt, and sleep refused to come. No matter which way she looked at the puzzle, someone lost. Two men were in love with her and that was entirely her fault. She had fought and manipulated and lied and now all her chickens were coming home to peck her eyes out. She had done awful things, in the name of the mission. Ah, the mission, her hunt for the truth. Was it worth it? Was uncovering the secrets of Faroust the god worth the destruction of Faroust the man?

She looked at her god-lover. For months now, apart from his jealousy-fuelled trip to Connemara, she had only seen the good in him. Which role was the mask? Who was the real Faroust? The man who said he loved her, or the Fae-monster?

Silently, she moved from the bed and into the bathroom. Her head pounded. Opening the cabinet, she swallowed a pill. She pushed the mirrored door shut and jumped back. For a split second, her reflection had not been her. There had been a flash of blood-red hair and black eyes. She stared at the mirror again but the illusion was gone. She shook her head, putting it down to exhaustion and an overactive imagination, but she left the bathroom in a hurry.

The clock in the kitchen told her it was five-thirty. Cornelius would be out for his run. She changed into her running kit and scribbled a note telling Faroust where she was. Automatically, she signed it with a kiss, then shuddered at the new implication of that tiny sign of affection.

She slipped out of the apartment through the gardener's lodge, trying to guess where Cornelius would be. Every day, he ran four laps of the grounds and the property was far from small. If she was quick, she might catch him as he passed the orchard a second time. She sprinted over and waited.

She arrived just before he did. He smiled when he saw her.

'Hello. Not chained to a bed, I see.'

Eliza scuffed the ground with her feet, refusing to make eye contact with him. 'I need to talk to you,' she said.

'Okay. Summerhouse. No cameras there.'

The floor of summerhouse still bore the marks of Eliza's panic attack of the previous year.

'We really should tear this down,' Cornelius said. 'No one uses it anymore since the gazebo went up.'

Eliza sat on a window seat, eyes fixed on the floor.

'You going to tell me what's going on?'

She took a deep breath. 'Faroust told me he loved me.' She screwed her eyes shut as pain flickered across her face. The seal must be burning her.

Cornelius leant back against the wall, digesting her words. She got up and went to him.

'What if it takes me years to discover his secret?' she said. 'What if I never do? I can't expect you to wait for me. You have the right to a life . . .'

'Oh no,' he said. 'You don't get to end this. You don't get to turn my whole life upside down, ruin my faith, make me a traitor, put me in danger and then walk away when it gets too hard. You don't get to make me fall so in love with you I can barely breathe without you, and then leave when you decide.'

She reached out to him but he smacked her hand away.

'I don't want to break up with you,' she said. 'I really don't. But Faroust's feelings change everything. This isn't just sex for him anymore. It means he won't be willing to end this when I want to end it. He'll fight to keep me until he decides it's over. That isn't fair to you. It would be selfish to ask you to stay with me.'

Cornelius folded his arms and sucked his teeth in annoyance. 'Now you suddenly understand what selfish is? Just my luck.'

Eliza shrugged and looked away from him again. Something occurred to him that he didn't much like.

'Look at me,' he demanded.

She did not.

'MacTir, I said look at me!'

Eliza's head snapped up, her eyes wide.

'Do you know what I think, MacTir? I think you're getting cold feet about your mission. You thought there would be no collateral damage. You've been trying to ignore the fact that you've been stringing him along. Well, sweetheart, I have news for you. That's *exactly* what you've been doing.'

Eliza opened her mouth to protest but he cut her off.

'I didn't give you leave to speak, MacTir! You had the opportunity to get out of this mission before it began. But because of what you saw in the Veil, you felt morally obliged to investigate. That meant you were prepared to manipulate him in whatever way necessary to get the information. The fact he has fallen in love with you is irrelevant! You've lost your objectivity in this situation. You've become a danger. Again. If it were any other mission, you'd be pulled out and dismissed. As it is, I can't do that.'

He grabbed her by the shoulders and forced her to make eye-contact with him.

'What does Faroust do every year?'

'He rapes a girl publically and drinks the blood of a boy, almost until the point of death,' she said.

'How may Rituals have you attended?'

'Eight.'

'Making sixteen sacrifices. And of those sixteen people, how many survived?'

'F . . . five.'

'In your experience of the Ritual, eleven people have died. Eleven young lives taken. That amounts to thousands and thousands of innocent people over the millennia. And it turns out it isn't enough. According to you, the soul of every Family member is bound to the Veil for no apparent reason.'

Oh, this was painful but he had to do it, even as he saw Eliza press her lips tight in an effort not to cry. He was so rarely angry at her these days and now he'd been furious with her twice in the space of a week.

'What did I say last week? About my job?'

'You said you protect the Family from threats.'

'That's right. Including this one.'

'What are you implying? Are you classing Faroust as a threat?'

Cornelius nodded firmly. 'Each one of us is willing to be the sacrifice to renew the magic, willing to give everything we have in worship of him. And it's not enough for him. Not even death releases us from our obligation. Our souls are trapped, to be abused however he wants. That is a threat. And you're going to help me deal with it.'

He let go of her shoulders and stepped back, crossing his arms.

'Wow. I really did turn you into a blasphemer.'

'You opened my eyes, yes,' he conceded. 'So no more talk of ending things with me.' It was a statement, not a question. 'I promised I'd wait for you. So I will. End of.'

Eliza smiled. 'Okay, boss.'

'Glad to hear it.' He glanced at his watch. 'You've interrupted my run. And I can't be late this morning. I have a meeting with your dad at eight.'

'Sorry, Sir,' Eliza replied meekly. 'Should I not have come to you?'

Cornelius grabbed her and held her against him, burying his face in her hair, breathing in the scent of her shampoo, the scent of her.

'Of course you should have. You don't love him back, do you?'

'No!' she cried. 'I love you. I was just . . . knocked for six when he said it.'

Cornelius moved his mouth from her hair, down to her neck, leaving butterfly kisses down to her collarbone.

'What are you doing?'

'You interrupted my run. I still need to work up a sweat.'

Thirty minutes later they stumbled from the summer house, sweating and breathless. Cornelius risked another passionate kiss before sending her away with a sharp smack on the backside. Eliza decided to jog around the grounds, just once, to lend credence to the idea she had gone for a run. If Faroust was up by the time by the time she got in, hopefully she would smell of sweat and not sex.

As it was, Faroust was still sound asleep. Eliza threw her clothes in the washing machine and stepped into the shower. By the time her god-lover woke, she had breakfast on the table. She accepted his morning salutation, his kisses and his affection, her faith in her mission restored.

Chapter 24

ELIZA FROWNED AS she opened the door to the apartment. Faroust was blasting loud music from the living room.

He'd been in a strange mood since the beginning of August. The Ritual was so close; it could be messing with his mystical mojo.

'Baby?' she called. 'You okay?'

'Fan-fucking-tastic,' he answered, his voice oddly slurred, before the music cranked up.

She rushed into the living room and switched the system off.

'Hey! I was listening to that!' He grabbed her and twirled her around.

'What the Hell is wrong with you?' She pulled away. 'Are you drunk?'

'Not enough booze. I'm high.' He cackled.

'How the fuck did you get high?'

Faroust triumphantly produced a silver pill packet. Every blister was empty. Eight co-codamol.

'You took all of these? Faroust, last time you had two and you were floating. You shouldn't take medicine like that. What if you hurt yourself?'

He collapsed on the couch 'I won't hurt myself. I always get antsy before the Ritual. I have to be here all the time . . .'

'Because the magic is weak?'

There was a menace in his smile that made Eliza uneasy.

'Sure baby, whatever. Come get high with me.'

'I'd rather not. Unlike you, I could get seriously hurt.'

He tutted, but let the matter drop. Eliza moved behind the couch and wrapped her arms around his shoulders.

'Will you make dinner?' he asked.

'What would his royal high-ness like?'

The god snorted. 'I see what you did there. As for dinner,' he grinned at her, 'I want you.' He grabbed her by the nape of the neck and dragged her over the sofa, pinning her beneath him.

'Careful!' she cried. 'You could have really hurt me.'

Faroust disregarded her complaints, pulling at the buttons of her shirt with his teeth.

'Faroust, stop it. I'm not in the mood.'

He ignored her, pulling the garment open. He kissed along her neck and collarbone, before moving down to her breasts, encased in violet lace. He lapped at her nipple through the material, making the nub hard despite its owner's protestations.

'See? Your body wants me. And I want it. So we're all happy.'

'I'm not. My body is not your plaything. I don't want to have sex with you,' she said. 'Despite the reactions of my treacherous bosom.'

He dissolved into giggles against her. She groaned. She could handle horny Faroust, angry Faroust, sulky Faroust and jealous Faroust. She could not handle this snorting, giggling man-child. She flicked him sharply in the ear and he jumped back with a yelp.

'Meany,' he pouted.

'Don't pretend you don't love it,' she said. 'What's wrong with you, that you want to get smashed out of your gourd?'

Faroust rubbed his face vigorously. 'Fucking Ritual. I can't just take off if I want. Jacob calls me every fucking day. Readings need to be taken, Family members gathered in, the seals need to be observed and it's all fucking bollocks.'

Eliza knelt in front of him and took his hands. 'I've been meaning to ask you something, about the Ritual. It's a little sensitive.'

Faroust leant forward, his eyes crossing as he tried to concentrate on what she was saying.

'I was wondering when you'd begin to . . .' she paused as she considered how to phrase it, 'degenerate, I suppose, and if you'd like some privacy . . . Why are you laughing?'

Faroust had dissolved into fits of laughter, gasping and stomping his foot in his amusement.

'Didn't you hear me, darling? It's all fecking boll-ocks.'

Queasiness rushed over her, as if she were about to faint. *No, please no.* 'I . . . I don't understand.'

The god made an exaggerated pantomime of looking around the apartment to make sure no one else could hear them.

'It's all shymbolic, baby. Shymbolic. I don't need any of it. It's a gesture of the Family's gratitude to me for sharing the magic. My degeneration is part of the symbol. Is not real.'

Eliza felt the blood drain from her face. If she hadn't already been kneeling, she would have collapsed. Faroust took her by the shoulders and pulled her closer.

'Do you want to know a secret?'

He put his lips to her ear and unburdened his final great and terrible secret. Vomit surged up her throat as the truth was revealed. The last affection she had for him died in that instant, and the rage that had been quiet for so long resurrected in her heart.

Her lover sat back on the sofa, chuckling to himself. Eliza stared at him, from the floor, groping for words that would not come.

'Baby, you look upset. What's wrong?' He reached for her hands.

'You're a monster.' The tears began to fall. She couldn't move to brush them away.

'No . . . no . . .' he said. 'I shouldn't have told you that.' His fingertips brushed hers.

'Don't fucking touch me!' She jumped up so quickly she wasn't sure how she'd got on her feet. 'Don't you dare touch me! Fucking Hell! I can't . . . I can't . . .' Her chest rose and fell as she gasped for air, fought the dizziness.

'Baby, it was centuries ago. They tried . . .'

'I don't care! It doesn't excuse what you've been doing to us ever since!' She covered her face, digging her fingers into the roots of her hair as if she could tear him free of her.

Faroust clambered to his feet. Eliza shoved him and he stumbled backwards over the furniture. He landed awkwardly, his body blocking the entrance to the Ritual room, to safety. Eliza scrambled away, tearing through the apartment, towards his office and the back door. She needed to get away, she needed to get to people.

She was halfway up the drive, far from the warmth and safety of the Family, when he caught her. She screamed as he snatched her, but it was short-lived. In an instant she was back in the apartment, lying on the floor, staring up at Faroust in his Fae form. He swayed back and forth.

'Oh shit.'

'We were going to fuck earlier. Maybe I should fuck you like this,' he said.

Eliza had a split second to react. She could placate him, or she could fight.

She chose to fight.

'Why would I let a monster touch me?'

'I'm not a monster,' he said.

'Your actions suggest otherwise.'

'I am not a monster! You have no idea what it's like, what I've suffered.' His hands moved into his hair as he pulled at his horns. 'I am not a monster!' he screamed, kicking the coffee table into the air.

She threw her hands up as it shattered, raining glass and splinters down on her unprotected form. She braced herself for a blow, but nothing came. Faroust dropped to his knees in front of her, weeping into his hands.

'You have no right to cry,' she snapped.

'Being Fae doesn't make me a monster!'

'I never said it did, you self-pitying bastard. I said your actions made you monstrous.'

'They tried to . . .'

'I already heard your disgusting story.'

Faroust lifted his face. His whorled cheeks were wet with tears. 'I thought you loved me!'

Eliza took a deep breath, forcing herself to be gentle. She had an opportunity here, an opportunity to make things better for those above them.

'I do,' she said, taking his hands, careful to avoid his talons. 'I love you but you have to understand that what you did, what you are still doing, isn't right. We don't deserve it. No matter what happened.'

Faroust was calming down, sniffing and gasping, but no longer really crying. Eliza pressed home her advantage.

'Would you change it back?'

'I don't . . . know if . . . if I could . . .'

'Of course you *could*. My question was, would you?'

He hesitated. In that moment of silence, Eliza played her dirtiest trick, hating herself for it even as the words left her mouth.

'Do you love me? Do you really love me?'

His head lifted, his eyes filling with fresh tears.

'More than anything.'

'Then change it back. For me.'

Faroust rubbed his eyes with his arm, like a small boy trying to mask his tears. Eliza pulled a tissue from her pocket.

'May I?' She crouched lower, under his horns, to dry his face. She was tender, blotting the tears away, rather than wiping them. She chucked him under the chin.

'I'm not a monster,' he repeated.

'By changing it back, you can prove it.'

Eliza ran her eyes over his strange Faerie beauty. Despite herself, and what he had revealed to her, she was hypnotised with it. With tentative fingers, she reached out and touched his face, feeling the tips of his ears. They were pointed, like all the pictures of Faeries she'd ever seen.

She ran her hands down his neck and over his shoulders and arms. His skin was soft, as if covered in a sheer layer of velvet. She followed the path of a whorl on his arm with her fingertip.

'That feels nice.' He sighed. 'You're not frightened of me like this?'

'Maybe a little,' she said. 'The last time I saw you like this, you tried to kill me.'

'More proof of my monstrosity.'

Eliza knew that was her cue to tell him she hadn't meant it, or to kiss him, but she couldn't bring herself to do either. They sat in silence on the floor, surrounded by the remains of the coffee table. Faroust was the first to move. He gathered her to him and lifted her up, picking his way through the debris to the bedroom. He placed her on the bed and knelt in front of her.

'I'd set the world on fire for you, Eliza,' he said, 'I love you so much. I promise, *promise*, I will change the Ritual back. I promise to be a better leader for the Family.'

Eliza stared at the floor. Now he was calm again, her anger was back. It was impossible for her to look at him. She pulled her head away as he tried to look her in the eye. He growled in exasperation and pushed his mouth against hers as they tumbled back on the bed. She flinched as he dragged his sharp nails over her body, cutting her out of her clothes. In moments, she was naked, breathing in sharply as his fingers brushed over her torso. But the talons were gone now. His fingertips were warm, so warm, against her skin.

Despite everything, her treacherous body wanted to surrender to him. He was casting some new spell over her in his Fae form. He smelt like rain and fresh air, a heady perfume. Her limbs were loose and heavy as if she was drunk, intoxicated with him. He finally broke the kiss, regarding her with those black eyes, but there was warmth in them now. She knew she was staring at him but she couldn't help it. Her vision lingered on his horns.

'May I?'

He watched nervously as she touched his face, her fingers travelling up to explore his horns. She laughed in delight as flowers bloomed under her touch.

'You are beautiful.' She'd never felt like this around him before. It had to be some unknown magic of his Fae self. She ran her hands over his shoulders and, after a moment's hesitation, touched his wings. The feathers were as soft as cashmere.

Faroust relaxed under her tentative explorations and lowered his mouth to kiss her again.

'I want you so much,' he said, pulling away from her to sit back on his heels. He reached back and plucked a long feather from his wings. It glinted in the half-light, green-black like a magpie's wing.

'What are you doing?' she asked.

He pressed a finger to her lips. 'Trust me.'

He lowered the tip of the feather to her neck and drew it down gently She gasped as her flesh goose-pimpled. The feather continued its downward journey. He dragged it across her nipples. She panted as he teased her, moving it in tiny circles on her belly. It felt like a fire building inside her, yet she shivered in anticipation as he reached the apex of her things.

She convulsed as he pulled the feather down the tiny gap between her thighs and across her outer lips.

'Open your legs,' he said.

He moved the feather slowly, making Eliza mewl and gasp in need. When the tip touched her clitoris, she climaxed, her body climbing and crashing in orgasm, skin flushing as she burned under his touch.

The god waited as she collected herself. He wiped away her tears.

'If we do this, you will be the first mortal woman I have had while in this form. I could really hurt you, so I can become the man you know if . . .'

'No,' she begged. 'No, no. I want you like this. I want all of you.'

He smiled, and sank into her. Eliza's body spasmed once more as his raw magic entered her. She curled herself around him, holding on to him, crying his name.

As the tremors faded away, Faroust began to move, slowly at first, savouring this new experience. She tightened her hold around his shoulders and wrapped her legs around his hips.

'Tell me if it's too much,' he breathed. 'I don't want to hurt you.'

But Eliza couldn't reply. She was lost; lost in her intoxication, in the power that roiled off him and into her. If he hurt her, she wouldn't know. Faroust withdrew and flipped her on to her stomach, dragging her off the bed by her ankles until her feet rested on the floor. She arched her back and shrieked as he slammed into her. He pulled her back by her shoulders so she was almost standing. She felt his heavy breath on the nape of her neck. He wound his fingers into her hair and pulled her head back. She yelped, but his lips on her cheek softened the roughness of the action.

'Come for me,' he whispered, as his fingers found her clitoris.

For the third time, she spasmed under his touch. This time her climax was sharp and painful. She howled with the intensity of it.

She dropped on to the bed as Faroust withdrew, as suddenly as he had entered her. In an instant, the Fae creature had her pinned against the wall, using it to balance her as he fucked her hard. She was lost in the thrill as he broke this last taboo with her.

'You are the most amazing creature,' he gasped.

Before she could answer they were back on the bed, but this time he was beneath her.

'Finish me,' he begged. 'I need you.'

She rode him hard and fast. He tilted his head back as he reached his release, shouting her name as he came. She collapsed against him, dragging the air into her lungs in ragged gasps. Beneath her, Faroust trembled as she slid off of him. He thrashed his head from side to side as if looking for something. She laid a hand on him, and he stilled.

'You okay?' she asked

'That was . . .' he shuddered as his Fae-self retreated, 'there are no words. That was utterly wicked and stupid. I've never fucked a mortal in my Fae body. I feel like I'm burning. Did I hurt you?'

She shook her head, but he lowered her onto her back and examined her body all the same.

'You're a little swollen,' he said. 'I can fix that.'

She watched him kiss her swollen labia, hissing as his tongue swept over her outer lips. A lazy heat unfurled in her belly as he explored her with his mouth. She groaned as the discomfort passed and her need for him resurfaced. His tongue passed over her throbbing clit and she came again, but so gently, so quietly, that all the tension left her body and warmth and happiness replaced it.

Faroust made his way up the bed to lie beside her once more. His horns were gone and his eyes had returned to navy blue. His skin was its usual hue, but the green and blue swirls remained. His raven wings still cast their shadow against the wall. It was only when she reached out to touch them that he pulled away from her. The last of the Fae faded away and her Faroust was lying beside her. He ran his hands over her body.

'You don't have a scratch on you,' he said. 'I love you.'

'Love you too,' she whispered as sleep reared up to claim her.

Eliza's head felt heavy and her vision was foggy, like she'd had too much red wine. Her mouth was dry and her body ached. She stumbled to her feet to find water. She was unsure of her surroundings and she blinked to clear her vision, but the grey fog remained.

There was a soft hiss behind her and she span around to confront the sound. The fog shifted, and with a jolt she realised she was back in the dead world inhabited by her ancestors.

'Oh, no. No! I didn't go near it!'

'Eliza,' a voice called, distant and plaintive. 'He's trying to make you forget.'

Eliza turned towards the voice, but she could see no one. 'What?'

She dropped to her knees, screaming as a sharp pain stabbed at her ears. There was a deep vibration coming from this world, something she couldn't hear, but which caused her to writhe in agony. The world around her pulsed and shifted in and out of focus. A low chorus of voices were speaking, but she couldn't see anyone. They were beyond her sight, somewhere in this Hellish reality.

'Don't forget!' they cried, over and over again, growing louder as the vibration throbbed within her. 'Help us! Save us!'

There were screams now, wails and cries of pain and panic. Shapes formed out of the mist. Eliza's own scream caught in her throat as the altar of the Ritual emerged through the fog. Sophie lay on it, weeping and howling. Blood poured from between her legs, splashing onto the floor. Eliza gagged. She turned to run but smacked into a new altar. She looked down, into Tom's open chest cavity. A pair of hands wrapped around his organs. Her hands. The iron tang of blood and bile and noxious rot rose up towards her. Her scream finally escaped from her throat as Tom sat up and grabbed her.

'Don't forget, Eliza,' he gasped. 'Don't let us suffer.'

She stumbled backwards, falling over yet another blood-drenched altar. Anna-Beth stared vacantly at the ceiling, her brains trickling out of the back of her head onto her brother's drained corpse. Her head snapped towards Eliza, her eyes white and full of maggots.

'Do not forget,' she said.

A cold hand closed around Eliza's ankle. Jonathan was trying to pull himself up to speak to her. She kicked him away and tried to run, but she was trapped. Everywhere she turned was another altar, another victim begging her to act. She saw her mother violated again and again by their god, silent tears of pain falling down her beautiful face. She watched a thousand young men have their rib cages broken open to expose the tender heart. She heard the snap of bone and the tear of muscle, the howl of lost innocence and humiliation. Again and again and again. The sacrifices repeated over and over, a thousand years of pain and fear pressed down on Eliza, surrounding her, trapping her, filling her senses, searing her brain, following her as she tried to escape the horror.

Eliza crumpled under the strain. There was no way out of this Hell. There was blood on her hands, the blood of her ancestors. Warm liquid dripped down her neck. With shaking hands, she reached up to her ears and discovered they were streaming with blood. She cried out in panic, her wailing combined with the plaintive voices of the Veil.

A pair of bare feet appeared in front of her. Eliza raised her head to gaze at the figure. Anna-Beth stood there, her eyes shut.

'Help me,' Eliza begged.

Anna's eyelids opened. Where her eyes should be, empty sockets burned with blood-red flame.

'It's not over.' The terrible vision spoke in a voice that skipped and scratched like a scarred record. 'Do not allow yourself to forget. There's blood, so much blood on his hands. If you forget, it will be on yours too.'

The spectre drew her hand back and grabbed Eliza's face. She screamed as a searing light entered her head, pouring out through her open and weeping eyes.

'Do not forget!' the creature ordered, shoving Eliza backwards.

She woke with a small scream. She was in Faroust's bed. She covered her mouth to keep from vomiting. She was trembling and unable to get her breath. She felt hot, so hot. Leaping out of the bed, she stumbled to the bathroom. Clambering into the shower, she turned on all the jets and let the cold water batter her aching body.

'Eliza?' Faroust called from the doorway. 'What are you doing?'

'I'm hot,' she said. 'Need to cool down.'

'You'll catch a cold.' He pulled her back from the water and pushed the wet hair out of her eyes. He uttered a harsh cry and jumped back.

'What?'

Even in the semi-darkness of the bathroom, she could see he was ashen. He took a faltering step forward and a slow smile of relief spread across his features.

'Nothing. A trick of the light,' he said.

'What was?' Eliza reached for a towel.

'Your eyes . . . They looked black.'

Eliza's head span as his words sank in. Either it *was* just a trick of the light, or something else was happening to her. She swallowed.

'Seriously? Faroust, no more pills, okay?'

'Okay, baby. Have a proper shower and I'll make breakfast.'

When Eliza entered the kitchen, Faroust was busy at the stove. She took a moment to watch him. If she lived to be as old as he was, she'd never understand why he did what he'd done to her family.

He turned, holding the grill pan. 'Bacon sambo sound good?'

She nodded, unable to speak. He laid the pan on the table, and she crossed to him and threw her arms around him. He turned in her embrace.

'You will keep your promise, won't you?'

There was a split-second of silence as he hesitated.

'Of course I will.' He smiled, pulling away. 'Now food.'

She sat down, watching him warily as they ate.

He hesitated. If he doesn't keep his promise, there's only one thing that can be done.

Chapter 25

CORNELIUS SAT DOWN heavily on his desk, his eyes wide as he digested Eliza's request.

'That's insane!' he said. 'There has to be a different way.'

'There isn't,' she said. 'Baby, I tried, but it didn't work. I need your help.'

Cornelius rubbed his bottom lip with his index finger.

'But to go to such extremes . . .'

'Cornelius, I know everything. Everything.' She leant forward. 'But I can't do anything with it if it's all locked away.'

'It'll hurt.'

'I know.'

'Do we have to do it?'

'Yes.'

'Why?'

Eliza couldn't answer him. What was she going on, after all? A hunch? The fact that Faroust took a moment too long to answer her? Her nightmares? She couldn't explain it, but her gut told her everything was coming to a climax, and tomorrow night their world would change forever. She had to be prepared for every eventuality. She shrugged at Cornelius.

'Fail to prepare, prepare to fail?'

He embraced her. They were both silent as they contemplated the gravity of their situation.

'You really want me to do this?'

She nodded.

'And there's no other way?'

She shook her head.

'Okay.' He sighed. 'I'll get my tool box. Take off your clothes.'

Eliza closed her eyes and inhaled. She removed her jacket and shirt, laying them on the back of the chair.

'And the rest.' Cornelius passed her a pair of scrubs. 'You're going to bleed. A lot.' He sealed his office as Eliza removed her trousers and underwear and pulled on the scrubs. She watched Cornelius pluck his tool bag from under his desk, shuddering as he pulled out a thin knife and a syringe. A sad smile crossed his face.

'It's funny. When we met, I wanted to cut you up. Now I can't think of anything worse. I've got a local anaesthetic for you. Might help the pain.' He laid a towel in front of his desk and moved her into place. She leant forward on her elbows. 'Let me know if it's too much,' he said.

She jumped as he rubbed the skin on her back.

'I'm going to inject you now. It might pinch.'

She curled her toes against the scratch of the needle. As he pulled it out, numbness spread across the seal.

'Can you feel that?'

'No.'

'Good. That was the first incision. Tell me if it gets bad.'

She felt the knife slip in deeper, felt the pull and drag of the blade as it sliced through layers of skin. It pinched and grew hot as he went deeper.

'Oh fuck.' She whimpered as electric shocks shot up her back. She slapped the table as the pain swelled into agony, and as the brand fought back she dug her nails into the wood, cracking the surface. Her body stiffened and her knees locked, paralysis creeping up her legs.

'I'll stop.'

'No.' She pushed back at the stiffness, forcing it down.

'Eliza . . .'

'Keep going,' she said.

The knife came again. The pain was worse. The seal knew she was removing it, knew it was under attack. And it fought back. She howled as every nerve burned, feeling every slice of the knife, every movement Cornelius made. His movements quickened as he cut with less care, in an effort to remove it as quickly as possible. She heard it come away with a soft squelch, and she collapsed on the desk.

'Is it broken?' he asked urgently. 'Is the spell gone?'

'Faroust hates raspberries.'

'What?'

Eliza pushed upwards. 'He hates raspberries. Little pips get stuck in his teeth.'

'Why the Hell would I want to know that?'

'Because I can tell you, and I couldn't before.'

He sighed, his relief tangible.

'Hold still. I'll clean you up. I should be able to heal it. Might scar a little.'

'Don't care. Nothing is as bad as that 'F'. Give it to me.'

'Why?'

'I have my reasons,' she said, as he laid her own skin in front of her. She touched it, and the wet blood instantly darkened and dried.

Eliza lay in the dark for hours, her mind swimming with all the possible outcomes of the next day, the day of the Ritual.

Faroust climbed in beside her at three am. He pressed himself against her but when she didn't respond, he rolled away.

Even though the Ritual did not begin until the evening, they rose early. Neither of them had slept well, a few snatched and interrupted hours. As far below the house as they were, Eliza felt the panic and excitement mounting as the appointed hour grew near. Faroust drew his robe over his beautiful, young, frame, and turned to her.

'I have a consort's robe for you, Eliza. A queen's robe. Wear my mother's necklace with it.'

Her robe was blood red. It was lighter than it looked and fitted perfectly, as if it had been made for her.

Faroust drew her hood up and kissed her. As he pulled away, he assumed the guise of the walking cadaver. She grabbed his arm, and he frowned at her.

'May I make a suggestion? If you want to change the rules, perhaps don't dissolve completely into a corpse? It's going make it hard to sell the change to them.'

Faroust smiled at her, decaying lips over tombstone teeth. She shuddered at the ghoulish vision.

'You are a very clever woman. What do you think I should do?'

'Silver fox?' she ventured.

The god's eyes lit up at her suggestion. He rebuilt himself, choosing to remain unbent, but greying his hair and deepening the few wrinkles around his eyes and mouth.

'How do I look? Believable?'

Eliza nodded. Faroust pressed his lips together, frowning at her distance.

'It'll be over soon, baby, and we can get back to us. Let's be really wicked. You refused me twice yesterday.'

'You're always wicked,' she said, as he pushed her against the wall, but she didn't refuse him this time. He was already suspicious of her. The sex was hard and fast. He came just as Jacob began the chant.

'Happy anniversary, baby.' He laughed as they hastily rearranged their clothes.

Before she could answer, the Faithful reached the end of their chant. Faroust opened the door on cue, and Eliza felt the hungry eyes of her Family upon them. There were whispers at her appearance, hushed awe at the beautiful robe and necklace. She stood behind the god's throne and waited for him to speak.

'My children,' his voice was warm. 'We gather again, as we have always done to renew the magic. Tonight, however, things are different.'

A rustle of concern passed through the congregation. Their god was not the same; his voice, his posture, it was all different. What had happened?

'Long ago, we were attacked before I was fully restored. In my efforts to protect your ancestors I was reduced to this, and I required more from your sacrifice. A great deal of my magic was lost. But a wondrous thing has happened.' He reached back and took Eliza's hand. 'The love of my beautiful Eliza has saved the magic I long thought dead. Your burden, which has been so great, for so long, can be lessened.' He dropped his hood, to a collective gasp from the Family.

The atmosphere instantly changed; there was palpable relief and joy. Eliza caught Cornelius' eye and risked a brief smile. He risked one back.

Faroust turned at the wrong moment and caught the swift exchange. Eliza stiffened as he glared at her. Oh God, he *knew*.

'Tonight will be the last time I perform the Ritual as you have known it. This last time will restore all my magic. Cornelius and Susan, step forward.'

Eliza's head snapped up. He was going to kill Cornelius. The fury returned; it engulfed her and all sense and reason vanished.

'You will not touch them,' she snarled from the shadows as Cornelius stepped forward, Susan cringing in his wake. He showed no fear, and her heart swelled at his courage.

Faroust turned towards her. 'I am the First-Father,' he said. 'I will have whomever I choose.' He seized Cornelius by the hair. 'Jacob, the knife.'

But Jacob didn't answer. He was staring at Eliza, and there was no recognition in his eyes. The cup and dagger dangled loosely by his side. Faroust reached for the knife. It flew out of the Patriarch's hand and clattered against the far wall. There were shrieks of terror from the younger members of the assembly.

'Jacob!' Faroust hissed. 'What are you doing?'

'That wasn't me.'

'What do you mean?'

The goblet was snatched from Jacob's hand by an invisible force and thrown into the crowd.

'It was me.' Eliza's voice echoed around the cavern. She stepped forward into the light, and saw her father's eyes widen with terror. In the crowd, someone screamed. Her hands were wreathed in green-blue flame. She blinked slowly at the crowd.

'Her eyes! Look at her eyes! They're black. She's a demon, a demon!'

Faroust let go of Cornelius and took a step towards his consort. His mouth worked, but no sound emerged. Behind him, Cornelius grabbed Susan's arm and hustled her off the stage, Eliza's parents hastening after him.

'Eliza?' the god whispered.

She tilted her head to one side, like a demonic Red Riding Hood.

'Not as you know me,' she said.

'Eliza, don't fuck with me. I will have your Cornelius, if I say so.'

He raised his hand. In the front row, Cornelius ducked as the god gathered power in his palm, white flame so hot his own skin blistered. It shot towards Cornelius. Eliza twisted her arm and her lover shot upwards towards the roof of the cavern, away from the angry god. Faroust snarled and launched himself at her. The flames dancing around her hands leapt instinctively away from her body. They wrapped themselves around Faroust and dragged him down, forcing him to his knees. She set Cornelius down behind her, away from the others.

There were cries of outrage from the crowd. A few men rushed forward to help their god. Eliza twitched her wrist and flame sprang to life along the edge of the stage, driving them back. Beneath the fiery crackle, deadly silence filled the cavern.

'Eliza?' Ruby cried. 'What have you done?'

Eliza pulled down her hood. Her white-blonde hair was gone. Now it flamed blood-red, like her mother's. She turned to the fallen god.

'Reveal yourself, Faroust,' she said. 'Show your children the truth.'

'Fuck you!' He spat, pulling free of her restraints, red light at the end of his fingertips. Eliza kicked him in the ribs as he reached for her. She felt bone snap and he cried out, falling to the floor and clutching his side. Eliza bent over him and wound her fingers into his hair. She yanked him upwards and he yelled as the mirage faded away. The beautiful young man she had been living with for a year knelt before her.

The silence stretched on as realisation began to sink in.

'But . . . but the Ritual . . .' Jacob said.

'Shall I tell them the truth, Faroust? Shall I tell them how our entire existence is built on a lie?' She snarled at the creature kneeling at her feet.

'Please, don't,' he wheezed. 'I won't hurt Cornelius. I promise.'

'Your promises are worthless.'

She faced the Family. The pain and anger on their faces made her hesitate for an instant, but she ploughed on.

'This is our god, ladies and gentlemen. This lying, pathetic, piece of shit is our god. Our god who gives us our magic, who protects us, who we think loves us.' She laughed, ironically. 'And the price for the magic? The rape and murder of thousands and thousands of our children. A Ritual which we permit and celebrate. But it is all a sham. Faroust does not need the Ritual. He does not wither and decay as the year goes on. His power does not fade. Our magic will not die if we don't make these sacrifices, just as we will not die if he leaves the grounds. It's all lies. Everything we built our faith on is a lie.'

'Shall I tell you when it started? A thousand years ago, some of our ancestors knew they could do great good with their magic. They sought permission from him to join the Church so they could help others with their powers. And at first, he agreed.

'But then these children of Faroust began to read the Bible and listen to sermons. Their hearts turned away from him and he couldn't have that. They might take everyone with them to this new religion. So the hoax began. He enchanted those who turned away from him, so that they would attack him. As they did, against their will, he suppressed the power of his other children, implanting the fear in them that without him they would fade and die. Not wanting to lose the power their god granted them, those who remained loyal tore the traitors to pieces with their bare hands and vowed to do anything their god demanded.

'In his outrage at the betrayal he had suffered, he took the blood of the eldest sons of those who went over to the Church, and he raped their daughters. All the while he told the Faithful his magic was forever damaged by the betrayal, that this price would have to be paid again and again. He rewrote our history, claiming we had been attacked by Christians. But there was no Bishop with his knights, no attack, no great loss of magic on his part. He was a man desperate to hold on to the power and adoration he'd enjoyed his whole life. We did not matter to him, only our worship did, and when a handful found something more fulfilling, he punished us all.'

A few people sobbed as she spoke. Eliza pressed on.

'He lives in the lap of luxury. He takes off for months at a time and only returns for this ceremony where he can get off on your stupidity and devotion. We mean nothing to him. He enjoys fucking with us.'

Jacob stared in horror at his daughter. 'What about the seams? What about the Veil? I've seen them myself. That can't be a lie.'

Eliza's heart softened. 'No, it wasn't always a lie. We used to guard the pathways between the worlds, stop the monsters coming through. But since the Fae first left this world, the creatures of the Otherworlds have long since lost the inclination to come here. They don't even know we're here.'

'But . . . but . . .' Jacob stammered, 'people have tried to get to the magic.'

'A handful. One or two who don't know what they are doing and often die in the process. They aren't a real threat. They never have been.'

She felt the anger pouring off the Family now, anger at Faroust, at her, anger at everything. Faroust wept on the floor.

'How can you be telling them this? I sealed you!' he cried.

Eliza looked down at him.

'I will not wear your robe,' she spat, pulling it off. 'I will not wear your necklace.' It chimed as it hit the floor. She threw something leathery and hard in his face. 'And I will not wear your seal.'

He gazed down at the item on the floor and gagged. It was the branded flesh from her back.

Jacob drew closer to the barrier of flame. 'My lord? Tell us it isn't true.'

Eliza glared at Faroust like an avenging Fury. She'd had her boyfriend cut deep into her back to remove his seal. It should have killed her, but she was powerful. She might be even more powerful than him, but she wasn't sure she was human and more, wasn't sure what she was capable of. Who knew what she could do to him, if she let him live? Faroust dragged himself to his feet.

'It's true. All of it.' He looked strangely relieved, and in that instant Eliza understood what she hadn't before. The spell was broken. His own imprisonment ended with his confession. 'I hate you all. I am bound to you by your need, your prayers and your adoration, bound by a vow I made to my dying mother thousands of years ago. You're not the ones who are trapped, I am!'

Cries of denial sounded in the cavern.

'I enjoy the Ritual. I enjoy abusing your ignorance and blind faith. I laugh at you and spit on your sacrifices. I revel in the deaths of the boys whose blood I've drunk and the screams of the girls I've violated.'

It was like a dam had broken and five thousand years of hate poured down on the Faithful. Eliza didn't need to inflict pain on him to reveal his truths. He spoke what had brewed in his soul for eternity.

'Why didn't you just leave us?' she asked, her voice shaking.

He span towards her. 'I was *betrayed*. I gave you everything. I'm stuck here because of you insects and your ancestors who had the audacity to abandon me for the Church. I bound my soul to this plain and what did you do? You threw me away! I wanted to inflict pain on those who betrayed me. I wanted my revenge.' His laugh was full of pain. 'And I had it. A thousand glorious years of it.'

'What do you mean, you're stuck here because of us?'

Faroust released a deep shuddering sigh.

'I knew, all those years ago, that the *Tuathane* were coming here. I felt them from miles away, felt their hatred and their intent to rip open the Veil. I could have walked through and closed it behind me, left you to your fate. But I couldn't.' He glowered at the people in the cavern. 'You raised me. Not my mother or father, but you. I knew you wouldn't stand a chance and I couldn't protect you and the Veil. I was too young, I didn't have the strength. So I gave your ancestors my blood, passed my magic to them, made them strong.

'It was incredible. All my warrior men and women transformed into Fae, like me: tall, strong, creatures of the Otherworlds who could fight with weapons and sorcery. The *Tuathane* were massacred. We slaughtered them under a Harvest moon and fucked in their blood. From that night the Ritual was born, a symbolic gesture, a tiny blood sacrifice from my strongest children as thanks for my great gift.

'Not long after, the Hound of Ulster slaughtered my mother. He left her on the battlefield, the fool. He had no idea what he had done. He condemned all the Fae, including those who fought for him, to death.' He turned to Eliza. 'It was I who ate her heart. I had no choice. The magic would escape as her body decomposed. I didn't want to die. I was only twenty-one, and I wanted more.

'In time, the Fae began to leave as the world of the *Gnáth* expanded. Our holy places were damaged and this plain was no longer attractive to us. They gathered in the clearing where your fucking awful house now is and began to pass through.

'I planned to go too. The tribe was strong with my magic, it would be fine without me. But I could not pass through. The Veil blocked me. My lover Bridgit crossed into the Otherworlds to discover why. When she returned, she had bad news. In sharing my magic with you in the way I had, I bound myself to this plain of existence and I would never be able to leave. Until,' he raised a finger, 'one was born who was stronger than I. They would be able to manipulate the Veil, to force it to take me home. But that was not the end of it. I had to condemn all the souls of my people to be consumed by the Veil. The magic had to return to its natural place.

'I could not do that. You were my people, loyal and loving. I committed myself to being your god, to leading and protecting you for eternity. But you cast me aside when Padraig brought his Middle-Eastern mythology with him. You had a god who loved you and cared for you, and you left me. Half of you ran away and committed yourself to this never-seen Nazarene. I would not be abandoned. You are mine, every last one of you from the dawn of your race until the end of time, until the one who can send me home is born. I dragged the souls of the departed back from the afterlife and pledged you all to the Veil. If you were going to abandon me, well . . .' He laughed again. 'Fuck you.'

'Why not just kill us?' Eliza asked.

'Were you not listening? I need you; your existence keeps the pathways alive, keeps the magic flowing. I can't go home until one of you parasites is strong enough to open the door. Dead things can't open doors. Was that what you wanted to know, Eliza? Bet you thought you'd heard the worst of it last night.'

Eliza didn't answer. She stared unseeing at the floor as the horror sank in. He walked towards her and gripped her by the shoulders.

'How were you able to do this to me?'

'I blossomed,' she said. 'I can copy magic. Any magic.'

Faroust smiled. 'You're the one Bridgit spoke of. The one who can send me home. Come with me, love. Be my queen on the other side. End the lives of everyone in here and rip the Veil open.'

Eliza stared up at him. 'No.' She shook her head. 'No. You don't get to go home after what you've done to us.'

Faroust leapt backwards, throwing a column of flame at her. She raised her hand and deflected it towards him. It knocked him backwards, shattering the last mirage he wore as he hit the floor, and his true form was revealed at last.

He lumbered to his feet, rolling his shoulders and clicking his neck. He stretched his bone white fingers as onyx claws emerged from the tips. His face was still beautiful, but it was more pointed and angular. His eyes were liquid black and from his head sprouted two horns, twisted from a thousand tiny branches, adding another foot to his height.

Eliza took a step back as he grinned at her. His teeth glinted black and jagged and his wings cast shadows against the flame.

'I am going to eat you,' he whispered.

He leapt towards her. Eliza threw her hand forward, throwing out a sharp gust of wind that thrust Faroust off course. He crashed against the wall. The earth quivered and shook beneath Eliza's feet as, with a scream of rage, he slammed his fists into the ground, extinguishing her fire. The earth cracked and Eliza's hands flashed out, knocking back a handful of the Faithful who were close to the chasm opening up in the floor.

'Run!' she called to her Family.

'No!' Faroust bellowed.

The Family juddered to a halt as Faroust cast a spell to stop them fleeing. Eliza charged him, knocking him back, breaking his hold. She tore away from his snatching fingers as he tried to grab her.

'You will take me back!'

'Never,' she said. But she was running out of space, uncertain of the magic she'd stolen. Eventually he was going to catch her. She made a misstep and the Fae prince grabbed her around the waist. He wrapped his arm around her neck and squeezed hard.

'You will take me back, or you will die.'

She squirmed her fingers under his arm, creating a gap between his flesh and her throat. She dug her nails into his flesh, sending electricity dancing along his arm, blackening his skin. He swore, but he didn't drop her. She swung her legs, fighting against him as his hold tightened.

'Cornelius,' she screamed. 'Help me!'

Cornelius pushed his way through the frozen crowd, a knife glinting in his hand. He drove it into Faroust's arm. The god howled as he dragged the blade down, carving Fae flesh. Eliza hit the floor as Faroust dropped her. Stunned into an instant of immobility, she looked up to see Faroust smack Cornelius with the back of his hand. She screamed as he flew through the air and crashed into the wall. He dropped to the floor and didn't get up. She tried to run to him, but Faroust grabbed her hair and pulled her back.

She lashed out at him, catching him on the chin but his hold remained firm. He pulled her back into his arms.

'Anna-Beth,' she shouted. 'Now!'

There was a thunderous rumble, and a painful crack as the Veil entered their plain. In the golden gateway, five thousand years of dead Family members stood in front of her and Faroust, stretching back as far as she could see. Eliza stretched out her hand towards them. And they reached back. She pushed her craning fingertips into the Veil, and Anna-Beth smiled and took her hand with cold, dead fingers. The girl vanished into Eliza, followed by her brother, her parents and a thousand generations of Familial ancestors, filling her until she felt she might burst from the pressure.

There was a flash of hot light, and a crack like a gunshot. Eliza howled as the light flooded her, making her skin sizzle and pop. Her body twisted and her back snapped as the power filled her. She pushed her arms down and back and Faroust was forced away from her, landing with a thump on his knees, his skin smoking. The light pulled away from Eliza and gathered in front of her. She stared at it as its surface calmed and grew reflective, showing the cavern behind her. She gasped.

Another Fae creature stood in the cavern. It was as tall as Faroust but its skin was bone white. Instead of blue-green swirls, its body was decorated with flicks and flames of scarlet blood. Eliza jerked forward and the Fae did the same. She laughed as the realisation dawned on her; she was a Fae. She was like him.

She was completely naked, her breasts covered in a pair of blood red whorls. She jerked again and grunted, feeling the skin on her back crack open. She swallowed against the burning pain as two pairs of wings emerged from her spine. One pair stretched upwards from her shoulder blades, the other swept the floor. Her feathers were white, long and perfectly straight, each one ending in a sharp point. A sharp point that looked as if it had recently been dipped in blood. She smiled at her reflection. Oh, this was good.

Faroust found his voice.

'Who are you?'

She rolled her shoulders and six sharp protrusions of bone popped out from the tops of her arms. She turned towards him, her movements fluid and graceful.

'Don't you recognise me, lover?'

Faroust balked. 'Your eyes. They're red.'

Eliza stalked over to him, grabbed him by the hair and dragged him to his feet. Screams rang out from the Faithful. He tried to wrench himself from her grasp but she held tight. He gazed in panic at her, terror giving way to a recognition that brought its own unique fear.

'Eliza?'

'Yes, lover. Eliza. Eliza the powerless, Eliza the weak, Eliza the useless.' Her harsh laugh echoed eerily in the cavern. 'But I am so much more than that now.'

Eliza released her grasp on the son of Mebh and stalked around him in a tight circle, her wingtips brushing his skin.

'I don't understand . . .' he began, but she cut him off with a punch to the face. He crumpled under the force of the blow.

'I am more than your plaything. I am more than my magic, more than the magic I've stolen.' She lashed out at him again, her foot connecting with his stomach. 'I am every lie you ever told,' she snarled, slapping him as he came up for air. 'Every drop of blood you spilt, every girl you raped, everybody you murdered, every mother who lost a child, every father who had no choice but to watch, every howl of pain you caused.' She grabbed his hair again and dragged him backwards. 'I am the soul of every innocent person you denied their eternal rest and trapped in a dead world through the Veil.'

Faroust flew forward as Eliza threw him towards his throne. It smashed into a thousand pieces as he collided with it. A few larger pieces flew towards the crowd. Screams rang out as the Family braced itself for impact. Eliza extended her hand and pulled the debris out of the air. She threw the pieces away to her left, before turning back to Faroust.

The fallen god struggled to his knees. In the impact with his throne, one of his horns had snapped off and he'd broken his nose. Blood poured from his mouth where a few of his jagged black teeth had fallen from his gums. She sauntered over to him. She was going to enjoy this. As she crouched beside him, Faroust span and punched her in the stomach. She flew across the room and smashed into the limestone wall, grunting as the breath was punched from her lungs by the hard stone.

'I've been doing this for five thousand years, bitch!' Faroust cried. 'Did you honestly think you could beat me?'

Eliza pulled herself from the cavern wall and shook the dust off. She tilted her head to one side as she considered her foe.

'Was that supposed to hurt?'

Faroust's eyes widened. She could see the panic in his face, smell it on his skin. He rotated his hand and a swirling wind sprang up in the middle of his palm, a tiny tornado growing bigger and bigger. He pushed his hands forward and the storm leapt at her. The wind whirled closer and closer. Eliza put her finger to her lips.

'Shh.'

The wind died. Faroust swore. He clicked his fingers, a column of flame erupting. She leant blew it out like a candle on a cake. He reared back, electricity dancing in his hands as he fired off two shots. She caught the thunderbolts and devoured them. They didn't even sizzle as they touched her mouth. Finally, he just gave in and charged her.

Thunder echoed around the cavern as they collided. He stopped dead in his tracks, his arms around her waist. Eliza raised him to his feet, grabbing his right arm and twisting it behind him. He screamed as the bone snapped and shattered. He fell to his knees, clutching the ruined limb. Eliza walked around him again, stroking his hair.

'Faroust, you are guilty of the worst crimes against us . . .'

'Eliza, please . . .' he wept.

'This is not a trial! This is a sentence!'

On his knees, he flinched as her voice reverberated through the cavern.

'I have several choices,' she mused, running her hands through his hair, tugging at the roots. 'I could re-open the Veil and send you and all this vile magic back to the Otherworlds. But then you wouldn't be punished for what you did to us. I could kill you. A simple execution. Or I could rip you to pieces, slowly, cell by cell, on the altar where you have ruined so many innocents. But death, no matter how slowly, would still come to you before this day is done. Death would release you. So again, what punishment would you really face?'

She crouched in front of him and kissed him. He tried to grab her hand as she stood up but she slapped him away.

'Please, Eliza, please!'

She ignored his begging. 'Faroust, false-god, liar, murderer and rapist.' She held her hand against his forehead. 'I take it all from you,' she whispered. The light went out of his eyes. He toppled to the floor like an ancient tree falling, and lay still.

Eliza turned and ran to Cornelius, still lying on the floor. He was crumpled at an odd angle, limp and twisted like a discarded toy. She knelt beside him and turned his head.

'Oh no.'

A patchwork of livid bruises was already forming under his skin, his nose sat at an angle, blood dripping from his nostrils. His cheek had caved in where it collided with the wall. She closed her eyes as she ran her hands over his body, searching for injuries; ruptured spleen, broken ribs, punctured lung. Broken neck. His breath rattled in his chest. His heart was slowing.

'Hold on, baby,' she whispered, tears running down her cheeks, 'I'm going to fix this. I won't let you die.'

Gently, she arranged his limbs, taking care with his neck. She put her hands on his chest. A soft light shone from her fingers and sank into his body. She sat back and watched it travel up to his neck and head before it wound its way down again, touching all the places he was hurt. She held her breath as she waited for her spell to take hold.

Cornelius' eyes flickered open as he sat up, gasping. He gazed around in confusion, his eyes finally settling on her. He cried out, scuttling back across the cold floor of the cavern until he hit the wall and had nowhere to go.

'It's all right,' she said, discarding the Faerie form, 'it's me. It's over.'

He stared at her for a long moment before taking the hand she offered. She helped him to her feet and wrapped her arms around him.

'Shit,' he coughed. 'I thought . . . I thought . . .'

'Shh. It's all right. It's over.' She shivered. 'May I borrow your robe? I appear to be in the nip.'

Cornelius shrugged his robe off and pulled it over her head. Eliza hugged the material to her, trying to warm up. She turned, looking for her parents. Her heart sank. Everybody, every single member of the Family, lay prostrate on the ground. They were bowing. They were bowing to her.

'No. This isn't what I wanted.'

There was a golden light and then there was only silence.

Epilogue

Eighteen months later

THE BUSTY YOUNG waitress slipped her number to the dark-haired, navy-eyed man in the expensive suit, along with his whiskey and soda. He glanced at her and smiled wryly. She was small and dark-skinned, her black curls held back by an Alice band, her eyes warm and inviting.

'I get off at eleven,' she said.

'If you're lucky, you'll be getting off again at eleven-fifteen.' He chuckled, tucking the phone number into his wallet, where it nestled amongst a dozen other such invitations. The girl's sultry smile broadened. Someone bellowed for service and she sashayed off.

The man stared around the hotel bar. It was mass produced, neutral chic; the floor was pale laminate, the chairs of the same blonde wood. The bar was jammed with irate office workers on mid-week conferences, glugging down malt without appreciation because it was on the company's bill rather than their own. The lighting was dimmed to give the clientele the privacy they would get in American hotels they'd likely never see.

He was seated in an empty booth, where there were thick, leather-clad cushions on the seats. He'd looked briefly at the menu before discarding it and plumping for the numbing whiskey.

He was on his fifth double, this time without the soda, when she came in. A rhapsody of auburn curls, fine tailoring and expensive shoes. She wore the black trouser suit like a second skin. He couldn't bring himself to look at her face, so he stared down at her blood red shoes. She stood above him.

'Hello, Faroust.' Her voice was soft and melodious.

He swallowed the last gulp of whiskey, for courage.

'I don't go by that name anymore. These days I'm called Henry. Please sit down, Eliza.'

She sat down. The pretty waitress passed by their table, throwing them an irritated glance.

'Were you planning to fuck her later? Sorry if I spoiled the fun.'

Faroust shrugged. 'It'd be nice, but tonight I've had too many of these. When I was a god that was never a problem.' His voice was thick with accusation.

'I remember.'

They sat in awkward silence for a long time. It was Eliza who spoke first.

'Perhaps we should have this conversation in private? Are you staying here?'

'Yes.'

'I'll get a bottle of wine and we can go up.'

The former god and his former concubine rode in silence in the lift, avoiding eye contact. Eliza crossed her arms as they travelled up to his floor. Her jacket gaped and he caught a glimpse of the lingerie she wore beneath it. Dove grey lace, understated and very sexy. Exactly what had captured him three years ago.

They entered his suite and Eliza barely concealed her amusement at its cream and gold opulence.

'Expensive. Some things never change.'

'I'll pour you a drink,' Faroust-Henry offered, ignoring the barb.

Eliza sat down on the sofa and gracefully accepted the glass he offered her.

'So,' she said, 'what did 'Henry' do with the money, and the second chance he was given?'

Faroust held out his business card. 'Henry Smith, CEO of MediaMonster Productions. We've recently acquired several smaller companies, a few newspapers and three TV stations.'

Eliza laughed. 'You'll give them all a run for their money at this rate.'

'Henry' shook his head. 'Nah. I just wanted to do something interesting.'

The questions he was burning to ask were on the tip of his tongue but he couldn't bring himself to voice them.

'I didn't think you'd have kept the phone,' he said. 'I didn't think you'd come.'

Eliza gave him a crooked half-smile. The memory of hundreds of afternoons spent naked in bed with her filled his mind.

'Ask your questions.' Her pale eyes were kind.

He licked his lips. 'How's the Family?'

'Happy. They don't remember anything of what happened that night. They don't remember you, to be honest. They don't even know there's a cavern below the house.'

'Henry' took a deep breath as he settled into an armchair. 'You got rid of me completely then?'

'I did. It was surprisingly easy to remove you from their memories and the house, and remove the seals from my parents. It took next to no time to clear out your apartment and seal the cavern. It must have been all the magic I took from you. And the Veil. And them.'

Her last statement hung heavy in the air as he realised what she was implying. 'You took it away from them too? Why?'

She took a deep sip of wine. 'Too dangerous. Without a god to guide them, who knows what they might have done?'

'You could have become their god.'

Eliza laughed bitterly but gave no other answer.

'So you're the only magical one left? All that power . . . How will you control yourself? Do you have my immortality as well? Because I don't have it anymore.'

Eliza took another sip.

'Fuck no. I sent it into the ether. Why would I want to live forever?' She paused. 'Do you want to know what happened when I took their magic away?'

'What?'

She leant forward conspiratorially. 'All that Familial paleness and whiteness went away. Variety came back to them. Cornelius has brown hair now.'

Faroust-Henry cracked his knuckles in annoyance. 'All that magic and power. What will you do, Eliza?'

'I don't have any magic, Faroust. I sent that away too. I'd lived my whole life without it. Once we were freed, and I include you in that statement, I didn't need it anymore, so I let it go. It vanished into thin air.'

He put his head in his hands as he tried to process what she'd told him. 'You just gave it up? How is that even possible? Did you wish it away? Shrug your shoulders and poof! It was gone?'

Her silence only served to fan the flames of his rage.

'You utter cunt. Why would you do that? I gave you everything!'

Eliza drained her glass and got to her feet without replying.

'I loved you!'

'It had to end. I couldn't let you kill any more boys, or rape any more girls. You're a fucking monster. '

'What would you know, you little bitch?' he snarled. 'I protected your incestuous, festering boil of a family for five thousand years! I made them what they are. I gave you the tools to rule the world.'

'You changed the rules. You condemned us to limbo until you found the one who could send you home. How is murder and rape a fair price for a few paltry parlour tricks?'

Faroust gasped at her blasphemy.

'Parlour tricks? Parlour tricks? I had the power to mould reality. I could do anything . . .'

'And yet you still chose to spend eternity wanking and watching TV. Well done.' She smirked. 'Face it, Faroust, you were nothing. The nominal leader of a tiny clan. One we only paid reverence to once a year.'

She took a step towards the door. 'We hated you. And in reality we didn't need you, did we? You'd served your purpose when you gave us the magic. You were a spoilt child, desperately trying to remain the centre of attention. You're pathetic.'

Faroust lashed out, blinded by rage and grief. Eliza stumbled backwards, gasping for air. He'd hit her in her stomach. She crashed to the floor, clutching at the carpet.

'You fucking bitch,' he panted. 'You took everything from me!'

Eliza looked up at him. He could hardly see her through the haze of sudden tears.

'You made me believe that you loved me.' His voice a bare whisper. 'And you took everything from me.'

'You . . . you had to be stopped.'

Faroust bent over her. He wrapped her auburn hair around his hand and pulled her to her feet.

'Your Family betrayed me. They needed to pay.'

Eliza tried to kick him but even as a mortal man he was strong, and he didn't let her go.

'And now,' he said, 'you're going to be the one who pays.'

He threw her down on the floor. She fell to her knees, and he followed up with a swift kick to her ribcage before she could scramble to her feet. Once, twice, three times his foot connected with her ribs. She didn't have the breath to cry out.

Once more, he pulled her upright by her hair. He threw her on the bed and straddled her, pinning her down with his weight. He closed his hand around her throat.

'I am going to fuck you. And then, I am going to kill you.'

His former bed-mate clawed his hand, but he tightened his grip.

'Good bye, Eliza.'

Faroust looked down, expecting to see fear in eyes. She was smirking again, the bitch. He raised his hand to smack the grin off her face.

Or at least he tried to. He couldn't move.

He was paralysed, unable to make a sound or movement. Eliza gently prised his hands away from her throat and eased the fallen god onto his side. She got off of the bed, sat down on the chair and glared at him.

There was a knock at the door. 'Come,' Eliza ordered.

A tall man with russet brown hair and navy eyes entered the room. *Cornelius!* Of course! She'd destroyed his legacy for this second-rate Family member who'd done all the dirty work. He should have known she wouldn't have met him alone.

The torturer crouched in front of the armchair and checked his lover's body for cuts and bruises. Faroust seethed inwardly at the movement of his fingertips, but there was nothing he could do. Eliza took a sharp intake of breath as Cornelius' hands swept over her ribs.

'You're badly bruised,' he said. 'I told you shouldn't have come in here by yourself.'

'Darling, it's fine. I can heal myself in a jiffy.'

Cornelius cursed as he pulled back her jacket collar and winced. 'That bastard could have ripped your head off. You're going to have a lovely crop of bruises. Fuck's sake Zee, you couldn't just paralyse him? You had to wind him up, didn't you?'

Faroust tried to force himself to move as his captors left his sideways vision, but it was impossible. He could see and feel but not move or speak. His back ached from being frozen in this crouching position. His shoulders burned and he longed to flex his numbing fingers. This was agony. Were they going to leave him here like this?

For an age he lay there, paralysed. He closed his eyes, absurdly grateful for that one small mercy Eliza had granted him, and tried to gather strength in the darkness.

He must have passed out from the pain for when he next opened his eyes Eliza stood in front of him, wearing a new suit and with not a mark on her. Cornelius appeared in his line of sight, sleeves rolled up.

'Shall we then?' he asked Eliza.

She nodded, idly chewing her thumbnail.

With Faroust's limbs screaming in agony, Cornelius guided him into a sitting position and adjusted his arms and legs. Hot tears slid down his face. His whole body felt like it was roasting on coals.

Eliza adjusted his head so he was looking up at her.

'Cornelius and I are here to finish the sentence,' she said.

The sentence? He wished he could speak. She must have read his mind, because she leant forward until her eyes danced in front of his, filling his limited vision.

'Oh, Faroust, did you think you had got away? Darling, it was all part of the punishment. '

The fallen god felt sweat gather on his brow. Had Cornelius taught her well, or had this cruelty always lived in her? She twitched. This wasn't the woman he knew. All that magic must have changed her. Being transformed into a Fae must have changed her.

She brushed a lock of hair out of his eyes. She smiled and he grew cold; she looked as if she wanted to eat him alive. He understood for the first time the terror his former acolytes must have felt when he addressed them.

'We needed time to create an adequate punishment. We thought about it for a long time, to make sure it was fitting. What does Faroust value more than anything? And then, of course, it was obvious. Cornelius, fetch his things.' Eliza put her hands on either side of Faroust's head and silently commanded him to follow her.

He jerked to his feet and walked behind Eliza and Cornelius, like a living mannequin, as they exited the hotel. He was made to sit in the back of a gleaming Aston Martin. Cornelius got into the passenger side while Eliza drove. They purred off into the night. Terrified and exhausted from the pain, Faroust passed out once again.

Cornelius looked over his shoulder and shuddered. Eliza flashed him a concerned look.

'Are you all right?' she asked.

'It makes my soul cold,' he said. 'The reality of what he did to our family. What we allowed him to do. It was all so unnecessary.' He frowned and fidgeted with his fingers, a habit born out of the guilt that dogged him now. Eliza reached across and squeezed his hands.

'I did awful things, Eliza. All for a lie.'

'We all did,' she said, indicating left and turning towards a concealed drive. 'But things are better now.'

'Only because you took action. You are amazing.'

She brought his hand to her lips and kissed his knuckles. The car cruised to a halt on the gravel. She sat very still for a long moment, as if steeling herself for what was to come. The door of the house opened.

Between them they manoeuvred the unconscious Faroust out of the car and into the house. As they climbed the steps, he opened his eyes, and screamed and screamed as Eliza and Cornelius marched him to his doom.

He faded in and out of consciousness. Eliza's spell, the pain in his muscles, his panic, all stopped him focusing properly. He was aware of people speaking, talking about him but everything else escaped him. He wriggled his fingers, the first action that was truly his own since he had his hands around Eliza's throat. As his understanding sharpened, he became aware that his body was his own again. He stretched his arms and a whimper escaped his lips. His flesh felt like it was on fire.

'No, no, Henry. Don't move,' a quiet voice reprimanded. He squinted to focus on the person speaking to him. It was Cornelius.

'Where am I?' he said.

'Back amongst Family. We're having a party.'

Faroust glanced around in panic, expecting an avalanche of enraged relatives eager to tear him apart. Cornelius laughed, cold and mocking.

'Don't worry. You have nothing to fear from them. They don't even know you existed.'

The captive man looked around. They were in the ballroom. There were a dozen or so circular tables dotted around and soft music played as the Family chatted and ate. A dark haired woman slipped in front of him to pass Cornelius a glass of champagne.

'Thank you Sophie.' Cornelius waited until she moved away before he resumed talking. 'You'd never recognise her, would you? But then, would you ever have recognised one of your victims? I mean, I was pretty bad, but I never fucked anyone against their will.'

'Let me go,' Faroust said. 'You've taken everything from me; my power, my family, my life. What more could you do to me?'

Cornelius' eyes lost their humour and the smile left his face. He whispered in his prisoner's ear.

'If I had my way, I'd rip you to shreds, peel your skin off and slowly, painfully, drag the life out of you.'

Faroust tried to slow his breathing as the Cruel's threat flowed over him. The boy was a monster too, a monster Faroust had helped to create. He knew one wrong word could mean Cornelius, with a few gentle touches, would inflict a whole new world of pain on him. As a god, he had experienced very little pain in his long life, but he was aware of Cornelius' reputation. On a whim, the bastard could paralyse him and he'd spend his life in fiery, agonising pain. In days gone by, he could have crushed this insolent cunt as if he were an insect. Now Faroust was the insect, and Cornelius the boot ready to crush him.

'There you are, darling. How is Henry doing?'

Eliza smiled down at them, stunning in a beautiful ivory lace dress. Cornelius moved from the fallen god's side and into Faroust's view. The young man wore a sharp grey suit. Ruby appeared behind them. There wasn't a flicker of recognition on her face.

'He's fine, sweetheart. A little uncomfortable, but after his accident that's normal.' Cornelius' cold gaze turned from his prisoner to Eliza and all the aggression vanished. Love filled his eyes, his face iridescent with joy.

'You look wonderful,' he said.

'I should do. This cost enough.'

'It's your wedding and we have money!' Ruby interjected, loud and happily drunk.

Faroust's heart constricted as he heard those words. *Oh, Eliza.* He had truly loved her. Whatever else had been false about their twisted relationship, his love had been real. The woman in front of him would not afford him the kindness of his love for her being another one of her tricks.

'Just like my Eliza,' Ruby sniffed. 'So thoughtful. So concerned about her family.'

Eliza bent her head to whisper in Cornelius' ear. Her husband nodded, took Ruby by the elbow and led her away from Eliza and her former master. There was a long moment of silence.

'They think you had an accident. That you were in hospital for a long time. They have no idea who you are or what you did for them so long ago,' Eliza whispered.

She moved behind him and he tried to stand, choking back a sob as he realised he was in a wheelchair. Eliza hummed as they made their way through the throng of wedding guests. Not one of them recognised their fallen lord and master. She pushed him towards Jacob's study.

For one heart-stopping instant, Faroust thought she was going to seal him alive in the Ritual room, but instead they swung left into a ground floor bedroom. Eliza eased Faroust into position in front of the window and locked the brake. The room overlooked the front lawn and the drive. Something was wrong, something was missing.

'What happened to my hydrangeas?'

Eliza smiled viciously down at him. 'I pulled them up.'

'Why?'

She leant in closer, a grin twisting her face. 'I hate hydrangeas.'

He stared at her in disbelief. 'I brought those back from China. I nurtured each one from seed. I grew those for my children.'

'I know.' She shrugged off his pain.

Faroust fought the tears gathering in his eyes. 'Why did you bring me here, Eliza?'

'Isn't it obvious, my lord, my god, my love? Your punishment.' She knelt down in front of him. 'You are to remain here, trapped for the rest of your life, to watch us grow and live and die without ever knowing you existed. We will feed you and clothe you and love you, we will help you recover and become strong again, never knowing the harm you once caused us.

'We will never know that all our wealth and privilege was because of you. You will be doomed to watch us live as ordinary mortals, with the knowledge that your descendants were once gods among men and you were their leader. You will rot in our love and kindness, guilt-ridden at how you mistreated us, unable to tell anyone the truth, unable to resist the love we lavish on you.'

Faroust opened his mouth to speak but she placed her finger on his lips. His throat constricted and his voice died. She ran her hands over his arms and legs and the pain returned a thousand fold. His mouth opened in a silent scream as tears streamed down his face.

'Your recovery will be hard earned. You will take many years to get better. You won't even have the ability to piss on your own at first.' She got to her feet.

'For your violations against the Family, for your millennia of rape and murder, I sentence you to life and love, with no relief from your guilt. The slowest and cruellest death I can think of. Now, I've put you by the window. Keep an eye out for the fireworks. Cornelius and I are finally going to send this poisonous magic away. It should make for quite a show.'

She turned away from the man who had once been a god, walked back into the light and warmth of her family. She left him alone, silently weeping in the dark.

About the Author

Ellen Crosháin is a Northern Irish writer, now living and working in South Wales. With a Northern Irish father and an Irish mother, she is the eldest of four children. Her entire childhood was spent with her head either in the clouds or in books. Her love of mythology, especially Greco-Roman, was sparked by her father who studied Classics at Cambridge, before becoming a Christian minister. Her love of a good story came from her mother who gave her book after book to keep her entertained as they moved around for her father's job. These factors eventually led to Ellen studying a joint Bachelor's degree in Ancient History and English Literature at Cardiff University.

After graduating, Ellen trained to be an English teacher and is currently working in a school in South Wales. After completing her teacher training, she returned to Cardiff University to study for her Masters degree in English Literature, while teaching part-time.

She has a wide range of interests. She is a classically trained singer and is a member of her local Church choir. She loves to cook, especially baking. She makes an excellent chocolate and Guinness cake. Oddly enough, she loves to read and really does read everything from comic books to classic literature. If it's interesting, she'll read it but Fantasy and Gothic or Horror are her favourites. Currently, she is researching about the Celtic Otherworlds as she works on her second novel, the follow up to 'Cruelty'.

She collects Pop Funko Vinyl figures, Nightmare before Christmas memorabilia, interesting salt and pepper shakers and Anne Rice memorabilia. She is also an avid Lego builder.

Every draft of everything she's ever written is done by hand in a series of beautiful notebooks. She finds that there is something more organic, more real, about the process of creating a story if it's done by hand first.

Ellen currently lives on the outskirts of Cardiff, with her Scottish husband and a small army of guinea pigs.

Acknowledgements

I keep having to pinch myself. I can't quite believe this is real. Five years ago, I had the idea for *Cruelty* and now it's becoming a reality. There are so many people to thank, without whom this book would not have happened.

First of all, I would like to thank my wonderful husband, Adam, who has brought me endless cups of tea, rubbed my shoulders, made me laugh when I would get stuck and left me alone when I was in the grip of a creative burst. Secondly, I would like to thank my mum and dad, Yvonne and Nigel, for all their support as this project has taken off. From an early age, they instilled in me a love of reading and the idea that everything is within reach if you work hard for it. I would also like to thank my brother, Christopher, and my sisters, Kathryn and Rachael, for their love and support. My in-laws, Mary and Jim, also need a mention. They have been proudly proclaiming that I am going to be published and have been drumming up trade already. I do have to say my sister and brother-in-law, Alison and David, were very understanding when one corner of the baptism of their daughter Jessica became a marketing opportunity for me. Finally, I want to thank my own large Irish family and both sets of grandparents, James, Eleanor and Ronnie, who have passed, and my granny Joy who is still with us.

None of this amazingness would be happening if it wasn't for the incredibly talented Sammy HK Smith who took a punt on a novella and helped me make it something incredible. I am blessed to call her not only my publisher but my friend. Thanks, too, to Joanne Hall, my amazing editor. She was amazing fun to work with and she even convinced me of the validity of the Oxford comma. A talented writer in her own right, Jo saw my vision and helped me achieve it. Thank you, too, to Evelinn Enoksen for my stunning front cover. I love it. Thanks to Ken Dawson for the lettering and Zoë Harris for the blurb. Thank you to all the Grimbold Team for helping me make *Cruelty* what it is. I am so fortunate to be amongst the fantastically talented people that make up the Grimbold family.

Finally, I would like to thank those who supported the Grimbold Books Kickstarter campaign and to all of you who read the book. I hope you enjoy it. As we say in Ireland, *sláinte*.

A Selection of Other Titles from Kristell Ink

Darkspire Reaches by C.N. Lesley

The wyvern has hunted for the young outcast all her life; a day will come when she must at last face him.

Abandoned as a sacrifice to the wyvern, a young girl is raised to fear the beast her adoptive clan believes meant to kill her. When the Emperor outlaws all magic, Raven is forced to flee from her home with her foster mother, for both are judged as witches. Now an outcast, she lives at the mercy of others, forever pursued by the wyvern as she searches for her rightful place in the world. Soon her life will change forever as she discovers the truth about herself.

A unique and unsettling romantic adventure about rejection and belonging.

March 2013

In Search of Gods and Heroes by Sammy H.K Smith

Buried in the scriptures of Ibea lies a story of rivalry, betrayal, stolen love, and the bitter division of the gods into two factions. This rift forced the lesser deities to pledge their divine loyalty either to the shining Eternal Kingdom or the darkness of the Underworld.

When a demon sneaks into the mortal world and murders an innocent girl to get to her sister Chaeli, all pretence of peace between the gods is shattered. For Chaeli is no ordinary mortal, she is a demi-goddess, in hiding for centuries, even from herself.

But there are two divine brothers who may have fathered her, and the fate of Ibea rests on the source of her blood.

Chaeli embarks on a journey that tests her heart, her courage, and her humanity. Her only guides are a man who died a thousand years ago in the Dragon Wars, a former assassin for the Underworld, and a changeling who prefers the form of a cat.

The lives of many others – the hideously scarred Anya and her gaoler; the enigmatic and cruel Captain Kerne; the dissolute Prince Dal; and gentle seer Hana – all become entwined. The gods will once more walk the mortal plane spreading love, luck, disease, and despair as they prepare for the final, inevitable battle.

In Search of Gods and Heroes, Book One of Children of Nalowyn, is a true epic of sweeping proportions which becomes progressively darker as the baser side of human nature is explored, the failings and ambitions of the gods is revealed, and lines between sensuality and sadism, love and lust are blurred.

June 2014

The Sea-Stone Sword by Joel Cornah

"Heroes are more than just stories, they're people. And people are complicated, people are strange. Nobody is a hero through and through, there's always something in them that'll turn sour. You'll learn it one day. There are no heroes, only villains who win."

Rob Sardan is going to be a legend, but the road to heroism is paved with temptation and deceit. Exiled to a distant and violent country, Rob is forced to fight his closest friends for survival, only to discover his mother's nemesis is still alive, and is determined to wipe out her family and all her allies. The only way the Pirate Lord, Mothar, can be stopped is with the Sea-Stone Sword – yet even the sword itself seems fickle, twisting Rob's quest in poisonous directions, blurring the line between hero and villain. Nobody is who they seem, and Rob can no longer trust even his own instincts.

Driven by dreams of glory, Rob sees only his future as a hero, not the dark path upon which he draws ever closer to infamy.

June 2014

Atlantis and the Game of Time by Katie Alford

A tale of two great powers and a battle across the breadth of time as Atlantis, a peaceful culture of academics intent on conserving the flow of time, struggles against a new rising power determined to reform it.

After decades of quiet time watching, the Atlanteans are caught off guard by a sudden wave of destruction, travelling up the timeline from the distant past, threatening to destroy all known civilisations and even, finally, that of Atlantis itself.

All that remains behind the time change is a single culture, one world and one history. Can the peaceful culture of Atlantis find the power to battle this new war ready culture and return history to its former glory or is the history they have protected for centuries doomed to be lost forever?

August 2014